Liar's Song

Book Two of The Wayward Light Saga

A. Samuel Bales

Cassian Press

ISBN: 979-8-9884875-5-5 (paperback)

ISBN: 979-8-9884875-6-2 (hardcover)

ISBN: 979-8-9884875-4-8 (ebook)

First edition 2025

Published by Cassian Press

www.asamuelbales.com

To those who lift their hands, voices, and pens against evil, tyranny, and ignorance.

Damn wisdom! Damn it all. It's done. It was necessary. It was necessary. It was necessary. Swords must be spread. The power must be spread.

Damn it all. I thank The One that Syladrya slept already, or surely I could not have clung to sanity. But it matters not. My end is near. Sweet silence. Let it end. Let it all begin.

—Vincet Ellemere

CHAPTER ONE

J eld knelt and ran his fingers along a hoofprint in the snow, its shape barely visible in what lingering sunlight pierced the canopy overhead. A faint whisper drew his gaze deeper into the trees. Staring into the shadows, his breath slowed as he opened his senses. Three auras filled his mind, each distinct in its own complex flavor. He sampled them before focusing on one in particular. The grains of the bow within his grip grew distant and soon tears welled in his absent eyes.

Blinking, he gave one final scan of the forest before smoothing over the hoofprint and coming to his feet. He crept onward, each carefully placed step leaving not a trace behind nor casting a sound ahead. The whispers grew louder with each delicate step until he ducked a final branch and emerged in a small hollow.

Fen pulled Lionus's saddle free and glanced over to Jeld. Jeld saw the frown beneath Fen's growing beard on realizing it had been another fruitless hunt. Fen nonetheless gave a nod before setting to brushing the horse. Beyond him, Benam was preparing a meal, and Lira was laying out bedrolls. Her hair was short and ragged. A mere smudge of dirt upon her face still managed to appear jarringly out of place, despite their lengthy travel together.

"Don't worry," Lira whispered as he approached. "It's best that we don't have a fire anyway."

Nonetheless, she wrapped her arms around herself to ward off the cold. Jeld forced a smile and set to helping her arrange the last bedroll. The bed of pine needles in the hollow was dry and clear of snow. The same could not be said of the forest floor without. Jeld had only rarely traveled through winter, when the odd job paid his father too well to turn down, or an unseasonal snow took them by surprise, but never had he endured the full of winter off the King's Road. As such, the group had come to rely heavily upon the winter fieldcraft of both Fen and Benam.

"We'll have a fine meal," Benam said. "Beans with a side of beans. More than many get."

The old knight was kneeling before an unlit firepit of the very sort he prepared each night despite never lighting it. Benam's sleeve was rolled up to reveal a thick wrap of bandages. He scooped a meager helping of beans from a pot of water at the firepit's edge and divvied it into four still smaller portions.

"We must remember our fortune," Benam said. "Thank the Idols for our freedom, and our meal, and one another. We have much."

"Praise the Idols," Jeld muttered, taking a plate. "It is only by their good graces that we've got more inquisitors trying to kill us than we have beans to eat."

Benam frowned as he handed Jeld a bowl.

"Jeld," Fen urged. He sat against a nearby tree and put a single bean in his mouth.

"Bless their guiding hands for shoving us into the woods for months when we should be trouncing Naelis."

"We're lucky to nearly be to Delvarad now at all," Benam said.

"May they just continue to watch over us," Jeld continued. "To *kill our families*, and—"

"Jeld!" Fen barked.

But Fen needn't have said a thing. A wave of anguish striking his heart silenced him and he looked to Lira.

"Sorry," Jeld said. "It's just—"

"No, I'm sorry," said Benam. "Hope and faith can belittle loss. I should be more sensitive."

"There's nothing wrong with a little hope," Lira said. "What else do we have?"

Sitting beside her around the would-be firepit, Jeld plucked a bean from his bowl and dropped it into hers.

"Sorry," Jeld said.

The group fell silent. Jeld placed another bean into his mouth and just sucked on it as he stared out into the woods. The first stars glimmered through the trees.

"We'll have our fill tomorrow," Fen mused.

Jeld felt everyone tense.

"Must we go into town?" Lira said. "We're close, why not just push through to Delvarad?"

"Not close enough," Benam said, his voice low. "We *might* make it if we faced no setbacks, but that bet would not have paid well along our journey thus far."

"But the whole kingdom is on the lookout for us," Lira said.

"There's travelers everywhere," Jeld said. "We don't have to be invisible, we just have to blend in."

"It was town last time," Fen said, digging at the pine needles with his heel.

Lira nodded. "They almost had us. We won't be so lucky next time."

"*They* were the lucky ones," Jeld said. "What were the odds of them being there, out of all the little towns and all the other days? They got lucky."

"Still, I don't like it," Fen said.

"It's not without risk," Benam said, wincing as he unraveled his bandages. "But that trip got us these very beans. We would have died of hunger by now had we been unwilling to trade off a certainty of death for a mere risk of one."

A twig snapped somewhere outside the camp and they all turned toward the sound. Jeld's own breath seemed to grow loud as he strained his senses. Seeing not but shadows, he closed his eyes and opened his mind. Only the familiar presences of his companions touched his mind.

"It's nothing," Jeld said.

"Perhaps we should split up," Lira suggested. "Stagger our arrival. They expect a group such as ours."

"Eh, splitting up has its own dangers," Jeld said. "Glendmill is no Tovar but it sees a fair bit of travel. We won't stand out. Plus, you'll be a boy again for good measure."

"Lovely."

Benam stood. "Rest your worries, my friends. Tomorrow will bring us only full bellies, and into our final stretch to Delvarad at last."

He crossed to his bedroll at the edge of the small hollow and laid down. "We wake early."

It couldn't have been three blinks before his breaths slowed in sleep. Lira took a final bite of beans and retired next. Rising to follow, Jeld gave Fen a gentle rap on the shoulder.

"Turning in soon?" Jeld asked.

Fen held his hands to the would-be firepit as if warming them. "Yeah, soon enough. Get a few things organized, then turn in."

"Need a hand?"

"Naw, all good. Thanks."

Jeld eyed Fen before putting a hand on his shoulder.

"Roba will be fine, Fen. They don't come any tougher."

"Yeah. Yeah, she will. She will."

"Get some rest."

Fen nodded. "You too, little prince."

Jeld grinned, gave Fen a final pat, and joined Lira. Their bedrolls lay beside one another. Lira was seated upon hers, suring up the straps of her pack. Her apprehension beat against Jeld, setting his own fears rising.

"We'll be fine," Jeld said, cinching a strap on his own pack. "It's not as if *every* town we've passed through had inquisitors."

"It's not that. Not *just* that. It's Delvarad."

"We'll make it. We're close."

"We're *late*. The usurpation is... cold. What if the moment has passed?"

Jeld eased her pack from her grip and laid it beside his own.

"Naelis murdered the king," he said. "That moment doesn't pass. There will never be loyalty there. The lords will heed your call. You're the rightful queen."

"What difference does it make to them whose head the crown sits upon? The kingdom is still intact, why should they risk their lives for me?"

Jeld took her hand. "You forget. Naelis is not just another king, he's a monster. If there is even a chance of stopping him, we have to take it. Not for you, but for the kingdom."

"If they don't come, a lot of good people will—"

"They'll come. I don't know anything of lords and politics, but I know you. And I know Benam. Even Dralor, sort of, and I know if the three of you agreed on a plan then it's a good plan."

Lira nodded hesitantly and set to smoothing out her already perfectly set bedroll.

"I think it's good," Jeld said.

She took a breath and laid down. Jeld followed suit, and together they stared up at the stars. The great star Hearth shone through the canopy in the northern sky, bright as ever.

"Finally got your stars, at least," Jeld said. "Had your fill by now though, yeah?"

"I only wish I'd met them on better terms. There's no denying their beauty, it's just... in my fantasies the stars were always freedom, where now they are a prison."

"They're not going anywhere. You'll have your chance again soon. Just one more bag of beans away."

"Delvarad is only just the beginning. If it isn't the utter end, anyway. And if town tomorrow isn't the end before that."

Jeld watched the stars twinkle in Lira's eyes. "Perhaps the adventure has already begun."

Lira met his gaze and gave a halfhearted smile before turning back to the stars.

***

The city of Glendmill boasted cobbled streets, a modest wall, and no fewer than four avenues lined with shops. Most called it not a town but a proper city, if only narrowly. With its position as the sole crossing over the Cairnich river for leagues, and its famed Glend flock wool, it stayed quite busy. Even at the early hour, today was no different.

Jeld veered through the market toward a corner store, his eyes and Idolic sense flicking about from face to face, mind to mind. After so many days in isolation his sense burned like an eye emerging from darkness. Each aura was an inquisitor, a soldier, or bountyman, until it wasn't. There was a troubling anxiousness of sorts in the air. Merely the early hour, perhaps. Or maybe it was just the ripples of usurpation. After all, rumor had it that war had broken out up north, with Lord Ralegus refusing to kneel to Naelis. Killing kings had consequences.

He peered over his shoulder to his companions following closely behind. Lira's flitting eyes landed upon him. Benam stood stoically at her side. Behind them, Fen scanned the market suspiciously. Jeld offered Lira his best reassuring smile and pressed through the door of the corner store.

The moment the door opened, a sound startled Jeld. His hand closed in an instant on the hilt of his blade, pulling it halfway from its sheath before his eyes locked upon an innocuous shop bell hanging above the door. The bell gave another pleasant jingle as the door closed behind Fen.

Jeld drew a deep breath. Behind a counter at the back of the shop, an older woman in an apron tried unconvincingly to appear as though she hadn't noticed Jeld's reaction. Benam and Fen went to the counter and exchanged pleasantries as Jeld and Lira browsed.

"Better be good beans," Jeld whispered.

"Idols know I could use some socks, too," Lira answered.

"I'd forgotten about everything but my stomach." Jeld grabbed a handful of bandages from a shelf and turned down another aisle. "You know we might just pull this off."

"Buying beans?"

"No, I mean… everything. Delvarad. Naelis."

"That all feels very distant. My concerns today are of beans, blisters… not kingdoms and wars."

Jeld spotted a pair of tall wool socks upon a shelf and held them up. Lira gasped and took them with a grin, then grabbed three more pairs.

After gathering a few more items they joined Benam and Fen at the counter. Lira kept her face turned from the shopkeeper.

"Three and five should do it," the proprietor said.

Benam placed three bricks and five pebs on the counter without so much as the slightest of haggling. The woman eyed him suspiciously before seeming to shrug.

"Safe travels," she said. "Safe as one can hope these days, anyway"

Benam shouldered a bag of beans. "Thank you. You as well."

Fen grabbed up the second bag, Jeld and Lira the remaining items, and they made for the exit. The brass shop bell bid them farewell, and as it fell quiet behind them only a heavy silence greeted them from the usually boisterous market.

Jeld froze. At once the tension in the market was palpable. He scanned the crowd and his breath caught as he spotted two robed figures on horseback. Inquisitors. A man and a woman, talking to a local guard. They were escorted by several Tovarian soldiers in crimson tabards. The very menace of the inquisitors sent a chill down his spine.

"Other way!" Jeld hissed to his companions. "Don't run. Steady."

"Our horses..." Lira said, nonetheless starting the other way.

"We'll circle back for them."

Jeld looked over his shoulder as he followed his companions, his every muscle screaming to run. Behind, one of the inquisitors suddenly went very still. She slowly turned, her eyes closed. Just as she came to face Jeld, her eyes suddenly opened and locked onto his.

"There!" came her voice across the market. Her mount reared and charged, the other close behind.

"Run, we're spotted!" Jeld yelled.

Jeld's companions were off at once. The bags of beans bounced on Fen's and Benam's shoulders.

"The alley, there! Horses won't fit. And drop the bleedin' beans, already!"

Benam carried on several bounds before frowning bitterly and dropping his bag. Fen only sped onward and into the narrow alley, beans and all. Behind them, the inquisitor leapt from her mount and raced into the alley after them.

"You guys go right!" Jeld huffed. "Circle back toward the horses. I'll meet you in Delvarad if not before."

"What!" Lira said.

"We'll never outrun them. I've got to slow them down. Trust me!"

Jeld sped into the lead so the inquisitor wouldn't see which way he turned. Fighting the urge to look back to Lira, he turned to the left. He hurried to a fruit stand and played at examining an apple.

"A fine crop," Jeld said to the fruit seller, peering past to the alley.

The inquisitor spilled from the alley and chased after Jeld's companions. He threw the apple back to a confused merchant and pursued, but after mere steps the inquisitor abruptly stopped and fixed her cold gaze upon him.

His eyes wide, Jeld slid to a stop and fled the other way as the inquisitor gave chase. How did she keep finding him? He searched frantically for some means of evasion. Cursing under each heavy breath, he turned onto a busy street only to find a horse barrelling toward him.

Jeld jumped aside, the horse's flank nonetheless sending him tumbling. He looked up to find the other inquisitor reining in the horse. Coming quickly to his feet, Jeld fled again. He turned into another narrow alley, then another, and another. He searched for his next move, but it was a dead end. Behind, the inquisitor woman appeared at the mouth of the alley and charged inward.

There must be a door. A window. *Something.* But none came, only smooth stone walls. Inescapable. He drew his sword and turned. The inquisitor slowed and pulled a needle-like sword from her robe.

Jeld's pulse pounded in his ears as he stared across drawn swords into the cold eyes of the inquisitor. He took a deep breath and took in the aura of the inquisitor. Though thick with hatred, it was not without subtleties. Patience. She liked her opponent to strike first. To lure them in. Still, with another inquisitor close behind, he had little choice but to oblige.

"Give me the bag," the inquisitor said. "It's all he wants. Your friends will be spared."

Jeld feinted high, then swept toward her legs. The inquisitor ignored the first and jumped his attack. Jeld sensed a flash of angry red from the inquisitor, and with it came a thought—*her* thought. He ducked as her blade shot out just where his head had been. Fast as he was, he nonetheless felt the inquisitor's blade pass through his hair.

He wouldn't avoid many of those, Jeld considered as he jumped backwards. His eyes flicked back to the impending wall behind. She preferred to counter... that meant he controlled the fight. He controlled when she attacked, and *where* she attacked.

He pressed forward with a barrage of conservative attacks. A body shot, a flick at her grip, a ring of her blade. Nothing committal. Nothing that would spring her trap, just make her hungry for his own. Finally, he put all his weight behind a high slash toward her neck, leaving his chest completely exposed. She ducked his attack, and plunged her blade deep into his chest.

Jeld charged into the inquisitor until half her arm was buried in his chest—into Kelthid's bag—then twisted his body until there came a cracking of bone. The inquisitor cried out and fell to the ground, her arm pulling free of the bottomless bag affixed to Jeld's shirt.

Jeld pressed his sword to her neck. "How did you track us! And how did you spot me!"

The inquisitor only glared venomously, her breath sharp through clenched teeth as she cradled her arm. Jeld pressed his sword deeper.

"The sense," the inquisitor said through clenched teeth. "Some of us can sense Idolics." She was growing pale. "You cannot hope to escape. This is our life. Our trade."

"Where do you all come from? Where do you learn this?"

When the inquisitor said nothing, Jeld shrugged and started pushing the point of his sword into her neck. She gritted her teeth and roared before finally crying out.

"The citadel!"

"The citadel... in Khapar? Where Master Sinwo teaches?"

Just then, the other inquisitor appeared at the mouth of the alley along with a squad of soldiers. The fallen inquisitor took full advantage of the distraction and rolled away before Jeld could finish her off. Jeld backed towards the end of the alley. His heart sped, mind racing for a way out—any way but the one way he already dared imagine.

The newcomers sped toward him. Jeld cursed and began unfastening his bag from his shirt. Back pressed to the wall at the alley's end, he stared at the closing inquisitor while his fingers fumbled with the buttons.

Just a moment away now. He tore the bag free with a rip and pushed his arms through the shadows within. He stared with wide eyes at the black void as he plunged his head inside. Somehow he expected to emerge, as if to pass through a waterfall to take a breath, but the nothingness only continued. He pressed his arms to the stoney floor or ceiling within and pulled himself inside. Looking back through the small hole—a window of light in the black ground—he saw the inquisitor draw a sword and lunge toward him.

Jeld reached out through the hole and grabbed the side of the bag. He stood frozen in the void for what seemed an eternity, heart filling with dread at the mere thought of what must be done. In the very moment the tip of the inquisitor's sword bit into the back of his hand, he jerked the bag in after him until there was only darkness.

CHAPTER TWO

L ira ducked in her saddle, narrowly missing a tree branch barely visible against the starless sky. Her breaths came quick and loud, punctuating the terrible bouts of barking behind them. She urged her mount onward with a kick, and despite the uneven footing and thick darkness, the blessed beast pressed on through the snow. It was the third day of nearly continuous riding since narrowly escaping Glendmill, and Lira wouldn't have blamed Jeld's old horse if it decided to throw her, or even simply to die. Even in desperate flight, Lira's stomach twisted at the thought of Jeld.

"They're gaining!" Fen yelled, riding up beside Lira.

"Faster!" Sir Benam yelled from ahead, slowing and waving them past. "There are too many to fight."

Suddenly the barking was not just behind but also ahead. Lira gasped and turned aside, charging nearly blindly through the forest. Her mount whinnied but she rapped its side and it pressed ahead, hooves splashing across some unseen stream.

Lira heard Fen cry out, then a loud crash beside her. She turned to see his horse standing back up without him. Benam reined in and climbed down, kneeling over what she now recognized as Fen lying on the ground.

"No, keep going!" Fen yelled.

The drum of hooves, cracking of branches, and barking of dogs grew louder from all around them.

Fen rose with a groan, hobbled a single step, then buckled again. Benam caught him and eased him to the ground as Lira too dismounted.

"No. Get to Delvarad," Fen said, struggling to rise.

Lira pressed a hand to Fen's shoulder. "We aren't leaving you."

"It was all for nothing, then" Fen breathed.

"One cannot regret failure, only never trying," Benam said.

The sounds of their pursuers closed in.

Fen let out a breath and nodded. "Help me to my feet."

Lira and Benam obliged and they stood together arm in arm as torch-wielding riders encircled them. One of the riders dismounted and drew his sword. Lira imagined the feeling of the blade pressing through her gut, the sound it might make. The meager contents of her stomach threatened to rise up.

"You stand against Liraelle Tovados, queen of Avandria!" Sir Benam boomed, drawing his own sword. "Cease your treason at once!"

The figure only drew closer. He wore black armor. Lightweight. Dressed for movement. For pursuit. For night. Lira's eyes fixed on the sword glimmering in the light of the man's torch. It was no longer her own death that gripped her, but that of Fen and Benam. And for what? For a crown. *Her* crown.

Lira stepped in front of her friends. "Do with me what you will, but spare them. They are nobody. Hired swords."

The man held his torch out. Lira flinched from the brightness at first, then forced her eyes open, waiting for the blade to pierce past the flame.

"You look like hell," came a woman's voice.

Lira looked past the flame to find not a man, but a woman. She looked perhaps the age Lira's father had been, with a strong jaw and thick eyebrows. She was looking at Benam.

"Tetchmira?" Benam gasped.

Lira knew the name, and faintly recalled meeting the woman in her former life. She was Benam's much younger sister.

"You never were around, but I can't have changed much. Idols, you look like an old man now, though."

Tetchmira turned to Lira and sheathed her sword. "Princess. We met once. You were a baby." She looked back at Benam and swatted his sword aside. "Oh put that away."

"Why the bloody mother are you chasing us through the woods!" Lira yelled.

"Father wants you. And he doesn't want that known, so I can't exactly go around shouting your names."

Lira's scowl broke and she loosed a single sob of relief. They were saved.

"What does he want?" Benam asked, his suspicion interrupting Lira's moment of relief.

Tetchmira frowned. "Hmm? Perhaps his son? His princess queen?"

The other riders began to set up camp around them. A pair of them were wrangling Fen's horse into the perimeter.

Looking unconvinced, Benam sheathed his sword. "How did you find us?"

"Whole world knows you were in Glendmill, and where you're headed. I figured you would take the hardest route to shake the inquisitors, a way only a Visleigh might know. Speaking of those inquisitor bastards, I heard the other boy fled from them into some magic bag. That true?"

Lira gasped. "What did you hear?"

"Told ya what I heard. Climbed into some bag, somehow. Pulled it in after him and—poof, gone. Same source said the boy did a number on one of the inquisitors first though, so I say cowshit to the whole of it. No boy can so much as scratch the sort that bested Handan Tovaine."

"Pulled the bag in?" Fen said. "He'd be stuck in there... at best. Right?"

Lira imagined Jeld inside that black void. Did it even have air? Dralor had survived going inside, but that had been for but a blink. Did the space even exist if Jeld had pulled the bag into itself, or was he just... gone? She wondered if maybe that wouldn't be for the better, simply to disappear instead of slowly starving or suffocating in the darkness.

Tetchmira shrugged then pulled a sack from her saddlebag. She produced a strip of jerky from it before eyeing Benam.

"Before I'd seen the look of you all, I'd thought you stupid for stopping in Glendmill." She threw the sack to Benam.

"Thank you, Tetch," Benam said, passing a handful to Lira, then Fen.

Lira took a huge bite and her eyes fell closed.

"Thank you," Fen said through a full mouth.

"Plenty more, and plenty else," Tetchmira said. "We travel light but not on food. Your leg alright?"

Fen nodded. "I can ride."

"Good." Tetchmira turned. "Abrol! Hot one tonight!"

"Aye, ma'am," came a youthful voice from someone among the shadows.

"Keep the fire small, mind you."

"Aye, ma'am."

"Do you think that's wise?" Benam asked.

"Your inquisitor friends turned east," Tetchmira said. "They could reach us yet, but we've a few days at least. We could all do with a warm bite, you lot especially."

Soon they were sitting around a small fire, stomachs full but nonetheless eating still. The flames only made the night all the more black to their eyes. The men of Delvarad encircling them could faintly be heard, offering a sense of security Lira hadn't felt since fleeing through the gates of Tovar.

"What of Delvarad?" Lira asked softly between mouthfuls of stew. "Has Lord Relthid..."

"Bent his knee?" Tetchmira offered. "Somewhat. My father has assured Naelis of no resistance, but also refused to lend his army. Or rather, he's managed to excuse them thus far without refusing outright."

Benam shook his head. "First he stands against the Idols, then against Beloros, and now he bows before Naelis. It's an embarrassment."

Tetchmira eyed Benam.

"Has he written the other lords?" Lira asked. "Surely they share a detestation of Naelis."

Tetchmira's eyes flicked to Lira. "Best let you discuss that with my father."

"Perhaps his stance will change once we put the odds in his favor."

Lira surveyed Fen, who pursed his lips not so reassuringly before returning to stitching a saddle for one of Tetchmira's men.

"You expect too much, dear princess," Benam said.

"Not the optimist I remember, then," Tetchmira said.

"Not in matters of our father, no." Benam bit his lip. "But... perhaps the Idols did shine upon us today."

Lira grinned. She wasn't convinced Relthid Visleigh wouldn't behead her to retain his lordship—nor, it seemed, was Benam—but considering she'd been expecting to be killed on the spot by inquisitors, perhaps the Idols had indeed shined upon them. She thought of how Jeld would no doubt react to Benam's albeit unconvincing faith, and her grin fell away as she pictured him forever falling deeper and deeper into the black void.

"Why did he send you?" Benam asked.

Tetchmira seems to consider her next words. "Why not? He's got Peyt. No matter if I fall in a ditch."

"He has more than his children."

"There are few he can trust. If Naelis finds out we have Lira..."

"I... see."

Tetchmira stood and kicked dirt on the small fire. "Rest up. Ten days to Delvarad."

With that, Tetchmira walked off into the darkness. Despite heavy thoughts and deep worries, sleep came quickly to Lira and her companions.

***

The howling wind pressed the front of the sleet-drenched bag over Lira's head against her mouth as she tried to draw a breath. She tried to raise her hand to pull it free until a tug about her wrists reminded her of the restraints. She turned her head aside and drew a breath, cut short as the hands upon her either elbow jostled her.

She felt the wind ease, then its whooshing suddenly disappeared with the rattle of a door closing behind her. Her captors tugged her onward. Lira tried to wipe her face against the bag to catch the water dripping down her face but managed only to collect more. She started to blow the water off her lips, then drank it instead. How the last months had changed her, she thought.

"Who're they, then?" an unfamiliar voice came.

"Can't say as I know, exactly," answered a deep voice. "Some folks who are thought to know things, I'm told."

Lira recognized the second voice as Arlaum, one of Tetchmira's men and the owner of the hand upon her right elbow, if she wasn't mistaken.

Several more jostles left or right. More muffled exchanges. Another tug ahead. Then Arlaum spoke again.

"Steps."

Lira reached out a foot, feeling for the steps. She shuffled forward and searched again. This time she struck something and planted her foot upon a step. She stumbled on the next, but her captors steadied her. Up they climbed.

Finally they came to a stop. There came the rattle of a door latch, another tug seemingly through the doorway, and a door closing behind. The grips upon her fell away, then her restraints, and then the bag over her head pulled free.

Lira flinched from the light. Reopening her eyes, she found herself in a room that was actually quite dim. Fine quarters even by the standards she'd left behind in Tovar. Arlaum stood to her one side, another of Tetchmira's men to her other. Yusch was his name, smaller in every way than Arlaum, with drooping but kindly eyes.

"Apologies, Your Grace," Arlaum said. "Your companions are in the adjacent rooms. You're free to leave your quarters but Lord Relthid insists it best that you remain in this wing. And he begs your forgiveness for not greeting you, but thought you might prefer to meet midday tomorrow. If it pleases you, Your Grace."

Lira's mouth hung agape as she stared into the room. Purple silken drapes hung from an oversized plush bed. Upon a dresser was a platter of fruits and sweets. Finally her eyes fell upon a doorway that could only lead to a lavatory. A small noise escaped her lips before she masked it by clearing her throat.

"Ah—Yes. Yes, it pleases me very much."

Arlaum bowed. "Good night, Your Grace."

Yusch bowed and both left the room.

"Good night," Lira said distantly as she drifted slowly into the room.

She reached out gingerly toward the billowy bed as if any sudden move might shatter the illusion, but her hand fell upon a velvety blanket. She let her fingers slide along it as she continued past to the lavatory. Inside, clouds of steam rose from a bathtub.

Lira peeled off her soiled clothing. Movement caught her eye and a hand sped to where her sword usually hung before she glimpsed merely her reflection in a floor-length mirror. The bath at once forgotten, she slowly approached the mirror, staring at the stranger within. She raised her hand to her face and the person in the mirror placed her hand on a gaunt, sun-baked cheek.

Lira let out something like a sob. She had seen her reflection in the odd stream or puddle or pale of water, but those rippling images could have been anyone. When was the last time she had truly seen herself, she wondered? It could only have been in Tovar, no doubt fussing with her hair or some outlandish outfit. No, actually it had been at the theater, in a polished plate used to direct a spotlight. Jeld had shown it to her. Even then, after a night sleeping atop some rooftop and another beneath a theater, it would have been a princess staring back. It would have been her. But now...

She stared into the mirror. Were she coming home from some grand adventure, perhaps a victor marching home from war, she could smile at the sight. She never cared to be some fair-skinned, dolled up princess, after all. But this was no adventure. She'd won no victory, only fled. Fled those that had killed her father. Those who had banished Benam and imprisoned Handan. Those who had killed Jeld, or worse.

Lira found herself wondering about her mother. In all likelihood she still danced her balls and held her winey socials all the same. Did she ever spare a moment to think about her daughter? Did she never feel even a spot of hatred at the sight of Naelis for murdering her husband?

She wiped away tears and a clean spot appeared on her cheek behind a smear of dirt. This returned her thoughts to the bath. It would be a mud bath if she didn't get some of the filth off first. She gave herself a quick once-over with a wet cloth, then lowered herself into the tub.

Her eyes fell closed and she leaned her head against the tub. A moan escaped her lips. She laid there until the steam had long gone and the water grown moderately cool before setting to cleaning herself. She scrubbed with exuberance, as if rather than toiling she were unwrapping some much anticipated gift.

Emerging from the lavatory wrapped in a towel, Lira plucked up a sweet roll from a platter and held it between her teeth whilst searching the dresser drawers. She was pleased to find ample clothing, having resolved to discard her ragged travel clothes even if it meant wearing a towel to her audience with Relthid. But clothing could wait. She stuffed what remained of the roll into her mouth, grabbed a second, and melted into the bed.

Her thoughts turned at once to the challenge she'd face the next day. She could already hear Relthid's refusal—*just a naive girl begging for a crown.* And he'd be right, wouldn't he? Of course, if he didn't refuse then things became even harder. Rallying the lords, then war. Troubling thoughts or not, she fell quickly into dreams.

***

Lira started at the sound of knocking at the door. Pressing closed a book on the history of Relthid's House Visleigh, she stood from a desk and started for the door.

"I'll get it," Sir Benam and Fen said together from a sitting area in the corner, both coming to their feet.

"No," Lira said. "I'll get it."

She paused with her hand on the door latch, frowning as she straightened her opulent green dress. Dressing in simple trail clothes had been a sure thing just two bells earlier when she'd woken, having resolved never again to fall into a life of decadence so long as any serving her suffered. But this had changed not long before the knocking. The dress wasn't for her. It was not a luxury, but a burden. A symbol of defiance. A symbol of the kingdom's perseverance.

Lira pulled open the door. Lord Relthid Visleigh stood alone in the doorway. He stood quite straight despite his years, gravity having claimed only a moderate drooping of the shoulders. His deeply lined face was cleanly shaven, his long white hair disorderly, and his eyelids pink as if of only a single layer of skin. He wore a black doublet and carried a substantial cane, its handle carved in the likeness of a rearing horse.

"Your Grace," he said.

His voice was cordial but stern. For a moment he looked almost disappointed, as if he'd hoped having the escaped princess of the kingdom in his guest quarters might have been just some dream.

"My lord," Lira greeted.

Lord Relthid walked past her without invitation. "Come, we have much to discuss."

Lira's temper flared. It was all she could do not to chastise the mere lord for barging in and leaving her to close the door like some servant. She took a slow breath. No, there might come a time where showing her teeth was necessary, but entitlement would offer a poor first impression. Here, Relthid was lord, and until she'd earned his loyalty, she was but a guest.

Lira closed the door and followed Relthid to the sitting area.

"Father," Benam said stiffly.

"Ben," Relthid breathed, coming to a stop before his son. "My, Tetch told it true."

Benam shook his head. "Yes, she was quite unrestrained when we met. Well, the journey has not been kind."

"You misunderstand. I mean to say you look the spitting image of my younger self. Like an old portrait of mine. Perhaps you recall the one?"

"In the western wing. Third level, in the hall between the aviary and the study."

Relthid forced a smile before turning to Lira. "Your Grace. You honor me with your visit."

"I am in your debt for seeing us here safely," Lira said. "We have gone to great lengths to reach you."

"Yes. Well, here you are, now."

Lira cleared her throat. "This is our companion, Fendrith."

"My lord," Fen said.

"Thank you for seeing the princess safely along." Relthid said. "Shall we sit?"

They did. A silence ensued, not long but heavy, until Lira spoke. "What of Naelis, my lord? What of the kingdom we are charged with protecting? What of the other lords?"

Relthid stared appraisingly back.

"Father," Benam started, "we don't mean to—"

"Enough! Do not sugarcoat her words. The princess has the decency not to waste my time talking around matters."

Benam said nothing, but his jaw set, a muscle tensing up his cheek.

"Naelis has a firm grip on Tovar," Relthid began. "Of the kingdom, less firm, but... he's faced little opposition. Our friends to the north have left the kingdom and have skirmished with Naelis a bit. Odsgaard only ever joined the kingdom for their countryman Tovados, so this was inevitable. Overdue, really. Warrinton... Lord Terich has managed to keep from lending his armies, citing pressures from the east, but there has not been a great need for them. Naelis has not asked for pledges, painting himself as but an extension of the line. This avoids opening the door for rebukes. So, barring any opposition, the kingdom simply... carries on."

"And you would just carry on, then?" Lira asked.

Relthid sighed and came to his feet with a grunt of effort. He filled four cups from a decanter on a nearby table and gave one to each of his guests. After, he slowly lowered himself halfway down into his chair before collapsing the rest of the way.

"Perhaps," Relthid said finally.

Lira sipped her drink, a puckery old brandy wine. "Why take us in? Unless you mean to turn us over, what purpose do we serve if you mean to let Naelis win?"

"He's waiting," Benam said, his drink untouched, eyes fixed on his father. "You want to see whether Naelis's grip will hold or not before you play your hand."

"Yes!" Relthid spat. "I'll not have you get us all killed and throw the kingdom into a bloody war until I know we'll win."

Lira considered Relthid's words. Perhaps he was right. Why should so many risk so much just to put a crown on her head?

"This isn't about you, Lira," Fen said, as if hearing her thoughts. "It's about stopping Naelis."

Lira smiled at Fen then turned to Relthid. "Taking us in is a poor hedge if you mean merely to wait. The kingdom waits for *us*, not we for it. Naelis will win if we do nothing." Lira's eyes grew distant. "But you know this. You are not waiting, you are hiding."

Relthid slapped the arm of his chair. "If Naelis falls I will welcome it! But I'll not have another generation of war for nothing!"

"You don't grasp the extent of Naelis's evil," Benam said, his voice low. "I've walked the death camps. I've seen the mountains of bodies. I've tended the starving, the stricken, the hopeless. You must do more than welcome Naelis's fall. You must instrument it."

Lira spoke. "I commend your hesitancy to shed the blood of our people. Too lightly do many resort to war despite its horrors. But here, in this, more would die under Naelis's rule than in a stand against him. I know you keep us here merely to stop us from opposing Naelis. Let me raise an army and stop him."

"*Raise an army!*" Relthid scoffed. "You don't understand. This all started under Dralor. To the people, Naelis is—Naelis is as the Idols taking down the mad king. An army is made up of people, and people don't war against their heroes."

Lord Relthid suddenly turned a glare on Benam. "And I know what you are thinking, so stop! The Idols were no heroes by the time I stood against them. They were—"

"I know," Benam said, his eyes rising to meet his father's. "I begrudged you for many years, but no longer. I may not fully agree, but I understand why you stood against the Idols."

Relthid's lines deepened in a surprised frown. He hid it behind a sip of his drink. "Yes, well. In any case, opposing Naelis will not be so easy as courting lords. Here in Delvarad, the people danced in the streets when Naelis took down your uncle. If I oppose Naelis, they'll just send him my head. Trenton fell from within only a week after Tovar. Plemenol days later. Then Caldemoor, even so far west. Those cities that did not fall immediately to uprisings still saw their people falling under the spell of Naelis's priests."

"The Sayers?" asked Benam with disbelief.

Relthid gave him an appraising look. "You didn't hear, then. Naelis established a new priesthood. Loyalist. Idol devotees. Red priests, some call them."

"Naelis will have them doing public stonings for drinking by springtime," Lira said. "The horrors of his camps will not long be secret. Soon all will know the truth of Naelis. Let us make preparations for that moment."

Relthid fell silent and his eyes grew distant. Finally, he shook his head. "There are few lords I would trust enough to broach this with. Naelis would waste no time in raising my city should he find out, and I assure you he would."

Lira considered. She'd had no qualms imploring the lord of Delvarad to at least gauge what support they might garner, but Relthid was right. The very first letter might well spark the war, and alone

Delvarad would fall. It would all have to be done in secret somehow. Hardly seemed possible, unless... Krayo.

"I will write to the lords under my own name," Lira said. "I know a way we might correspond without revealing that we're operating from Delvarad."

Relthid grunted dismissively. His eyes fell closed, his chin lowering to his chest. Lira couldn't help but wonder if he'd fallen asleep. She glanced at Benam, finding him staring intently at Relthid, then to Fen, who shrugged with a frown.

"How?" Relthid said finally.

"I cannot say, except that there is a man of great discretion whom I trust deeply."

Lord Relthid glanced to Benam then back to Lira. "Oh, very well."

Lira let out a breath and fought back a laugh of exuberance.

"But you'll confer with me on what lords we treat, and how!" Relthid chided. "And we'll make no promises of war until our support is known."

Benam stared at his father with a mixture of reverence and disbelief.

Lira came to her feet. "My lord, you honor me. You honor the kingdom. You will not regret this."

Relthid grasped the arms of his chair with bony fingers and fought his way to his feet. "No, I'm quite certain I will." At that, he rose with an effort, and left.

CHAPTER THREE

P rince Dralor roared with effort and flung his sword through the gate of Tovar. It spun end over end, whooshing through the air. Somehow the inquisitor charging after Liraelle upon his horse turned just in time, but hardly for the better of him. The sword slammed against his face and sent him toppling from his mount.

Dralor let out a breath and looked out through a cloud of dust to the wagon, finding Liraelle staring back from atop it. Their eyes met. Perhaps she would make it. Perhaps there was hope for her. Hope for what he'd left of the kingdom.

He turned and picked up a sword from the cobblestones beside a fallen watchman's body. No less than ten watchmen formed a semicircle around him, their swords leveled. Lira was off, he thought. The air was fresh and clear. Better to die now by sword than dangle in a public square tomorrow.

Dralor slapped aside the sword of a watchman at one end of their line. This pushed the watchman into his comrades and left an opening along the wall. Dralor charged through the gap, bringing his sword down behind him against the watchman's exposed neck. He kept right on running, making it out of the gateway before more watchmen cut off his escape and all encircled him once again.

"Press in!" barked a watchman with a sergeant's spaulder upon one shoulder. "Take him alive!"

Dralor lunged at a watchman, not bothering to knock aside the sword in his path. Sometimes you had to bet that your opponent cared more about living than about killing you. Even better when they meant to take you alive. The watchman pulled away, falling onto his back. Dralor pressed ahead to plunge his sword into the man's neck, but the others closed the gap at once.

The next watchmen were not so careful to leave Dralor unscathed. One slapped his sword aside and another swung for his upper arm. Dralor cried out as the blow struck true. He swung his sword in a wide arc to keep the watchmen at bay then passed his sword to his other hand. Without pause he charged again, piercing a watchman's shoulder before a sharp pain in his calf brought him to a knee.

Three swords pressed his own lower, the flat of another slamming against his wrist and sending his weapon to the ground. A heavy kick slammed square against his back, knocking him breathless onto all fours. Another in his ribs sent him to his side, and then they were all upon him, kicking and punching and stomping. Gritting his teeth through the blows, he stared through blood and flashing boots toward the city gate, just faint lines through the dust.

"Enough!" came the sergeant's bark.

A last blow to the back of his head sent a flash of light before his eyes, then he was dragged to his feet. The ground seemed to lurch from side to side beneath him, no less than three hands steadying him. His leg was wet with blood and managed to hurt over the general pain radiating throughout his entire body. Each step sent a shock of pain through his battered head. Otherwise, he was very much alive. He cursed to himself.

"Out of the way!" barked one of his captors.

"Move it," came the roar of another, followed by the hiss of drawn steel.

Dralor looked up from his half dragging feet just as what looked to be a large potato slammed into a watchman's cheek. A thick crowd had gathered around them, and while it gave berth to the blades of the watchmen, it gave little more.

"Dogs!" someone shouted from the crowd.

"Let him go!" said another.

"Aside!" yelled a watchman. "Aside or we'll have the lot of—"

Suddenly a piece of a cobblestone hit the watchman square in the temple. He folded to the ground, motionless. Two of his counterparts hoisted him up and carried him between them while others drew their blades, swinging them before the encroaching crowd. A woman at the crowd's forefront held her ground and spat on the lead watchman. He backhanded her with his swordhand.

The shouts of the crowd rose and more debris flew into the watchmen. The formation slowed then stopped as the watchmen fell and cowered beneath the onslaught. Something hard struck Dralor's shoulder with a sharp pain. The blow turned him halfway around and he realized nobody was holding him. Still, he only stood there. Beside him, several people were kicking a downed watchman.

A hand closed on Dralor's shoulder. He turned to find a woman with thick, curly gray hair before him.

"Come!" she said with a tug. "Quick now, there'll be reinforcements soon."

As if on cue, a horn blared deep and ominous. The woman released Dralor from her grip and started off through the crowd. Dralor looked once more over the chaotic scene then limped after her. The woman led him off the main road, snaking through narrower streets. They paused at an alley's end as the summoned reinforcements thundered past, an inquisitor at their center. Once it was clear, Dralor followed the woman onward as she wove south and east, toward Riverside.

She finally slowed to a walk as they spilled onto a busy street. Dralor looked up at the many windows and balconies above the shops lining the street. A woman on one such balcony was hanging wet clothes upon a line. An old man upon another sat whittling what looked to be a spoon. Recent mob notwithstanding, life went on. *Lives* went on. Lives that before had always been just a personified mass. Commoners. Averages.

He shook his aching head. The matter of whose head bore a crown had little influence on how fast clothes could be dried, or whether a spoon could be crafted in time for supper. Just then something struck his shoulder and turned him halfway around.

"Watch it!" barked a man in a sweat stained shirt, struggling to keep a cart of mussels from toppling.

Dralor steadied the man with a hand on his shoulder, and the peddler righted his cart with only one mussel lost.

"That's a peb, you owe me!" the man snapped.

Dralor only stared back. It all felt so surreal. Walking the city. Squabbling over a mussel. He felt as though he wore another man's body. Another man's life.

"Oy!" came the peddler's shout, jarring Dralor to the present.

Then the woman he'd been following was there, pushing a peb into the man's hand. Without a word, she took Dralor's hand in her bony grip and again they were off. This time, she did not let go as they walked. Dralor's head pounded as they went. The pain in his leg where he'd taken a blade radiated further down to his ankle and up past his knee. Everything ached. A heavy sweat dripped down his forehead.

"We'd best clean you up, you're getting looks," the woman said, stopping in a quiet alley. "And you could use a moment."

"I'll be fine," Dralor said, nonetheless leaning against the wall.

"Yes, because you'll rest."

Dralor slid down the wall to sit, his head lolling back against the bricks. The woman pulled a scarf from a small bag and began wrapping Dralor's leg.

"I don't mean to discount your injuries," she began without looking up, "but I've never seen so many watchmen try so hard *not* to kill someone. Why?"

Dralor long considered before giving a slight shake of his head.

"I see," she said finally. "You'll forgive my caution, but I need to know what I'm dealing with."

"I'll just be on my way," Dralor said, beginning to stand.

"Oh sit," the woman chided, continuing her bandaging as Dralor sank back down. "I don't imagine they were preserving you to do nice things to you, and anyone the watch wants to do such things to is likely a friend of mine."

She cinched a knot over the wound, Dralor wincing, then stood with a groan. "Very well. Keep your secrets. Come, let's continue along."

Dralor fought his way to his feet, his head and ribs and leg and everything protesting angrily.

"Where are you going?"

"*We* are going somewhere safe. Come, let us get off the streets. You'll see for yourself soon."

Dralor stared after the woman as she started down the alley. *Somewhere safe.* But to what ends? To kill Naelis? To reclaim the throne? He wanted none of that, but what was he if not the prince of Avandria?

The woman stopped at the alley's end and looked back to him.

Still Dralor considered. What else would he do, hobble about the city until he died or was taken up by the watch and hanged in a square for all to see? Perhaps merely to survive, then? Yes... it would have to be enough for now. To survive.

He followed the woman on through the city. After a time the stench of excrement in the air began to thicken. He had not spent much time in Riverside, but enough to recognize its scent. It was a welcome stench, for unless this woman meant to take him into the countryside, it meant their grueling walk must nearly be over.

He limped on, gasping whenever the odd step would send a jolt of pain radiating from one rib or another. Just when he could no longer bite his tongue to keep from asking how much farther they had to go, the woman stopped before a door. She produced two keys from her shirt, and her veined and bony hands deftly navigated the locks. Pulling the door open, she stood beside the doorway and turned to Dralor.

"I'd ask that you use the side door going forward," she said. "Too many comings and goings and we'll get undue attention."

Dralor peered inside. Light from two high windows illuminated a broad room littered with tables bearing candles of all shapes and colors. The thick scent of countless perfumes wafted out from the shop. Shelves lined one wall, packed with vats presumably of wax or tallow, as well as a range of tools. A boy was pouring the contents of one such vat into a cylindrical mold, another boy holding a wick in place. A woman was meticulously carving some design into a large purple candle.

"I don't do as much myself as I'd like to anymore," Dralor's guide said. "Oh I can manage, but I haven't the time. Too busy cleaning up the prince's mess."

Dralor went still.

"You alright? Look like you've seen a ghost. It's the talk of the prince, isn't it? Would you believe I once stopped a boy from sticking him with a knife at a parade? Never a day goes by I don't kick myself for that one, I'll tell you that." She gave a smile. "Well, with any luck

High Priest Naelis will right things, but they all come with their own messes. Right, come in, then, come in."

Dralor drew a breath and entered. The woman closed the door behind him then barred it and turned two locks. She led him inward, stopping before the woman carving a candle.

"This is Callie," the older woman said of the carver. "My only proper apprentice. The rest I teach well enough, but it's sheltering that brought them here. Callie, this is—" She laughed. "Well, who is this, then?"

"Del," Dralor said after too long a pause. He'd thought first of his father Beloros, then of his own shortened name before settling on something in between.

"And pardon my not saying so before, but I'm Raf."

"Again Raf goes to market for nails and meat but returns only with a person," Callie said. Only the slightest traces of girlhood lingered upon her face, but none of time's lines. Her blond hair was drawn back in a tight braid.

Raf smiled, but it fell away and her eyes grew distant. "Would that it were not necessary, my dear."

Suddenly she gasped then turned to Dralor. "Idols, forgive me. Making introductions when you can barely stand. Come, Del, let us get you settled."

Dralor limped after her as she headed for a staircase at the back of the shop. The boys continued their work with little more than a glance. Dralor paused behind her at the base of the stairs before setting his jaw and following her up, a hand pressed to one wall and a shoulder to the other.

Reaching the top, sparkling motes danced before his eyes. Cots packed a broad room that once must have looked quite nice, with maroon papered walls and quaint furniture since crammed aside. As he followed Raf across the room, the walls seemed near, then far. They spun and he staggered, but Raf's grip steadied him with surprising strength. He took several slow breaths until the world settled, the grave look upon Raf's face coming into clear enough focus.

Dralor offered Raf a firm nod, and she stared back for a time before picking some folded blankets from a pile and leading him across the room toward two doorways. Inside the first, two young girls played some game with yarn woven between their raised fingers. A broad shouldered man with a bushy beard, and a tired looking woman both sat upon a nearby cot in quiet conversation. The woman gave Dralor a look somewhere between fearful and threatening.

Raf led him through the second doorway. The small room beyond was unoccupied, the floor bearing a makeshift bed of piled blankets.

"We'll squeeze you in here," Raf said, setting out the other blankets to form another bed. "It all gets a bit cramped come evening, but what can we do?"

Dralor slowly lowered himself to the newly placed blankets, hissing through his teeth as a stab of pain shot up his leg. He leaned back against the wall, drawing a breath and slowly letting it out.

"You... shelter people," Dralor said, lifting his injured leg onto a chair. "Criminals."

"Are you a criminal? The watch seemed to think so."

Dralor fell silent. His mind turned to the sprawling camp at the foot of the prison tower looming just north of the city gates. *Prince's Prison*. He hadn't expressly ordered the worst of it, but deep down he'd known the horrors that went on there, and yet he'd done nothing. He thought too of the countless people that had been sent to various other jails throughout the city in his sweeps. Maybe Naelis had deceived and provoked him, but that was a poor excuse. No, he'd done far worse than any criminal.

"Never mind," Raf said, holding up a hand when Dralor made to speak. "It matters not. Whatever you did, the crown did worse."

Dralor's eyes fell.

Raf gave a comforting smile. "I'll have Eshal come see to your leg. Rest up, we'll talk more tomorrow over breakfast. Or lunch. Sleep as long as you need." She gave the doorframe a pat then left.

Dralor let out a long breath. Eyes half closed, his gaze fell to his clothes. A mud of dirt and blood caked the whole of his tunic. The pant leg that was not bandaged was ripped halfway off. It was no wonder the mussel peddler had treated him like a street dog.

Suddenly he gasped, hands shooting up to his collar. Fingers closing upon a pin on the underside of his collar, he eased back down against the wall. He pulled it free and looked down at it, a beaming sun set in gold. He'd taken it from his brother before the pyre. Somehow it had gone unnoticed by the guards during his imprisonment, and somehow it hadn't been beaten loose by the gate.

The pin had been their father's, a gift from Tovados. It had come to represent their rule after decades upon the monarch. Dralor had borne it for only days before the kingdom collapsed. He shook his head at his failure, wishing very much that his brother were here with his calming smile and hopeful counsel.

A slight cough drew Dralor's attention to the doorway, his hand closing around the pin. The large man he'd glimpsed in the other room stood there, broad of shoulder and a full head taller than he. He had a bushy beard, and held a bucket of water in one sizable hand. *Eshal*, Dralor presumed.

"Need a hand with your leg, I hear," the man said with a surprisingly soft voice, entering without pause.

Dralor forced himself to sit up. "That'd be wise."

Eshal set the bucket beside Dralor's feet and set to unwrapping Raf's makeshift bandages. "Whose blood on your shirt there?"

Dralor said nothing. The folk here had no love for the watch, yet he didn't figure being branded any sort of murderer would do him much good.

"If it was yours I'd have been asked to tend more than your leg," Eshal added, surveying the gash on Dralor's leg. "Whose blood, then?"

"The watch," Dralor said finally.

Eshal's hands stilled, his eyes growing distant. After a long moment he blinked and gave a grunt. "Probably for the best."

Eshal set to washing Dralor's wound with a wet cloth. "I'll pick up a salve first thing tomorrow. Should heal up just fine if we keep it from festering."

Dralor nodded. Eshal finished in silence then wrapped it in a fresh bandage.

"That should do for now," Eshal said. "I'm going to go see if Raf needs anything, but I'll check on you later."

"Thank you," Dralor said.

He found himself wondering what might have brought Eshal here. What circumstances might bring together a prince and whatever it was Eshal considered himself? He recalled the man's children at play in the next room and his thoughts turned to his own broken family, if it could even be called a family.

"You are fortunate to have your family with you," Dralor added.

"Hm?" Eshal said as he stood. "Oh. That was Jollel and her children there. Just arrived yesterday. No… my own awaits me."

The large man's face reddened with anger and his chest began to quickly rise and fall.

"My apologies," Dralor said. Though curious, he dare not pry lest he invite such inquiries of himself.

Eshal closed his eyes and looked aside. His breathing slowed and he nodded as if reassuring himself. "Taxmen came. It was a poor crop, and I was short of what they asked. They threatened us, and—I should have kept my mouth shut, but..."

"Taxed at your farm?" Dralor blurted. He'd never approved such a practice. Rather, Loris never had. *Naelis,* then.

They fell silent for a time before Dralor spoke. "Can you not return?"

"I will. On foot if I must, but I haven't the coin to get through the gate or make the trek. I hadn't even any shoes when first Raf freed me. She gives what she can for my help, though it's I that should be paying her." He shook his head. "Plus, if I return too soon and men go looking for me... it'd put my girls in danger."

Eshal suddenly bared his teeth and punched the wall with a huge fist. He roared, then looked to Dralor and lowered his voice again. "Apologies. Apologies."

Dralor accepted the apology with a shadow of a smile. He offered another thanks and bid his roommate farewell. Left alone, he laid upon his back, bunching a bit of blanket beneath his head and letting out a deep breath. His eyes fell closed, but seeing only Lira's fleeing wagon, he opened them to stare instead at the ceiling. This fared no better, with the memory of General Handan falling beneath the blows of two inquisitors playing upon the wood. He saw Benam's eyes as he banished the old knight. Then, his mind turned to Loris. His dear brother, dead at the hands of a mob that never should have been. A mob Dralor had as good as created.

He rapped his head against the wall and his splitting headache shot a sharp pain clear to his shoulders. He pinched his eyes closed, and despite the haunting thoughts, he soon fell into dreams.

Chapter Four

Lira stood before an open window within her quarters in Delvarad. Fen was beside her, Benam at the desk re-reading one of the many letters strewn about it. She might consider her apartments nice, were they not a prison. Truth be told, she wasn't actually certain what Relthid might do should she try to depart, but it mattered little seeing as she could think of no better place to go.

Outside, the legendary plains of Delvar stretched as far as the eye could see. The sunward slope of each of the rolling hills peeked through the snow. Lush green grass showed beneath the edges of streams swollen by the melt.

"We might as well have waited in Tovar for the snow to melt," Fen mused. "We'd have arrived here at nearly the same time."

Lira grunted. "We couldn't have known we'd be fleeing off the road the moment we left the gate. And probably they'd have found us there. Besides, we'd still not have arrived quite this soon, and these weeks have been invaluable."

"Invaluable? We've got a few small lords perhaps, but not enough. Even if we did, who's to say whether Relthid would truly let us act, let alone fight for us."

Benam stiffened at the disparaging talk of his father, but could not bring himself to disagree on that point. "And Warrinton. And Odsgaard," he said without looking up from a letter.

Lira pursed her lips thoughtfully. "Yes, but Warrinton will spare little. Lord Terich is as loyal to me as he is to his duty defending the kingdom from the East."

"It's something," Fen said. "I suppose just knowing they won't stand against you is something. Beats dreamin' *Caldemoor*."

The wound was still fresh for all of them. "I'm sorry," was all Lord Ashlun's letter had read, without so much as a signature. One might forgive his quick surrender, with Naelis marching upon them even before Tovar had fallen, but their loyalty was another matter.

Benam soon joined them by the window and they watched the sun set. Afterward they settled around a small table for a game of Scratch, so named for the varying number of lines marking the stone game pieces. The sky grew dark as they played, the room with it.

Fen moved a stone marked with two scratches onto the cloth in a square beside one of Lira's pieces. He stood and added a log to the glowing embers that remained of their fire. Sparks swirled up into the air as the log settled down through the lighter char with a soft rustling. All three started as a knocking sounded at the door. Lira wondered at its purposes before realizing they'd not been brought dinner yet.

"Come in," Lira called.

She turned back to the game until Benam suddenly stood. The young attendant boy Relthid had assigned to them stood in the doorway. He bore not a tray, but a letter. Lira stood, frozen in place. She'd been giddy with excitement at the first such letter, but as the rejections piled up, they had begun to bring about a very different mood. This was the first in weeks. Could very well be the last, and what then? Then it would be over. All of it. Her father would have died for nothing.

She exchanged a look with Benam. The old knight was plainly holding himself in place only with great restraint.

"Go on," she said, but Benam only shook his head and reclaimed his seat.

Lira took a breath, then started slowly toward the door. The attendant boy shuffled his feet nervously. Lowering his gaze, he held out the letter. Lira's world was reduced to the seal upon it. Firelight and shadows warred across the surface, revealing little more than meaningless bumps and grooves upon black wax. The light shifted with each step. Still she hadn't her answer as she took the scroll in her hand and turned it to the light. The ridges in the wax became walls of a towering keep.

"It's from Havaral," Lira whispered, her feet carrying her back toward the others as the attendant closed the door behind her.

Like the firelight and shadows upon the wax, emotions grappled within Lira at the revelation. To call Lord Annend Cross her grandfather was to do little more than name the blood in her veins. A rejection from him would almost be refreshing for the lack of pretense, if not for also crushing any hopes of victory. Without Havaral there were few paths to mustering the force they'd need. With it, they'd still need Relthid, and that seemed increasingly unlikely. Even with an army, it all seemed more likely the beginning of a far deadlier march to the same outcome. Would it not be better to just let it end now with Havaral's refusal? Must so many more die for nothing as her father had?

She sat, Fen and Benam leaning forward in their chairs beside her. Her fingers slid habitually beneath the seal despite it having already been broken by Relthid like all the others. She unrolled the scroll, eyed her companions, and began reading to herself. Benam and Fen stared. The fluttering and popping of the fire grew loud in the ensuing silence until, finally, Lira lowered the scroll.

"Lord Annend pledges his support," she breathed, her eyes staring still where the message had been. She turned to the others and spoke again, louder. "Lord Annend pledges his support."

Benam's eyes welled and he nodded slowly. "All will be set right."

"Down to Relthid, then," Fen said softly.

Lira huffed, hope already melted away. "He'll never go along. Without him we'd need every other little lording to go along, and that won't happen. Why did we even bother?"

"Perhaps when he hears that Havaral—"

"You *know* he's heard, he reads my letters before I do!" Lira shouted, coming to her feet and pacing away. "What fools we've been. He won't risk it. Why should he? He'll just lock us away here to keep things as they are."

Fen leaned back in his chair. "Until the dust settles. He'll have little need for us then."

"Ease your worries," Benam said. "Will he fight... I don't know. But he will not *execute* us."

"Execute, exile, cage... they are all endings," Lira said, sitting at the hearth. They all fell silent for a time before she sighed and spoke again. "It may be for the best. It's as Relthid said, Avandria needs peace more than it needs one person or another on the throne."

"No," Benam said quickly. "There is no peace under Naelis. War is a terrible price, but it is a price we must pay to save Avandria from decades of persecution."

The door burst open and Relthid hurried in, cane tapping. He was pale and breathless, his eyes wild.

"Liraelle," he said between breaths. "I'm sorry, but—"

"Yes, I know!" Lira spat, already on her feet. "You won't fight with us. You saw Havaral's pledge and must finally come to terms that you never intended—"

"Inquisitors," Relthid shouted, silencing the room with a word. "They are here. I don't know how—"

"Here?" Lira said, her voice coming out smaller than she'd intended. "You have to stop them. They are powerful, but no army."

"They are in the keep. I couldn't stop them, but we've delayed them below, if only a little."

"You let them in…" Lira breathed, drawing a blade from her hip. Fen and Benam had already retrieved their weapons and were taking up position between her and the door. "You've already surrendered!"

"I had no choice!"

"You told them I was here, that—'

Just then there came the rapid slap of footfalls. They all turned to the door and Tetchmira rushed inside, her teeth bared and chest heaving. Blood streamed from a gash on one hand, and she clutched at her side with the other.

"They come!" she hissed breathlessly. "I'm sorry, father. We could not stop them!"

Tetchmira glanced out the doorway and her eyes widened. She darted back inside and slammed the door closed. She pressed her back to the door and dug her feet against the ground. Despite Tetchmira looking the spitting image of a battle-hardened warrior, Lira was reminded of a child as Tetchmira looked desperately to her father. The shared look did not last but a blink before the door burst open, slamming Tetchmira against the wall, where she crumbled to the ground.

Two inquisitors stood in the doorway, a man and a woman, both with the telltale white robes, shaved heads, and pale skin. The woman entered first, empty-handed despite a thin blade sheathed at her hip. One of her arms was splinted to her chest. The man followed, a curved blade held casually at his side. He was older and a head taller than the woman. They stopped across from Fen and Benam, the woman flicking a glance to her partner.

Lord Relthid slunk along the wall toward the exit, the inquisitors seeming either not to notice or not to care. At the door, Relthid turned and met Lira's scathing glare before hurrying from the room. Despite the more pressing danger of the inquisitors, Lira stared after him, shaking her head. She could hardly blame anyone for fleeing an inquisitor, but it was more than that. It was the complete affirmation of the cowardice and deception she'd already known lurked behind his hospitable front. He'd handed her over to the inquisitors, and didn't even have the courage to stay and watch the bloody fruits of his betrayal.

"Is that the one?" asked the taller inquisitor, his eyes upon Fen.

"No. I don't think so," the woman said, her eastern accent even thicker than the man's

"Are you certain?"

The woman narrowed her brow at Fen. "Yes. The other was smaller."

The other flashed his teeth in something like a curse. His curved sword rose to point at Fen even as his eyes fixed on Lira. "Where is the other? The young man, from Tovar. Arvin Emry."

Lira looked to Fen. His eyes were wide, breath coming fast. A sweat gleamed upon his forehead. He was a man caught before a viper, a man who knew he could not run, could not fight—that whether he would live or die was out of his hands, left only to the viper. Yet still Fen held his sword out at the ready. Beside him, Benam held his larger sword steadily in a two-handed grip. She could not tell if he looked resigned or confident.

She wanted to command her friends to stand down, as she had in the woods, but the inquisitor's message was clear. How could she ask him to stand down when already the inquisitor threatened her with his death?

"We don't know," Lira said through clenched teeth, suddenly furious. "We were separated. *You* chased him! So, where did he go?"

The inquisitors exchanged glances, and Benam lunged. His sword just touched the man's robe before the curved blade rang against Benam's in a flash and twisted it from his grip. Fen charged the same inquisitor. In a blur of speed, the other was suddenly there. Her small knife stopped Fen's larger sword overhead with seemingly little effort, then flashed toward his side.

"Stop!" bellowed the man.

Fen cried out as the tip of the knife bit into his side, then the inquisitor froze. Fen's eyes flicked down at the rest of the blade still showing above his shirt. With a wicked sneer, the woman swirled the blade and Fen groaned through his teeth.

"Enough, Jital!" the male inquisitor shouted, his blade at Benam's neck. "We do not take pleasure in what we must do! Are you still a *clati?*"

The one called Jital scowled at her partner and pulled the knife free. Even as another pained groan escaped Fen's lips, he brought his sword down hard upon the woman. In a flash, she sidestepped the blow, stabbed Fen through the forearm, and kicked him behind the knees. Fen fell to his knees, clutching his bleeding arm.

"Enough," the older inquisitor said again, almost a whisper this time. "The other, he had a bag, yes?"

"You know he did," Benam said before Lira could deny it. The inquisitor's sword whispered over his whiskered neck with every breath. "We know little of it."

"Where did he get it? What was inside?"

"We don't know."

"Where did it lead?" the inquisitor pressed. Benam backpedaled half a step as the sword pushed harder against him. Blood trickled down the blade.

"To darkness!" Lira spat. "To emptiness! To death!" She sobbed the last.

"They lie," Jital said, her words full of venom.

The man met Lira's gaze, then Benam's and Fen's in turn. On his feet again, Fen glared back, his broad shoulders rising and falling. Blood seeped from between the fingers pressed over his wound.

"Perhaps," the man said. "It led to darkness. Very well. Where did he get it?"

Lira said nothing until the woman took a step toward Fen. "A dream!" she said quickly. Her eyes fell to the ground as she considered her betrayal.

"A dream," the inquisitor repeated, ignoring an eye roll from Jital. He drew a breath and spoke again, louder. "We will continue this conversation on our journey to Tovar. The high priest has many questions about this bag. And this boy. And your little letters."

Suddenly the inquisitor's blade swept across Benam's neck in a flash. Lira's breath caught, a primitive, quavering cry escaping her lips before terror froze even that. She met the eyes of her beloved tutor, protector, and friend above a line of red crossing his neck. The sickening cold of horror twisted its way through her, but the gushes of blood that had in an instant terrorized her imagination did not come. The line stayed fine, only a few beads of blood trickling down Benam's neck. A cut. Just a cut.

Benam's nostrils flared above a shaky frown, but his shoulders did not sag nor his chin fall. He would not give them the victory of fear.

The inquisitor waved his sword toward the door. "Go."

Jital sheathed her knife with bored indifference and started for the door. Lira shot the remaining inquisitor a cold glare, then nodded to her friends. Pressed between their Idolic captors, they followed.

Jital stepped through the doorway, then in a sudden flash her knife was drawn and raised defensively before her face. But no sooner was it there than it was gone, and the top half of her head lifted then fell in an explosion of red. Only then did Lira hear the clang of steel.

When Jital's body folded lifelessly to the ground, there was a man standing behind her. He had receding charcoal hair peppered with gray, a full beard of similar hue. He was fairly tall and broad shouldered, but not imposingly large. Yet, the air about him filled the room as if a bear stood in the doorway. Lira stared past his beard and bloodied sword into his deep brown eyes. They were unblinking, wide not in surprise but rather in grave purpose.

"Handan," she breathed.

Handan Tovaine flowed into the room, sparing not a moment of attention for anyone but the next inquisitor as he circled toward him.

The inquisitor leveled his sword at Handan. "You will *pay* for robbing the Idols of a servant!"

Handan said nothing, only closing the distance slowly until suddenly his blade shot out. The inquisitor's curved sword was there before Lira saw it twitch. Steel clashed. Their blades locked overhead for only an instant before the inquisitor's eyes widened and his blade gave way. He jumped aside and Handan's blade sliced a shallow cut down his shoulder.

The inquisitor bared his teeth and charged forward toward the impassive Handan. Their swords whirled and rang, Handan seeming never on the defensive but rather *attacking* the blows that rained upon him until he was the storm. The inquisitor did not again make the mistake of attempting to catch the incoming blows, only turning them and dancing aside. He deflected another, then three more until the next sliced him across the side.

Wincing, the inquisitor tried to force Handan back with a broad sweep, but the once-general slapped it aside and attacked in the same swing. Steel shrieked until the inquisitor's blade caught in one of the many deep notches now scarring Handan's weapon. Blades crossed, they pressed against one another like great antlered beasts. Handan grit his teeth and the muscles in his arms bulged. Slowly, the inquisitor's feet began to slide across the stone floor. Sweat shone upon the inquisitor's brow and he dug his heels in, but still he slid.

Behind, Benam retrieved his sword from the ground. Lira fought not to betray him with even the slightest flick of her eyes. Then he lunged. Suddenly the inquisitor jumped aside, spinning and swatting away Benam's attack as Handan's sword came down where he'd stood. The old knight swung again, but the inquisitor caught it overhead, and pulled both their swords down against Benam's neck.

"Stop or he dies, and the girl next!" the inquisitor shouted. He circled toward the door, dragging Benam with him.

Handan slowed his pursuit but not completely, only matching the inquisitor's retreat. He looked to Lira and waved her behind him with a tilt of his head. Lira obliged but a single step before halting, realizing Handan's intent. She shook her head, not wanting to risk Benam.

When the inquisitor reached the doorway, his eyes flicked to Lira and she knew the terrible fault of her logic. He was going to kill Benam regardless. The inquisitor's lips pursed in a bitter frown and the muscles in his arm tensed.

Suddenly the inquisitor grunted and his eyes widened. Whatever happened, he wasn't finished. He snarled and spun. His sword lashed out at whatever or whoever must have stood in the doorway beyond him, but Handan was there in a blur of speed. His blade cleaved up the inquisitor's side through flesh and ribs and the vitals within then crashed against the inquisitor's sword, stopping it cold.

The inquisitor followed his entrails to the ground. Lord Relthid stood in the doorway beneath Handan's still raised sword, a long bloody knife held in both hands. Benam held his father's gaze and something passed between them, respect or understanding or some blending of the two.

Lira looked about the room and everything seemed to lag behind where she turned. A ringing seemed to fill the room, yet she felt it more than heard it. The tunnel of her vision fell upon the disemboweled inquisitor, then the other just beyond in another pool of blood. She saw Fen sitting upon the ground, Benam wrapping his arm in a strip of cloth.

"Their escort," Tetchmira's voice came through the ringing. She was sitting up against the wall now. "We must stop their escort."

"It's done," Relthid said, staggering into the room and collapsing into a chair. "Our men have them."

"Your Grace," a voice came and Lira turned. She stared as her vision caught up with her before settling on Handan. "It's over, Liraelle. Take a breath."

Lira felt herself nodding, but nodding turned into the shaking of her head as if in disbelief or denial. Handan grasped her shoulders firmly and she met his eyes. So immense was the strength within him that she could not help but feel it. Suddenly the ringing stopped and she sucked in a breath as if emerging from deep water.

"Handan," she whispered. "But how..."

Handan turned to the sound of men rushing down the hallway. Soldiers of Delvarad came to a stop in the doorway, eyeing the bodies of the inquisitors before surveying the room.

"Have someone see to this mess," Relthid barked.

"What would you have us do with the inquisitors' men, my lord?" a brawny soldier with a sergeant's band asked.

"Kill them," Relthid said. "Likely Naelis knows the princess is here, but then perhaps not. In any case, we want to slow news of today's events." His eyes flicked to Benam. Again their gazes met, but Benam was not so proud this time.

The sergeant gave his orders and his men split to their tasks. Most departed to deal with the inquisitors' men. The three who remained helped Tetchmira into a chair then turned their attention to the mess. They stood over the bodies looking rather uncertain where to start before departing presumably to retrieve supplies.

Lira took Handan's arm and he led her to a chair beside Relthid.

"How did you escape Thenally Island?" she asked. "How did you find us?"

Handan did not sit, but sheathed his sword. "It is not a short tale."

"Then do not tell it all, but tell it some."

"As you wish. In truth, I never reached the prison. Naelis was careful to strip the crew of any who might be loyal to me, but my men pursued under the guise of an escort ship." He swelled with pride. "There is much more to tell here, but suffice it to say the ships were both damaged when my men attacked, and we were adrift for weeks before a ship from the Isles discovered us and took us to Caerghallad."

He shook his head. "It was there that I learned of Tovar's fall. And of Dralor's death, and that you'd gone missing."

Lira's hand jumped to cover her mouth. Dralor was truly dead, then. Often she had wondered whether Dralor had died at the gates that day they had fled Tovar, or by execution in the moments or days to follow, but never had she doubted his death. Yet, hearing it stated as fact for the first time set her hand trembling.

Handan continued, his eyes staring past Lira. "I have been searching for you ever since." Suddenly his eyes narrowed and he turned to Relthid. "You told me you didn't know her whereabouts. I've been here for *days!*"

"Yes, yes. You've every right to be angry," Lord Relthid said. He sighed and pushed himself back onto his feet. "Rest and clean yourselves up. We'll dine in the great hall tonight. No sense continuing this charade. We have much to prepare."

Benam cleared his throat. "To prepare... for what?"

Lord Relthid reached the doorway and turned back to face them all. "For war."

Chapter Five

Dralor searched past the large basket of linens upon his shoulder to try to glimpse what seemed to be the last bird still singing the morning's song. It carried over the rumble of wagon wheels and the street chatter that was only just beginning to meld into a more homogenous chorus. The bird's song was familiar, one he must have heard a thousand times before. Perhaps on marches with his armies, or at the highest windows of his palace. Yet he wondered now if he had ever truly listened to it.

Then he spotted the small red bird in an unlikely tree rising from the cobbles at a fork in the road. It flitted out, pausing in the air to loose what may have been a threat or a greeting, but in either case sounded just as pleasant. It then circled straight back to its perch.

Dralor had seen little meaning in even the finest arts gracing the royal palace, nor felt much in the songs of the greatest bards of Avandria. Where others might stop, stare, tear up, find meaning… he'd seen nothing. Heard nothing. Had he not scoffed at, even ridiculed men for such sentiment? Now here he was staring at a bird.

"You coming, Del?" Eshal said.

Dralor started and turned to Eshal. The big man bore a similar basket upon one shoulder, though it looked much smaller on him. "Yes. Yes, continue."

Eshal gave him an inquiring look then went on his way. Dralor glanced back once more before following after Eshal, the bird's song trailing after for a time before being lost in Tovar's waking voice. They made several more turns, then Eshal dropped his basket beside a long trench between two women washing clothes. Grunting as he lowered his own basket, Dralor squeezed in beside Eshal.

Dralor took the first cloth from his basket. It was one of the bandages from his leg, among the earliest from the week prior, judging from the sizable stain of blackened blood. The bleeding had quickly slowed in the days to follow, the wound closing nicely. He watched Eshal work before dunking the bandage beneath the foamy surface of the water.

"It works best if you don't ball things up," Eshal said. "And do not just squeeze with your fingers, scrape it against the trough. Be firm. Better to rip a thread than to rot a garment."

Dralor's eyes flicked to Eshal before nodding and applying the recommendations without a word. When his companion pulled a blanket up from the trough and wrenched it dry, Dralor did the same with the bandage, then again as it continued to drip. He felt Eshal's eyes upon him.

"What?" Dralor said irritably.

Eshal laughed. "Like this," he said, taking the bandage. "Start at one end. You're just moving the water around."

When Eshal had twisted the last drips from the corner of the blanket, he hung it over the side of his basket and Dralor started on the next cloth.

"Don't do much laundering, then?" Eshal asked as they worked their way through their mounds.

Dralor scrubbed a heavy woolen blanket as he weighed his words. "It was never my task."

"No judgment," Eshal said, holding up a big hand in apology. "I should not have laughed. Anyway, I wasn't laughing at your washing ability so much as your reaction. No, we've all got our strengths. Milk a cow, plant a field... swing a sword."

At the edge of his vision, Dralor saw Eshal eyeing him and he felt his hackles rise up. But no, only curiosity. Only natural.

"And today I learn another," Dralor said. "Washing."

Eshal smiled, not pressing further as they continued their chore.

"My wife did more than her share of the washing," Eshal said distantly, his smile long since faded. "But I am proud to say I am no stranger to it. And she can work the fields and the animals as well as anyone. My girls, too. I suppose they are getting along just fine without me then, eh?" Eshal's big knuckles went white around a cloth. "Just fine, I'm sure. Just fine."

"Just fine," Dralor affirmed. "You've seen to that. Nonetheless, they will be glad to see you very soon."

Eshal turned to meet Dralor's gaze, forgotten hands lowering the wrung cloth back into the water. He pursed a quivering lip and nodded, first to himself, then to Dralor. Turning back to his work, he again wrung out the cloth and they both resumed in silence. When Eshal finished, he helped with what remained of Dralor's load. Dralor's fingers ached with fatigue by the time they were through, and the baskets far heavier despite his best wringing. They walked toward Raf's in silence.

He looked for the bird when they passed the lone tree, but did not see it. Enough for the morning, Dralor supposed, glancing to the sky. The sun was just peeking over the city wall now. *Tovarian dawn*, he recalled that Arvin boy calling it. Suddenly he was awash with shame. How out of touch he had been, not knowing a common phrase used by all those beneath the hill he'd ruled from. And not even knowing how to properly wash linens. It was no wonder Naelis had so easily turned the people against him, and he against the people.

Dralor's stomach rumbled as they passed a man hawking meat sliced from a haunch of game simmering over a fire. He knew they hadn't the coin, though, and continued past. On arriving back at the shop, they hung the linens around the hearth in the workshop while Raf served a more mundane meal of porridge from her pot. They joined her at a low table by the hearth and set to their meals. The warmth of the fire radiated through Dralor's cold hands.

Many others came down for a bowl, most returning upstairs to eat, others taking their meals in various places about the workshop. Jollel and her two girls joined them at the table, the youngsters making faces at one another in jest as they ate without complaint. She looked as tired as she had the first time he'd glimpsed her, and her hair had likely not known a brush in some time. Even so, there was a beauty to her that was only amplified by her unmistakable resolve. A glob of porridge fell to the table from the younger girl's mouth amidst her performance.

"*Gaiyla,*" Jollel chided, then turned an apologetic look to the others. "I'm sorry."

"Do not be," Eshal said. He showed the contents of his own mouth to the girls then gave a smile both joyous and melancholy. "They are wonderful. These are times to be treasured. Do not waste a single moment, Jollel. Not a moment."

"We'll treasure them just as well with closed mouths and straight faces, thank you," Jollel said, nonetheless offering Eshal a smile. She turned to Dralor. "Little ones of your own, sir?"

Dralor blinked. "I... no." He took another bite, meaning to leave it at that, but found himself speaking again. "My wife... died. In childbirth. The baby did not make it."

Jollel made a small sound, the table falling otherwise silent save for the slow clink of spoons. "I'm so very sorry, Del," she said finally.

"It's done," Dralor said, eyes distant.

Jollel put her hand on Dralor's atop the table and gave a squeeze. It snapped Dralor back to the present. Not an altogether pleasant place, but better than where he'd been. Far, far better. His eyes flicked from hers to their hands, then back. He cleared his throat and gave her a nod. She took her hand back and watched her children as they resumed their meals and their play.

Dralor swallowed another bite of porridge and filled his spoon, but froze before lifting it to his lips. He tilted his ear toward the front door of the shop. Everyone fell silent, even the children. The crackle of the fire came loud to his ears, but otherwise there was only silence. Not the call of merchants, nor the beat of hoofs. Only terrible silence.

A horse nickered nervously and Dralor turned suddenly to Jollel. "Get them to the safe room. Go, quickly!"

Jollel did not delay, pulling her girls to their feet at once and dragging them to the stairs. Halfway up, she pulled open a hidden door in the wall. The girls began climbing in, two others from the workshop lining up behind them.

"Hurry!" Jollel said. "I'll get the others." With that, she disappeared up the stairs.

Dralor pushed aside a spool of woolen yarn on Raf's supply shelf and grabbed his sword.

"No," Raf said. "Feign innocence. We cannot win in a fight, so we must not start one."

Dralor reluctantly let his hand fall from the hilt of his sword and pushed the spool back in front of it. He heard quick footfalls overhead and then others emerged from upstairs and scrambled into the secret door. Jollel was not among them. They needed more time.

He raced toward the door and slammed a shoulder to it just as it burst inward. Pain flashed in his shoulder and he bounced off the door, but he charged it again and rammed it closed with his other side. It held for a moment but then the resistance doubled. Dralor's feet began to slide and he dug the edges of his boot soles deeper into the planks, staying it once again.

"City Watch!" a strained voice barked. "Surrender or die!"

Dralor glanced to the stairs, his head scraping along the wooden door as he turned. Jollel was there now, as was Eshal. They helped two others into the hole, then the burly farmer set to helping an old woman.

Dralor's face was fully red, his wide eyes and neck bulging as he pushed with every muscle and bone and very skin. His head bounced as someone slammed into the door, and again his feet began to slide. His eyes met Jollel, the kindly, motherly, and beautiful woman he barely knew, and he shook his head. Jollel's eyes went wide with understanding, and she pressed the small door closed behind the old woman as the shop door beat Dralor aside and watchmen charged in.

"Get in the corner!" yelled a short but thick watchman, waving his sword to an empty corner beside the fireplace.

"Let them in!" Raf chided with motherly disapproval. "They're watchmen, not those robbers, dear!"

Another rounded on Dralor, leveling his sword at him as three others fanned out across the room. Five more charged straight to the stairs, their leader pulling Jollel and Eshal down into the corner and the rest disappearing upstairs. It was a thorough raid, Dralor considered as he watched, his quick breaths fogging the sword at his neck. Drilled by his own order, no doubt. Jollel was trembling on the floor. The children were no doubt distraught in the hideaway. Eshal stared, broken, after his last shattered hopes of seeing his family again. All his doing.

"Drop it, lady," the one with a sword to Dralor said without turning. "This is the bastard that held the door. Ought to—"

"Stop," barked a sergeant. "You'd be doing him a favor. Let him put those muscles to use in the quarry."

The sword at Dralor's neck brought him to the corner with Eshal, Jollel, and Raf. It made a shallow cut as the watchman released him with a flick.

"Where are the rest?" demanded the sergeant.

Raf tilted her head. "Rest of what, our guests? It's been a light season, sadly. All the trouble up the hill, I wager. And the taxes, no doubt."

"We know blazin' well what this place is," the sergeant said dully then turned toward the sound of footsteps.

Dralor followed his gaze to the stairs. Unable to see beyond the first steps from his position, his breath caught as he awaited the sight of Jollel's children being escorted at sword point. Instead, only the watchmen returned, the one in front shaking his head and giving the sergeant a shrug.

"You'll smell nothing of tar here, if that was your worry," Raf added. "Just travelers with coin enough for a bed."

"Rest of you are travelers too, I suppose?" another watchman said.

"We are," Eshal said. "Came—"

"Stop," the sergeant barked at his man. "We ain't here to talk. Commander knows what they're doing. Where are the rest?"

"Had four other guests," Raf said. "Went out on errands. Not like to come back, either, if they see or hear of what's going down. But you're welcome to wait and see for yourself. Please, stay. Share a drink with us."

Two younger watchmen turned inquiringly to their sergeant, but the sergeant only grinned humorlessly. "I think we'll not, and nor will you." He turned to his men. "Out. Take them out."

The watchmen split, some leading the way from the shop and others prodding their captives ahead from the rear. Raf went first. Eshal took a single step but stopped. His jaw set and he looked about at the watchmen surrounding them, violence in his eyes. Violence completely covering him, for that matter. Dralor patted the big man's shoulder and eased him along. Jollel followed. Something between relief and panic, there. Her girls would be safe, for a time. But what of later? What about herself? Dralor shot the closest watchman a look then followed.

Four prison wagons awaited them outside, two full and two empty. Dralor looked about but quickly dismissed any thought of escape. Three mounted watchmen surrounded them, several others atop the prison wagons adding to the dozen or so who had raided Raf's shop. No crowd had gathered as it once might have. Instead, the market square was empty save for a few merchants with stands too large to cart off themselves. Dralor and his companions filed into one of the cells and the door slammed shut behind them.

"That's it?" a watchman said from atop his horse.

"One less place to hide, anyway," another said casually.

The wagon jarred into motion and Dralor grabbed a bar to keep his footing. He eyed the bench then looked about. Eshal too still stood, but all the other prisoners were seated. Given up, like cattle to the slaughter. Then he let out a breath and sat.

"Prince's Prison," Raf mused, Dralor's gaze dropping to the cage floor.

"I should have gone back to them sooner," Eshal said, his voice a low growl.

Jollel wiped tears from her face. "No. It's as you said, that would have endangered them. You protected them."

Eshal grabbed two bars and throttled the cage, rocking and rattling it fiercely. "I should have gone straight back. They are safer with me, watchmen be damned!"

"She's right." Dralor said. "Go proudly, you protected them."

The wagon stopped and the bark of watchmen came over the rattling. Eshal stood and shook the cage more, pausing only to turn to Dralor.

"We can tip it," he said. "Rock with me, all of you!"

A watchman reined in his mount beside the cage and shouted. "On your ass, now!"

When Eshal didn't stop, the watchman drew his blade and slapped the flat of it against the bars. Eshal jumped back from this, but his lips peeled back in a snarl. The watchman raised his sword threateningly as Eshal glared at him like a hungry wolf.

"Easy," Dralor whispered to the both of them.

Eshal's eyes slowly widened as a mad, hopeless rage filled him, then he lunged forward. Dralor slammed into Eshal, knocking him away from the watchmen and into the side of the cage. He wrapped Eshal up, hands barely clasping behind Eshal's broad torso. But he might as well have been wrestling a bear. Dralor was on his back before he knew what happened, Eshal raising a fist over him.

Dralor might have got a blow in, might have rolled away, but he only stared back. Eshal heaved several great breaths, his huge fist rising and falling like a ship upon a stormy sea. Sanity slowly returned to Eshal's eyes and his fist fell. Dralor came to his feet and eased Eshal to the bench, sitting beside him. Outside, the watchman sheathed his weapon and turned his mount away at a trot.

"Live," Dralor said. "That is what you can do for them."

Eshal said nothing, only staring off into the distance. Their rolling cage continued along. Dralor watched the passing city that was his no longer. Worse than not his, he was an outlaw here—no, a prisoner. He considered his narrow escape from the castle jails and his equally unlikely rescue by Raf at the city gate. Likely he would die in his own prison now. A slower, more miserable death, but one he still greatly preferred over swinging from a rope before his subjects, eyes bulging out and pants soiled. The people of Tovar would cast stones as he dangled. Death to the black prince. At least now his death would be as a nobody, his body forgotten instead of desecrated.

Dralor caught glimpses of the prison tower looming in the distance as their convoy wove toward the western gate. When they reached it, the guards waved them ahead of the line. It was odd leaving the city. Last he'd done so he'd been a prince under escort, amidst a retinue of nobles and commanders and guards.

The city grew smaller, and the black, windowless tower and its surrounding camps larger as the wagon rattled on. The faces of his cellmates echoed the horrors of the camps that Benam had tirelessly begged him to abolish. The horrors he had long ignored, even enabled. He felt closer to these companions after mere days sheltering together than he did to most he'd known for years at fickle court, but oh how they would rip him to pieces if they discovered who he truly was.

The wagons turned off the main road onto one of hoof-beaten mud. Dralor forced his gaze from the tower. Low grass and moss covered a rocky countryside. Beyond it, the glistening sea, almost green beneath the cloudy morning sky. For all its beauty, he could think of nothing but its enviable freedom.

An evil scent breaking through the cool sea breeze turned Dralor's attention back to the prison as they neared. Death. Burning flesh. Filth. His mind drifted back many years to the battlefields he tried never to recall but too often did. Still, there was something worse in the air. A slower death. Humanity at its most deprived. The tap of hammers or picks rang in the distance.

Their convoy stopped before a gate in a modest wall encircling the tower, and only then did Dralor grasp the scale of the camp. One of the other filled cages was emptied first. The captives were filed toward a door set into the wall near the gate. Three prisoners wept. Two attacked their escort, earning one a gash on her arm and the other several broken teeth. The sun was directly overhead before the second group was forced in, this one without incident.

Finally the watchmen returned for Dralor's cage. Eshal glanced at Dralor, looking very much like he wanted to be dissuaded from another altercation. Dralor obliged with a shake of his head. A sweet moment of open air, then they were through the door. Inside was a room of the same plain stone of the outer wall. A barred door on one side, a barred window into the next room on another. A wiry watchman manned the window.

"Name," the watchman demanded of Raf.

"Rakelle," she answered quickly.

"Raf," the sergeant who had led the raid corrected.

Raf barely flinched before nodding. "Rakelle Raf, that's right."

The watchman in the window wrote something in a thick ledger then looked up to the sergeant. "Crime?"

"Harboring," the sergeant said. "Twenty counts."

The wiry watchman winced then looked up from his book and surveyed the room. "More outside?"

"No."

Behind the bars, the watchman's long mouth curled up at one end. "Got it." He made another note.

He took more details on the raid from the sergeant, and from each of the prisoners in turn. Jollel claimed to be Raf's apprentice, though at the shake of the sergeant's head the other watchman seemed not to write that down. Eshel gave the name *Essa*, but confessed to having farming experience.

"You?" the wiry watchman asked of Dralor.

"Del Baez," Dralor answered, thinking of a ship captain he'd once ridden with. "Scribe." Light duty, with any luck.

The watchman smirked and finished his notes. He walked out of sight, then appeared at the barred door and pulled it open. They were herded through, Dralor at the front. A long hall, at its end an open door and accompanying watchmen. Daylight streamed in through the door. Dralor slowed at the end, but a hand at his back pushed him through.

He stumbled out into the shadow of the tower. Walls reached out in either direction behind, turning to encircle him somewhere in the distance. Countless rows of long wooden barracks in a perfect grid filled the wall's embrace. An avenue ran down their center toward the black tower. The terrible smell was stronger now.

A line of men pushed carts laden with stone toward a heaping mound of it beside the wall. They were thin, but even the most frail managed their burdens. Others went about various chores in a less orderly fashion, these ones looking even worse off. Knees knobby, faces gaunt, limbs frail and seeming somehow too long. Most wore a uniform of a long linen shirt with simple matching pants and sandals, though some were garbed in what might have been remnants of their original clothing. A dozen or so guards bearing bows milled about atop the wall.

A gate slammed shut behind Dralor and company, then a heavy lock clanged. Dralor did not turn, just stared through the endless buildings to the tower. The prince's prison. Jollel gave something like a sob and Dralor finally tore his gaze from the tower. Jollel was looking about the camp in terror, Eshal and Raf close by. Dralor made to say something and then flinched back. To comfort those you've damned... what sort of sick, devilish thing to do was that?

"You two, with me!"

Dralor found a mounted guard looking their way. Several men stood before him already, all from the other prison wagons save one tall man with a slight limp and the typical ragged linen uniform.

"Best go then, boys," Raf said.

Dralor could think of nothing to say, instead offering her a shallow nod. Jollel cried out and clung to Eshal.

"Survive for them," Eshal said with a glance to Dralor.

She sniffed and wiped her eyes. "Go. Quickly, now."

And so they did. The rider led them west along the wall. When Dralor looked back, Jollel was staring after them, her arms wrapped around herself. He did not look back again, walking on through sucking mud. They passed a stone building with black smoke billowing up from a chimney, that evil smell thickening. Worse still, it smelled of meat. His mouth watered, stomach rumbling then twisting in revulsion at his hunger.

It was only a furious guilt that distracted him enough to keep his stomach down. How could he have been so blind, so vindictive against the phantom dissidents that he himself would make real. Naelis may have stoked the hatred, but he hadn't sparked it. He thought back over the many years of calm counsel from Naelis. All deception. All biding time, moving him like a game piece. Turning him against his own people. He'd as good as killed Loris himself.

The ragged man followed Dralor's gaze to the black smoke and smiled knowingly. "Most don't realize at first. Soldier?"

Dralor frowned. "Scribe."

The man gave only a slight smile, but his tight skin still looked as if it might rip. Dralor ignored a curious look from Eshal and they walked on.

They passed a dozen cohorts of prisoners at work. Mass bakeries. Sewing and sandal operations crafting the uniforms worn by most there. Largest was a group of several hundred people chiseling bricks from stones, presumably building the very walls that imprisoned them. Each group had a supervisor that looked neither like a guard nor a prisoner. Hired hands for carrying out dirty work inside the prison, most like. Taskmasters.

Their mounted escort led them to a gate in the southwestern wall. It stood open and guarded only by two watchmen. Seemed a light force to keep between them and freedom, Dralor thought. He whispered to Eshal to be ready, but as they neared his hope flickered out. Beyond the gate lay not freedom, but a long passage that stretched into the distance. The walls were not of brick, but sheer stone. It was like a gorge, carved into the very hillside behind the prison.

Eshal pushed Dralor back into motion and Dralor looked back at the big man as they walked down the gorge. Had it been the first time he'd ever been pushed, watchmen notwithstanding? When Eshal raised an eyebrow, Dralor bobbed a nod and marched on. The tap of chisels from the camp faded behind them, giving way to more of the same ahead amidst a clattering of rumbling carts and the shout of men.

They parted for a stone filled wagon, then stepped out of the passage into a vast circular quarry. Hundreds of men slaved inside, chipping away at the walls or heaving rocks into wagons at the quarry's center. Several terraces ringed the walls, each lined with more men. Ramps with shallow steps connected these tiers, though a sheer cliff had been retained at the top, no doubt to better contain the prisoners.

Numerous shafts had been built into the base of the wall at odd intervals, for what purpose Dralor could not imagine. There was virtually no talking beyond the shouts of more taskmasters. Mounted guards patrolled ominously around the perimeter.

"*Khapar*, we missed lunch," cursed the man in the ragged linens.

Dralor's stomach rumbled again at that as they pressed deeper inward, but his hunger was soon forgotten. Eyes turned upon him as he passed by, eyes that saw not him but their own first days in the quarry. Two bodies were heaped in a pile, buzzing with flies. Every so often their escort would stop his horse at a taskmaster and deposit one or more of the new arrivals there.

"I need two," a taskmaster near one of the shafts said, then turned to Eshal. "Oh, that one definitely."

Dralor stepped forward beside Eshal. Their guard shrugged and shouted at the rest to follow, leaving Dralor and Eshal behind.

"Grab picks," the taskmaster said, pointing to a nearby cart then continuing as Dralor and Eshal complied. "Now listen here. You newcomers often think this is your chance to bash someone in the head and run away. But that's not going to get you out of here, it's just going to get you dead. Now, top level, and get to work."

Dralor exchanged a look with Eshal, then they started up a ramp. Reaching the first tier, they walked past countless men at work to the next ramp. A man with a laden cart was working his way down, his arms shaking. The cart tottered wildly and the man's sinewy muscles strained, neck bulging and eyes wide. Dralor hurried up to him and reached to help.

"No!" the man shrieked, startling Dralor back.

The cart swayed one way, then the other, then dragged the man onto his knees. Shouts rose up, echoing off the walls, and men scattered below as the cart slipped from the man's grip and tumbled downward. One man was too slow and a large rock struck his knee with a loud crunch heard even over the ruckus. He fell to the ground, screaming only after he saw the bone protruding from the lower part of his leg set off at a grotesque angle.

The man who'd fumbled the cart glared up at Dralor then broke down in sobs as a taskmaster started down the ramp toward him. "I can do it!" he pleaded. "It was him! He made me fall!"

"Maybe," said the taskmaster, "but I think you were about done anyway. Up, now. Come with me."

"No! I'm strong enough!"

The taskmaster waved his arms and Dralor looked down to find two watchmen veering toward the ramp. The man who'd dropped the cart continued his pleas, but the sounds of labor resumed all around them. Either this was commonplace enough as to no longer be interesting, or they all feared the repercussions of being caught idle. Both, Dralor surmised.

Meanwhile, the man with the mutilated leg had fallen unconscious, or perhaps died. The taskmaster who'd first taken ownership of Dralor gestured to two prisoners and they lugged the man into a cart. Without prompting, one of them began hefting the cart toward the mouth of the gorge.

Turning away, Dralor led Eshal up to the top, where another taskmaster waved them toward an available space along the wall. To one side worked a stocky bald man with a red beard. On the other side was a gangly young man little more than a boy. He was among the few without a beard, though scraggly hairs were beginning to work at it.

"Just keep swinging," the redhead said, his voice showing plainly the many teeth missing from both his jaws. "Not so hard that you make more rock to carry, and not so soft you earn a beating, or lose quarry duty."

Dralor swung his pick. Even the light blow rattled his bones. "What is worse than quarry duty?" He swung again.

"Oh it's mother-bleedin' awful, but we are fed better. Beats wasting away. And you don't wanna be housed with the skinnies. Sicknesses sweep through those places always. People don't last as long there."

"Ah," Dralor said, swinging again. It did not leave so much as a mark on the stone. This irritated him, though he couldn't say why he should care. Beside him, Eshal broke off a sizable piece of stone on his first swing.

"You'll need a goodly pile to keep them happy," the stocky man said. "They prefer big pieces for brick. Smaller serves as ore fine. Dust is worthless."

Dralor swung again, to little effect. Though no bells marked the time, Dralor judged it couldn't have been a single bell before his hands were both so tired, aching, and blistered he could barely keep a grip on his pick. The rest of his body was hardly better. Alternating between hands helped, as did a two handed grip at times, but neither was enough. Soon he was driving the pick with his very bones to spare his muscles.

Every so often, the taskmaster who patrolled the nearby lines—a scrawny man the others called Chesh—would stop and task a prisoner with collecting. The selected prisoner would then push the cart down the line, and the laborers would load their hauls into it. Each time he passed by, dread gripped Dralor's heart.

Then, finally, Chesh stopped directly behind him. He certainly couldn't handle the cart when he could barely hold a pick. So, this was it, then. Not even a single day. Pathetic.

"No good," the taskmaster said, surveying Dralor's meager pile. "Fill that up before the next pass or I'll put you with the skinnies."

Dralor stared down at his useless hands as the taskmaster walked on. Then, moving as quickly as his aching hands would allow, he ripped a ring of cloth from the bottom of his pants and tied it tightly around his palm. Stuffing the pick through it, he tried a swing. The cloth didn't do *all* the gripping, but it helped. He did the same with his other hand, then set to work.

Tap, tap, tap. That dreamin' sun had never moved slower. His shoulders were next to go, his swings starting lower and lower. His hands bled. Even his feet were blistered. He swung again, a feeble thing, more like turning his body with a pick in his half closed hands than truly swinging. It struck without so much as a tap, a faint wisp of dust rising up.

His eyes fell closed and he just lay against the stone wall. He felt a sob rise up in his throat. *A sob!* He forced his eyes open, and swung again. He fell into a pattern of using different muscles on each swing. Back and legs this swing. Shoulders and arms the next. Switch sides. Repeat. Slow and steady, better a few productive swings than a dozen for less rock.

The cart rumbled down the line toward him. Well, he'd avoided another cart duty at least, but would he have enough? He glanced at the hauls of his neighbors, then back to his own, and his heart sank. The images of the starved hordes that would be forever burned upon his brain flashed anew. He'd be among them soon. How long would it take before his eyes sank? Before the vacant stare, the sunken abdomen, the knobbly knees. The long teeth.

As Dralor stared at his pile in dismay, a hefty boulder rolled into it. He looked over at Eshal, but Eshal only swung his pick again, loosing another stone just as big. Dralor couldn't help but smile as he resumed his labor.

Chesh came and went without incident, making no mention of his threat as Dralor filled the cart. The sun traversed its course overhead, and darkness fell. Perhaps it too was enslaved, Dralor wondered as his mind ventured from his pained body. Several people fell from exhaustion. Others were hauled off for failing to meet quota. But when at last a call to return rose up through the quarry, Dralor was still standing.

The army of prisoners shuffled back through the gorge. They remained organized by taskmaster, Dralor and Eshal walking with Chesh's crew. Dralor began to shiver as his pounding heart eased. A cold rain began to fall. Already entirely soaked through with sweat, it could chill him no further. Nor did he have any last embers of hope to extinguish. Might as well rain on the sea. He trudged on, stiff arms hanging at his sides, eyes on the black tower looming like a shadow in the dark sky ahead.

Reaching the end of the channel, Chesh led his crew along the prison wall to a large stone building, the smell of filth growing in the air as they neared. Those in the lead filed in. Dralor waited outside with the rest, stomach tight, until the crush carried him through the door. A long, low trough spanned the large room, countless men unabashedly shitting or pissing into it.

Dralor swallowed hard. He'd done his business in trenches plenty on campaign, but this was something else altogether. *Khapar,* they looked like penned animals. That's what he was now, he supposed. All anyone was. Just animals. He joined the ranks over the trough and did his business with the rest of the stock.

He shuffled into the next room. More bare flesh, the stink hardly better. Men hastily scrubbed themselves with soiled rags from buckets of brown water that too closely resembled the contents of the trough in the room before. Dralor looked down into the closest bucket, then shuffled on, certain a wash would only make him filthier.

Filing outside, Dralor scanned for Eshal. For Chesh. For any familiar face. His chest fluttered. *Khapar* but he felt like a lost child. Eshal aside, they were worse than strangers, yet he clung to them like his own mother. But there they were, of course, and he rejoined them with unreasonable relief. Fen emerged soon after, and together their crew shuffled on.

They came to a structure with open walls and a long trough reminiscent of the one Dralor had just made use of, except this one offered a savory smell that set Dralor's mouth watering. The memory of roasted flesh twisted with the smell and his stomach heaved, but it passed. Hunger prevails. Gaunt faces working the kitchen ladled slop into bowl after bowl. To Dralor's dismay, Chesh led them right on by, then past four other kitchens before finally stopping at the next.

Dralor followed the lead of the stocky man with the red beard, grabbing a large bowl from a central counter and filling it in a trough of slop. Behind the trough, starved men and women tended the kitchen under heavy guard. It was a cruel fate, Dralor considered. To starve while surrounded by food. This did not stop him drinking from his bowl like all the others as he followed his group on through the night. The slop was a foul amalgamation of flavors, but it was hot and hearty. Altogether, foul or not, it was wonderful. The sole prize of the day's labor.

They peeled off from what remained of the mass to walk down a dark aisle between barracks. It occurred to Dralor as he followed his group that he had yet to see Chesh glance back. Could he not simply slip away? But then, what would he do next? Perhaps another day. Perhaps with a plan beyond hiding all night and being executed the next day. He followed like a dumb, juicy lamb, and soon they reached the barracks. It was indistinguishable from the countless others, save perhaps for its own distinct collection of scars. They filed in through doors on either end.

In the darkness within, Dralor could just make out a narrow walk running between tightly packed bunks organized in pods of four beds. The current of people pushed him deeper and he cupped a hand over his bowl to protect it. Twice he sat upon a bunk but was forced back into the aisle. Finally he stood alone in the aisle save for the occasional person slinking past. He looked about in a panic for Eshal before spotting a large silhouette and finding his friend down the way.

Together they walked the aisle in silence, peering between each bunk for a vacancy. Dralor was surprised to find most men sitting at the edges of their bunks in conversation, all savoring their meals. There was humanity left here, then. Their cold acceptance of the torture and death of fellow captives in the day was not for lack of compassion then, but rather for survival.

Dralor was halfway back to the entrance he'd come through, with still no sign of a single empty bunk yet alone two, when Eshal's hand closed on his shoulder. He turned and found the stocky, red-bearded man with them.

"This way," their quarry neighbor said, starting away without delay.

They followed the man nearly to the opposite door before turning into a row. Seated upon one of the upper bunks, the young man who'd worked beside Eshal looked up from his bowl.

"The bottoms are yours," the stocky man said, climbing onto the other upper bunk and taking a sip from his bowl. "I'm taking the upper now. I didn't use to get so blazin' cold."

Dralor and Eshal both sat at the edges of their bunks, neither showing the same restraint with their food as they had witnessed with the others. Dralor peered through the bunk to the other set pressed against his, finding an older man looking his way. His ragged gray beard had somehow been trimmed, a square jaw showing through. The man offered a nod, which Dralor returned.

"I'm Yanick," the stocky man said through his nearly toothless gums. *"Yan* is fine. Boy there is Taupry."

"Taup's fine," the young man said over a mouthful. His eyes were closed, cheeks puffing out as he swished the soup around.

"Essa," Eshal said before tipping up his bowl again.

"Del," Dralor said in turn. "I owe you thanks."

"It's nothing," Yanick said. "Anyone would do the same."

"And yet it's only you who have aided me. Twice."

"Oh it's a good lot here, really. Of course, most are criminals just as the black prince wanted, but not many of the worst sort. Most will help so long as it doesn't cost them much, seeing as all us here have so little to give."

"And what sort are you?" Eshal asked.

Dralor winced. Eshal had asked the same of him, but here it felt far more likely to get them killed in their sleep.

"Fair to ask. For me it was Tar," Yanick said, hugging himself as if suddenly cold. "Used to hide it, but why bother? Well, sure, I did some bad things to chase it, too, but I'm off it now. Suppose I'd be dead if I weren't here." He nodded as if reassuringly to himself. "Yeah, yeah there's that."

Dralor had once had a soldier executed for selling tar on a campaign, and several imprisoned for using it. His mind drifted back over his life with such a different perspective that it seemed the life of another man. The bunkmates continued to converse—mostly Yanick—with Dralor offering little by way of his story. The occasional distant scream, frequent sobs, and inescapable scent of death reminded Dralor of the hell he was in despite the warmth of camaraderie filling the barracks.

After a while Dralor lay like so many others upon his bunk beneath a thin blanket. The older man in the bunk just beside his was soundly asleep already. Dralor knew sleep would never come that night, so he resolved to consider means of escape. *Escape*, he told himself, then nothing more before dreams took him.

CHAPTER SIX

Jeld fell back against the stone floor, cowering beneath his arms as the sharp pain of the inquisitor's sword shot through his hand. Darkness. He'd flinched, he realized in a panic, Handan's voice already chiding him. *Good for dust and wind, not so much for sharp steel.* He forced his eyes wide to spot the next attack, but they wouldn't open. They wouldn't—he blinked.

His eyes *were* open, but everything was dark. Darker than night. Darker than the grave. But those were substantial, thick. This was... emptiness. This was the void. He lowered his raised arms, his bag in one hand. He'd crawled into his bag, pulled it into itself. But what were they in if not the bag, then?

The warm sensation of blood streaming down his arm tore his mind from the conundrum, until he unthinkingly reached toward his collar to retrieve bandages. If he and the bag were here, then what was in his bag now? Cautiously, slowly, he pulled it open, tensed to squeeze it shut should he find himself starting up at inquisitor or blade, but there was not even a single point of daylight within. With nowhere else to turn for bandages, he set his jaw and reached slowly inside.

A sound gave him pause. A slight rustling, like a small creature approaching. Jeld looked about, seeing only black and hearing only his quick breaths and the patter of his blood slapping against the ground. Probably just a mouse, he told himself, having found the creatures in every one of the many dark holes he'd previously resided in. He reached farther into the bag, ignoring more skittering.

His fingers brushed something and in the same moment something touched his leg. Crying out, he dropped the bag and scrambled back, only to trip and land on his back. Neither cry nor tumble echoed, the sounds just swallowed by the void, leaving only a metallic hissing like a coin settling. He reached toward the sound and his fingers closed upon what seemed like a small metal ball. His sparker, he realized.

He twisted the sphere. Sparks flashed in the darkness. A stone floor, somehow seamless as if from a single slab. Again he twisted to more sparks. There was the bag he'd dropped in fear, beyond it a host of objects. More sparks and he plucked up a lamp, lighting it with another twist. The wick caught and flared to life, its light reaching out around him

The objects he'd glimpsed were arranged in a perfect ring around a black circle that was all too familiar, the same void that lived at the bottom of his bag. As intimately familiar with the items as he was, they were almost unrecognizable from such a perspective. Dozens of bags tied to ropes leading to the void at the center like spokes of a wagon wheel. Props, Handan's massive sword that he'd impulsively stolen the night he'd set fire to the gardener's shop. The old sock he knew to contain Lira's golden coin, an empty sack where he kept a stock of food in better days, his father's long knife

Jeld picked up the knife and stuck it in his belt, then looked about. The light only revealed more of the same stone floor before fading into blackness. Above, there was no stone, only the same emptiness. Nothingness. Like a stone floor floating through the place beyond the skies, only with not a single star to light it.

He walked an arbitrary direction, holding the light out before him as if to cast it farther. More of the same. Darkness. He thought of his lamp burning out, leaving him in the darkness to die. What good was the lamp anyway, if it only revealed more darkness? But somehow it mattered.

He took a few more steps, but still nothing more. Idols, did it go on forever? Could he wander forever, lost in the—he spun in a panic. Only darkness the way he had come, with no sign of his belongings. He took a few hesitant steps, eyes locked straight ahead to hold his course.

Khapar but everything looked the same. He must have curved. Must have spun too far, or not enough. His heart pounded, loud in the otherwise silent void. A scream was rising up in his throat when he glimpsed something at the corner of his vision. Careful to leave his feet pointing in his original heading, he looked over to it. Just a slight glimmer in the darkness.

Jeld held his lamp aside to let his eyes adjust and stared out until the glimmer took the faint shape of Handan's sword. He let out a shaky breath and hurried toward it, his ring of familiar objects coming into view. He sat amongst them all, his raft in an endless sea. Gradually, his panic faded, breath slowed.

Another slap of blood and he held his hand to the light. It was a bloody mess. He winced as he wiped it on one of his costumes and inspected the other side. Yes, clean through. It still seemed to open and close, at least. He set to bandaging.

Mind grounded, he finally thought of Lira, Fen, and Benam. Had they made it? He'd managed to get them a fair lead. Of course, there could have been more men blocking the gates. Even if they'd made it out of the city, what then? And did they have the horses? Did Fen still have a bag of beans? It all felt so far away. So long ago, but they'd barely even be *to* the gates. They were fighting to survive and he was sitting in the dark bandaging a little poke.

One end of the bandage in his teeth, he cinched it tight with a groan. Then he turned his attention to the center of the ring of items. There, a black circle stood in the center of a flattened bag. It looked to be a perfect copy of his own. He picked up his bag and dipped his fingers inside, eyes intent on the black circle at the center of his ring of possessions. Slowly, fingertips rose up from the void, then a hand. His hand. Another shiver ran down his spine.

Coming to his feet, he stood in the faint light thinking before quickly retrieving a coil of rope from his ring of items. He fastened it to Handan's sword, the only object heavy enough to secure it with any confidence, picked up his lamp, and turned back to the shadows. His pulse drummed in his ears. With a deep breath, he walked into the darkness.

How silly this all will feel when he finds himself merely in some dark room, he thought. The levity lasted only until a glance over his shoulder showed his rope fading into the darkness, his belongings lost in the shadows. Eyeing the lamp, knuckles white around his end of the rope, Jeld continued deeper. The press of the stone against his feet and the unfurling of the rope was the only indication that he was even walking, the uniform floor and shadows around him remaining unchanged with each step. The lamp running out wouldn't kill him, he thought as he walked. It would be thirst and starving that managed that, but somehow it was the darkness that terrified him.

The rope pulled taut, a distant scraping of Handan's sword upon stone reaching from the distance. Though it couldn't have moved the sword but a finger or three, his fear rose higher still at the thought of following his rope back to nothing but the sword. Carefully, he turned and began walking a circle, keeping the slack out of the rope. After several breaths he stopped. How would he know when he'd completed a circuit? Perhaps by marking the floor, but any give in the rope would put him off his mark. Couldn't he just walk a reasonable distance? The rope he'd bought was ten leaps if he remembered correctly, it couldn't take all that long to walk a circle with it. He recalled that Tutor Reiman had covered something of the sort in his lessons on shape mathematics, but couldn't conjure the details. Surely it would be less than walking a square of four such lengths, right? Ten leaps would be twenty paces. Four of those, eighty paces. Eighty paces.

Jeld walked. Every so often he'd hear the sword scrape the stone and his stomach would twist. Twenty steps, and nothing. Thirty. He really was in the void. The void inside the void. Endless emptiness, it could only be so. The lamp flickered and he quickened his pace. Sixty. The sword scraped along stone. His heart pounded. Seventy. Seventy, it would have to do. He could see far enough ahead, right? He turned and followed the rope back in, dreading the moment he'd glimpse it alone in the darkness, but his ring of possessions took shape and he ran to them.

Sitting, he tried to think, but the lamp flickered again. He tried to peer into its oil well but it was too dark. He had a small bottle of extra oil, a few candles. Afterward he'd have to resort to burning clothing, but that wouldn't last long. Wondering whether he would need his other clothing or not, he realized it was neither hot nor cold in this strange place, but a perfect temperature. Or... no temperature?

The lamp sputtered. Escape. How to escape. He needed to explore further. He had a bit more rope, perhaps he should extend the other and try a broader search. Jeld reached for his collar instinctively then shook his head. No need for that, he was already inside it. He grabbed up the extra rope but stopped as an idea struck him. What if he didn't need a rope? It seemed another length of rope was as likely to allow him to reach an exit as it was to connect two stars in the night sky.

The bag though... he could search as far as he wanted and simply crawl through the bag to return should he get lost.

He picked up his lamp, gripped his bag with white knuckles, and started off once again into the darkness. After only a few steps though, something caught his eye. A difference where the endless void should be unchanging. A mark upon the ground. He walked over to it and knelt. It was a scratch, a line in the stone angled just a little ways off his course. Pointing?

On a hunch, he matched its heading and continued, hand tight on his bag lest he be lost forever beyond the stars. Only a few breaths passed before he came to a matching mark, then another. This continued long after Jeld had lost count. *Idols,* the place really did just go on forever. Or he was walking in circles somehow despite never seeming to turn. Panic rose again and quickened, then more until he was almost jogging. He felt like he was drowning, as if kicking toward the surface from the depths, lungs aching for breath. More marks flashed by.

Jeld looked up from another mark flashing by at his feet, and suddenly a wall stood before him, an arched door set within it. He didn't stop, instead throwing himself against it, not to force it open but rejoicing in its substance, its mere deviation from emptiness. He tugged, surprised when it actually opened. A cruel disappointment seemed more fitting of this place. Perhaps the cruelty lay beyond. More emptiness? Worse?

Beyond the door was a stairwell. Up he went, slowly, fighting the urge to run up. It leveled off onto a landing, then a wall of nothing but solid stone. He laughed and fell to his knees. Lira was on her own, if she wasn't already dead. He'd be stuck here forever, or at least a few days until he died of thirst.

Then he narrowed his eyes and held his lamp to the wall. Iron bars set into the wall rose up into the shadows. Jeld grabbed the first wrung and pulled himself to his feet. He looked up into the darkness once more, then looped the handle of his lamp around his wrist and started climbing. His breath was loud in the narrow shaft as he worked his way higher. When he could no longer see the ground, he had a moment of panic that this climb might go on forever like the void below. Only this time when he tired he would fall to his death.

Not a moment after this terrible thought, a fine square of light took shape above and his panic subsided. He reached what looked to be a trapdoor. It was heavy, but pressing his shoulder and head to it, it gave way and crashed open beside him.

Jeld pulled himself up and looked about in awe. The massive chamber was easily twenty times the scale of the grand hall of Tovar. It was shaped somewhat like a star, with five main avenues, each running a good way before turning out of sight. Countless narrower hallways lined the whole place, at such a scale they could be hairs on some great beast. He peered down the nearest one and found it ran seemingly without end, punctuated by doors after door, no two alike. He shivered, reminded again of the void below.

He started slowly toward the closest of the main avenues. The vast chamber he crossed was dimly lit and flickered as if from firelight, yet Jeld saw not a single torch. Things at the edges of his vision seemed to fog, only to return to crystalline focus under his gaze.

Jeld's mind spun as he continued on slow, careful steps. Five halls, inside a bag pulled from a dream. Pulled from the Traveler's tavern. There seemed only one place he could be, but his mind searched for any other explanation. Alas, mundane explanations were not easy when one has arrived via magic bag. This could only be the Halls of the Idols.

He stood transfixed for a time before a question came to him. How did one *exit* the Halls of the Idols? By awakening, if such stories of the

Idols—the Dreamers—were true. And what of his own brief visit to the Traveler's tavern? When that vision had ended, he'd been staring at a candle upon one of the tables. Maybe he could find the Traveler's tavern and repeat this? But then, he'd entered the Halls with a vision or daydream that time, not through a bag. There was nothing to awaken *from* this time. In any case, he had no better idea.

Jeld reached the broad avenue and started down it. Peering down one of the many endless corridors lining either side, his stomach tightened and face paled. He locked his eyes forward and continued past, taking comfort in what looked to be a turn ahead—anything but the horror of infinity. He was pleased when after a time these side corridors ceased and there was just the main hall.

It was not a turn, he saw now, but two great doors. As he neared, that fogginess at the edges of his vision faded and by the time he reached the doors, everything was in sharp focus. Runes adorned the large doors, just like the doors of the Temple of One. He reached out and grabbed the handle. *Idols*, could these truly be the same doors the Idols had walked through so long ago? He pulled, and to his surprise the doors opened with ease.

Beyond was more hallway, only it was paneled with rich, dark wood. There was a familiar scent in the air, prompting Jeld to realize he had not actually smelled anything at all in the Halls until now. It was the same smell of leather, paper, and perhaps ink that pervaded Lira's library. His pulse quickened with excitement and he chided himself. This was no exploration, this was a search against time for an escape. He had to save Lira. *Dreams*, had to save himself. He hadn't a single bean tucked away anymore, and his water skin was not half full.

A four way intersection, all paths looking much the same. He stowed his lamp in his bag, drew out a peb, and set it down to mark his path before continuing straight. He turned another corner and froze.

A room, roughly the size of the royal ballroom of Tovar, only filled by a maze of tall bookshelves. In the distance, in what looked to be the center of the room, a cylindrical tower of bookshelves rose through a hole in the ceiling, a staircase spiraling up with it. Upon a table just inside the library was a candle holder with a single burning candle.

Jeld took up the candle and stared at the flame. It looked real enough, yet how could it be, sitting unattended and full in this strange place. He held his hand over it and jerked it back. Real enough. Staring for another moment, he frowned and pressed inward through archways set into the shelves.

Reaching the tower at the center, he looked up and found what looked to be two more floors above. Up, then. The books he passed were all numbered but otherwise without title. He thumbed through one. He was no librarian, but it seemed to be an index. Same another dozen steps upward. The whole column, an index with more books than most libraries.

Jeld continued past the second story, which looked much like the first, and the spiraling staircase deposited him upon the topmost floor. This one was far smaller than the others, with a lower ceiling and only a few bookshelves. Jeld took in little else about the room before his breath caught. A window, set into the back of a nook. *Sky.* Cloudy, but bright.

Hurrying to the window, he climbed up onto a cushioned reading bench beneath it to peer out. A distant bird rose on a current to soar higher with a flap of its wing. A great, rolling ocean stretched from the horizon to beat against rocky cliffs below.

The Halls had an outside, then? Outside of what though? Where could it lead? Where could it end? Or did it end? Those awful corridors didn't seem to, but somehow their uniformity made that easier to accept. How could something as rich as the outdoors go on forever?

He wondered again if he might indeed simply be in some far off, but very real place.

A cool breeze blew in, Jeld's frantic pulse easing at the freedom in its touch. When the breeze settled, he reached his hand out of the window, longing for more. Instead, his fingertips began to fade just as had the edges of his vision back in the great hall. He jerked his hand back, stumbling backwards off the bench and into the side of a desk. Something hit the ground with a clap.

A book lay on the ground beside the desk. He picked it up. It was bound in a soft leather that reminded him at once of the Traveler's bag still clutched in his other hand. There were no words inscribed anywhere upon it. He opened it up and read.

When the last flame dies and the frigid cold of a winter night tightens its grip beyond the very bones… when even the most tenacious have succumbed and by all logic our only hope should be for a swift end, faith draws yet another breath.

But how many faithful lie frozen in the snows? And why—because robed men the world over preach their tales with illogical conviction? Should not this deceit earn our rebuke? Yet, if faith helps but one survive the night, was it not just? Need not the human soul a beacon to guide it? Is it not just as vile to hold decency and peace in one's hand, yet not administer it?

Jeld flipped to another page.

What better serves the common good, swords in the hands of the few, or in the hands of the many? Simple logic would seem to suggest both models are equal, that so long as we are more good than not, decency will prevail just the same, in time.

In time… A handy measure to those afforded eternity, but the stricken care not the odds of being struck. What if this sole sword should fall into the hands of a power so absolute, so devastating, that humanity cannot recover? What will time do with naught but ashes?

Like the other page he'd read, this one was only partially filled. Looking ahead, he found most were much the same. A journal of sorts, he presumed. Could it be Vincet's? Jeld riffled through the book, finding the second half empty still. He backed up toward one of the last of the populated pages.

Long do I dream now. Even in wakefulness my mind is in the Halls, some foreign shell of me left walking Avandria. I dread this wondrous place, where once I was whole. Every quiet corner and warm hearth is a reminder of dear lost Syladrya and our treasured talks. My other beloved brethren remain, yet I must distance myself, lest I be unable to do what must be done next.

Suddenly Jeld closed the book. Philosophy would not help him get back to Lira's side. Then he wondered why he'd come into Vincet's library at all, instead of turning around once he'd figured out it wasn't the Traveler's tavern where he could find a lamp that might wake him should he stare into it. He blew a breath of humorless laughter from his nose at the fanciful idea. Probably as likely to escape just sitting here with a good book. Nonetheless, he set the book upon the desk and started back toward the junction.

Again everything took on an ephemeral cast as he passed beyond the wood paneled halls. Again with the dizzying, endless hallways. He turned up another of the broad avenues. It led to a door indistinguishable from that of Vincet's library. This door came open just as easily.

A cool, wet breeze greeted him. Blinking, he found himself staring into a dusken valley, a light rain falling from the gray sky. The silhouette of a tall ridgeline rose up to one side, the other descending toward a thick forest. Ahead, a path wound up a slight incline to a lodge. The edges of the lodge's shuttered windows glowed a perfect heartlight orange. Woodsmoke rising from its chimney carried a hint of something savory. A burning lamp hung beside the door in the traditional welcome to travelers.

Jeld walked outside, leaving the door ajar. He breathed in cool highland air as he started down the path. It seemed so real. Beyond real, even. It was perfect. For a fleeting moment he wondered how far off the path he could venture before fading as his hand had outside the library window, but the Traveler's tavern beckoned. He had a slight chill when he reached the building and slipped inside.

The wondrous orange light inside wrapped around him like a warm embrace. The place was just as he'd remembered, every last detail he'd vividly carried ever since his visit. There was the low stage with instruments hanging on the wall behind it, the blazing fireplace with a broad stone hearth. The stone and plaster walls crossed with old beams. The fire's crackle was muted by the ghostly murmur of unseen travelers and the faint lute's song that seemed to come from both everywhere and nowhere.

Jeld walked slowly to one of the many tables. Like the others, it had a lamp upon it. There was a lighter stripe in the wood atop the back of one of the chairs. Running his hand over it, he found a slight groove as if it were worn down by use. It was the spot where he had first discovered his bag hanging by its tie.

He sat in the chair and looked into the flame atop the lamp, the very one he'd been peering into when he woke. This would never work, he told himself. Still, he leaned forward until the flame was warm against his forehead and light filled his vision. He pinched his eyes shut then opened them and looked around.

"*Khapar!*" Jeld cursed, jumping to his feet, chair crashing over behind him.

The chorus of voices quieted in the wake of his outburst. After a few breaths the bustle resumed, just as a real tavern crowd after a disturbance. Jeld sat back down, head in his hands and staring through the table.

So it would be starving, then. The thought did not terrify him as he expected it might. Instead, he found himself worrying about Lira. At least he knew his fate, though. At least he could stop trying to escape and just appreciate this wondrous place. He leaned back in his chair, sagging as he let out a long breath.

Jeld's eyes fell on a beautiful lute hanging on the wall behind the stage. It stood out from the other instruments despite looking more ordinary than most. He went to it, climbing the single step onto the low stage. The lute was quite small compared to Master Edlin's, worn in places, outright scratched in others. Still, its scars only made it all the more beautiful. He'd heard stories of the Traveler playing lute at the everyday watering holes he was known to visit. Could this truly be that very instrument?

Jeld carefully lifted the lute from its hanger. He plucked a few strings, their notes rich and resonant. Sitting on the edge of the stage, he strummed a chord Master Edlin had taught him. He'd never really taken to it despite the master's efforts, just somewhere well shy of the basics. He played more, slow and steady. Poor as his form and sour as his notes might be, a melancholy song began to take shape. A mood, anyway, if not a song.

Suddenly he stilled his fingers and looked out over the room. The voices were lower now, the song absent. The mood of the room had darkened somehow, though he could not place it. Just a reflection of his own mood, perhaps. He began to play again. Then he felt it, a tugging at his Idolic sense as he poured out his song. A presence—no, *many*, pressing against him as if the room were packed with people, yet nowhere to be seen. Not real, certainly? The whispers of spirits, long since trapped as he was? Or could they be people in the world dreaming even now?

Plucking on, he let his music flow with these unseen currents. They seemed to fall with his despondent mood, then brood with him as he again faced his helplessness. An audience, no doubt about it. Somehow. Somewhere.

The harmony ended abruptly with a dissonant note and Jeld set the lute beside him. His mind churned on the horrors and oddities of his long day, and he wondered at what bell it must be. Past due for a meal. Only, he wasn't hungry? He couldn't remember the last time he'd not been hungry, but there it was. Not tired, either. Was there no time here? It had been bright with daylight outside the library window, then dusk outside the tavern only shortly after. Had even a second passed in the outside world? Had years?

With a sigh, he picked the lute back up, and began plucking another somber tune.

Chapter Seven

Lira stood upon a low bluff overlooking the sprawling war camp in the fields below. She wore a polished leather jerkin with a shining steel spaulder over one shoulder, tall black boots, and thick padded undergarments at Handan's insistence to ensure she could quickly don armor. A beautifully crafted short sword hung at her waist, a gift from Lord Relthid.

Countless campfires were already aglow, though the sun had not quite dipped below the distant treeline. Crude walls of felled trees had already been constructed, and with each passing bell they grew higher and thicker as thousands of soldiers hurried about their work. They toiled also at digging trenches for waste, cooking, sharpening, and all manner of fieldcraft. Lira had read many books on the subjects of logistics and the movement of large bodies, but still the challenges of humanity at this scale had surprised her in their journey south.

The modest castle of Plemenol stood well out of arrow shot behind her, effectively besieged between their dug-in army and a lighter element supporting the supply trains to the north. Their lines below did not face Plemenol, however. Instead, the line faced south, toward Caldemoor and Tovar. The bulk of the western portion was dominated by the black banners and dress of Havaral. The march south to join Lord Annend Cross's army had been largely without conflict, only the better part of spring lost.

Lira turned toward the ringing of swords. Benam sparred with Fen beside a modest command pavilion, its walls drawn open to the late spring breeze. Her old knight called out lessons as he warded off blow after blow. She couldn't help but smile as she looked on, for a moment forgetting how the men below would soon die for her. Would that she could think so objectively as the books of war, of numbers, of victories, of crowns won. Never had they told of the young soldier who had marveled at her as she'd taken a meal from his line, nor the old spearman who had straightened his posture and bowed when she passed.

Her smile faded and she walked to the pavilion. She forced a calm to her face and smiled to a boy standing beside the pavilion.

"Wesslund," she greeted.

The boy had been lent to her and Benam to serve as a page of sorts, running errands, donning armor, and the like. He'd proven quite capable, his common sense and quick learning far exceeding his experience. He followed her inside, taking up an unobtrusive position in a chair against the wall.

Handan stood looking over a table covered with a large map. One of the many captains coming and going as emissaries to the commanders was addressing him as the general moved a piece upon his map. Lord Relthid sat nearby, speaking quietly to Tetchmira. Lord Annend Cross was seated opposite them. Her grandfather, technically. The more time Lira spent with him, the more she found herself forgiving her mother for her vanity and socialite ways, and the more she found herself thinking of her mother back in Tovar. Annend was cleanly shaven except for a short gray goatee, and managed to look quite young in his gilded armor compared to Relthid across the table.

"Then tell him to drill contingencies with the officers, and leave the men to their tasks." Handan told the captain. "We can sacrifice neither."

The captain pressed a fist to his chest in salute and hurried off, bowing to Lira as he passed. Lira went to Handan's side and looked over the map and the many carved wooden markers upon it.

"How go the preparations?"

"Well enough, Your Grace," Handan said.

Lira considered that. "And will that be sufficient?"

Handan nodded, looked over the map, and nodded again. "In all foreseeable scenarios, we are well prepared."

"And in the other scenarios?" Lira asked.

"Ishdalar could threaten Warrinton from the east, forcing Lord Terich to fall back. Not so unlikely, as the eastern kingdom has never truly acknowledged our claim to the west. Naelis could use Tovar's fleet to sack Havaral and cut off our supply lines, then simply dig in while we starve. Few things are certain in war."

Handan turned his attention to the map, moving his hands over it as he spoke seemingly more to himself now than to Lira. "Odsgaard is one week out from joining us, Warrinton two, in part. Caldemoor is getting close, we know, but they are outmatched by our present force, and so unlikely to attack."

His hand fell on a group of five red pieces to the east of the river Kline. "Tovar could do many things. They could stay east and face Warrinton, but that would leave us and Odsgaard to crush Caldemoor and advance. Most likely they will hurry to join Caldemoor and face us before we are four armies, but they'd need to leave a force behind to defend Tovar, and this would see us with superior numbers. Once Odsgaard arrives, Naelis will have no choice but to fall back, and we'll likely see a lengthy siege of Tovar."

Handan turned back to Lira. "I cannot say with certainty that we will win, though I think the odds are with us. What I can promise, though, is that if we remain idle and isolated, we will lose."

"Why not declare Havaral the seat of Avandria once again, put a crown upon my head, and dispatch Naelis at our leisure?" Lira asked, Lord Annend perking up at her words.

Handan considered this. "The greatest appeal there would be pulling our army together before advancing. But, the more time we give Naelis, the better he can secure everything south of the river. We've already crossed the river, taken Trenton, taken Plemenol."

"Agreed," Lord Relthid said. "This is our best chance."

Lira sighed, then nodded. "I as well."

Another officer entered and began reporting to Handan on logistics. Lord Annend rose from his chair and came to stand beside Lira.

"I wish your mother could see you like this," her grandfather said distantly. "She would be proud."

"I suspect if she were here, she'd be too busy complaining about the mud and waste trenches to take much notice."

Lord Annend frowned. "Do you truly not miss her?"

"I see her nearly as much now as I did then." Lira felt a pang of guilt at her own words. "I do worry for her. I know you said she's fine, but—if she's not being held captive, how can she stand beside the man who killed my—killed her husband!"

"Not all captives are held behind bars," Lord Relthid said without looking up from a letter he was penning.

"Indeed," Lord Annend said, wiping a tear from his eye under the guise of scratching. "She has sacrificed so much for the kingdom. She may enjoy aspects of court life, but she was not keen to be married off to a stranger. Used by the kingdom like some pawn. But she did it, and now she makes an even harder sacrifice to hold the kingdom together."

"Well, she was, perhaps," Relthid muttered. "But Naelis will have little use for her now."

Her grandfather went pale.

"She might be okay," Lira said quickly. "Likely just jailed, at worst. Or kept at his side still, to help unite with Havaral should he... should he win." Her eyes grew distant. *Yes, she'd likely be safe. She must be.*

Lord Annend nodded, but said nothing. Soon after, the clap of galloping hoofbeats rose over the roar of the camp. Lira turned to find a female captain named Sylitha reining her horse in just outside the pavilion. Sylitha was the leader of Delvarad's scouts.

"Caldemoor has drawn close today, my lords," she called in a loud voice as she dismounted.

Tying her horse off with a few quick flicks of her wrist, she marched quickly to the table and bowed her head to Relthid, then Handan. The scout captain had light red hair, pale skin, and blue eyes, together with her name marking her as from the Syl people. Benam and Fen followed her into the pavilion, both sweaty and panting.

"They kept a good pace all day," Sylitha said. "Didn't stop to establish their lines as we'd anticipated. If they march through the night, they could be upon us as soon as morning."

"They should be keeping their distance," Handan said. "I'd have liked to wipe them out before Tovar arrived, but I didn't think they'd be so foolish as to pursue this far. Perhaps they just want to give us less room to work with. Or they mean to lure us out... draw us further west. Further from our allies." He bit his cheek. "You're certain Tovar is still a week out?"

"Certain, General."

"And no signs of any other forces?"

"None, General. Well, only the small town militias we've already discussed, but alone they are not even a threat to our rear guard."

Handan turned back to those around the table. "Your Grace. My lords. We must attack at first light. Defeat Caldemoor before Tovar joins them. Anything else would be foolish. Hopefully they are foolish enough to march through the night again to save us the trouble."

Relthid gripped the table with his knobby fingers and pulled himself onto his feet. "They will have little time to prepare a defense. None, if they are foolish enough to attack. Our losses should not preclude a victory over Tovar afterwards, so long as we get dug back in before they arrive. Yes, The One will not give us such a gift twice."

Benam gave his father a curious look, but Relthid gave no indication of having noticed. Handan turned to Annend, who returned only a slight nod of affirmation. Afterwards, all eyes turned to Lira.

Lira looked over the map. "Best to face them on our terms. While they are alone. Yes, Handan."

General Handan turned to Sylitha. "Go have someone fetch the high commanders at once, then get back to your scouts. I want constant eyes on Caldemoor. Keep me informed of their movements."

She pressed a fist to her chest and hurried back to her horse, galloping off into the camp. Lira exchanged a grave look with Handan before he summoned a page and went about a flurry of preparations. Fen soon dismissed himself to go join the craftsmen. A meal was served to them at Relthid's request before the old lord rose to retire.

"I know well I'm damned old," the lord of Delvarad said. "If I'm to be of any use tomorrow, I'd best rest this insufferable body."

The ease and efficiency with which Handan went about preparations reminded Lira of how he moved with a sword. She was pleased to find her plentiful reading of war prepared her well in the areas of macro tactics, when Handan would graciously ask her opinion or approval. What she realized though as she marveled at Handan's swift decision making and issuance of orders was that these larger bits of tactics she'd studied left countless questions unanswered and variables unconsidered.

This went on until the sun had fallen, the camp quieted, and Annend too had long since retired. Benam slept upon a narrow cot to one side of the tent, Wesslund in a chair. The flaps had been closed save for one section, a guard standing just inside before it. Lira and Handan sat near the table around a small brazier of glowing embers, a light rain rapping on the tent.

"Do you ever think of the lives lost?" Lira whispered, watching a small flame lick out from the brazier.

"I would be a poor general if I did not care for my soldiers. But, I would be a worse general were I unwilling to trade lives for victory."

Lira was silent for several breaths. "I hope this victory is worthwhile." *And I hope these deaths earn a victory.*

"If just the cruel were willing to fight, the world would be run by the cruel. Naelis alone bears the blame for any blood shed tomorrow. There is a time to question the spilling of blood, my queen. This is not such a time."

My queen. Lira met Handan's gaze and he nodded gravely. Just then the guard at the door stepped aside and Sylitha entered again, the water upon her cloak catching the firelight.

"Your Grace," she said, lowering her voice as she spotted those sleeping. "They march yet."

Handan leaned his head against the back of his chair and stared up at the roof of the tent. After a time, he sat back up and shook his head. "I suppose we must act as if they will attack. Wise One alone knows why Lord Ashlun would do such a thing, but that's what we'll assume. If they stop, we'll attack. If they don't, they can crumble against our defenses."

He stood and went to the door. "Kelv."

The guard turned and spoke with a gruff voice. "General?" He was on the younger side of middle years, eyes bored enough to imply this wasn't his first eve of battle.

"Get word to Relthid and Annend that Caldemoor will be upon us shortly after dawn. Tell him to have everyone up by first light, and ready to march by sunrise. Understood? *Everyone up by first light, ready to march by sunrise.*"

"Understood, General." And with that, he disappeared into the night.

Handan turned to Sylitha. "Sir Tennv has night operations. See that he is informed and have him double the guard and patrols. Then get some rest, we'll need you sharp come morning."

Sylitha saluted and was off again. Handan walked back to Lira's side and put a hand on her shoulder.

"I'm going to get some sleep," he said. "I suggest you do the same."

"Sleep, yes," Lira said, but did not move.

"We can rest easy knowing we have made all the necessary preparations."

Still Lira didn't move. With that, Handan bowed and laid in his cot not far from Sir Benam. His breath slowed quickly.

Lira shook her head, even snorting at how easily sleep came to the general at such a time. She stared into the burning embers for a short while before forcing herself to rise. She laid on her cot, eyes falling again on the glowing brazier.

It was fruitless trying to sleep, she considered. Tomorrow could decide the fate of thousands of men. The fate of a kingdom. They had superior numbers, at least, but that only left her wondering about Caldemoor's curious tactics. Perhaps Lord Ashlun was merely a poor tactician. Had not Lord Relthid said as much when still she'd been entreating for his aid? But then, more likely it would be Naelis's doing, and she had no doubt he would throw away every last life in Caldemoor if he thought it would win him the war. Trading lives for victory... just as she was.

Lira woke with a start to the sound of men shouting. She sat up at once, heart pounding, but what she'd mistaken at first for alarm she began to realize were merely calls to wake. Benam was sitting in his cot lacing greaves onto one leg, Wesslund fastening the other. Handan was not on his cot or anywhere she could see. A glance at the open doorway told her it was the tail end of night. The guard there had been replaced with another. Beyond him, more figures stood outside conversing, words lost in the waking war camp.

Handan entered a few moments later. "Liraelle," he said loudly before his eyes found her. "My apologies, Your Grace, I only meant to wake you."

"What news?"

"They are not stopping. I still suspect they will halt soon and try to draw us out, then fall back to bait us toward Caldemoor. They want to keep us from joining with Odsgaard. We'll oblige, but not let them get far. I'm sending the cavalries from both armies out in preparation to flank from either side, with mounted archers in case Caldemoor has the same idea."

Lord Relthid appeared in the doorway, quickly releasing Tetchmira's arm before leading her in. He was wearing intricate leather armor with polished steel bracers and a blue cape over one shoulder.

"My cavalry will depart soon," he said. At the table, he swept all of Caldemoor's pieces slightly closer to their line and shook his head incredulously.

"Tend to Her Grace first," Benam told Wesslund.

"No, go ahead," Lira said. "I'll be right back."

She stood and ducked through the tent, waving Benam off when he made to stand. Outside, Lira could faintly see men going about their preparations. The clouds had cleared and there was a chill in the air. The night was without a moon, but the great star Hearth glowed brightly to the north amidst the lesser stars. Wondering at the time, she found the Wise One's eye. *Dawn comes when the Wise One looks upon the hearth.* The words came to her in Jeld's voice. Raising her hand to the sky as he had taught her, she counted perhaps half a bell until dawn.

Lira walked down the hill into the camp, past men dressing, donning armor, tacking horses, eating. Most were more subdued even than she'd noticed was typical of men beneath the stars. Handan had made sure to spread word of their numerical advantage to keep morale high, but battle was battle.

Though she did her best not to disturb anyone, faces turned toward her as she moved through the camp. Soldiers had a way of spotting rank, she'd learned. It would propagate by some imperceptible signal, like alarm over a predator spreading through a group of animals. Her breath caught at the simile and she came to a sudden stop. Murmurs rose up around her as she stood frozen.

"Your Grace," came one.

"Princess Liraelle," said another.

"Queen Liraelle," another still.

A handsome young soldier held a bowl out to her. "Join us, Your Grace?"

"I—" I what? Can't be bothered, now go die for me? She gave a smile and took the bowl. "Thank you, soldier."

"Would you join us?" the soldier asked, turning his boastful grin to his comrades.

"I have much to do, I'm afraid. But now I have one less." she said, holding up the bowl.

"Of course, Your Grace."

Lira gave him a nod then started off. After only a few steps, she stopped and turned. "What's your name?"

The soldier's confidence melted and he swallowed. "Noleerce."

"How about this, Noleerce. After we win this battle, I will share drinks with you all."

Noleerce managed only to stare back until the other soldiers began to laugh and cheer. He breathed a little laugh then saluted.

"We will win swiftly then," he said, then received an elbow from an older soldier. "Er, Your Grace."

She considered her next words. Thank you for your service? This is no squabble for a crown, but a fight for the sanctity of the kingdom? Forgive me for playing your lives like pieces in a game of Scratch?

Instead, she pressed a fist to her chest in salute. "Fight well."

To a man, the soldiers saluted back. Lira nodded to Noleerce and walked on. She relieved herself into a waste trench, trying her best to ignore the many eyes she knew were watching. Turning back toward the pavilion, she found herself worrying over Fen, but convinced herself he would just be off fixing things, not holding a spear on the front lines.

Back inside the pavilion, a dozen knights and soldiers stood before the map table, Sylitha among them. Lira went and stood beside Handan, Lord Relthid, and Lord Annend, several men murmuring their greetings quietly as Handan spoke. How had this gathering been called, she wondered. So often the army moved as if on Handan's will alone. It was so little a thing—a meeting—and yet she marveled. More mastery that might never be found in a book.

"But we're going to bet they won't so foolishly attack," Handan said. "I don't want to give them a chance to dig in either. So, we'll advance immediately,"

Wesslund tapped Lira gingerly on the arm, holding up a polished steel greave. She nodded and he began donning her armor as she stood there before the leaders of her army.

"Lord Relthid will run a standard advance south. Half of Lord Annend's forces will take the west end of the line, the rest split evenly between mobile reserve units and flanking elements. Cavalry will follow on the flanks as well. Our superior numbers will do us little good if we simply lock lines and trade man for man, so we'll flank hard to fully exploit this advantage. Eyes on the signal flags, ears to the horns. Your Grace? My Lords?"

Lira looked to the lords. *Her* lords. Annend was so pale she looked to Relthid just to see if it was merely a trick of the light, but the older lord's wrinkled complexion was no paler than usual. Lord Relthid looked her way and gestured for her to speak first, but she bid him proceed. His wrinkled lips frowned in thought, then he cleared his throat and spoke.

"It's always simple in principle. Around the map. Any army can have a good plan, but greatness... greatness comes in how we execute once swords are crossed. In our order, our communication, but also in our independence. Our initiative. In the countless decisions every leader makes. So as the general says, heed the signal flags and horns, but above all be smart and lead your men. You are their flags. You are their horns."

Tears glistened in Benam's bright green eyes. The men murmured their agreement and offered quiet salutes, most looking next to Lord Annend. Annend's mouth opened and closed, then he shook his head. All eyes then turned to Lira. Wesslund secured the last buckle of her cuirass, then strapped a short crimson cape onto her spaulder and stepped away.

"I would address the whole army," Lira said. "Ready them for movement, I'll share my words from their front before we march."

Somehow she expected to be questioned, but instead the soldiers saluted, then hurried off at Handan's dismissal.

"We'd best be off as well," Handan said.

Lira nodded and turned to her cot. Wesslund was already there, stowing the last of her few possessions into a pack. He strapped it closed and shouldered it over his own.

Thank you, Wess," she said, then left the pavilion.

Attendants stood ready with mounts outside. A squad of signaleers, personally trained by Handan during their journey south, stood outside a nearby tent hurrying their food down. Lira mounted her white beauty from Relthid's stable and looked to the sky. The eye looked almost directly at Hearth now, the sun's glow showing just above the horizon. She waited until Tetchmira had finished helping Lord Relthid into his saddle, then wheeled her horse and started toward the front.

Lira looked out over her army as she descended the hill. Their defensive walls had been parted and the men were amassed beyond it now. A lot of work wasted, but better to have a wall and not need it, and all that. Men stretched beyond her vision in either direction in the dim light. She could not help but look west for some sign of the enemy army, but saw nothing.

Reaching the parted wall, she waded into the army, retinue close behind. Again her presence spread like a ripple and a path appeared where before there had been only endless lines of men. Commanders of two of Havaral's reserve companies saluted as she passed between where they'd split. Past line after line of archers, then swordsmen, then spearmen.

A row of swordsmen with full shields parted and she emerged into empty space. There was grass underfoot, a rarity of late given her typical position behind the thousands of feet tearing up the ground. She trotted her horse out from the army, eyes on the brightening horizon. At first she was searching for the enemy, then merely delaying that final turn to face her army. Finally she drew her sword then wheeled her horse.

From above, the force had looked massive. From here, incomprehensible. The gradual incline that had been the basis of their defense now ensured not only that she could see every last man, but that the army towered over her as if filling the stands of some great colosseum. The clouds beyond them were faintly touched with pink and yellow. Handan, Relthid, and Annend fell in behind her. All was silent.

"My good soldiers," she called into the dawn, surprised by her own volume. "Of Delvarad. Of Havaral. Of every place between. Except Plemenol," she said to laughter, pointing with her sword to the tower peaking over the hill.

She was quiet for a heavy moment before speaking again. "I almost did not do this. Almost did not call you to fight. I thought any peace, even one under Naelis, would be better than war. But I was wrong. Naelis is truly evil. Perhaps giving him Avandria would save more lives, but his stain upon our kingdom would cost all our spirits. So do not fight for me today. Fight for Avandria."

The army erupted with cheers. They did not raise goosebumps upon Lira's neck, only guilt in her heart. She sheathed her sword and turned to General Handan. "March when you are ready, General."

Handan nodded, his eyes full of pride. Saluting, he looked out over the army as several blue signal flags marking the ready rose from the masses to stand unmoving. Two red flags waved on the northern line, and Handan patiently waited, the sky brightening over the hillside. Sylitha rode out to them from somewhere to the north as they waited and confirmed that Caldemoor was about three leagues out, dead ahead. When the last of the red flags was replaced with a still blue one, Handan exchanged another nod with Lira, Relthid, and Annend, then looked to his army.

"With me!" he called, his booming voice stoic. He turned his horse and trotted west, toward the enemy.

Chapter Eight

The ringing of Dralor's pick echoed through the dark mineshaft, then the scuttle of broken stone. A single dim lamp burned behind him, casting a thin shadow on the wall that could almost have been him. He swung again, striking the small fracture he'd made at the perfect angle and knocking loose a sizable chunk of stone. Eshal worked just beside him, the ringing of his own swings steadily following Dralor's.

Dralor wore the standard uniform of loose linens. He'd retained his outsider clothing until a worsening rash had forced him to swap them out. They would have been laundered, and in all likelihood someone else in the prison wore them now. His boots clung to life still, if only barely. It would be a sad day when they went. The cold, the bugs, the sting of stone chips against his feet, but worst of all the mere loss of it. He'd lost flesh. Lost cleanliness. Lost a tooth, albeit in the back of his mouth. Lost pride. Lost hope. Don't take the damned shoes.

"So a fever, then?" Eshal said quietly.

"I'd prefer something less easily refuted," Dralor said. "If someone at med feels our foreheads or sees we aren't pale or sweaty, they'll send us right back, or worse."

"And with an injury we'll want a quick enough recovery. Gut issue?"

Dralor lowered his pick and considered. "They couldn't refute it… unless they cared to watch us in the—oh."

"The privy. Right where Raf wanted to pass off the pick."

"Not bad," Dralor said.

Eshal's pick was silent for a few beats before the big man grunted and swung again. "Could work. If she gets the blazin' pick anyway."

Dralor did not reply as he thought through the plan as he had a thousand times before. Upon first arriving in the prison camp, they'd been escorted to the quarry by a single guard. A prisoner who had finished recovering at the medical station accompanied them. Dralor had confirmed that these midday runs moving new and recovered prisoners was a standard practice, and that they almost always had just a single guard. So, he and Eshal would fake an injury, recover in time to join such a movement, kill the guard, and climb the gorge wall to freedom.

The walls were sheer, though. That is why Raf would *somehow* pass them a pick in the privy after she'd *somehow* acquired it from the brick crews back in the camp. They would make holds in the rock as they climbed. What they would do after reaching the top, they did not yet know. Not a perfect plan, especially the climbing part, but it was something. It could work.

"If we could make do with a chisel that would certainly be far easier for Raf," Dralor said. "It's the least we could do. *Dreams,* I wish there was a way to get her out too. And Jollel…"

"Chisel won't do," Eshal answered. They both paused to listen for Chesh or another prisoner, then continued swinging.

"We could climb side by side," Dralor said, unconvinced. "One holds a chisel, the other strikes it with a rock."

"The rock would probably crumble."

Dralor wiped his brow. "More holds to make that way, too. Take twice as much time. No good."

In the wake of the ring of Eshal's pick, there came a sharp hiss and Eshal cried out. They both jumped back, colliding in the narrow shaft.

"What—" Dralor felt a mist of water against his face. He moved aside to let lamplight pass and found a narrow band of water shooting from the wall.

Eshal bent and rinsed his face. Laughing, he opened his mouth and drank from the stream. Dralor smiled and took a turn. Then, without preamble, they began frantically scrubbing themselves clean. They were on perhaps their third wash, and still drinking their fill, when Dralor heard the rumble of the cart.

"Oy!" came the voice of Taupry, and a short while later he appeared around a bend in the tunnel. "I hope this isn't piss I'm walking in."

He stopped the cart nearby with a groan. Spotting the jet of water, he laughed and started drinking, a hand on his injured hip. Eshal began filling the cart, Dralor following his lead while the boy drank and, just as they had, began washing himself.

"Underground stream?" Taup asked. "Or a spring? Is it a spring if it pops out in a cave?"

Dralor exchanged a look with Eshal as they both dropped stones into the cart. Though Taup had been quiet the first day they'd met him, he'd quickly revealed his true loquacious self.

"Last cart, ya know," Taup said. "Rain blowin' in."

Eshal grunted. "Doesn't usually stop them working us."

"Looks like a storm. Plus, there was that escape attempt yesterday, so..."

They fell silent at that. Often when there were executions to be displayed, it meant cutting out a bit early. The youngster continued bathing and drinking until Dralor loaded the last bit of loose rock.

"No, no," Eshal said as Taupry reached for the handles of the cart. "I can at least take it to the exit. Damn Chesh and the rest of them for not letting us help each other."

Eshal drove the cart to the exit, past several passages where Chesh had ordered the tunnel turned for one reason or another. Taupry took over with a groan and led them from the mine. Dralor squinted severely as they emerged. The sky was dark with storm clouds, but blinding compared to the deep mineshaft. The storm's early wind was a biting cold against his drenched clothes.

"Pick up the pace, boy," Chesh said as Taupry limped past with the cart. "I ought to pull you off quarry." He stopped and frowned. "Why are the three of you all wet?"

Dralor's jaw clenched, as it always did at the sight or sound of their taskmaster. "We hit a spring."

Chesh cursed, grabbed Dralor's pick, and walked past into the mine. Dralor and companions joined the thousand other sorry prisoners stowing picks and moving rock. Chesh returned a short while later and pointed his pick at Yanick.

"You. You're in the mine tomorrow, yes? I marked the wall about ten leaps back. You'll turn the shaft there. Make sure everyone knows it, we aren't making a swimming pool."

Chesh shoved the pick into Yanick's arms then turned and started his usual cadence of threats and curses to hurry them. When all was in order, they began their daily shuffle back toward the prison. Halfway back, it began to rain. Dralor stared at the prison tower looming before approaching storm clouds. Sheep plodding dumbly to watch one of their own get slaughtered.

He forced his eyes from the tower and searched the cliff walls. Beside him, Eshal was doing the same. Dralor recognized their current favorite spot as they passed. It was sheer like everywhere else, except for a small divot partway up and a bump a bit farther. It wasn't much, but two holds they didn't have to carve while climbing could very well make all the difference.

Dralor looked over to Eshal as they reached the gate to the main camp. The big man shook his head, no new discoveries. The lingering daylight as they filed through the food lines was a constant reminder that they'd returned earlier—a reminder of what was to come. Dralor spotted Raf behind the serving line and veered toward her station. As usual, she feigned a pronounced stoop, convincing given her years, for any who hadn't known her prior. While many men tried to appear strong for the well fed quarry duty, Raf's best bet was to earn herself the lightest duty possible while staying out of infirm.

Raf smiled and reached out a bowl to him with a shaky hand. "I'm close, she whispered. A few more days, I think."

"Good," Dralor said quietly, filling his bowl in the trough. "Privy still seems best."

Raf nodded.

Dralor felt his usual stab of guilt. How could he force her to risk her life for an escape she couldn't even be a part of?

"Thank you," he said as the masses pushed him along. "Be careful!"

Behind him, Eshal leaned in and exchanged a few words with Raf. She patted his hand and the farmer followed after Dralor. They shuffled with the currents toward distant yelling, then poured into the broad clearing at the foot of the black tower. Perhaps ten leaps up, a triangular landing pierced out toward the east. In stark contrast to the dark stone, an inquisitor in white stood to one side of the landing, hands clasped in front of him. At the narrow tip of the platform, a woman stood with her feet shackled to the ground, an iron collar around her neck.

"Is this the Idols' will, priest!" the woman shrieked. "Murder those who try to escape enslavement? You are a farce! You are Discord!"

Fury and horror and shame twisted Dralor's insides as the woman strain against her bonds. More prisoners pressed in behind him until the crowd stilled. Two guards atop the platform pulled a chain through a loop upon a low wooden pedestal. The chain fixed to the woman's collar went taut and dragged her screaming to the ground, neck against the wooden platform.

"There are thousands of you, fools!" she spat. "Fight, you fools! Just fight before you're too broken to fight!"

The inquisitor walked to the edge of the platform, the crowd quieting. Dralor's thoughts turned to the night Handan had confronted him, and the inquisitors had first revealed their strengths in dispatching him. The shame brought a wordless groan to his lips, but it was lost in so many others.

"Crimes are not the most vile sin," the inquisitor said, "because crimes can be served with justice. The vilest sin is justice left undone."

The woman screamed curses at the inquisitor and the crowd alike. Dralor felt a cold sweat on his brow even as the rain grew heavier. His vision tunneled inward and he blinked to clear it. Was there nothing he could do for her? She was right to curse them all. Thousands of them cowering, like a herd watching idly as a single little predator plucked one away. Beside him, Eshal looked ready to charge the platform himself. Dralor put a hand on Eshal's arm, as much for the both of them.

"We can't," Dralor said. "Much as I'd like to kill an inquisitor, what then? A rain of arrows? More executions?"

"They don't have a thousand arrows," Eshal hissed.

The inquisitor nodded to another guard, who pulled a huge sword free of its sheath and handed it to the inquisitor.

"We might take control of the prison for a time," Dralor whispered. "But we wouldn't escape. They'd make us pay for it. Maybe we could do it with a plan, but not like this."

Eshal glared at Dralor then turned his back on the platform. Dralor averted his eyes as the inquisitor reached the sword high. The screams stopped suddenly with the clap of the blade against the block. A chorus of groans followed, then silence.

"Your time here is justice," the inquisitor said, soft voice reaching. "Do not seek to escape justice, or it shall be delivered."

Eshal began pushing his way back toward the barracks. The rest of the masses unfroze shortly after, Dralor shuffling along with them. But just as Dralor reached the first row of barracks, he stopped. Was he such a coward that he could not be bothered to look upon her? This after first standing by as she was executed. No, first had been building this wretched place, and locking her up for likely petty crimes. He'd as good as swung that sword, and whether out of a debt to her or justice unto himself, he'd damn well look upon her. Dralor turned over his shoulder, but the crowd jostled him away before he could see more than a glimpse of the blood spattered platform.

A short man with forearms as thick as boulders and eyes too close together stood before the barracks as Dralor approached. His clean clothes and the lost look upon his face marked him as a fresh arrival. He was squinting at a small sign upon the barracks reading "5 x 9", marking it as the ninth building in the fifth row.

"Fif... fifxynine," the man said.

A skinny, loudmouthed man from Dralor's section named Kopal laughed hysterically. *"Fifxynine?* It's *five by nine!"* He burst into more laughter.

"You can't even read, Kop," said a wiry man they just called Shrew.

"Oh sure, fine, but I know you don't read numbers like letters!"

"No, you can't!" came a shout from behind. Dralor turned to find Yanick and Taupry walking toward the barracks with Chesh.

"We're running a quarry, not a temple," Chesh said. "He's out. Look at him, he can hardly walk!"

"I managed today!" Taupry pleaded. "I'll be even faster soon. Just a few days."

Yanick squared his shoulders and took a step toward Chesh, hands squeezed into tight fists at his side. Dralor gulped down his soup and edged closer.

"It's done!" Chesh yelled. "He's out. Now back away before we have another execution to watch today. Into the barracks! All of you, get in there!" He stabbed a finger toward Taupry. "You, with me."

Yanick charged at Chesh and took a swing. Dralor caught his arm and wrestled him away.

"I should have your head!" Chesh said.

"No no," Dralor said calmly. "No need for that, we're just going to go wind down."

"Come take it you bastard!" Yanick spat. "He's a boy! Just a boy! What's wrong with you!"

"I'll be fine, Yan," Taup said. "I wasn't built for breaking rock anyway."

Eshal took Yanick's other arm and together he and Dralor dragged him toward the door.

"No!" Yanick shrieked in roaring sobs. "No! Taup! Help him, you bleedin' cowards! Taup!"

The decrepit door swung as near as it came to closed behind them. Yanick only redoubled his efforts, and even big Eshal struggled to keep hold. Finally Yanick went limp and they set him against a bunk, both staying between him and the door.

The sturdy ginger's head hung, then he looked up at Dralor with hateful, bloodshot eyes. "How could you? How could you!"

He jumped up and charged at Dralor, grabbing the front of his shirt and slamming him against another bunk. Dralor did nothing to defend himself, his eyes growing distant. Yanick was right, of course. It was worse than letting a predator take their young—he'd *protected* the beast as it took Taupry. The lighter duty might let the boy's hip heal up for a time, but it wouldn't last.

"Del saved your life, Yanick," said Nethe, a pale-skinned easterner with a gray beard and bald head. "And your death would not have helped Taupry. It is just as the story of Karetas and Holmed, when the prime took—"

Yanick snorted, gave Dralor another jostle, then pushed him away. The odd fellow who'd been trying to read the sign shouldered between them, muttering to himself and walking down the aisle.

"Watch it, *fifxy,*" came Kopal's voice shortly after from deeper in the dim barracks.

Yanick wiped tears from his eyes, shook his head at Dralor, and strode toward his bunk.

"I'm sorry," Dralor said softly. Sorry for more than Yanick would ever know.

"Join us, Del."

Dralor turned. Down the aisle, Nethe beckoned to him then disappeared into a bunk row. Dralor wasn't feeling keen to socialize, but then, he was even less keen to retire to his bunk next to Yanick.

Eshal patted Dralor on the arm. "I'll go help the newcomer. He'll need a bed." He hurried after the squat little man.

With little else to do, Dralor went to Nethe, finding the old easterner sitting upon a bunk sipping his meal. Kopal lay on his side on the bunk above, head propped on his hand, and one knee kicked up.

Across the row, Jo and Pyt sat beside one another on the lower bunk. Jo had skin like tanned leather, bright blue eyes, and a long blond beard streaked with gray. Pyt was one of those who actually seemed likely to belong in such a place. A skittish fellow with a wispy dark beard and shifty eyes. Not the usual quarry sort, this row, but they were tough enough to make their quotas just fine.

Nethe watched Dralor as he took another sip, then offered a comforting smile. "Sometimes there is no good choice, but there is always a best choice."

Dralor frowned at that, then nodded. In the silence, his thoughts turned back to the girl who had been executed.

"If every last man and woman in here were to revolt, do you think we'd stand a chance?"

Nethe smiled and looked to Jo, who held up a finger and swallowed a mouthful of soup.

"We've dreamed up some right good plans," Jo said with a deep, scratchy voice. "A dozen ways we could kill every last tasky and guard in the prison. Maybe the inquisitors too, or wait 'til they are out. How to get out though? Well, I figure we could get a person or two out, but hundreds would have to die for it. It's just too hard to get enough people on the wall, and to do it fast enough before reinforcements arrive. Did you know there's a whole mess of soldiers garrisoned just outside the wall?"

"I did not," Dralor said, straightening. Curious. Might Naelis be preparing to move troops to the west? Would he march against Havaral? Or Caldemoor? Were they marching upon him?

"It's usually the guards that get people out," Pyt said. "If you have something to offer. Dirt on someone, or make their job easier, or off someone. Coin, usually. Now, these guards seem different. Got the fear of them inquisitors keeping 'em straighter."

Dralor wondered at the criminal's words. He didn't have even a single coin to his name anymore. Perhaps he could promise riches upon his return to the throne. Maybe that other criminal Krayo would put up coin for him, though he could hardly see how that would benefit the man. Or, there was always offering himself. Probably they'd execute him even sooner, hang him in the streets. Maybe he could turn that into an escape plan somehow? Or could his life at least buy the freedom of Eshal, Raf, and Jollel?

Shaking the thoughts aside, he found Pyt staring at him. He hoped the beady-eyed little man had done horrible things to have arrived in this place, but he knew better than to ask. It wasn't supposed to matter here.

"Mostly just common stealin'," Pyt said, flashing a grin at Dralor's surprise. "Sometimes odd jobs for people. Hey, the way I came up, I coulda done a lot worse, princey."

Dralor shook his head. They'd started calling him that despite his best efforts to sound lowborn.

"What did you do, then?" Pyt said, his eyes darting away. "Too much salt in some topper's food?"

Jo laughed, sharing a smile with Nethe.

"What?" Pyt said.

Jo only shook his head.

Dralor didn't answer, and Pyt shrugged it away. The row talked for a good while longer before Dralor excused himself so as to not keep them up. When he reached his row, Yanick lay staring at the ceiling, not acknowledging him in the least as he climbed into the bunk beneath.

Dralor cursed himself a fool as he too stared, sleepless. Every missed moment of sleep or bite of food was a step closer to the inevitable death the prison promised. Even so, it was not long before his thoughts turned from his own fate to that of the many he'd seen beheaded at the foot of the tower—*his* tower. And to sweet, good Loris. Benam. Handan. Lira. Oh how he'd failed Lira, in the end.

For the first time since he'd sat waiting to be executed in the palace jails, he thought of the one person he had both never wronged and never failed. Those deep, clever eyes. The way they would narrow and she would cock her head when he told her a story. She was so skeptical. So brilliant. Then the eyes were wide and she was screaming. The blood... blood everywhere. He was helpless. So damned helpless.

"The baby?" she managed, voice soft now.

Dralor's wide eyes were thick with tears. He pursed his lips and managed something like a smile, then nodded. He kept nodding until finally he could speak.

"Fine," he lied. "Just fine. She's—she's beautiful."

"Her? A girl..." Her face lit up, eyes still closed. Her words were faint, so tired. "I want... to see her. Let me...see..."

Dralor glanced toward the door to the next room, where the other healers would be operating on their child. He took her hand and squeezed it. His eyes pinched closed and he shook his head, fighting to keep his voice from cracking.

"Soon, my Dot," Dralor said. "You'll see her soon."

He started awake from the dream, and sobbed silently into his hands.

Chapter Nine

Jeld sat upon a large stone amidst the short grass, a stream trickling past beside him. Sunlight filtered through a thick canopy overhead. His fingers moved nimbly over the lute strings to a song that spoke of adventure, full of wonder and promises. It was by no means masterful, and often he grew frustrated with his inability to produce the sounds he imagined, but he'd come a long way. It could only have been a few weeks since he'd been trapped in the halls, but he'd had nothing but time to practice.

Sleep, he had discovered, was not necessary in this strange place, nor was eating. His hair had not grown. Candles did not burn down. A thrown ball still fell, and yet time seemed frozen in so many other ways. He often wondered what this meant for the real world outside the Halls, whether time could be flying by as he spent an eternity here, or if instead it stood frozen. Were he to finally escape one day, would he discover Lira was an old woman? Or long dead?

He felt the moods of the presences around him fall as his dark thoughts soured the music. As with the Traveler's tavern, something—countless things—listened. It was not the unnerving sense of being watched, but rather like butterflies rising and falling on the breeze of one's passing. Whatever it was, it was *something* to share this lonesome place with.

Jeld's fingers stalled as his mind drifted to days spent wagoning across Avandria with Niya. No notes seemed good enough, or happy enough, or sad enough, or just...right enough. When finally inspiration struck, he couldn't play it. Clearly his untrained note plucking was insufficient to convey this complex amalgamation. He needed more chords, new techniques. If only he had a teacher, or a—or a book.

Coming to his feet, he followed the meandering stream through the woods. It widened and with it the gap in the canopy above, until the stream ran glimmering in the sunlight over a bed of smoothed stones. Jeld picked his way over the rocky riverbank beside, ducking beneath a willow tree and continuing as the stream narrowed again to press into verdant old growth.

A door stood in the middle of a small grassy clearing. Jeld passed through it into the Halls, all traces of the forest gone as he closed the door behind him. He wound his way toward the nexus, as Vincet's books called the grand central intersection. The edges of his vision grew more surreal with each step, as they always did outside the individual Idols' spaces.

The nexus just ahead, he stopped before one of the countless narrow hallways that lined the broader corridors to each Idol's Hall. Punctuated by all manner of mismatched doors, it stretched without end into the distance. As usual, standing before it his gut clenched as if he were looking down over a deadly drop. He'd etched five day marks into his tavern table since first resolving to venture down one of the unfathomable hallways, but had gone not a step.

Jeld stumbled back from the hallway. Tomorrow. Perhaps tomorrow. He crossed the nexus to the corridor leading to Vincet's library and soon was digging through books. He found one that looked promising and started toward Vincet's room upstairs, where he'd taken to doing much of his reading.

Over the next perhaps several bells, he slogged through an entirely too scientific text on the lute and broader music theory. Twice he closed the book, resolving to learn on his own, before relenting and continuing through. The third time, he did not reopen the book, nor did he resume his practice. Instead, his gaze fell upon a small leather bound book amidst a mess of others he'd been plying through for a means of escape.

Vincet's journal. An affixed ribbon of leather marked where he'd left off, near the end. He slid the book before him and tapped the desk nervously. Then, blowing out a breath of probably fake air, he took the journal to the reading nook and opened it to the marked page.

In these final days, I find myself pondering the meaning of it all. I can conclude only that our purpose is our pleasure. That ultimately, we will never make a single selfless decision. Why do we give? Why do we take? Pleasure, and pleasure only.

The spider preys. The thief steals. But I fear we cannot fault either, only stomp and stone them in kind for impeding our own pleasures. This thought leaves me feeling filthy as I make my final arrangements. I acknowledge it must only be for my own pleasure that I aim to serve the greater good, but if I must spin a web to do so, am I not a spider?

Jeld skimmed ahead through several more pages of philosophical musings on the topic of necessary evil, then slowed as something caught his eye.

> *I have long shied from writing down this anathema, for fear it would cast my path in stone. Yet now I know that is precisely why I must. It must be done.*

> *I have written at length of the hypothesized cyclical destruction and rebirth to which the world as we know it is bound. The hungry fire, said the legend of one lost people. The red destroyer, another called it. Never by the same name, but always, always it is there in these tales of old.*

> *Only a hypothesis, yet one with consequences so severe that extreme measures were warranted. Surely anything is better than the complete, or near-complete destruction of humanity. This must be slightly balanced against the possibility that this fabled destruction is merely legend, but even so the formula quite necessitated the rule by we five.*

> *It seemed so clear before—swords in the hand of the few wins if we can guarantee the wielders of these swords*

are benevolent. We were the Idols, of course we were benevolent. And we were, for centuries. But then, it was our very pursuit of order, even peace, that led to war. To Syladrya's murder. To Khapar.

It was then that I realized my mistake. There is no perfect, benevolent leader, and when power is in the hands of the fallible, a destruction more absolute than any that could be produced by the many becomes possible. This destruction resulting from the consolidation of power into the hands of the few, and the fabled cycles of destruction, are likely one and the same. There is no destroyer but ourselves. It has been our very quest to hold the world together that has put it again onto the path to destruction.

We could right this, I long maintained. We could abdicate. But nay. It is not enough to share the seat of our power, so too must we distribute the power itself, this gift of The One. I knew I could do both, but how could I be certain the others would follow? Were any to refuse while others should not, we would leave power even more concentrated in the hands of those who remain.

I have searched for another way, One believe me, I have searched, but there is none. It must be done, and so now let my words cast my most terrible path in stone and lend me the strength to let wisdom, not sentiment, guide my hand. My brethren, and I, must die.

Jeld read those last words again, then again. His heart was racing, his muscles tightening as if for a fight. He closed the book, opened it, read the words twice more. The Idols had not ascended in some final act of sacrifice, nor had they abandoned the world. They were simply dead. The Idols were truly dead. Killed? By... by the Wise One?

Jeld's chest grew tight and his lips trembled. He had never been a particularly faithful person, yet this felt terribly wrong. Of course, this meant there was probably no Discord, too. He should rejoice in that, yet somehow it too left him feeling hollow, as if meaning had been stripped from life itself. His hand shaking, he turned the page. Passing over a line he took to denote a new day, he read on.

It will be poison. Poison, One forgive me. But my misgivings are irrelevant. The world cannot be sacrificed just to save one old man some pain, nor to preserve the lives of five. Thank The One I too must die, lest my deeds forever torment me. They might never know of my betrayal, or at least will not suffer the knowledge long. Yes, we have merciful death to console us.

But, Naelis. My dear Naelis. It is enlisting his aid that pains me most, for this marring of my most loyal follower's soul will not be quenched with death. No, he must long carry this terrible deed, this terrible knowledge. And still I ask more of him. Though I conclude we alone are the destroyer we feared, this truth will not resonate with men. For most, evil needs a name, and so I name it Discord. I know no one stronger than Naelis to carry this burden and spread my most terrible but necessary lies, yet... I can only pray these fissures I so regrettably rend upon his soul do not shatter it.

A sound jarred Jeld from the words. He strained to hear, but there was only his heart thudding at Vincet's revelations. Perhaps it was nothing, this place had an odd way of—

The sound came again. And was that a distant voice? He jumped to his feet and ran to the stairs. Slowing upon the spiraling stairs, he looked down over the second floor but saw nothing. He did the same for the next level and something caught his eye. A light near the entrance was slowly moving through the shelves. The little table that usually held a single burning candle stood empty.

"Hello?" Jeld found himself calling. The light shook then froze. "Wait, I'm coming!" A stab of panic when his descent brought him too low to see the light. He retreated upward a step until he could see it again, frozen in indecision. Then he ran down the stairs.

"I'm coming! Wait!" Jeld called, weaving through the aisles, vaulting over a couch.

He slid to a stop at a narrow aisle along the outer wall. An old man with a tattered black robe and a long gray beard held the candle out toward Jeld.

"Vincet," Jeld breathed.

The old man stared back for a long moment, then suddenly burst into laughter.

"Did you know his beard was actually quite short?" the man said, his voice high and croaky. "Though I suppose it would be quite long by now if he'd been stuck here all these years." He looked down at his robe. "He *was* fond of black, though. A symbol of how little even the wisest know."

"Hair doesn't grow here," Jeld said.

"Hmm? Ah, ah! Fascinating." The old man's eyes darted in thought.

"You just became Idolic, then," Jeld realized.

"Mm, yes... yes, that *is* the logical conclusion. Either that or I've become drunk again."

"You'll wake soon."

"Yes, that is my understanding." His eyes narrowed. "Why are you here?"

Jeld searched for an answer, not quite knowing what to say.

Suddenly the old man gasped. "You're Reverie's boy. How—"

The man *vanished*. The candleholder clattered to the ground, its flame sputtering out.

"No!" Jeld shouted, reaching out as if to pull the man back from nowhere.

An anguished sob escaped his lips and he staggered, grabbing the bookshelf to keep from falling. He slid to the ground, unblinking eyes staring where the man had stood.

So he remained for what might have been the better part of a bell before coming quickly to his feet. He lit the candleholder with his sparker and hurried toward the stairs. Halfway up, he thumbed through one of the index books, then replaced it and tried another. His scanning finger stopped and he tapped a word before returning the book and rushing off into the second floor. He passed beneath a low archway of shelves filled with still more books into a particularly dark corner he had yet to explore. Holding out his lamp, his eyes traced the volumes before coming to a stop on one bound in black leather, along its spine, etched in gold, was the word "REVERIE."

Jeld sat on the floor and began to read. The tale of Lord Reverie was not an unfamiliar one at its surface. Jeld had even done a small part in one of Director Sammel's plays that touched a bit on the story, but it had done little to realize the extent of the tragedy that was the life of Lord Reverie. Like many of the other early Idols, Reverie had managed to extend his life. His wife refused to let him preserve her youth with the power, and so while Reverie remained timeless, his wife grew old, and died. Their children grayed and stooped and died. Then their grandchildren.

Reverie was broken by the losses. He wished for death but had not the courage to let it take him. So, he escaped into fantasy. Such was his power that his fantasies, his dreams, took shape. The beginning of the Halls were born. Not yet split into the five by Tholomas, these took a shape reminiscent of her home. Even his wife manifested there, and his children. In the real world he slept more and more, distant even in wakefulness, until one day he never woke. Not present to work his magic, his body simply withered, and he died.

Tears ran freely down Jeld's cheeks as he read. It was the worst imaginable story for his already despondent mood at the old man's disappearance, being stuck, being alone. Luckily what followed in the book was a quite dull analysis on noteworthy writings by Reverie. One particular section caught his eye.

Though consumed in his fantasy, Reverie still took a scientific interest in the Halls at times and was the first to note many of its oddities. So too was he the first to explore the dream halls and discover what we now agree to be some embodiment of The One. It was this that led him to posit that the Halls operate much like a heart, with energy from The One passing into it and feeding the dreams of men through narrow vessels, while pouring into the main hall and fueling the vast power of the Idol, at that time singular.

Tholomas the Wise later wrote that this visualization of the Halls formed the basis for his strategy to split the halls into the five aspects we know today. Even he could not control the vast power lent by The One, but by reshaping the Halls—the focus—the power flowed like blood to fill the new pathways. He would later go on to also liken the Halls to a prism, splitting the power like light into its many hues.

Jeld frowned. Could *dream halls* mean those terrible endless halls? He'd looked through several of the countless doorways lining them and found their contents to be ethereal and seemingly random. People's dreams, perhaps? The One's connection to all humanity? And if so, could that truly mean these hallways led to The One? Intriguing as the thought was, if the hallways led to The One, that meant they *didn't* lead to freedom.

He returned to Vincet's chamber and sat staring out the window at the rolling sea, wondering if Lira still lived. How he wished for sleep... some end, some escape, a way simply to reset in this place without time. But there would be no such respite here, and so he kept reading, searching for any means of escape, mind always returning to those endless hallways.

Chapter Ten

The enemy dipped out of sight as Lira rode down one of the rolling hills then up the backside of another. Handan rode at her side, Lord Relthid alone at the head of his army to the south. In truth the bulk of the line was Relthid's altogether, with only half of Lord Annend's on the line at the northern edge, the rest making up the flankers, reserves, and otherwise distributed amongst Relthid's.

Lira crested the hill and the low eastern sun behind her set her armor gleaming. So too did it set aglow thousands of weapons on the enemy line stretching across the plains below. They were so close now she could almost make out the shapes of individual faces.

Idols but they looked just like us. Just other Avandrians come to the slaughter over a crown. Mighty as her army was, no matter how likely her victory, thousands would die today.

"The blame lies with Naelis alone," Handan said, as if reading her thoughts. He shook his head. "They should be stopping. Digging in. Making us pay for rushing into them."

"Yes," Lira answered. "Perhaps Naelis wants to take a bite out of us and Caldemoor at the same time. Maybe he sees them as a threat."

"*We* will stop, then," Handan said. "Position the archers on the crest of the hill and let the fools come to us. The extra range the height affords will make all the difference."

He turned his mount and called for a stop. A few shouts, a handful of spoken words, and the army made his will done. It always awed her, his leadership. His mastery of the army. It was not the majestic single mindedness of a school of fish or swarm of bees, but the beauty of a rider driving a willful steed.

Lira and Handan stopped just behind the archers with a small handpicked elite guard, the signaleers, a few mounted runners. Benam was there, Fen, and, to Lira's horror, her young page Wesslund. A child, brought to battle. Lord Relthid joined them a short while later, an old man to go with the child. Hardly a pitiable one, but still she'd dragged him here at great risk. She wondered, what was the worth of one child's life against that of an old man and his army, his city.

When the enemy's front spilled back into view down a final rolling hill, they were so close it seemed her army should be doing something. Seemed *she* should be doing something. She looked over to Handan as if he might have missed the enemy army, but of course the general watched patiently, calmly. A predator waiting to strike.

The enemy pounded their weapons to their shields and chests as they marched. Lira's already racing heart pounded, loud in her ears even over the enemy's terrible racket. Her hands began to twitch, whether by adrenaline or fright or both, and she drew her sword, if for no other reason than to occupy herself. All around her rose the hiss of a thousand men drawing steel.

"Archers draw!" Handan roared, others echoing his order.

Lira's eyes flicked between Handan and the approaching army. The general looked up at the cloud-speckled sky as if casually contemplating the heavens on a morning stroll. No, he was looking at a banner to check the wind. He didn't flinch as a cry rose up from the army of Caldemoor, and then they began to charge.

"Free fire!" Handan roared.

A hail of arrows loosed overhead. Enemy shields rose but still hundreds of men in the front ranks fell. Archers drew and loosed again and again as the enemy closed. Caldemoor's archers finally came into range and began firing. Shields rose all at once without an order. With their broader shields and stationary position, her men fared better under the barrage than had the enemy. Nonetheless, the first of her army's blood was spilled in her name.

The armies came together with a booming crash that shook the very ground. Weapons rose and fell, rising again red with blood. Her vision began to tunnel and she pressed it away. She forced herself to focus on the battle, not the individual men, not the screams, not the blood, not the bodies. It struck her as odd that such destruction could happen in the morning sun, then finally she began to see the battle at scale.

Their line was largely holding firm as far as Lira could tell. Handan policed up a few potential weak points that she couldn't even identify, giving orders to the mounted runners. Something did catch her attention, though. Lateral movement in the enemy lines toward the north, a swelling of their numbers there. She started to speak but Handan was already staring toward the north.

"All rear reserves north!" Handan shouted.

A signal flag shot up, another behind the line acknowledging it. Handan sent a runner off with the order as well, then half turned to Lira while surveying the southern line.

"It's a smart enough move," he said, "but our cavalry and other flankers will be on them soon."

Lira looked to Wesslund. He looked both horrified and restless. She'd never before seen the boy idle. Always he went about some work in her service, but there was nothing to be done now but wait. Wait for victory, or for death. She too itched for something to contribute, feeling very much like a mere banner. Wess looked to her and they shared the horrors of battle before the boy gave a nod and turned away. *We're alright*, he seemed to say.

"They're not moving yet," Fen said.

Lira surveyed the battle and frowned. "Who's not moving?"

She realized he was looking to their rear and turned. Several clusters of Lord Annend's reserves remained in their positions distributed across the line. Even the company just behind their command position, beyond a thin rank of Relthid's men, remained in place.

"Handan!" she yelled over the melee, but again he was already looking.

"*Dreams*," Relthid cursed. "I thought Annend had those signaleers trained."

Handan was shaking his head. "No matter, the rider should be there any—"

Finally the reserve companies began to move. Handan nodded and turned back to the battle. The northern line had lost ground with the delay, but would hold out long enough. Parts of the main line itself had already moved to bolster the north a bit. Handan swelled with pride over his commanders for their initiative. A willful beast at times, yes, but a trained army should run itself in the fog of war.

Suddenly the northern line gave way. Handan gasped as the enemy spilled through and began to encircle Annend's men. He lifted his reins but forced himself not to charge to their aid. His flankers would descend upon the enemy soon, and the reserves would patch the line up shortly. His men needed a general more than a warrior. *Dreams,* though, they'd seemed ready enough despite the abbreviated training.

"*Dear Mother,*" Benam breathed beside Lira.

"It will be fine—" Lira's words cut off as cries rose up from behind.

She turned and paled as the men of Havaral plunged swords and spears into the unsuspecting rear ranks of Relthid's line. Men in Delvarad yellow turned to fight, but unprepared, uncoordinated, sur-rounded, they fell.

"Reverse!" Handan barked, shaking a signaleer until he started waving the command. He turned to a runner. "Spread the word down the front, Havaral has betrayed us. They are the enemy! Go!"

"Damn your maneuvers, Handan, get the princess out of here!" Lord Relthid spat.

Handan drew his sword. "I'm going to salvage this fight."

Relthid moved his horse to block Handan. The horror on Handan's face that looked so foreign there turned to a more familiar icy stare.

"We didn't merely lose half the army, Handan, the enemy *gained* half our army, and behind us! There is nothing to salvage. It's already over."

Handan bared his teeth and turned his mount to bypass Relthid. He looked all about the battlefield. Caldemoor had completely pressed through in the north and was pressing Relthid's men from both sides. Bodies littered the ground, virtually all of them bearing the yellow of Delvarad. Down the line, the men had split to face both fronts. In some places to the south, their men seemed not to have realized the betrayal yet and the men faced only west as Annend's soldiers butchered them from behind.

"I didn't know!" shrieked a lone Havaral soldier nearby, an engineer judging by the tools at his belt.

A Delvarad soldier plunged a sword through the man's neck. The Havaral soldier fell to the ground, blood seeping through fingers pressed to his neck. His mouth opened and closed, wide eyes to the clouds above. Lira blinked and again there was fighting all around them.

"Take point, General," Relthid ordered, then turned to his guards and a spattering of nearby soldiers. "V formation, on Handan!"

They mustered perhaps two dozen men and soon Lira was riding at their center through the carnage. There was no longer any shape to the battle, no particular direction friend or foe might face or approach from. Just men fighting, fleeing, dying.

They cut through a squad of Havaral men with hardly a pause, emerging from the melee only to ride straight into the side of perhaps fifty more enemies overpowering a Delvarad platoon. Handan charged toward the skirmish, but suddenly the line beside them collapsed and countless enemies spilled toward them. Handan turned their party between the closing tides and kicked his horse into a gallop. Benam and others warded off blows and ran down those in their path as Havaral and Caldemoor men closed around them like two tides. Lira's breath came fast as the beats of hooves beneath her, a curse in each.

"We've got to pierce through!" Handan shouted over his shoulder. "Be ready!"

He blocked a blow from another rider, grabbed the man's arm, and threw him into another. Just ahead, an archer raised a bow toward him and loosed. Handan swatted the arrow from the air and lobbed off the man's head whilst charging past.

"There!" he bellowed, turning sharply.

They plunged into a line of Havaral men. The enemy did not part around them, rather Lira and her soldiers poured into them like water through rocks. Suddenly there were enemies all around. Lira ducked a blade, parried another. Benam blocked a third, smashed another from the saddle. Another came up behind him and Lira's sword flashed as if on its own accord, plunging into the enemy's armpit.

Wesslund remained at her side, mud and blood spattering his face. His eyes were wide but focused, shocked but not panicked. Lira looked about the madness for Fen but couldn't see him. She winced as her horse stepped straight through the gut of a fallen man, losing its footing for a terrible moment before steadying.

Finally Lira burst from the melee. The battle was thinned here, men fighting alone or in small groups. Handan took down a charging knight in full armor with a single blow then turned and started waving their men past.

"Go! To the treeline!" Handan called.

Lira stopped, looking back toward the heart of the battle. No more than ten of their men emerged, most charging straight toward the treeline, but a few slowing and falling in around Lira. Wesslund appeared, then Lord Relthid with Benam at his side. Where was Fen?

"To the treeline! Move, Liraelle!"

"Fen's not here!" Lira called.

"Move!"

Benam raised his sword threateningly to a Havaral spearman running to rejoin his countrymen, but made no move to attack. One of Relthid's elite guards drove his mount the few steps to the man and cleaved him through the shoulder, Benam wincing.

"I... I can't leave him," Lira whispered.

She couldn't move despite the battle raging just behind. The thought of losing Fen was debilitating, but it was more than that. It was happening again. She was losing everything again, and this time the failure—the blood—was on her hands alone.

Relthid grabbed her shoulder. "Your life is not yours to give, Lira. It belongs to Avandria, and while you live, so does she. Now go, this day cannot be for nothing!"

Lira shook her head, but already Relthid had her horse moving. Somehow the momentum was enough and she kicked her mount faster. She turned over her shoulder and found the old lord unmoving. She stopped as Benam came up beside his father.

"You're not coming..." Benam said.

"We don't have time for more *dreaming* speeches, there's a damned battle going!"

"Enough, come now!" Benam called over screams and hoofbeats and the ring of steel.

"I'll just slow you down. I'm old, son. This is no worse than withering in a bed. Maybe I'll save a few men, send them your way. Maybe I'll stab Annend through the neck. That's the end of the blazing speech, now go."

"You—"

"Go!" Lord Relthid roared.

Stern as he sounded, his eyes brimmed with tears. He smiled at his son, a true and proud smile, then turned to the few soldiers that remained with them. There were six in total, four of Relthid's elite guards and two swordsmen.

"Go with the princess or fight and probably die with me."

Without another look back, he rode off toward where two Delvarad men fought three enemy. One of the elite guards rode after him, another cursing and following. The rest moved closer to Handan.

"On me," Relthid bellowed as he rode toward the adversaries. "Group up! Let's make them hurt for this!"

Any frailty seemed to have vanished from the old lord. Soldiers flocked to him like a beacon in the chaos and devastation. Lira lost them in the battle. Grief consumed her for only a fleeting moment before she pushed it away. He was right. This day must not be for nothing.

"Come on!" Lira called, grabbing Benam's reins and tugging him into motion.

Benam looked back several times until they charged from view down the back of a hill. Stray soldiers melted out of the path of the nine. They spilled into the treeline, slowing only slightly in the sparse underbrush. The terrain descended, the canopy thickened, and the roar of battle quieted. They rode into a low mist.

Lira's breath came rapid and ragged, loud in the relative silence. Her wide eyes shot toward a distant scream. Then toward a long, low wailing. Then toward the thunder of hoofbeats rising, then falling. More hoofbeats somewhere through the mists, and suddenly a group of riders took them from the side.

Two of Lira's soldiers fell. Lira deflected a sword and slashed her assailant across the face. A second blade slammed into her chestplate, knocking the wind from her. Doubled over, she turned and could only raise her thin blade feebly as a burly man brought his sword down.

Wesslund slammed into the man and the falling blade smashing against his shoulder. Both fell to the ground. Wesslund writhed as the burly soldier came to his feet and raised his sword over him. Lira plunged her blade through the back of the man's neck and tore it out the side.

Wesslund struggled to his feet, and Lira fought to keep the shock from her face. The boy's shoulder had been split so deeply that Lira could see the ends of bones on either side of the gaping wound, like some piece of meat at a butcher's. He raised his sword in his other hand and looked about for enemies.

"Oh Wess..." Lira breathed.

At that, the boy looked over to his shoulder. He stood frozen for the longest time, then he staggered and fell onto his back.

Handan raced over to them, face spattered with blood, and a dozen bodies behind him. Benam hurried down from his horse, a large bandage already in hand. He rapidly bound the boy's gaping wound. It looked to Lira to be a fruitless gesture, but all the same she was grateful the boy would not be able to see his terrible wound any longer.

Handan waved Benam over. "Give me the boy. We need to move."

"I'll take him," Benam said. "We need you free to fight."

Benam mounted and one of two remaining soldiers helped seat the boy in front of him. By the time Wesslund was situated, he'd gone ghostly pale and was nearly limp in Benam's embrace. Lira began to shake. Her skin crawled. She pressed a hand to her cheek, then rubbed her arms, then tried to clench her chest but her armor was in the way. She blew out a breath and set her jaw.

"We need to move," Lira said, flicking the reins.

The others followed. They rode on through the misty forest, leaving even the sporadic screams behind. Lira could hear Benam's low singing in Wesslund's ear as they followed the edge of a stream. After probably three bells of hard riding, they stopped to let the horses rest and drink.

"Will he... be alright?" Lira asked, fingers running through Wesslund's hair.

She was seated beside the unconscious boy, his head propped on her rolled cape. Benam knelt over the boy, stitching his wound closed.

Benam pulled a stitch through. "If we stop for the day and I can properly see to him... perhaps. But perhaps not. If he does live, there will likely be lasting effects."

"Then we stop," Lira said.

"We need to distance ourselves more," Handan said.

The general took his reins from one of the remaining Havaral soldiers, who'd been watering his horse in a nearby stream. Lira really looked at the soldier for the first time. *Lukan*, she'd heard Handan call him. He couldn't have been older than twenty. Tall, clean shaven, handsome. He looked about with stern, suspicious eyes like he might be attacked at any moment. Not scared, but alert. She turned to the remaining soldier sitting against a tree. *Jaret*, this one was called. One of Relthid's elites, he was a broad shouldered man with a short beard and dead eyes.

Two soldiers? Had she really just abandoned her entire army to die, save for two soldiers?

"It will kill him to keep riding," Benam said.

Handan watched Wesslund's chest shakily rise and fall. He looked out beyond the stream where the forest thickened and the ground looked to be swampy.

"Can he make it perhaps another league?" Handan asked. "If we can't distance ourselves more, at least we can go someplace we're less likely to be followed."

Benam followed Handan's gaze into the thicket. He sighed. "We should try."

Benam finished his stitching and redressed the wound, then they were off again. Looking about to ensure everyone was accounted for, Lira's heart wrenched when she caught herself searching for Fen. The mud deepened, then turned to standing water. The brush thickened around them upon countless little rises peeking above the water. So too did the buzzing, biting insects thicken as they ventured through the swamp.

"This way," Handan said after a long ride in silence.

He led them up a slight incline. They slowly worked their way through the underbrush, Hanadan's sword melting through even thick branches in their path. They'd just slowed in a tiny hollow to consider it for a campsite when Handan froze, looking off into the distance.

"A cabin?" Lira said.

Jaret clucked. "Not where you'd find the best sort."

Handan nodded. "Still, the boy could use shelter."

Jaret clucked again and rode off toward the cabin. Lira and the others followed. They emerged from the dense underbrush into a small clearing just big enough for the cabin within. As cabins found in swamps went, it couldn't have been near the worst. Its walls were of small logs, held off the ground by large stones in each corner, and it was topped by a mossy lumber roof. Judging by a small walk framed by sticks, they were approaching from the side.

Handan waved Jaret back, dismounted, and handed the soldier his reins. Circling to the front, he knocked on the door. No response. He knocked again, but still nothing.

"We mean no harm," Handan called. "We have a wounded boy who could use shelter. The rest of us can manage outside. We have coin."

"Alright, alright," came a voice from behind.

Lira spun. A wiry man with a bushy brown beard emerged from the underbrush and started toward them. A dog—no, a *wolf*—plodded along behind. He squeezed through them, the horses snorting and jumping aside at the wolf's approach. The man glared at Handan before his eyes fell on Wesslund. Softening, he hurried to the door and pressed it open.

"Get the boy inside, then." He sighed. "And the lot of you. You'll end up inside anyway with the storm coming. Tie the horses off under that tree there."

They did as the wiry man bid. The inside of the cabin consisted of a single open room with a tiny desk, a chair, low bed, shelves, and a small mattress by the fire where the wolf was already settling.

Benam laid Wesslund in the far corner beside the fire and resumed tending his wound. Lira sat at Wess's side, taking his hand in hers and watching the others settle in. Fen gone, Relthid gone, Wesslund dying, her army massacred. Avandria fallen.

The cabin's owner sat in the sole chair, having turned it from the desk. Jaret stood against the door, no doubt to ward off unexpected visitors. Lukan and Handan settled upon the floor, Handan managing somehow to still appear imposing there.

"Well," the wiry man said, leaning back in his chair. "I'm Tirc. And you lot..." His eyes flicked from Handan to Lira, seeming to think better of saying something. "And you lot?"

"Survivors," Handan said. "Thank you for taking us in."

Tirc nodded, biting his lip. "Could be you were followed."

"Followed... no, I don't think so. But there could be a search."

Tirc's eyes flicked again to Lira, then to the door.

Lira sighed. "Yes. Princess Liraelle."

Tirc swallowed. "Queen, ain't it?"

"Of what?"

A loud boom shook the cabin, everyone jumping, Tirc nearly to his feet. The wolf barked once then laid its head back down. A low rumble of thunder followed.

"*Khapar*," Tirc cursed, giving Handan a glare. "Well, storm ought to slow down anyone following you. And clear your tracks."

The group fell silent as heavy rainfall began beating against the cabin. Then the wolf began a low growl and all eyes went to the door. Jaret, who had slid down the door to sit propped against it, was slowly reaching for a knife at his belt.

Lira glanced at Tirc. The wiry man's eyes were flicking between the door, Handan, and a knife upon his desk. Sweat beaded on his forehead. He had no reason to aid them, Lira considered, but every reason to turn them over and be rid of them. Lira casually crossed to Tirc as the dog continued to growl, disarmed him with a smile, then disarmed his desk. Tirc blinked as she stuffed the knife into her waistband and drew her own blade.

The wolf came to its feet and snarled, ears back and eyes fixed on the door. Handan waved the others against the walls and stood alone directly before the door. A knocking rapped thrice on the door and Lira jumped. To her dismay, Handan began raising the bar. She almost protested, but of course delaying things would hardly help. Best to face it now, on their terms, or something like that. Unless there was an entire army knocking at their door, it would be unlikely to get past Handan Tovaine anyway. Unfortunately, that's probably exactly what was knocking at their door.

Handan swung the door wide open. Rain streamed down past the open doorway, not a single person in sight. Lira stepped forward and stood beside Handan. The storm had darkened the day despite it being only late afternoon, and together with the rain Lira could barely even make out the shapes of the—

"The horses," Lira said.

Handan darted around her and was only a single step out of the doorway when a voice from somewhere outside gave him pause.

"Lira?" the voice said.

Lira froze, then realization swept over her and she charged outside.

"Fen! Oh my—Fen, where are you!"

Fen emerged from behind a tree. Lira ran to him and wrapped him in a fierce hug, though her arms couldn't quite close around him. He staggered and she released him quickly.

"You're hurt?"

"Just tired," he said. "Lots of running. Some fighting."

She led him inside. The firelight revealed ragged, bloodied clothing and a gash across his temple. Fen nodded to Handan, shared a smile with Benam, then stared at Wesslund.

"You *are* hurt."

Fen tore his gaze from Wess. "Maybe a little. It's nothing."

"What happened?" Handan asked.

"I got knocked down when we charged through those men. Few of us fought a bit. They all died... Then a horse knocked me down and I just... pretended to be dead. Some riding, then, well, lots of running."

Fendrith looked about the cabin, then frowned at Tirc. "Army engineer? This is a classic model. Well done."

"Yeah, yeah," Tirc muttered. "Did a bit of that."

"You served?" Handan said. "How did you end up in a swamp? What lord did you serve?"

"I, ah—Delvarad."

Handan eyed him. "I don't mean to judge you if you served an enemy, man. I mean to judge your lord for not taking care of you.

"Truly, sir! Didn't serve long, though. Enough for a few coins maybe, but I like it here."

"You deserted," Lukan accused.

Tirc's eyes widened, but he quickly recovered. "Maybe I prefer living in a swamp over serving some lord for scraps my entire life."

"You deserted," Lukan said again.

"I didn't! But what do you call *this* anyway," Tirc said, gesturing to them all.

"Retreating!" Jaret shouted.

"Bah!" Tirc scoffed.

Lukan jumped to his feet, sword in hand.

"Sit down, soldier," Handan said, voice almost a whisper.

Lukan froze, saluted, then sat.

Handan stared into the fire then finally spoke. "There was a time I would have hanged a deserter. I did, many. Now, though..."

Handan grunted, losing himself in the flames. The room fell silent save for the crackle of the fire, the heavy breaths of the slumbering wolf, the patter of the rain, Benam's song. Lira looked down to Wesslund. He was pale, chest rising and falling unsteadily with shaky breaths.

"Where will we go?" she asked, taking Wess's hand.

"Odsgaard," Handan said. "Ralegus will fall back. You'll be safe there. And you'll be with the largest of your armies."

"No... I'll not lead Naelis to Odsgaard. I've gotten enough people killed."

"Lira, it's as Relthid said, the people will turn still to you. You—"

"I know. But I won't make the same mistake again. Avandria isn't ready. We're not ready." She pursed her lips, thoughtful eyes darting. "We should lie low somewhere for now. We—" She looked up suddenly. "We should die..."

Handan frowned. "Liraelle?"

"The only way to keep Avandria safe is by making Naelis think we're dead. We'll wait for Avandria to be ready. Help it along, but wait. So, we'll go somewhere Naelis can't reach us. Somewhere out of sight and mind. And yes, somewhere strong in case we're found."

Benam retrieved a kettle from the fire and poured boiling water over a cloth in a bowl. He waved it in the air a few times to cool it then began to gently clean Wesslund's ravaged shoulder.

"The Isles," Handan said.

"Your new friends would take us in, I think?" Lira asked.

Handan seemed to consider this. "Yes. But they won't allow the sort of scheming Relthid granted you."

"Perhaps not yet. Perhaps not."

Again they fell silent. Lira watched Benam work, the flickering firelight dancing over him as hummed. She frowned. There was something odd about the firelight upon him, like it wasn't quite in sync with the flames themselves. And the color... it had an almost blue tinge to it. She followed it all the way down to his hands and onto Wesslund's wound. Before her eyes, the jagged red line down the stitched wound seemed to diminish.

CHAPTER ELEVEN

Dralor stood in one of a dozen lines of naked men packing the room. At the front of each, two men scrubbed themselves with soapy rags and brown water. Reaching the front of the line, Dralor set the bundle of his clothing on a nearby bench and started washing himself. He had skipped the filthy buckets for over a week after his unexpected shower in the mine, but with the sweaty labor, it could be put off no longer.

Dralor washed quickly, then wrung out his long hair and beard, dried with a damp rag, and dressed. He rejoined his section in something resembling a military formation outside. It was almost fully dark out still, the air biting cold against his damp body. Frost-covered mud crunched as he shuffled toward the food lines, and he whispered his thanks to the mother for his ragged boots.

"Actually looking forward to breaking rock," Dralor said, arms wrapped around himself.

"This bleedin' place," Eshal said, his voice tight and shaky. "Can't be bothered to issue gloves? Socks? Hats? Coats? Can't mine if we lose our fingers."

The food lines were slower than usual, a fact that puzzled Dralor until he stood before the steaming trough, his hands warming wondrously overtop it. His eyes fell closed, warmth radiating against him, until a hand closed sharply upon his. Across the trough was Jollel, smiling out at him. She had thinned already, and some of the light in her eyes had faded, but she was just as beautiful.

She grew serious not a moment later and leaned closer. "Raf says today. It must be today."

Dralor blinked. "Today. Why—you shouldn't be putting yourself at risk."

Jollel filled a bowl and pushed it into his hand, then another into Eshal's. "*Today*. Now go. Go!"

Dralor just stared back as the crowd carried him away. His heart pounded with thought of chains forcing him down to the chopping block. It was worth the risk, he told himself. A chance to get out, to...to what? Escaping the horrors and certain death of the camp was reason enough, but surely there must be something else, something to run toward rather than merely from?

He looked over at Eshal. His friend had a family waiting. A wife. Kids. A farm. A life. Dralor could not help but feel envious, but more than anything he felt resolve. He may have no life waiting for him, but *dreams* if he couldn't help Eshal return to his. Only... was that the best he could do? One life, of all the countless others here whose lives he had ruined?

Dralor shivered from the cold as he shuffled along with the masses. His hands were wrapped tightly around his warm bowl of porridge, holding it close to his chest so the steam rose up to thaw his frozen lips. Today? A moment ago he'd been headed toward another torturous but ordinary day beating rock. Now... probably death.

They were nearing the gate to the quarry when Eshal nudged Dralor. *Today?* Eshal nudged him again, harder. Dralor took a deep breath, set his jaw, and nodded. Yes, one life would have to do. Eshal's life.

He looked covetously down at the remaining quarter bowl or so of porridge, then took a big mouthful and flung the rest off beside the marching lines. He staggered out of the line, leaning over with his hands on his knees as if having just vomited. Stealing a glance back to Chesh, he found the taskmaster had stopped and was looking his way. Dralor staggered again and fell to one knee, hands clutched to his gut.

"What's this?" Chesh scoffed, arms wrapped around himself despite his heavy clothing. "Get up. Back in line."

Dralor spat out his mouthful of porridge with a loud retch. Going to all fours, he continued with loud, chest-heaving retches, finally spilling onto his back. Gasping for air, he started mumbling incoherently and shaking his head.

Chesh cursed, then turned as cries rose up from the prisoners. Amidst the crowd, Eshal was sitting slumped over on the ground. He heaved, and what only Dralor knew to be porridge sprayed onto the ground. He came to his feet and shambled with the masses before stepping out of the line and doubling over.

"Don't be babies, on your feet," Chesh said, looking more nervous than he let on. "We've got rock to beat. Up!"

Dralor forced himself to wretch more, rolling back onto his hands and knees, even managing to truly throw up a little.

"Enough of—" Chesh's voice was cut off by more cries.

Dralor rolled onto his side to get a look. Beyond Eshal, Yanick was writhing on the ground. Dralor muttered a curse. Not part of the plan. Two falling ill at once would be suspicious enough. Yanick jumped up, ran to the wall of a nearby barracks, and hurriedly dropped his trousers, groaning and shaking.

"Nuh-uh," Chesh said. "Up with you all. If we don't—"

Again his words cut off, this time by another taskmaster. "Get them to med before they get us all sick!"

Chesh looked at Dralor, Eshal, then Yanick. "Dream it! Keep an eye on my section while I move these three." He turned from the other taskmaster. "You three, med. Move it!"

Dralor tried to feign struggling to his feet. Idols, but he was no actor. Chesh at the rear, they slowly worked their way between barracks. Dralor heard Yanick retch and followed suit twice before they emerged onto a broader avenue.

They passed a smeltery billowing black smoke and came to the first of three large wooden buildings. Dralor leaned against the wall and pinched his eyes closed as if in pain. Suddenly he recalled a memory. He'd just snatched a sweet from Loris's hand, then when his older brother had rightfully pried it from his grip, he feigned injury to get him admonished. Odd, he might well have not thought of the moment since the very day it happened.

Chesh grumbled and eyed them suspiciously as he led the way through a rickety door. Rows of low beds were spaced slightly more generously than those in the barracks, most of them filled. The patients largely appeared no worse off than the emaciated walking dead making up most of the prisoners. The obviously dying or permanently injured were left in the barracks to rot without the overhead of treatment, if not simply killed.

They were greeted by a squat woman too clean to be a prisoner peeking out beneath a white apron. She interrogated Chesh about his observations of their symptoms, then their taskmaster departed. Next she questioned Dralor and his companions with enthusiasm, like a large cat eager for fresh meat. She prodded them several places, looked into their mouths with a mirrored lamp, and penned numerous notes.

Several beds down, a frail man with a blackened hand cried out. The nurse hurried toward him, face alight and pen at the ready.

"What's the angle?" Yanick hissed. He'd only recently begun looking Dralor in the eye again. "Wait 'til night? Then what?"

Dralor glared at Yanick.

"Should I go to the privy?" Eshal whispered.

Dralor glared at Yanick another moment then pulled Loris's gold pin back out from where he'd stashed it beneath the mattress a moment before. "I thought she'd be here. I thought we'd see her first."

"Angle," Yanick said again. "Don't want to blow it for you."

"We're getting out of here, with any luck," Dralor whispered, eyes on the nurse as she hurried into the next room. "We're getting a pick in the privy, then returning to the quarry in the midday run. In the gorge we'll kill our guard and use the pick to climb the wall to freedom."

Yanick started to rise. "I'll—"

"No," Dralor commanded.

Yanick frowned but settled back onto his bed. Dralor rose and passed through a doorway the nurse woman had directed them to use as needed. A short hallway ran seemingly between buildings before opening into a privy like so many others in the prison. Dralor was just about to stick his head through one of several toilet holes when he suddenly spun.

"That would be a cruel place to hide it," Raf said, grinning.

Dralor felt a surge of joy. He had not known the old woman particularly long or well, but always she'd been kind. More than that, she'd known him on the outside. He'd hardly been at his best even then, but she'd see more than a filthy, thin, broken creature. Then his smile fell away. He was leaving her here.

"I'm sorry, Raf. I—"

She tapped a board with a ragged mop. "It's here. Hurry, I must go."

Dralor lifted the board she'd indicated just enough to peer beneath. Sure enough, there was a pick upon the ground just within reach below. It was a smaller variety than those used in the quarry, but it would serve its purpose well.

Dralor replaced the board. "Eshal will get it a bit later. I'm so sorry, Raf. I wish—"

"I know. Go, friend. And good luck."

Dralor pursed his lips and nodded. "Thank you."

Raf smiled and put a hand on his shoulder. With that, she hurried from the privy. Dralor moved a small stone to rest atop the board Raf had indicated. Eshal was anxiously staring his way when he emerged.

"It's there," he said, his friend letting out a breath. "Probably best wait a few bells in case the nurse lady is going to prod us more."

"Why didn't you tell me about this?" Yanick accused. "Not bad enough you let them take Taup?"

Dralor froze halfway through laying back on the bed. He'd considered it, oh how desperately he'd tried to make it make sense, but each person they included seemed only to reduce the odds of Eshal making it back to his family.

"I'm sorry," Dralor said. "I tried."

Yanick grumbled, but said nothing further. They fell silent and the bells passed slowly, those distant chimes from Tovar haunting like whispers from a lost loved one. They took turns retching and groaning to keep the charade intact. With each passing blink Dralor more frantically racked his brain for some other way that might let more people free. Raf, Nethe, Taup, Jo. Fifxy, too. He'd grown quite fond of the simple little man. Everyone. It wasn't only that he wanted to find such a way, he *needed* desperately to know there *wasn't* one. How else could he live with abandoning them so—living when those he's condemned should be left to die?

It was almost a relief when the nurse came again to prod them. A distraction, if a dangerous one.

"Nothing?" the nurse said, palpating Yanick's abdomen.

Yanick shrugged. "Thought I was gonna shit myself to death not a bell ago."

"Feels a bit tight..."

"Just those slave muscles, hah!"

"All of you, nothing..." The woman pinched between her eyes and shook her head. She looked up and eyed them skeptically.

"Maybe that rat we ate yesterday, eh boys?" Yanick said.

Dralor blinked. "Ah. I told you we should have cooked it."

"Chesh gonna let us have a cookout is eh?"

"You... ate a raw rat?" the nurse asked.

"You seen what they feed us around here?"

"It's not that..." Her eyes darted over her notes. "Yesterday, you said? What time? Morning?"

"Mm," Yanick affirmed.

She opened Eshal's mouth and peered inside. "Usually it takes about three days before the sickness starts. Gray or brown?"

"The rat?" Eshal said through the nurse's fingers in his mouth. "Brown, I think?"

"Ahh. I meant your shit, but that's interesting. Brown you say?" She tapped her lip with a pen. "Could be something there."

She scratched more notes, then eyed them suspiciously again. Another tap at her lips then her shoulders fell. "Alright. You're free to go. You tell your taskmaster I want an update tomorrow, sick or not. If you experience anything odd, I want to know about it. *Anything.* Rash, shit, abdominal pain. Any boils on the neck or crotch, come back immediately, you hear me?"

Dralor nodded. "Thanks for seeing to us."

"Go to the front gate and someone will see you back," she said, already walking down the aisle surveying her patients, or subjects.

"Quick stop in the privy," Eshal said to Dralor.

The nurse stopped, turned. "Are you ill again? What do you feel? Cramps, is it?"

"No, no. Nothing like that. Just better to go before the quarry."

"I'll observe. This could be important."

Eshal shot a nervous glance at Dralor. "Er—observe?"

"It's nothing to fuss over. There is no room for modesty in science. I see the body no different than an engineer inspecting his work."

"Right. I... it's probably just piss."

"Hmm. Should be dehydrated, I'd think. Kidneys slowed, maybe? Either way, best observe. Come along, I've got others to attend to."

The nurse started off toward the privy. Eshal gave Dralor a horrified look, then followed her inside. After a while, Yanick sighed and started toward the privy.

"What are you doing?" Dralor asked, but already he knew.

"Going to help. Eshal doesn't have it in him."

"She could come out first," Dralor said.

"Maybe. Or she might not. Not going to get a better chance than this. Crazy bitch has it coming, anyway."

Yanick started off again without waiting for an answer. Dralor frowned, then followed. They were nearly there when Eshal emerged, face ashen and eyes wide.

"You take care of her body?" Yanick asked, peering around Eshal. "Didn't just leave her there, did—"

"It's done!" Eshal hissed, pushing him out. "I have it."

Eshal walked toward the front door, gait a bit stiff with the pick presumably fixed to his back. They made their way to the front gate without incident and approached a mounted guard loitering nearby.

Dralor eyed him. Average stature, well-enough muscled, with what looked to be a good reach for his size. He wore his sword on his right hip. Left handed then.

Two freshies in clothes Dralor once would have called ragged joined them from the gate before they began the trek to the quarry. Both had long brown hair, the older with a mustache and the young one the beginnings of a wispy beard Transfixed on their horrified faces as they all walked, Dralor realized they must be father and son. It was horrible enough to lose one's own self here, but to see your child suffer the same fate...

Dralor took no notice of the biting cold as he walked, his mind searching still for some way to save more people. Finally, they passed through the rear gate into the slave-cut canyon leading to the quarry. Here Dralor added a stagger to his step, a pause, a gripping of the gut. He gagged as he walked and stumbled, pressing a hand to the cliff wall to keep from falling. The watchman said nothing, but Dralor knew he was watching.

It was nearly time. There had to be some better way. Some way that didn't leave thousands to die. His thoughts raced through ploys—impersonating guards, paying off guards, tunneling, scaling the wall, a mass uprising. These and a thousand more, all dismissed as fast as they were dreamed up. Just then his breath caught as an idea solidified in his head. Tunneling... he'd dismissed countless variations of the storybook escape technique, each as ridiculous as the last, only, but this?

He drifted over to Eshal. "I've got it. I think I know how to get our whole section out."

"Dral, we're..."

"Remember where we struck water in the mine? We turned the tunnel, and Chesh never checks it. We could work that route but turn it upward, mine our way out. As long as we fill carts and make some progress in the main shaft, nobody will notice. We—"

"No," Eshal said. "How many months do you think that would take? Or years? Our whole crew could be dead or broken and off quarry before you'd break free. Honestly, you'd probably be caught and executed long before then. We have a real chance now, and I won't keep my family waiting any longer."

Dralor started to protest but stopped and nodded. "I understand."

"And *you* need to get out before you're just one of those skinnies waiting to die!" He lowered this voice. "And stop acting like this is all your fault. You deserve to live too. Now are you going to do this or do I need to?"

Dralor studied the passing cliff face until he recognized their spot. It offered a few natural handholds already. The concentration of tree roots and the hint of a canopy above suggested some degree of concealment if they actually made it to the top. It was time. *Dreams*, but it was time. He gave his friend another look, then lapsed into a fit of retching. Turning, he staggered back toward the watchman.

"Sick," he managed. "Still... sick. Need to... go back. Holding himself upright against the wall, he passed the watchman.

"Er—stop!" the watchman said, looking between his prisoners. "Hold it, we'll go—"

Dralor fell to the ground and started convulsing.

"*Khapar,*" the watchman cursed, sounding more irritated than horrified. "Pick him up, we'll—"

The watchman's words rose in alarm. The hiss of a sword being drawn. Dralor jumped to his feet as the guard was spilling from the saddle. Eshal got atop the guard, pinning his sword wrist to the ground and silencing him with a forearm across the throat. Before Dralor could reach the scuffle to assist, Yanick smashed the guard's head in with a rock.

Dralor blinked at Yanick, then turned sharply to secure the horses. He found the older of the two newcomers already holding the reins and stroking the beast's head. Nodding to the man, Dralor helped Eshal up and pulled the pick free from the straps around his back. Without another word, Dralor started swinging. Shards of rock flew, and Dralor brushed away the fragments to reveal a well shaped hold, precisely as they'd been practicing with their every swing in the quarry.

"You're going to climb out," the younger newcomer said.

"Yes," Eshal answered.

"And then what?" the older one said.

"Not be here!" Yanick said with a laugh. He finished rifling through the guard's pockets then started to strip the clothing off.

Dralor slid the pick into his tattered belt and pulled himself up on the new holds. Out with the pick and he swung, just one hand clinging to the rock. When it struck he lost his grip and fell the miniscule distance to the ground. He couldn't help but look up the wall, cursed at the distance, and tried again to improved success.

As Dralor and Eshal had planned at length, they traded off every few holds to give them practice while still near the ground. They let Yanick join the rotation as well, but decided the newcomers wouldn't have the stamina for it. Once they were high enough to make for a nasty fall, they took longer turns to minimize the climbing.

Rock and dust peppered Dralor's face as his pick rapped against the cliffside. More than halfway up, now. The sun, directly above the canyon when they'd begun, had disappeared beyond the cliff. The blue sky beckoned, but his aching hands didn't seem much to care as he feebly tapped at the sad little divot he'd managed overhead. His other arm, dangling from the last grip he'd managed to carve out, began to shake. Enough. Best left to the next person.

He started stuffing the pick through his belt to make ready to climb back down, but the heavy head of the pick dipped to one side. Dralor fought to pull it back into balance. His forearm burned, cramped. The pick wrenched toward the ground, then slipped from Dralor's useless fingers. He turned quickly to call out to his companions below—too quickly. His toe slipped from a hold. Sharp stone dug into his fingertips as his weight came down on his hand. Free of the pick, his other hand scratched at the rockface. His dangling foot felt blindly for purchase but found only sheer stone. His fingers began to slip, slip. Then his hand closed on the new hold, shallow but steady.

Dralor blew out a breath, knotted stomach easing if only a little. He slowly felt about with the toe of his shaking foot until he found a hold, then clung there with his cheek pressed to the cliffside, quick breaths blowing clouds of dust into the open air. When his shaking eased, he let his cramped arm dangle for blood flow before slowly descending. Near the bottom, all four of his companions grabbed him and eased him to the canyon floor.

"Don't be a hero, princey. I'll take over," Yanick said, but Eshal was already climbing.

"No time to spare," Eshal said without looking back.

"The big man has spoken," Yanick said with a laugh despite looking nervously over his shoulder. The two newcomers followed his gaze.

"This could go many ways, but I promise you the risk is well worth it to avoid this place," Dralor said, rubbing his arm.

The younger of the two seemed to find some calm in Dralor's eyes and managed a nod. "I'm Nithen, by the way. This is my brother, Tthal." He prodded the other, who only eyed Dralor suspiciously.

"I'd thought father," Dralor said, looking back up to Eshal.

"May as well be," Tthal finally said. "You'd think after twenty years without support, our ma' wouldn't take our father to her bed again, but there you have it."

Dralor managed an uncomfortable smile. Yanick blessedly intercepted the conversation, showing little sign of the animosity he'd been harboring for days. Dralor's eyes fixed on Eshal and the chatter seemed to fade. His heart thudded fast in his chest as his friend neared the top, moving slowly but steadily. Men his size were not built to climb, but they were born to swing a weapon.

The band of sunlight atop one wall narrowed. The sky darkened. Eshal reached up with one long arm and his fingers closed on the surface. Dralor marveled at the decency of the man as Eshal nonetheless set to work with a final hold for his shorter-limbed companions. Two steady blows, pick back to his belt, brush the debris, test the hold. Seemingly satisfied, Eshal hoisted himself to freedom. Nithin was next, Yanick next at Tthal's insistence, then Tthal at Dralor's.

Pulling Tthal up, Eshal looked down into the canyon, where Dralor stood holding the reins of the dead watchman's horse. Their eyes met, and Dralor saw realization dawn on Eshal.

"You're coming," Eshal said, just loud enough to be heard.

Dralor shook his head. "I can save them."

Eshal batted a hand off his shoulder. "Dying won't save them. Come!"

"Go! Go to your family!"

Eshal glared back for a time, then kicked his legs back over the edge and began to descend.

"Stop that!" Dralor roared.

Eshal did not slow as he answered. "If you won't come, then I stay."

"No! No, they need you."

Eshal only kept climbing.

"Stop! St—wait! Wait!" Cursing, Dralor ran to the wall and started climbing.

Eshal peered down. "You're coming?"

Dralor pulled himself up another hold. "Yes, *dream you*."

Dralor followed Eshal up to the top, taking Yanick's arm and rolling onto his back in the patchy moss. The smell of moss, grass, and trees filled him. Not ash. Not filth. Not stone. Not dust. Life! Wind. Freedom. He was free. A stab of guilt hit him at that, but still he breathed a sob of joy.

Chapter Twelve

Jeld stared down one of the endless hallways, mismatched doors stretching into the distance. *Dream halls*, Vincet had called them, or at least it seemed to be these unnerving halls he'd been referring to. Regardless of whether it truly led to this... *embodiment* of The One that Vincet wrote of, it seemed just as unlikely to offer any way out. Looking down the hall, Jeld's stomach seemed to drop as if he were teetering at the edge of some great height. Setting his jaw, he marched into the hallway.

Two steps. Three. He stopped beside the first door. Twice he'd peered through dream hall doors. The worlds beyond might indeed be dreams. They were not sane places, shifting and surreal, fuzzy like the edges of his vision here.

Jeld shuddered and glanced longingly behind to the nexus. As he'd grown accustomed, everything at the edges of his vision swam as his eyes cut through the space like a hand above water searching for purchase. He forced himself to turn away and took a few more steps before something gave him pause.

Frowning, Jeld again looked behind and scanned the immense nexus. There, something substantial where everything else was blurry. The moment he focused on it, there was nothing but an empty stone wall. Walking back into the nexus, Jeld again looked away and it came back into focus. A door.

It teased at the edge of his vision. Details were elusive, but it was unmistakably grand like those leading into each of the Idols' halls. Five Idols, six doors? He stopped before it, eyes averted to find the handles, and pulled it open.

A fresh breeze filled his lungs. As abruptly as waking from a dream, he stood before a beautiful grove. The trees were mostly green, some few with leaves turned a range of yellows and reds. Birds chirped. The ground was patchy with grass and dry dirt, a narrow trail woven with gnarled roots at its center. A huge house that managed to look both luxurious yet also rustic stood beyond the trees.

Jeld stared into the other world, eyes squinted to the bright sunlight. Birds chirped, and Jeld could hear the unmistakable sound of children playing in the distance. No doubt faceless echoes like the music and chatter in the tavern, but it brought a smile to his face all the same.

He walked into the grove toward the house, the nexus just a dark rectangle cut from the world behind him. The dirt felt so real beneath his steps. The birds, the laughter, the sun, the trees... He forced the smile away, steeling himself from disappointment. An illusion. Just another—he froze. Children, in the yard near the house. People, real people! They were running about at joyous play, yet doing nothing in particular the way only children can.

"Kits, dinner!" a woman's call came.

The door to the house was open now, and a woman started down the path toward the children. Like the house itself, her clothing seemed merely to be playing the part of rustic. Her gaze caught upon Jeld and she froze for a moment then waved.

"Hello," she called softly.

"H—hello," Jeld said, standing from a crouch.

"Will you be dining with us?"

"Dining—with—I, er... what—"

"It's no inconvenience. Please, join us if you wish."

"Oh, do!" said one of the children, a skinny little girl of perhaps seven years.

"Don't!" said a slightly older boy with a grin.

"Hacher!" chided the woman, wrapping her arm around the boy. "Please, I'm sure you're most welcome."

Jeld smiled again. The woman was every kind of beautiful, but it was her motherliness that shined brightest. His smile faded and his eyes widened. He couldn't remember the last time he'd thought about his mother, or rather the hole in his life that one might have filled, but oh what must that be like? To have a mother's arm wrapped around one's self... that unconditional love, that comfort, that security, that completeness...

"Sir?"

Jeld started. "Sorry. I'd really best... er, well, I suppose I don't have any place to be."

"Wonderful!" she said with a clap. "Come in, won't you? And you, children. Come along, now."

The children hurried toward the house without complaint, shooting Jeld glances and sharing looks of curiosity and excitement with each other. The woman waved Jeld after, and together they strode toward the door.

"Forgive them, we don't get company often," the woman said. She frowned and cocked her head. "Must have been a week or more."

They entered into a sitting room, with a couch and several chairs around a low table. Light streamed in through open windows. Potted plants on shelves and in corners made the place feel very much part of the grove. Jeld's mouth watered at the wondrous scent of a home cooked meal, like Evelyn's back at the theater.

"Revi!" she called. "Revi, we have company!"

She waved the children, then Jeld, into another room of similar decor. Several trays of steaming food filled a large dining table.

"Now isn't this wonderful, dear?" the woman said.

She produced a plate and cutlery from a hutch and arranged another setting at the table. "A guest just in time for dinner. A man fresh off the road is certain to have some interesting tales to tell, isn't that right?"

"I...do have some stories."

She went to a vacant spot between the children, a second empty chair beside her, but she didn't sit. The children didn't either, just stood there, hands resting on the backs of their chairs. Shifting uneasily, Jeld followed suit.

"Yes dear, we should," the woman said.

Jeld frowned and looked around the table.

After a few blinks of silence, the woman looked over at him. "Well? Would you care to say the whisper?"

"I...I'd really rather..."

The woman waved it aside. "That's quite alright. Hacher, after your little display perhaps you can share some kinder words with our guest. Go on."

The boy sighed, then bowed his head. "We thank The One for... our trips here to Tyaswood, and for father's blessing, and... and for peace and family and this meal. And we whisper that Billa's stutter gets better, and Oshy's gut too, and that there's peace so Father can stay with us more. With you, in dreams."

"In dreams," everyone echoed.

Everyone sat and set to filling their plates.

The woman took a bite of what looked to be roasted beef, then looked to Jeld expectantly.

"Hmm?" Jeld said, realizing everyone was watching him.

The woman turned sharply to the chair beside her. "Reverie! I'm sure he hears just fine, dear." She turned back to Jeld. "Never mind that, my lord was just asking you what brought you to our door today?"

Jeld's eyes flicked to the empty chair beside the woman. *Reverie*, she had said? And hadn't she said *my lord*? Jeld looked again to the empty chair, then the idyllic family in this picturesque place. This was his dream... Lord Reverie's fantasy. The origin of the halls. Again his eyes flicked to the place the others must still see their long lost husband and father.

He stood abruptly. "Beg your pardon, but I actually must be going."

The children gave a collective groan. The woman looked to the empty chair, nodding along to some unsaid words, then turned back to Jeld.

"Yes, do stay," she said. "Please."

Jeld forced a quick smile. "Thank you, but perhaps next time?"

Without further delay. Jeld spun and hurried from the room as fast as he could walk. In the next room he broke into a run toward the still open door. Perhaps he'd heard too many stories, but a part of him expected the door to somehow close before he could escape. It didn't, though. As he ran through the grove, he next expected the passage back into the Halls to be gone, but this dreadful worry proved unwarranted as well. He spilled from the scene into the nexus and slammed the door closed behind him.

Distancing himself from the door, Jeld turned and found it entirely gone before remembering to avert his eyes. There it was, hovering at the edge of his vision. Jeld shuddered. He had to get out. Had to escape, now!

Jeld ran to the nearest dream hall, felt in his collar to be sure his bag was still back in its usual place, and ran down the hall. Doors of all variety passed in a blur to either side. Two. Four. Ten. Twenty. He glanced over his shoulder. The main nexus was already only barely visible.

Thirty. Fifty. A panic rose up and he took a deep breath. It wasn't as bad as the void he'd first had to navigate. At least there was the passing doors to tell him he was even moving at all.

"Just one day," he panted.

That was the plan. One day, whatever that meant here, then return. Just don't get turned around. Don't get turned around. A simple enough task, that. Just keep facing this way. Yet, the more he fixated on it, the more his mind spun. The more it seemed it would betray him. Slowing, he pulled a piece of chalk he'd found in the Craftsman's Hall from his pocket and made a mark on the wall between two doors. He took a breath, then continued at a brisk walk.

Time was difficult enough to judge elsewhere in the Halls, but here in this seemingly endless corridor it was nearly impossible. He'd given up counting doors long ago, and reduced his marks to preserve his dwindling chalk. Not even hunger could be used to judge time in this place, nor sleepiness for that matter. His legs did tire, so there was that, and from days past he did have a good sense of how time dragged with nothing to do but walk the open road.

Jeld wrote the number thirty-two beside a small, dilapidated door, pocketed his chalk, and kept walking. He'd taken to writing numbers to better mark time. Thirty-two marks now, give or take a few he'd probably forgotten or double counted or skipped. That would be maybe... *Idols*, only around eight bells? With a sigh, he pressed on.

Nearly a full day in, he wiped sweat from his brow and sat, pointedly keeping himself oriented. Why was it he could sweat despite not requiring water here? It made about as much sense as any dream though, and that's what this place was, right? A dream? Well, a dream you could crawl into through a bag, anyway. Hadn't he heard once that if you realized you were in a dream, you could gain control of it? He'd never experienced that himself, but it seemed reasonable enough.

He stood and broke into a jog, willing himself to ignore the fatigue his mind must be fabricating. Unfortunately, he experienced no such control. and he was soon doubled over and panting hard. He peered ahead as he recovered, squinting to bring his vision into focus. Just more of the same. More doors.

He sighed. Perhaps one more day? The thought was not comforting, but what if it was just a little farther? If he turned back now, surely he'd end up returning some day and having to suffer the same stretch again. It would probably prove fruitless anyway, but if he did nothing... He shuddered, recalling his experience with Reverie. Would he fade like the Idol had? Or since his body was truly here, not just his mind in some dream, would he properly die here? Or... his hair didn't grow and he didn't eat nor sleep, so would he actually just... live forever? How long would that last before he went insane? He walked on.

Jeld marked another number on the wall. Two days now, if his count was right, and it probably wasn't. He pinched his eyes shut. He could walk for a month if only something around him would just bleedin' *change!* Doors. Doors. More doors. He yelled with frustration, laughed, sobbed, and yelled again. The noise helped. It was something, at least.

He drummed on the walls and passing doors, tapped and stomped and slid his foot along the stone floor. Then an idea struck him. He pulled his lute from his bag, and a great weight lifted at its familiar feel, its sound as he strummed each string. Even began to sing, mostly just hums with only the occasional lyric strewn about.

Jeld walked on. No more marks. No more doors. No more Halls. Just the music. It could have been several bells or closer to a day when he trailed off mid song and blinked. In the distance, where before there had always been only the endless halls stretching into infinity, there was instead a fine point of black.

His breath caught. Another void, probably, but something other than doors at least. He slowed to a stop and stared at it, then finally broke into a run. It remained a distant black dot when he stumbled to a stop panting, however. After maybe another bell walking, he seemed no closer.

Endless, then. Seemed rude, getting the hopes up with the black bit only to go on forever anyway. But then, there was plenty rude about this miserable place. He buried his face in a hand, fighting back tears. When he looked up again, the black point seemed a tad larger.

He blinked again, and hurried onward. The point grew, slowly at first, then faster, larger and larger. Something took shape in that blackness. A light. It took the shape of a circle as he drew closer. He could make out where the hallway ended now, a sharp edge against the blackness. A buzzing sound took shape in the silence, louder with each step.

Then he reached the end. A hand upon the abrupt edge, he peered into nothingness. No floor, no walls, no ceiling. Countless other hallways a mirror image of his own encircled the space, little windows like stars in a night sky. And the light at its center... For all its brightness, it seemed to make the room no less black. Not a circle, it was a sphere. It swirled and shimmered like a womb of lightning. An embodiment of The One, Vincet had written. Jeld's eyes fixed on the sphere. The buzzing grew louder. Not a single sound, but many. Voices. Thousands, millions of voices.

Jeld froze. He was standing on emptiness perhaps halfway to the sphere. He stood there in the emptiness, staring still into the undulating currents within the sphere, then took a breath and eased toward it, footsteps soft upon the darkness. It was thrice his height when he stopped beneath it. He reached a hand out, just above its surface. No heat. No pull. Nothing.

Then he felt something. Not against his hand, but rather his Idolic sense. He reached out with his mind. It felt so... inviting. A sense of welcoming, yet it was so vast. So powerful. The chorus of voices grew louder. He was nothing. Insignificant. A speck of dust in its magnificent storm. His mind tried to comprehend its majesty and he could feel himself tearing, breaking, searing.

He raised the walls around himself and took a few steps back. "The One," he breathed. The One, in all its magnificence.

He lost himself again in the eddies and flickers of the swirling light for a moment before shaking himself free. Still stuck, though. Sitting in the presence of the one true god, the very source of the power of the Idols, the Halls, and maybe dreams the world over, but still just as stuck. Perhaps he could touch it and be gifted power enough to free himself? That would probably work in one of Director Sammel's stories, but it seemed more likely to make him go mad or disintegrate him.

Jeld sighed. What had he expected, an exit? A friendly god to snap his fingers and cast Jeld back to Lira's side? Staring into divinity, he shook his head. Maybe it was omnipotent, and maybe it was benevolent, but it wasn't both. The world was too terrible, too unfair a place for it to be both. He turned his back on the glowing, floating sphere and took a single step toward the hall, then froze.

So many hallways. Even straight ahead, there were a dozen he could have originated from with just a few steps drifted one way or the other. Which one had it been? Did it even matter?

He thumbed the edge of his bag through his collar. Which was worse, another maddening multi-day march through a dream hall, or crawling through his bag for a short but terrifying trip through the void? Mulling this over for a while, Jeld finally unbuttoned the bag from his shirt and crawled through into darkness, pulling the bag in after him.

While far from pleasant, the trip through the void was less terrifying now that he knew the way out, and far shorter. He followed the marks through the darkness, mind on the glowing entity he'd left behind. What a waste that had been. Of course, eventually he'd be desperate enough to return and touch the dreamin' thing. Maybe it would get him out somehow, a win. Or maybe the majesty and power of The One burned him to ashes. A win?

He emerged only a short while later into the nexus. Wishing very much that sleeping were possible, he made instead for the Warrior's Hall and lost himself in Bantae. It had become his nightly ritual. Far from rest for the body, it was the closest he could get to sleep for the mind.

Eyes closed, Jeld imagined the weight of an enemy's sword against his. Keeping it perfectly balanced upon his, he circled his would-be foe. All around him he heard the flicker of flames, and despite having spent so much time around fires in his life, the first thing it brought to mind was the sound of Cobb shaking out an uncut leather. Handan's distant voice seems to nag Jeld to focus, but he ignored it and let his thoughts and body drift.

Realizing he hadn't even moved in quite a while as his mind wandered, Jeld lowered his sword and opened his eyes. He stood at the center of the Warrior's Hall. Inspired by the great halls of the north, it was a vast chamber with wooden walls and heavy beams running overhead, and several huge fireplaces. Long tables covered much of the floor, with torches strewn all about and several huge round iron chandeliers adding their light as well. Weapons lined one of the walls as they had Handan's training room. Two less grand longrooms intersected the main hall to either side.

Wiping his brow, Jeld breathed in the scent of smoke, wood, mead, even the snow outside. The place was so magnificent and rich with depth that it was easy enough to forget he was trapped, but he never forgot for long. He could still see that orb of white lightning as if he'd stared too long at the sun, a constant reminder of his latest failure to escape. Play his lute at the Traveler's tavern or the Mother's woods, tinker in the Craftsman's shop, read in the library, bantae here. Repeat. Repeat. How long could he go on?

Suddenly a person snapped into existence not four leaps in front of him. Roaring and flying through the air as if thrown, he crashed onto the long table at the room's center. A sword clattered to the ground beside him. He stiffened, looked about his new surroundings, then jumped up into a fighting crouch toward Jeld.

Jeld backpedaled and held up a hand. "Easy... It's alright."

The man took a step toward Jeld and barked something in some guttural language. His clothes were ragged, his face and arms badly scratched and scarred.

"Easy!" Jeld said. He realized he was holding out a sword and lowered it. "Easy, friend. Easy."

The man looked around the room again, at the beamed ceilings and weapon-lined wall, the long tables and smoldering fireplaces. He said something else in his tongue, and amidst the unfamiliar words Jeld recognized a sound.

"Tovados!" Jeld repeated. "Yes, yes, Tovados! Idols. The Halls."

"Tovados," the man affirmed. He climbed over the table and retrieved his sword, then started pacing around the room. He spoke more in his language, questions by the sound of it, but didn't seem to expect any answer.

"You were... in a fight?" Jeld asked. "You'll disappear soon. You'll return. Be ready."

The man went to one of the large fireplaces and sat backward upon the bench to face it. He leaned back against the table, breathed a short laugh, then broke into deep, joyous laughter. Amidst his laughter, he looked at Jeld. Jeld grinned, and when the man only laughed harder, joined him in laughter.

Yes, whatever his situation, this place was better than most he had known in his life. There was no pain here. No beatings by his father. No hunger, no cold. No beatings from watchmen, jails, cults, or conniving politics. Nor was there any need to steal, to threaten, to harm, or any of the terrible things he'd had to do to survive. It was a good place. A trap, maybe. A prison he would not stop trying to escape, but here and now he was by a fire, in the great hall of Tovados, safe, warm, as fed as this place required, and now he had someone to share it with, if only for a moment.

Jeld sat not far from the visitor. They shared another look and their laughter rose into hysterics. Howling, the man leaned over and rapped Jeld's arm. Wiping tears from his eyes, Jeld reached back to do the same, but the man vanished. Jeld's laughter turned to sobs, then screams. After a time he sat staring into the reflection of the fire dancing upon his sword where he'd thrown it to the floor, tracks of tears joyous and sorrowful lining his face.

Suddenly his breath caught. He glanced to where the man had been sitting, scanned the table, the bench, then the floor below. The man's sword was gone. It had disappeared, gone with him. When the first person he'd encountered had disappeared, the lantern he'd been holding had merely dropped to the ground, not gone with him. Perhaps only items from the normal world could return to the normal world? Did that mean Jeld's bag had originated in the real world?

Jeld jumped to his feet. *His bag.* He'd pulled it from the halls. That meant someone *else* could pull it from the halls. And if he crawled through its counterpart in the darkness below... he'd be free! Of course, it was usually weeks between encountering visitors, and he wasn't sure how he'd go about convincing a flustered stranger to take his bag, and to not kill him when he stuck his head out of it. And then there was the matter of not knowing where in the world he would emerge if it worked, but never mind all that. Anywhere was better than this nowhere.

Chapter Thirteen

Dralor dunked a bread roll into his steaming stew and interrupted his own hearty laugh taking a bite from it. He was seated on a stool beside a table covered in food. It was a small room. Eshal and Yanick sat at the edges of two small beds, stuffing their boyish grins. There was a time Dralor wouldn't have so much as tolerated the sight of such a bed, but it seemed a luxury now. Wouldn't have been caught dead with the likes of his two roommates either, but far from it now.

Yanick caught Dralor's eye over his upraised bowl and pointed to a stack of meat pies on the table. Dralor threw him one, but Eshal snatched it from the air and ate half in a single huge bite. The three laughed again through full mouths as Dralor tossed Yanick another. Far from it now.

Two weeks had passed since their escape, nearly all of it spent off road as they worked their way northwest toward Eshal's farm. The two newcomers had split off soon after their break from the prison, planning to return to their lives in Tovar after hunkering down for a while. The remaining trio arrived at the small town of Chesswick just that morning, sending Yanick in wearing parts of the clothing he'd stolen from the guard to secure the rest of them less incriminating garb.

Yanick set his bowl aside and went to the fire. Taking up a shovel from beside the fireplace, he scooped a large stone from the coals of the fire and lowered it into a pot of water upon the floor. Steam rose up with a hiss. He grabbed a small mirror from a table, bore his toothless gums at it, and shook his head.

"Well, it ain't pretty," Yanick said, dunking a cloth into the water and scrubbing his face. "But you're the poor saps that have to share a rag with it."

"Beats sharing it with you and a few hundred others," Eshal said through his roll.

"Still, I think I'll add another rock," Dralor said.

Yanick cackled and set to hacking his beard off with the knife he'd taken from the guard. Dralor watched, transfixed by the look in Yanick's eye as he seemed slowly to recognize the man buried beneath the beard and all it symbolized.

"I'm so sorry about Taup," Dralor said.

Yanick froze, then looked Dralor in the eye and nodded. "I'd do what I did over again if I had the choice. But, I hope you'd do what you did every time to save my stupid arse."

Dralor let out a held breath and nodded back. When Yanick was finished and looking like a new man, he sat at the edge of a bed and started putting his boots on.

"I'll start asking around to find us a ride while you two clean those sorry faces," Yanick said to their inquiring looks.

"I'll go with you," Dralor said.

Eshal set his bowl down and stood. "We'll all go."

Yanick waved them off. "Oh sit down. I snoop better on my own." He stopped in the doorway. "You're good lads. Good lads." A gave a quick smile, patted the doorway, and was off.

"He's a softy," Eshal said.

Dralor nodded and came to his feet. He shoveled another smoldering rock into the water then began to wash and groom himself.

"I was thinking," Dralor began, sawing at a fistful of his beard. "We should part from whatever ride Yanick secures a day or so out from your farm. If people come asking about escapees, it wouldn't do to lead them to your family."

Eshal grunted in agreement. "Guess you do have some criminal in you."

"Politics," Dralor said too quickly. "Tactics."

If Eshal thought it odd, he gave no sign. "I should have thought of that. Done enough hunting in my day."

"Not hunting," Dralor said, cutting another chunk off his beard. "*Hunted.* Prey, now."

"Two days on foot to be safe, then. Six on wagon." He seemed to grow almost anxious. "Eight days..."

Dralor turned to hide a grin. "Soon all will be well."

Dralor finished trimming down to a close beard, then dressed while Eshal took his turn. Eshal had half of his bushy beard tidied up when he noticed Dralor slipping a boot on.

"Going somewhere?" Eshal asked.

"Thought I'd check on Yanick."

Eshal sawed off another clump of hair. "He'll manage. Best stay together."

"Been out a while, hasn't he?"

"Eh. Unfamiliar town. Probably not too many groups heading toward the farm, either."

Dralor bit his cheek. "Still. Think I'll check on him."

"Wait. I'm almost finished. Let's not get stupid, now."

Dralor stood and headed for the door.

"*Khapar,* what happened to sticking together?" Eshal murmured.

"Isn't that what got us imprisoned?" Dralor said, then left the room.

He walked down the hall past a few closed doors and descended a staircase. A buzz of chatter grew louder as he emerged into the common room. It was typical as such places went, if a little subdued. He scanned the tables and bar for Yanick's bald head and what little remained of his red beard.

"Help ya?" a serving woman asked.

She had three heady mugs in one hand and a basket of bread in the other. Dralor mouthed his thanks but pointed toward the door and strode by. The darkness outside surprised him, having seen every sunrise and every sunset for so long now. He started in what looked to be the busier direction, looking over the heads of passersby to the shop signs.

Dralor peered into a pub with no luck, then two more. A lot of pubs for a small town, but such was the way of things. A corner store was no help, nor a brothel that brought a flush to Dralor's face. This brought him to the edge of town.

He frowned back the way he'd come. Most likely he'd simply chosen the wrong direction, or Yanick was occupied in one of the brothel rooms, or a privy, but that didn't stop a nagging worry quickening his steps back the other way. Halfway back and no sign.

A woman burst from an alley and slammed into Dralor. Dralor stumbled, but she got the worst of it, spinning and falling onto her back. He made to help her but she scrambled up and hurried off without a look back. Dralor stared after her, brushed himself off, then froze.

There was something on the ground in the alley the woman had emerged from. A still form, sprawled out between the narrow walls. Was that a bald head? Dralor's stomach sank and he slowly walked into the alley. Another step and red whiskers came into focus. Yanick lay still upon the ground, eyes open to the early stars.

Suddenly Yanick convulsed then sucked in a breath. His eyes flicked to Dralor. "I'm s-sorry," he stammered. "I'm sorry."

Dralor scanned Yanick for any sign of injury but found none. "What..."

The black of Yanick's eyes were barely a pin prick despite the darkness. His breath came slow and shaky, limbs twitching between long stretches of stillness. Tar, Dralor realized. And far too much of it. He looked Yanick up and down again, wishing for some injury that could be bandaged or sewn or anything useful.

"What can... what can I do?" Dralor said, voice cracking.

"Suppose my body—wasn't quite used to so much—anymore." His arm flopped up and slapped back down to the ground.

"What do I do? How do I stop it?"

Yanick managed a fleeting smile then grimaced. "It's alright, p-princey. Probably for the best. I'm no—"

"No! You're coming to the farm," Dralor said. He sat and pulled Yanick into his arms. "You'll have purpose. We'll take care of each other."

Tears welled in Yanick's eyes and a sad smile pinched them free. "I stole from my own mother, just like she said I would." His eyes fell closed, then opened as he gasped in another breath. "But not this time. Just took my share. Just took my share."

Dralor could only shake his head, helpless.

"I woulda hurt you and Esh," Yanick breathed. "Eventually. This is probably... for the best."

"Why!" Dralor demanded, suddenly angry. "Why endure all this? Why survive the camps, just to—just to throw it all away! I saved you! I saved you!" By the end he was yelling, but he cradled Yanick's head against his chest.

Yanick's eyes turned to the sky. His mouth opened in a smile that was somehow both euphoric and tragic.

"For this," he said, drawing another breath. Then he slowly breathed it out until he was still in Dralor's arms.

Dralor turned an escaping sob into a yell. Tears flowed down his cheeks as he rocked Yanick tightly. Yanick the loose-tongued. Yanick who had been the first in the prison to offer kindness, who would have let himself be executed before seeing Taupry hurt. Yanick the friend he had saved.

He lowered Yanick gently to the ground and backed away as his breath quickened, raced. Could he save no one? Could he change nothing? Undo nothing? He staggered, turned, ran.

Panting, eyes bloodshot, and clothes sweaty, he fell into a chair in the common room of his inn. The same server brought him a strong drink, though he didn't notice it, nor the next one. When the second was nearly empty, a large hand slapped another onto the table and he blinked at Eshal taking a seat across from him.

Eshal sipped his drink, concerned eyes fixed on Dralor. He sat in silence, then looked about the establishment and cleared his throat.

"What happened?"

***

Dralor lengthened his strides to keep up with Eshal. Leaves dropped ahead of the nearing winter blanketed the ground. Eshal had quickened his pace all morning and said little as they drew closer to the life he'd been torn from. It was getting toward midday now and finally the air had warmed enough to stop making their breaths fog.

Eshal's pace continued to accelerate for maybe another bell until he stopped atop a steep hill. Stopping beside him, Dralor followed Eshal's gaze past orchards and fields of crops and stock to a small house at the valley's edge. Eshal stood frozen there for a few long breaths, gave Dralor a wide-eyed look, then started running toward the farmhouse.

Dralor set down the little pack he'd purchased in town and sat against a tree. Letting out a breath, he nodded to himself. A woman came out of the house, a sword in hand. She stood her ground with a strong posture, then staggered as Eshal called something out. The sword slipped from her hand and she ran toward him. They melted into each other's arms.

The door to the house swung open and two girls emerged, one perhaps six and the other in her mid teens. The older one rushed to her father, burly Eshal swinging her in a circle then burying his face in her neck. Eshal set his daughter down and turned to the little girl standing frozen in the doorway. He took his older daughter's hand and approached the little girl. Kneeling, he opened his arms. A moment, then the girl flung herself into his embrace.

Dralor tore his gaze from the scene and wiped away tears. He stood, but couldn't bring himself to join them. Instead he sat back down, this time facing the open country back the way they'd come. Nobody awaited his return back that way. Not a single person. Most would wish him dead if they discovered his identity, and the rest would outright kill him themselves. No, nothing that way.

Even so, he didn't care to trouble this perfect family with another mouth to feed. A stranger to disrupt their peace, their familiarity. How could he take charity from a family he'd devastated, anyway? And why did joy terrify him so much more than pain? Perhaps it reminded him of what could have been. For him. For Avandria. Perhaps it was just that he didn't deserve joy. He deserved pain.

Sometime later he was jarred back to awareness by footsteps coming up from behind. Eshal stopped beside him.

"Come, Del."

"Eshal, I—"

"Oh shut it."

Dralor blinked. Even months spent publicly shitting in a trough and cowering at the crack of taskmaster whips had not accustomed him to being ordered about so. With another glance behind, he climbed to his feet and grabbed his pack. Eshal patted him on the back and they started down toward the homestead in silence. They passed into an orchard with rows of low cropped trees, branches fanned out within reach overhead

"Planted all these myself," Eshal said. "They give us a good haul now. Tough to get by those first years, though. Ate more deer than anything."

Dralor ducked a branch. "You've done well. Earned this peace."

"It might not be home for you, but it's a better place than most."

"It's wonderful," Dralor said. "I'm more likely to catch a deer than a carrot, but likely neither, I'm afraid."

"Farms are more complicated to run than people think, even little ones like this. But after the system is in place, it's mostly labor. You started off a little soft in the quarry, but you're as hard a worker as they come. You'll catch plenty of carrots, my friend."

They emerged from the orchard into a field of low grass. A flock of sheep grazed nearby. Eshal patted one of the sheep as they crossed. Beyond the field, Eshal's family stood just outside the house watching them.

"Sheared a bit late, it looks," Eshal said. "Well, they should have just enough coat for the winter. Good to know she can't run the place *perfectly* without me."

Eshal's wife stiffened as they approached, eyes on Dralor and re-sembling the woman he'd first seen bearing a sword. Eshal thumped him on the back then went to their side, wrapping one of his long arms around them all.

"This is my friend Del. You can thank him for getting me home."

"No!" Dralor said more forcefully than he'd intended, then soft-ened his voice. "No, please. You owe me nothing. It is I who owe you thanks for letting me visit your home."

"You set our da' free?" the youngest asked.

Dralor shuffled awkwardly, never quite knowing how to talk to children. "We aided one another."

"Well," Eshal's wife said. "That's Claritte. My other girl here is Tensley. And I'm Roschiel."

"I'm honored to meet you all."

Claritte gave a curtsy, Tensley a hostile stare until her mother shot her an even sharper look.

Tensley sighed. "Pleased to meet you."

"Well, won't you come in?" Roschiel said. "We've just eaten but I can put out some food to hold you both until supper. Surely you are hungry after your travels."

"I'm well enough fed, thank you. Please, don't let me interrupt your day."

"Nonsense!" Eshal scoffed, riffling Tensley's hair to a smirky scowl. "Interrupt everything, this is a day to celebrate!"

"No, he's right," Roschiel said. "We're dreadfully behind, and the snows will be upon us any day."

Eshal smiled, then squeezed Claritte and set her down. "My hard working family. I can think of no better way to spend the afternoon than working the farm with you."

"Watch, Da'," Tensley said, running to a wheelbarrow loaded high with some sort of tubers. With a straight back, she hefted it up onto its wheel and, face red with effort, got it moving.

Eshal cheered. "Look at you, my strong girl!"

The wheelbarrow wobbled and Eshal ran to her aid. He stabilized it from the side as she drove toward a little stone smokehouse.

"Impressive, but remember you don't want to burn yourself out, or break your back."

"We didn't know if you'd come back. I had to get strong."

The girl upended the load beside the smokehouse without Eshal's aid. Roschiel stoked the fire within, Claritte began chopping and loading the tubers inside, and Tensley worked at pulling up more tubers. It was clear Dralor was witnessing a practiced routine, and he looked about feeling even more out of place.

Eshal put Dralor to work pulling tubers and moving the barrow when Tensley let him. Afterwards, he moved on to hacking down the remnants of an earlier crop and tilling. Eshal said the tilling would jumpstart decomposition to better prepare the field for planting come spring, which sounded vaguely familiar from Tutor Reiman's lessons decades ago. Eshal did a bit of everything, all the while sharing huge smiles with his loved ones as they worked and shared tales of the days he'd lost.

Dralor lost himself in the labor, though on more than one occasion he found himself captivated by the beauty of the family. Had he ever spent a single day with his wife just working together? Doing anything together, instead of the wars, the politics, the kingdom? Probably she'd still be gone, but all the more reason to have coveted those days.

It was nearly dark when Eshal dropped a final armful of firewood beside the stump Dralor was splitting sections on.

"Enough," Eshal said, then turned and shouted toward where his family worked. "Enough, today! Let's celebrate!"

This time Roschiel did not protest. They tidied up then went inside. The house was cozy and beautiful in its simplicity. Everything from chairs to cabinets to the very walls was crafted for practicality. A wooden doll here or a bright homespun doily there gave the otherwise sparse home a warmth the finest decor could never match.

They all cleaned themselves up, then Eshal and his family prepared a meal and set the kitchen with honed efficiency. This time, Roschiel and Eshal insisted their guest be treated, so Dralor sat at their small table watching them work, the joy of their reunion plain in their broad smiles and Roschiel's chides alike. The heat of the fire at his back and the warmth of this family all around him, Dralor felt a peace he'd not felt in a very long time. The fire flickered regrets and popped with pains, even the joyful laughs stabbed with guilt, yet his heart was full and easy.

They shared a feast of homegrown food that managed to exceed the most opulent meals to grace the high table of Avandria. Dralor exchanged pleasantries while managing to share little about his true self, only that he'd been a soldier, then later a clerk. They all cleaned up together after, Dralor pitching in where he could despite Roschiel's protests. When it was done, Roschiel and Eshal took the children to bed, leaving Dralor alone.

Eshal's muffled voice told an animated story to little squeals and giggles. He emerged from the bedroom, Roschiel's sleepy song coming loud then muffled as the door shut behind him. Coals tumbled and popped as Eshal pressed another log onto the fire. He put a kettle over the fire, then gave Dralor a pat and sat at the table with him.

"You have a wonderful family," Dralor said, leaning back in his chair.

"Aye. That, I do." Eshal's glimmering eyes wandered around the room, as if every little detail brought back years of joyful memories. His lip quivered. "*Dreams*, I'm sorry."

"Don't be. Don't apologize for joy."

Eshal nodded, took a shaky breath, and finally let his hand fall away. "We made it, my friend."

The door creaked slowly open and Roschiel emerged from the children's room. Eshal retrieved the kettle, poured three cups of tea at the table, and sat beside her. She squeezed his hand, lip trembling as their welling eyes met.

Suddenly Dralor began to feel out of place again, burdensome. Perhaps the afternoon would have been largely the same regardless of his presence, but there was no denying Eshal and Roschiel's evening would have an altogether different feel were he not intruding. His eyes flicked around the room and to the bed of blankets she'd laid out for him by the fire. The place seemed so small now. So cramped.

Roschiel cleared her throat and turned to Dralor. "Well, quite a day it has been."

"Yes," Dralor said. "Thank you for hosting me. You have a most wonderful home and family."

"Thank you. The children have already taken a liking to you, I think."

"Even Tensley," Eshal said with a chuckle. "And she's not easy to win over."

Dralor took a sip of tea. "They're great girls."

Roschiel bit her lip, finger tapping the side of her cup. "Forgive me, but why were you in jail?"

Dralor stiffened.

"Rosch!" Eshal gasped, jerking his hand from hers. "I was in jail too, do you think I—"

Dralor held up a hand. "It's alright. She's right to ask. You must keep your family safe."

He watched the light of the flames behind him flickering across the polished table. Well, it was probably for the best, he thought. To end this fantasy, this undeserved peace before it truly started, before he hurt anyone else even more.

"I made many mistakes," Dralor said without looking up, voice nearly a whisper. "I placed order above humanity. Anger above decency. I hurt many people."

Eshal shook his head. "Del, we all—"

"The prisons were supposed to take the wicked off the streets. To punish them, and protect the innocent." Dralor's eyes were haunted, distant as he spoke. "In the end it was those needing protection that I hurt the most. I was the wicked. I was the monster."

Eshal shook his head. "Del, it's not your—"

"It's my fault you were taken from your family. My fault for the sweeps, my fault for every starving soul in that damnable place."

"No, you can't take—"

"I built it, Esh! I built the prison. It was all me. All my fault!"

"Del, I don't..." He trailed off, eyes darting back and forth as he pieced things together. He shook his head. "No, no that's not..."

"Prince Dralor Tovados," Dralor said, the name foreign, as if another person. Finally he looked up from the table and met Eshal's eyes. "I'm sorry, Eshal. I didn't want to lie to you, but..."

Eshal just shook his head in disbelief. He jumped up and started pacing with angry, abrupt turns past the fireplace.

"Prince..." Roschiel whispered. "All of this... Y-you murdered the king, you—"

"No!" Dralor said through clenched teeth. "I loved my brother. It was Naelis. He... was behind much of the horrors, but I went along with them. He deceived—" Dralor shook his head. "Many were my doing. But *not* Loris."

Eshal continued to pace, pitching another log onto the fire carelessly.

"I should go," Dralor said, coming to his feet.

Eshal abruptly turned back toward him and Dralor knew then what was coming. Eshal was right to stop him. To make him pay. It wasn't fear that filled him as death approached, but an immense relief. He forced his chin high, though he hadn't the courage to look Eshal in the eye. He couldn't bear the thought of seeing hatred in his friend's eyes, even if for but a moment before he died. Then a large hand closed on his shoulder.

"It's done," Eshal said.

Dralor blinked. "You... Eshal, I—"

"It doesn't matter. What matters is who you are now."

Dralor finally looked at Eshal. His friend's eyes were wide as if he'd just done battle. The anger wasn't entirely gone, but what remained wasn't hatred. It wasn't hatred. Dralor tried to speak but couldn't. Finally a forgotten breath stirred him and he nodded. His eyes fell closed and still he nodded, pursing his lips to still their trembling. Then, tempering his hope, he looked to Roschiel.

He found her staring at Eshal in awe and love. She went to him and placed a hand upon his cheek, then turned to Dralor.

"If Eshal thinks you're a good man, you are a good man. You are welcome here."

A lump rose in Dralor's throat. *Dreams,* when had he become so soft. He sniffed and straightened his shoulders. "Thank you," he managed. "Thank you."

"I'm going to bed," Roschiel said, patting Eshal's arm. "Good night, De—Dralor. Prince Dralor?"

"Best stick to Del, if you please. Not all are as forgiving as you."

She nodded. "Good night then, Del."

"I'll join you very shortly," Eshal said, setting a bottle on the table. "Just a drink or two with the good prince."

Chapter Fourteen

Jeld walked toward the back of the Craftsman's workshop. He passed a drafting table with an architectural sketch of a massive bridge suspended by lines of ropes, then between neatly organized shelves of supplies and tools that reminded him of Cobb's shop. The steeply pitched roof overhead with its exposed beams was structurally not unlike that of the Warrior's hall, and yet it felt entirely different. The wood was light in color, sparse and unstained by smoke or finish. It had the look of a new, half-finished project compared to the established, strong, cozy mountain hall.

His bag dangled from one wrist by a length of string he'd affixed to the drawstring, always at the ready. His first attempt to pass it off to a visitor three weeks past had ended in the man throwing it to the ground and fleeing. Afterwards, Jeld attached this string with a slip knot to tie it to whoever he'd encountered next. He'd used string from his own belongings, just to be certain it wouldn't disappear like anything originating from the halls seemed to.

Reaching an open space with a number of stalls, he peered into just three before spotting a stack of long, sturdy boards that looked promising. Despite a fair bit of investigation, Jeld still didn't understand precisely how they worked, only that they somehow managed to always contain whatever he needed.

Jeld hefted four boards onto his shoulders and returned to a work-bench at the front. He measured, cut, and affixed them like table legs to a wooden box of sorts suspended from the ground. At the device's center was a crossbow he'd borrowed from the Warrior's hall.

Ever since realizing he could escape, he'd been plotting new ways to exploit the power of this bag beyond simply using it as a closet. Any-thing to give him an edge the next time an inquisitor stood between him and Lira. Inspired by the device Alal used to practice catching crossbow bolts back at the theater, this weapon had been among the first of his ideas. Positioned above the entrance in the void, he could theoretically shoot a crossbow anywhere he could point his bag.

After another long while of making adjustments, he nocked an arrow and tugged a string attached to the contraption. With a twang of the bowstring, a bolt hissed out and clapped against a wooden target, nose buried deep and tail rattling. Not bad. Not nearly on center, but it would have made it through his bag at least. Probably, anyway.

He retrieved a hammer, ignoring the objections of his blistering hands, and turned back to his work. Only, he found himself just standing there, mind numb. He let out a deep breath and set down the hammer. It *had* been a long day.

Jeld stood in silent thought debating whether to go play his lute or read, then made his way to the library. Reverie's door lurked at the edge of his vision as he crossed the nexus. He was glad to shut the Wise One's door closed behind him and begin winding his way toward the library.

"Akhel?" a woman called in an eastern tongue, voice tight with fear.

Jeld froze for a heartbeat, then sped ahead toward the voice. He reached the library, bag free from his wrist and slipknot pulled open and ready.

"Where are you!" Jeld yelled, glancing down aisle after aisle.

"Here!" the voice answered in a heavily accented Avandrian

Jeld ran toward it, darting beneath shelved archways and over low shelves and couches.

"Who are you?" the woman called, much closer now.

As Jeld burst from an aisle, suddenly someone was in his path. He jumped aside, rolling and crashing into a bookshelf. Without pause he came to his feet and ran toward a woman just shy of middle years with pale skin, dirty white robe, and what looked to be a noose around her neck.

The woman cried out and punched at him but Jeld dodged and looped his bag around her wrist and pulled it tight. With a twist of his fingers he tied a lock knot behind the slip then stepped out of her reach.

She scrambled back, shaking her wrist. "What—"

"You're okay!" Jeld said quickly. "Please, you'll return any moment. Just take the bag with you, it's my only way out."

"What? Who are—where am I?" She pulled at the knot as she looked about.

"This is the Halls of the Idols. You're Idolic now." Eyeing the rope around her neck, Jeld put a hand atop hers over the knot. "Please, keep it. Just a little while longer."

"Halls of the... this is the Wise One's library?"

"That's right," Jeld said, releasing her hand.

"But... I'm not—I couldn't—I was never—" She frowned bitterly, turned, and seemed to shout at the very walls. "Is this some kind of trick! Or—"

Her hand went to the rope around her neck. "I'm dead... This is my punishment." She turned to Jeld. "This is my punishment, isn't it? I know it's too late for me, I know—"

She vanished. Jeld scanned the floor for the bag, but it was gone. It was gone! He raced out into the nexus toward his father's old pack near the junction to Kelthid's area. He pushed the pack aside, slid his fingers under the tile that had been beneath it, and hefted open the trapdoor. The black depths stared up at him.

Jeld climbed down into the darkness. At the bottom, he dug blindly through his pack. With a flicker from his sparker, a flame kindled atop his lamp and wrapped him in a small bubble of light. He hurried down the steps, passed through a door, sped into the void. He spotted the first mark upon the floor, then another, and another, fighting each step to hold a steady bearing as he ran.

Then a next mark did not come. He froze, heart pounding, breath loud in the silence. Always before, he'd had his bag on hand in case he got lost, but not this time. This time one wrong step could leave him wandering this infernal void for all eternity.

Head locked in place to keep from turning further off course, his eyes pressed at their edges, searching desperately for a mark. There, faint at the edge of his lamplight. He let out a shaky breath, steeled himself, and continued ahead, slower.

One foot after the other. Straight. Straight. He reached the next mark, then another. Working up his courage again, he sped into a steady jog. The marks came in the nothingness as if it were them moving and not him, until at last he saw shapes in the distance and came upon his belongings. They still formed a ring, at their center the black void of the other bag lying flat upon the ground like a hole.

Taking a deep breath, he plunged his head and hands through the hole. Pure darkness all around, his lamp light lost behind him. He felt the leather walls of his bag and pressed them apart until warm air and blinding light streamed in from above. *Sunlight.* Real sunlight. He reached both hands out the top of the bag to pull himself through but they only closed on skin.

"Ahhhg!" came a horrified cry.

Shapes above began to move. Clouds, spinning about. Nails dug into the back of Jeld's hand.

"Ow!" Jeld cried. "Stop, it's just me! Stop that!"

Then the bag was flying through the air. Sky, ground, sky, ground. Jeld felt a stab of panic, certain the bag would fall into itself, but the picture steadied. Just a still, blue sky. He heard her frantic breaths.

"I'm coming out. Just, take it easy."

"What is—how are..."

"It's just me. From the Halls. I'm coming out now. I'll explain everything."

A quick peek to ensure neither she nor whoever had tried to hang her were waiting to smash his skull with a rock. He spotted her lying on her back, propped up on her elbows as if she'd toppled over and scrambled away. Nobody else.

Jeld pulled himself through and rolled onto his back beneath the open sky, head in the dusty dirt, bright sun upon his face. Laughter burst from his lips for but a moment before he sat upright and looked about. How much time had passed? It was warm now despite having been nearly winter when he'd entered the Halls, so did that rule out the possibility that no time had passed? But then, if they were in Ishdalar as the woman's accent implied, it was known to be warmer there. Of course, if time had passed, there was no telling if it had been a single season, or a lifetime...

Jeld came to his feet. "What year is it?"

"What? Year... ah... twelfth cote of the two hundred ninety-fourth drishna."

"So that's... that's what year?"

"That's..." Her eyes pinched closed and she began mouthing something to herself as if counting. Wincing, she shook her head and continued. "That's... *peshjot!*" she yelled, seemingly a curse. "It doesn't matter anyway."

Jeld looked about. "Alright, then where are we?"

The terrain was dry and dusty, with little vegetation between the many barren trees. When no reply came, Jeld turned from the open country to find the woman staring up at a frayed rope dangling from a tree branch.

"Do you think they could still be nearby?" Jeld asked, searching the landscape.

She blinked. "Hmm? Oh. Maybe? I do not think it."

She stood, eyes now fixed on the bag as Jeld buttoned it into his shirt. "What is that thing? And who are you? Was that truly the Halls?"

Jeld started to answer but stopped himself, eyes on the rope around her neck. "What did you do? Why were they hanging you?"

She loosened the noose and threw it to the ground. "They got the wrong person."

A lie, Jeld noted, but he didn't press it. "My name's Jeld. From Tovar, in Avandria. The bag was Kelthid's. I was stuck in it—in the Halls—until you pulled it free." He looked up again at the sky, at the trees, at the dry, dusted ground, and laughed again.

The woman shook her head, incredulous. "How does—what do—" She shook her head more, then seemed to give up. "I'm Tejani. This is the Runwan. Of Ishdalar."

"Pleased to meet you." An awkward silence. "You're Idolic now, you know." Jeld looked again at the dangling rope. The tip was not only frayed, but blackened. Charred. "You burned it? You... can burn things?"

Tejani picked the noose back up and inspected its blackened end. "If I can, I don't know how." She scrutinized her hands. "What's your gift?"

Jeld blinked at her, then realized he didn't have even the slightest veil up and chided himself. Too much time away from people.

"Come now, tell me," Tejani said.

Jeld considered. It wouldn't do well to reveal he could read people, even deceive their senses. "Fighting. Good reflexes. Serves me pretty well."

"Fascinating," she said with her thick accent, searching Jeld's eyes.

Jeld tensed. An attack? No, a feint. No, now it was an attack. A high attack, now low, now... sadness? Guilt? *Khapar*, what was going on in this woman's mind? But, her once scrutinizing gaze only drifted away to the horizon.

Jeld cleared his throat. "I need to go. Do you know where I can get supplies?"

"For what purpose?"

"I need to find someone."

"Who?"

"Someone in danger if I don't hurry."

Tejani frowned. "Who is she?"

Jeld scowled. *Idols* he was sloppy. "Can you help?"

"Does one help a man who crawls out of a magic bag and won't reveal his aims? How could..." She trailed off, looking suddenly full of anguish. "It doesn't matter. Come on."

Without looking back, she started off in the same direction the long shadows of the trees stretched. Jeld followed, contemplating whether there was any way to differentiate east from west at a glance without knowing whether it was morning or evening.

"Where are we going?" Jeld asked.

"My house."

"How many days out is it? And what direction? I need to get to…
Delvarad."

"We'll be there soon," Tejani said, picking her way down a rocky
hill.

"Will the people who tried to hang you come here?"

"I think not," she said.

After perhaps half a bell they came to a stream. Beside it was a small
mill, little more than a cottage with a water wheel dipping into the
river behind it. The trees were more green here by the river, and more
prevalent.

Opening his Idolic sense, Jeld looked out over the scene for any sign
of whoever had tried to kill Tejani, but there was nothing. He might be
rusty, but if anything that should make him more sensitive, like every
time he arrived in Tovar after months on the road. Tejani stared at the
mill, sorrow, regret, guilt beating against Jeld's open mind. Her notes
tore at his own emotions, awakening and amplifying them until his
knees threatened to buckle.

The ring of what seemed a small bell jarred Jeld from Tejani's
thoughts in time to see her racing toward the mill. He followed after
her, peering in the door then stepping inside. The faint light from the
doorway set motes of dust aglow as he picked his way through a mess
of pots, tools, firewood, all scattered across the floor. Tejani's curses
led him into the next room. Her arms were wrapped under a large
wooden gear, straining at a thick lever. Beside it, a wooden column
creaked and strained. Jeld joined her and the lever gave, disengaging a
gear and freeing the column to spin without protest.

"Thanks," Tejani said, unshuttering a window. "Some food in that
pantry. Take whatever you want."

She laid down on a small bed with her knees raised, not bothering to relocate a stack of books now pressing against her side. Jeld opened the indicated pantry. It contained some pickled vegetables, jam, a bag of flour, and another of beans. Simple and limited, but his stomach twisted in hunger. He'd been starving, he remembered suddenly. *Sucking-beans* starving, and then nothing in the Halls for who knew how long.

In the midst of untying the bag of beans, he stopped and looked to Tejani, then back at the plentiful food. With a sigh he turned and sat in a chair near where Tejani lay staring up at the ceiling.

"Is there a place nearby where I can buy food?" Jeld asked.

"I told you, take what you wish."

"I don't want to take from you."

She snorted, then frowned. "You are kind. But, take it."

Jeld considered, then returned to the pantry and pulled out the beans. He got a fire going, grabbed one of the pots from the floor, filled it with water from a large jug atop a table, and hung it over the fire. A little flour, half a jar of pickled vegetables. A sprinkle of some seasoning he found that smelled unrecognizable but fittingly spicy. When it was finished, he filled two bowls and set one beside Tejani before settling into a chair with his own.

"Thank you," Tejani said, taking up her bowl.

Jeld nodded, and they both ate in silence for a time. It wasn't long before that old voice that had kept him alive on the streets began to whisper cautions. He dined with a criminal. Sure, he knew too well that even a relatively innocent crime could get one hanged, but the *guilt* pouring off of this woman... She'd done something truly terrible.

"You would not make it far," she said, taking a bite and giving a satisfied frown. "Not many western folk here. Some traders with enough influence and value to roam freely. Otherwise only slaves. You would stand out."

Jeld considered, but managed to conclude little owing to having no idea where he was. "Runwan, you said? Where exactly is that? Are we near Warrinton? Or is there another way to Avandria?"

"Warrinton," she spat. "Four weeks on foot if off road. But you would be captured. At the Mouth for sure, if not before. Unless you plan to use your gift to fight off every Ishdali you encounter."

"You don't like the west," Jeld said.

"I do not like Warrinton. I like the west more than Ishdalar."

Bait, maybe? Drawing out his intent. But then, he sensed no such deception.

"What do you dislike about Ishdalar?" he asked. "Everything I have read of this place... the incredible architecture, the cities, the universities, the—"

"Bah! The universities care more about the quality of their paper and their... how do you say it... *big words* more than their knowledge."

"But some of the most advanced mathematics and philosophy comes from this place."

"Yes, yes. But *why?* For show. Vanity. For competition. The whole realm is torturing their children for a chance at those *peshjot* universities. In the west, anyone can choose if they do not want this."

"No, Avandria just doesn't have them. If you are born poor you stay poor. There are some schools or tutoring, but only for the rich. It sounds like if you were in the west you'd still choose to be a miller over being a scholar, no?"

"But I could choose it without dishonor!" she snapped to more anguish, then looked away.

A long silence ensued, then Jeld spoke. "I need to help a princess in Avandria reclaim the kingdom from an evil priest."

Tejani cleared her throat, and ate another spoonful, back still turned. "How?"

"Rally her armies from Delvarad. Actually she may have already done that by now, depending on how much time has passed. *Idols*, she might already sit the throne again."

Jeld frowned. What could he do to help Lira anyway, if she had her army or even her throne? She was the politician. She was the strategist. She was the princess. He could find his way through the woods or navigate a city, but little else.

Tejani's brow narrowed. "You are some kind of Idolic warrior, are you not? Can you not go kill this priest?"

Jeld frowned. "You are some kind of fire shooter, can't you go destroy every university in Ishdalar?"

Tejani seemed to consider it, but said nothing.

"It's those dreamin' inquisitors!" Jeld blurted.

"You cannot defeat them? They are... Idolic?"

"Maybe one, if I'm lucky. There are always more, and they—" Suddenly he remembered what the inquisitor he'd interrogated at knifepoint had said. They can track Idolics. They can track him, and even if he made it to Lira, he'd lead them straight to her.

Jeld drew a breath. "Where is Khapar from here?"

"Same far, about. In mountains near your Warrinton."

"Would I be enslaved there too?"

"No, no. Khapar is different. People of all sorts. No soldiers. Not Ishdali, not Avandrian. On the way though, yes, you will. Probably die in the desert first, though."

Nodding, Jeld set his bowl aside and pulled his boots off. The remnants of old Cobb's once prized boots, pulled from retirement during his trek toward Delvarad. They'd probably die in the desert too, and likely before he did.

"Why do you want to go to Khapar?" Tejani said with a full mouth.

"The inquisitors are made there." Jeld pursed his lips. Maybe it was the isolation, but *dreams* he couldn't hold his secrets. "Trained there. The best way I can help Li—my friend—is to stop them."

There, a secret kept. Only, there was only one princess of Avandria anyway.

Tejani nodded, eyes distant, calculating. Jeld felt a swell of gratitude. She was halfway taking him seriously. He pops out of a bag and tells a tale of fighting priests and rescuing princesses, and she was neither laughing nor throwing her hands up. Couldn't be too many people in all of Avandria or Ishdalar like that.

"But you can only fight one..." she mused

Jeld shrugged. "If I'm lucky. They train Idolics there, right? I could use that to get in, maybe. Check things out." And surrounded by Idolics, the tracking would be of little use, hopefully. Or, not.

Tejani fell silent for a long stretch then spoke abruptly. "I will take you there."

"You—what? But, your mill. Your life here. It will be—"

"What life? Maybe I'll return, maybe I won't. I'm Idolic now too, remember? Somehow. Maybe Sinwo can teach me." Tejani looked to be surprising even herself as she spoke. "I can get you there safely."

"How?" Jeld asked.

"You will be my slave."

CHAPTER FIFTEEN

Dralor cinched Claritte's fishing pole to the side of her little pack and patted her shoulder. Eshal, Roschiel, and Tensley stood with them beneath the eaves of the cottage, where the ground was not blanketed in snow like the expanse of white countryside before them.

"Come with us," Eshal said to Dralor.

Dralor shook his head. "Thank you, but no. You all go. Bring home some fish."

"Dral, you—"

"No," Dralor said, the prince he'd once been showing through for a moment. "You welcome me every blink of every day. Go. Enjoy a day as a family."

Eshal grunted. "No changing your mind, I suppose. Very well. And what'll you busy yourself with today?"

Dralor raised a rusty old poleaxe that was leaning against the cottage. "Shaking snow from the trees in the orchard."

Eshal grinned. "It's a good thing you got to toughen up in the quarry. Good little warm-up for farming."

"The food is much better here," Dralor said, giving Roschiel a look.

She smiled. "I've just the thing for some trout."

"Da' doesn't usually catch anything," Tensley said.

Eshal gave her a little push. "That's because I'm too busy baiting everyone's hooks and untangling your lines!" He shouldered his pack. "Now let's go."

They all trudged through the snow toward a distant draw that would be the easiest passage through the hills toward their usual spot. Dralor followed for a short while then said his farewells and parted toward the orchard. He was shaking down the first of the fruit trees when suddenly cries made him jump. Snowballs pelted him from two directions. Laughing, he threw down his poleaxe and counterattacked, landing a few hits on the now shrieking girls. They gave him another good volley before their father called them away.

Dralor's smile lasted for half a dozen trees before fading. He hurried to another tree to busy himself before his idle mind could venture too far, then started with a high branch. Start at the top, or you'd end up cleaning the bottom twice. More wisdom from Eshal. It probably wouldn't have taken long to realize it himself, but there it was all the same.

It was a simple matter, yet thinking of it now, Dralor wondered what the years had granted him if not such basic wisdom. A tarnished legacy. Infamy. The fall of the Tovados line. No little farm, nor the skills to run it. No family. Only death and failure.

He worked faster, his thoughts clearing as he sweated and panted. When the orchard was clear he turned to repairs on the roof. That done, he saw to the animals and other chores before finally setting some broth over the fire should the others return with a catch. Late into the evening, he sat before the fire, awaiting the children's tales of fish that got away.

***

Dralor hiked up a hillside at Eshal's side, half a doe slung atop the big farmer's pack looking far smaller than Dralor thought it had a right to. He shrugged his own biting pack straps into a new spot to torture, the other half of the doe throwing him off balance on the muddy ground. Most of the snow had melted just days before, remaining only in drifts and the backsides of hills.

"Not bad for half a day's work," Eshal said. "Quicker kill than usual for this side."

"Quite preferable to breaking rocks," Dralor muttered.

"Far tastier," Eshal grumbled, then laughed humorlessly. "How about that blazin' porridge they served? Thickened with quarry dust, I'm thinking."

Dralor said nothing.

"Ah. Sorry, my friend."

Dralor looked over at Eshal and nodded, slapping him on the arm. "I might do a few bells in the quarry if it saved me slogging this *dreaming* thing home."

Eshal gave a proper laugh, punching Dralor back. "Glad to have you, else I'd be carrying her home myself."

Dralor groaned, then suddenly froze. Eshal fell silent at once, and together they scanned the woods. The hill crested just ahead, so Dralor couldn't see far. Nothing of note behind. Just, everything was so quiet. No birds, no bugs, no chittering chipmunks. Then, the snort of a horse.

Dralor hurried behind a thick tree, Eshal giving him a skeptical look before following suit behind a second. They'd encountered another hunter on a previous trip not terribly far from this spot, Eshal's look seemed to remind. But they'd both been talking loudly. Whoever it was knew they were here and chose to hide or stalk. Either way did not bode well for his intentions.

At the next tree, Eshal was frowning with an ear cocked up and all trace of his earlier skepticism faded. A twig snapped in the distance to one side. Dralor tried to slow his breaths for silence but couldn't. A rustling came from the opposite direction. At least two, then, and they were circling. Then, the whisper of drawn steel.

Dralor carefully lowered his pack to the ground, eased himself prone, and peered out from behind the tree through the concealment of some vegetation. His eyes widened. Three—no, four riders were fanned out in a search line, two wielding swords and the others bearing knocked bows held low and ready to be drawn. He slowly slid back behind the tree and stood to face Eshal.

"Four coming from there, two with bows," Dralor whispered. "Sounds like more flanking."

"Best attack, eh? You're the prince, but sitting in an ambush is supposed to be bad, right?"

"Mm. But charging mounted men uphill is worse, even without archers. No, they heard us but they don't know where we are."

Movement off to their right caught Dralor's attention and he barely made out a fifth man on a far flank. He was already past their position and moving deeper down the hillside.

"We wait here," Dralor continued. "Attack when they are upon us. Get your bow out. Try—"

Dralor noticed Eshal's hands were shaking, and he realized the big man probably had no battle experience at all, save for wrestling a prison guard from his horse.

"Give me your bow," Dralor ordered. "I'll try to take out at least one archer."

Eshal nodded, took a breath, and carefully set his pack down. He found a sizable stone and turned it over in his hand before settling on his grip. They both crouched low, waiting. Twigs snapped. Underbrush rustled. The breath of horses. Gentle hoofbeats. It all drew closer.

A horse snorted from what sounded like just behind Eshal's tree. Eshal's wild eyes fixed on Dralor as if for strength. Dralor held up a hand and shook his head. *Wait.* Eshal nodded back quickly, incessantly. *Khapar,* he was terrified. Strongest bastard Dralor knew, but may never have been in a single fight. Probably true, but there was a more distant terror in Eshal's eyes. His family... Had these men been to the farm yet?

A rider appeared just beside Eshal, and Dralor issued a sharp nod. Eshal didn't hesitate, jumping out and pulling the man from the saddle. Dralor drew his bow and spun out from behind the tree. He scanned the woods overtop his arrow. Rider, ten paces back, sword in hand. Another—one of the archers, bow drawn and fixed on Eshal. Dralor loosed his shot.

The arrow hissed through the air and stuck straight through the archer's neck, the man's own arrow going wild. Dralor darted back behind the tree and in the same moment another arrow hissed past him. Dralor nocked another and jumped out, but a charging horse slammed into him. He landed hard on his back, breath shooting from his lungs and bow falling from his grip. He jumped up, grabbed the bow, spun even as he scrambled to nock an arrow, but he found the other archer fixed already upon him. The man's chest tensed in that final preparation, and then something struck him in the head and sent him toppling to the ground.

Dralor turned to find Eshal catching his balance from a powerful throw of his rock. Then a rider was upon Eshal, lashing out with a long sword. Dralor took aim, then spun. Another rider's blade hissed through the air and cut the bow from Dralor's grip, the back of his neck had he not spun. Dralor drew his belt knife and circled behind the tree, rider wheeling and stalking back toward him. Beyond, another was coming closer from the distance.

He chanced a glance to Eshal, bracing himself for the worst, but he found his friend standing over the other archer, a bloody sword in hand. Like Dralor, he was keeping a tree between him and one of the riders.

Dralor's rider pressed in slow this time rather than charging past. A blow rang against the trunk beside his head. An explosion of bark and moss and dirt stung his eyes and cheeks. He jumped aside, tripped on a root, fell, scrambled to his feet. More were coming. It was attack now, or become outnumbered.

Dralor circled, circled, then jumped out behind the rider, stabbed the horse's ass, and charged Eshal's foe, a bald man in light armor. The man got his sword around just in time and steel rang. Dralor got a good shoulder in, but Baldy's sword was already coming again. Then Eshal's sword jutted out through the man's chest. Dralor pulled the sword from the man's fading grip, spun, caught a heavy blow from the next rider charging past, and went down on his back.

Dralor rolled, came to his feet, and dove right back to the ground, blade of yet another rider burning a line down his back. He cried out, crawled back to his feet against a tree, peered around. Just one rider there. Where was the second? He spun. Eshal was on the ground writhing on his side. A man with a black beard climbed to his feet near Eshal, head bleeding and horse running off into the woods behind him.

"Eshal!" Dralor called, running toward Eshal. Then the remaining rider was upon him again. He jumped aside at the last blink. It would have been wise to strike the mount, but he was angry. His blade caught the rider right across the bend of the waist. No ring of steel or scratch of mail, just a wet squelch, hoofbeats, and a scream behind Dralor as he spun and charged toward Eshal's final foe.

Black-Beard froze, eyes darting between the writhing Eshal and Dralor, then he turned and limped hurriedly away.

"Why are you here?" Dralor shouted, jogging after him.

The man looked back, eyes even wider, and quickened his pace. "If none of us return they'll send more! Let me go and I'll tell them— "

"Who are *they?* Tell who?"

Dralor got within striking range and Black-Beard turned and raised his sword, backing away with one hand over a cut on his thigh.

"The watch," Black-Beard cried, almost tripping. "They hired us to kill the big fellow. No need of you, just be off!"

Dralor glanced at Eshal. He'd managed to pull himself upright against a broken stump. His chest was soaked with dark blood. Dralor's face twisted in a bitter scowl.

"You don't want to kill me," Black-Beard said. "Let me go and I'll tell them you're dead."

"I *am* dead," Dralor whispered through his teeth.

Dralor slapped the sword aside and lunged. Black-Beard managed to parry, countered even. Dralor leaned just out of reach and the man's blade swept past his face. Black-Beard blocked another strike, Dralor stepped inside his guard, and headbutted his nose with a crunch and a cry. Catching Black-Beard's wrist, Dralor shouldered him to the ground.

Black-Beard groaned. "Wait! I—"

Dralor stuck his sword through the bushy black beard into its namesake's neck, as easy as pushing a shovel into mud. Eyes wide, Black-Beard clutched feebly at the sword. Dralor might have made more ceremony of it, acknowledged the death, whether with disdain, respect, anything really, but there was no time. He pulled his blade free and ran to Eshal's side.

Blood trickled down Eshal's nose and beard. High up his blood-soaked chest was a patch deeper, darker than the rest, like the sea as it descends from shallows into the beyond. It pulsed and seeped, more blood flowing into his lap and down to the green underbrush. Eshal's breath came raspy and quick.

"Just a scratch," Dralor said.

"Rosch," Eshal whispered. "Go... check them."

"I will. Let me get you bandaged,"

Dralor ran to his pack and cut the strap holding the split doe in place. The doe, red with blood and meat, fell still against the brush. The image of Eshal limp and red atop the ground flashed in Dralor's mind, froze him, clenched his racing heart. He shook it off, pulling his overshirt from his pack and setting to binding Eshal's wound with the cut strap.

"Stop!" Eshal said, teeth clenched. He broke into a fit of wet coughing then laid his head back against the tree. "Go. Go to them."

"They're okay, Esh."

Eshal tensed again and Dralor put a hand on his shoulder.

"I questioned one of the bastards, Esh," Dralor lied. "They shook your family up a little, that's all. They're safe. Your family is safe."

Eshal's shoulders sagged, a peace seeming to wash over him. Head still leaning back against the tree, he met Dralor's eyes and took his hand in a strong grip.

"Take care of them," Eshal whispered, eyes welling. "Tell my girls their Da' loves them."

Dralor stared back, tried to speak but managed only to nod.

"I will," Dralor finally managed. "Be proud, my friend. Your family is beautiful. Their life is beautiful."

A hint of a smile flashed over Eshal's face. He bit his lip and managed a nod, then his eyes fell closed. Dralor pulled his friend close. Eshal's chest rose and fell, rose and fell, then his hand slackened and he let out a final breath.

Squeezing Eshal, Dralor shook his head, swallowed one sob, but not the rest. They poured out until he was screaming. Another of his victims. He might as well have swung the blade. No better man, either, at least since the last he'd ruined. For all his efforts, it was the good men he hurt most. Men like Loris. Like Benam. Eshal. The innocents.

Take care of them, Eshal's voice reminded, and Dralor fell silent. With a final squeeze, he gently eased his friend to the ground. He propped Eshal's head up on his pack, then laid him flat instead, opening his eyes to the beautiful canopy and sky above. Dread twisting him nauseous, he took up a sword, a bow, arrows, then ran toward the cottage.

The doorway of the cottage stood gaping open. Dralor's feet dragged limply to a stop. His stomach churned, threatened to upset itself as he stared at that open door, certain at what must lie ahead. Roschiel would never have willingly directed men toward their hunting spot. It must have been torture. Or threatening her children. But they could be alive. Frightened, certainly. Hurt, probably. But alive.

Dralor closed his eyes, let his panic subside. If they were alive they'd need calm. If not... he'd need it. He gathered himself. Distanced himself. Rid himself of emotion and of humanity as he'd done in war. People were just animals. Just meat. This was just life. Meaningless. Natural. And with that, he walked inside.

Despite his preparations, Dralor staggered, clamped his eyes shut, but the image was still there. His stomach twisted, wobbly legs carrying him back, out, away.

Take care of them.

Eyes still clamped shut, he shook his head, slow, then faster, faster. His heart thudded, breath fast, bile in his mouth. Another step backward, outside now.

Take care of them.

Dralor blew out a breath, took a step forward, and opened his eyes. He tried not to see the broken haven, the blood, the still forms. Tried not to see the story the scene told of the struggle that ensued, the horrors they must have endured in their final moments. Tried not to consider whose doings had led to this moment.

He brought Roschiel out first, setting her in the soft grass beside the cottage. Tensley was next. He brushed her hair back behind her ear, shaking his head and burying a sob in the crook of her neck. He set her down beside her mother and covered them both with a blanket.

Why were these beautiful, wonderful, innocent people dead—murdered—and he was alive? He looked back to the door of the cottage. Claritte next. He hadn't seen her yet, could only imagine the position he might find her in. He couldn't. Couldn't. Idols, please. Anything but this.

Take care of them.

He trudged back inside, weak at the knees. He searched the great room, the kids' bedroom, Eshal and Roschiel's room, even the privy, his heart lurching with every turn of his gaze. She'd be outside then, face down with an arrow in her back, or worse. He patrolled the area but found no sign of her. An idea in the back of his mind, one from which he wouldn't dare to take even a whisper of hope, led him deeper into the woods.

After a short hike he came to a stream where the clear water ran over smoothed stones. The sight of Claritte's willow tree at the water's edge brought tears to his eyes, but rage began boiling away grief until there was nothing else. He would find her little body soon, and her death would be his doing just like the others, just like the prisoners, like Yanick, and Loris, and probably Lira by now.

Something caught his ear. A scuttling barely audible over the trickling water. He drew his sword and crept toward the stream, one ear cocked behind to help place the sound. There it was again, toward the willow. He peered around the tree and there was Claritte, curled into a tight ball with wide eyes, breathing with panicked little squeaks.

Recognition dawned on her and she sprang into Dralor's arms. Dralor lifted her in a tight embrace and clung to her even as his knees buckled. He had to protect her, had to comfort her, had to pay his debt to Eshal, and yet he clung to her like his own life depended on it, like she was the only thing keeping him afloat, keeping him sane.

She began to sob, then shriek, then everything just flowed out in a panic. "Ma'—Tenny—those—they—how can—dead! De-dead, they're—wh-where—where's D-Da'?"

Dralor cradled the back of her head in his hand and squeezed her tighter. He managed a slight shake of his head and tried to speak but no words came out.

"I'm sorry," Dralor managed, voice breaking. "So sorry. So, so sorry."

Dralor rocked her for a long while, then reluctantly carried her toward the cottage, circling wide to keep the bodies on the other side. He stopped at the edge of the orchard and set her down, taking her shoulders in his hands.

"You should wait here," he said. "Let me get things back in order."

She nodded and sat trembling upon the ground beneath one of the fruit trees, knees pulled up against her chest.

"We will... Everything is..." Dralor sighed and squeezed her. "I'll be just there."

Dralor gave her another hug and returned to the cottage. There, he cleaned up the grisly scene, peeking out on occasion to check on Claritte. Her shadow made a slow circle around her, but she herself remained still. Still save for bouts of chest heaving sobs. Still save for trembling, save for wide eyed rocking.

When he emerged, she watched in silence as Dralor began stacking wood for a pyre at the edge of the tuber field. He worked with a fury as he'd always done at the farm, but despite his best efforts his mind wouldn't numb from the labor. That anger was still there. That guilt.

He dropped another stick on the growing pile and a second landed beside it. Claritte, eyes bloodshot and distant. She threw on another, then returned to their wood pile and grabbed up a log that must have weighed nearly as much as she. Dralor felt a swell of pride at her strength of spirit, and they worked on in silence. The sun was low when finally Dralor stilled Claritte with a hand on her shoulder and they stood looking at the pyre.

"Go inside and clean yourself up. Put some food on. I need to go... retrieve your father." Claritte started to object but Dralor shook his head. "I know you are strong. But I'll handle it. You'll see him soon."

Her eyes flicked back and forth in thought, then finally she nodded and went inside. Dralor retrieved the barrow and returned to where Eshal's body still rested looking up at the darkening sky. He rifled through the pockets of the fallen mercenaries, gathering up a fair haul of coins, then loaded up his friend as gracefully as possible.

It was almost fully dark by the time he'd returned with aching legs and managed to get all three bodies atop the pyre. They picked at a small meal then returned outside, where Dralor started a small fire near the pyre. He pulled from it a long stick burning at one end and held it out to Claritte.

"I think it's best if you do this," Dralor said.

Claritte reached out to take the stick but lowered her hand.

"I can't. You do it."

"I know it's strange, but trust me. You'll understand someday."

Claritte considered this, the little fire gleaming in her wet eyes, then took the burning stick. She stood beside the pyre for a long while, staring at the still forms of her family, then pressed the stick into the smaller twigs at the base. Dralor put an arm around her and they stood in silence as the flames grew. She looked away as the first flames found her loved ones, until the blaze raged enough to mask the worst of the details.

They remained at the pyre, not a word shared between them, until late in the night when it was reduced to mere embers. Dralor carried her to her bed and sat with her for a while. Claritte's eyes were still open, staring up toward her sister's bunk, when finally he stood to leave.

"Stay," she said. "Please."

Dralor returned to her side and rubbed her cheek with the back of his hand.

"Alright," he said.

He climbed onto the bunk above and lay down.

"What will we do?" Claritte's voice came.

"We can't stay here," Dralor said, his eyes closed. "It's not safe anymore."

"Where will we go?"

Dralor considered this. They could make a life in some small town easily enough. Just enough to give her some peace and safety. Enough to live a normal life and forget the terrors of the past. Only, wasn't that what he'd been trying? And look what it had brought. It caught up to him. It always caught up to him, and as long as he hid, more people would die. No, this had to be faced.

"We must go stop the people responsible for this. Make sure that this never happens to anyone else."

Dralor considered his own words. *The people responsible for this.* Was that not he himself? But no, he'd no small role in sparking this fire, but that didn't matter now. What mattered was stopping the flames. Stopping Naelis.

"We go to Tovar."

Chapter Sixteen

A top his horse, Jeld held his breath as he and Tejani rounded another switchback, then sighed on seeing only more rocky hills ahead. The wide road of natural stone cut ever upward, steep rocky cliffs not far to either side. It had been a long three weeks through the desert and two days in these dry mountains. They should be nearly there, if the traveler they'd encountered that afternoon could be trusted, though Jeld had begun questioning that trust several switchbacks prior.

They'd also asked every halfway sociable traveler about the presumed inquisitor training, but if they knew anything they hid it well. Jeld wasn't exactly disappointed at the idea of being able to hurry to Lira instead of surrounding himself with inquisitors. But then, peace would be short lived and uneasy with the specter of the inquisitors looming.

"I think it is best if you remain my slave in Khapar," Tejani said, pulling alongside Jeld. "A free westerner is not completely unheard of there, but it could still stand out a bit. At the citadel, though, I think we can drop it."

Jeld tugged the reins to keep his oafish horse from veering toward a patch of grass and pressed on. "How could nobody have seen anything? Even if they were confined to the citadel, surely someone would have seen something."

"The citadel is a somewhat secretive place."

"But even that group from the citadel didn't know."

"Maybe they were lying," Tejani said.

Jeld didn't think so, but he'd been careful not to use his Idolic talents for fear of being detected by the inquisitors. Something caught his ear then, a low hum. It grew louder with each step and he soon recognized it as the same thrum of humanity sung by Tovar. His thoughts turned to the past as he rode on up the rocky road.

They crested a hill and with each step a vast plateau ahead rose into view. Soon it stretched across a valley of sorts between the now distant walls of the surrounding mountains. The sheer cliff walls of the plateau rose into battlements that looked to be carved directly into the stone. A small river wound around both sides of the plateau, passing beneath the road, which rose up an incline to a huge open archway cut into the wall.

Jeld followed Tejani toward the city. He made a quick audit of his character, a muscle he'd resharpened during the journey after it had atrophied so long in the halls. He mimicked the defeated eyes he'd observed on so many others. Then there was the stoicism, almost a calm, that came with having no control, no voice, no choice. Like a dog waiting to be ordered. There was little to the costume, with slaves of a certain station readily walking free of bindings and even carrying weapons in service to their masters.

They rode up the incline, Jeld feeling like he was shrinking as Khapar loomed higher. He was surprised to find there were no guards whatsoever at the entrance. They passed beneath the archway, gargantuan doors hanging open to either side. Jeld's mind went at once to one of Director Sammel's plays portraying this place with incredible accuracy, save for the scale. The Traveler had let Idol Tovados through this very gate, though Jeld could see no evidence of the terrible blaze that would follow. Vengeance for Syladrya's murder.

Jeld walled his sense off further still as the press of humanity beat against him. As with most cities, Khapar opened into a market, this one fairly crowded despite the relative isolation. Like the walls, everything in the city was constructed of the same pale stone, yet this monotony only made the many colorful awnings and tapestries all the more striking.

"What do we do now?" Tejani asked.

"Find a pub, of course."

"Pub?"

"Pub, yes," Jeld said, but Tejani only blinked. "Tavern? Bar? Drink house?"

"Ah," Tejani said, wrinkling her nose. "Your western drinks are not permitted in Ishdalar. I suppose Khapar *could* have one, but this is no time to poison your mind."

"It's not that! I just need a place where people talk. To ask about inquisitors. Ask someone, would you?"

Tejani stopped her horse. "Ask who?"

Jeld felt himself growing impatient and reminded himself that most people hadn't the misfortune of needing to learn the streets. Looking around for someone to ask for directions, he saw a skinny, filthy man with a long gray beard sitting against a wall. Suddenly his own misfortunes didn't seem so bad. Less than a year on the streets, and he'd practically let it define him. This man looked to have spent a lifetime there.

"Maybe just go buy some of those pies there and ask the lady?" Jeld suggested, pointing to a cart.

Tejani did, and a short time later their horses were stabled and they were sitting in a pub of sorts down a narrow flight of stairs beneath a spice shop. Pubs were legal and numerous in Khapar, it turned out, but distasteful enough to bury.

"Tovados razed a whole city for vengeance then didn't even kill Sinwo," Jeld mused, mind again on Director Sammel's story.

"Yes, I know the legend," Tejani said, sipping some sort of tea. "The Warrior and his fire crumbled the citadel atop Sinwo. The master emerged only after the Idols departed."

"Departed," Jeld scoffed. He took a drink of the same tea, first wincing, then frowning approvingly. "Do easterners believe in the Idols? Worship them, I mean. Or The One?"

Tejani gave a sympathetic smile. "There are many things nobody understands. Your Idols. Life. Death. The stars. Dreams. To most Ishdali, these are to be studied, not worshiped. Even if there were gods, what purpose would be served by worshiping them?"

Jeld found himself nodding. "Religion is just a con." His thoughts drifted to Prishner Walson. "Usually, anyway."

He took another drink and scanned the establishment for a good target. "I think I like these eastern sensibilities."

"Mm. Skepticism, realism, yes, I like very much. Yet here, where efficiency and pragmatism rule, men can take slaves freely, and heart and wisdom matter for nothing, only knowledge."

"Religion is worse," Jeld said. "Never mind what it teaches directly, it makes people blind. Makes them followers. Zealots. Facts don't matter, just what a robe says."

"Beliefs rule, or facts rule. I'm not sure which is more dangerous."

"But if something is unknown... there are no facts. Only beliefs."

"There is a fact. That we don't know is itself a fact. Maybe dreams are a connection to gods, or maybe dreams are just idle thoughts. Or, maybe they are both. We don't know. That is the only fact."

Jeld shifted in his chair. "Sure... but until something is known, surely easterners wonder? Or theorize? Believe?"

"Of course, but few here believe in anything as far-fetched as gods. And fewer would see reason to worship them."

"It seems Ishdali millers are as wise as Avandrian scholars."

Tejani smiled, then frowned and turned away. Jeld too said nothing further, just surveying the room. He spotted a young, bored-looking easterner drinking alone at a small table and sent Tejani to see what she could learn. They repeated this snooping for four fruitless bells. While bells came a bit quicker in this city, by the time they departed Jeld was very glad to be back out in the open air.

"You're sure this inquisitor was telling the truth?" Tejani asked as they rode deeper into the city toward the citadel.

Was he sure? He didn't recall using his Idolic sense to weigh the inquisitor's words, but he *had* put a blade to her neck. *The citadel*, she had said. Could she have been misdirecting him? Possibly, but somehow it felt right.

"No, I suppose I'm not."

"But you believe?" she said with a smile.

"We don't have to worship it," Jeld joked. "We just have to see for ourselves."

They passed a large cage filled with men. Easterners, mostly, plus a few western folk. All well enough fed, but with those defeated eyes. Another, cleaner man stood before it giving what Jeld could tell was a sales pitch despite not knowing the language. *Idols*, what was he doing here. Of course the inquisitor would say *something* to survive, and why not throw him halfway across the world, maybe get him enslaved while they were at it.

"Maybe we can just be quick at the citadel. Have a look around. Not enroll like we'd discussed."

Tejani looked stricken. "We can't. They are very exclusive. Very secretive."

Jeld eyed her, fighting to keep his Idolic sense shut tight while still getting a read. Then he blinked in surprise. "You *want* to go."

Tejani's eyes widened, then she shrugged. "Yes, well it certainly did not seem safe to stay at my mill."

A lie. Jeld raised an eyebrow.

"Okay," Tejani said quickly. "I suppose I just want to explore this new talent. Explore a new life."

Jeld bit his cheek. True? Damn inquisitors and their power tracking. Well, true enough. He nodded, and they walked on.

It was well into the evening when they arrived at a wall thrice the height of a man. Beyond it, several huge, ornate buildings peeked above the wall. The very front of one of the buildings straddled the wall and bore an entrance that felt grand without being particularly flashy. A black door stood open at its center, above it a symbol like two crescent moons facing one another with their points overlapping.

Jeld started to sweat. He and Tejani shared an uncertain look, then went inside. A broad room, dominated by a courtyard at its center. The walls were ornately tiled in colorful patterns, lit by the evening's light streaming readily through the open courtyard. A small stream flowed in a narrow rectangular channel in the floor.

Halfway between the entrance and the courtyard was a square counter of dark stone. Behind several tidy stacks of letters and ledgers was a woman in the common eastern garb of loose linens and a white shawl. Upon one shoulder of her shawl was the same double crescent that marked the entrance. Two young men poured over books at the counter opposite her, backs turned.

The woman bowed to Tejani, then said something in the eastern tongue. They spoke for a few moments, then Tejani turned to Jeld.

"She says they do not allow this," Tejani said. "Their students are selected, and they are... usually much younger."

Jeld stepped closer to the counter. "Did you tell her we are Idolic?"

"I did."

"But that doesn't make any sense! Everyone knows the whole purpose of this place is to push the limits of human ability. To craft the best. Tell her! We're Idolic. We're the best, and we can be better with training."

Inquisitors be damned, Jeld reached out with his sense and searched the woman's aura stretching out between them. He found the conviction. The skepticism. The impatient arrogance or perhaps pride. He softened them, worked them like strings of a lute. Tejani cleared her throat to speak but abruptly the woman turned to Jeld and spoke in his familiar western common tongue.

"We are all that, this is true. But, the best cannot simply be admitted, they must be forged from youth. So long as there is an imperfection in the bud, there can never be perfection."

"All the experiences the world has to offer and you think your training is the only path to perfection? Why then were none of the Idols your students? Why then was Handan Tovaine the greatest warrior since Tovados despite all those you train?"

There was something else holding her firm. Fear... but not of them. Perhaps of Sinwo? But it undulated nearly synchronously with her pride, her self confidence. She was afraid to fail. Jeld gently worked these notes. Softened her fear, her skepticism. Stoked her trust, her interest, her awe.

"You could be right, but we have no shortage of fighters anyways," She turned to Tejani. "And your... blackening of a rope, was it only the once?"

Tejani looked to the ground, shoulders sagging.

"I'm not *really* a fighter. I can read people. It helps in a fight, sure, sensing a next attack, but it's more than that. I can sense lies, guilt, anything, really. Fear... fear of failure. Fear of disappointing..."

The woman broke her gaze free and shifted uneasily.

"And her," Jeld continued. "Do you have any other buds that can burn things with their mind? Forget your policies, what would your master want?"

The woman said nothing, trying very hard not to look Jeld in the eye as she considered. The two young men behind her shared a look and tried unconvincingly to appear to be reading still. Jeld found himself wondering whether they could be inquisitor trainees.

"Very well," the woman said. "I'll write to him and he can decide for himself."

Tejani shot Jeld a gleeful look.

"Stay in this building and I'll find you when I have his answer," the woman said. "There are seats overlooking the courtyard back that way if you wish."

"Thank you," Jeld said.

The woman did not acknowledge Jeld, just began penning a letter. She passed it off to one of the other men, who departed hastily. Finally, she gave Jeld and Tejani an annoyed look. Point taken, they hurried off.

Jeld stopped atop a tiny bridge spanning the little man-made stream and leaned upon the rail, looking out into the courtyard. He marveled at the greenery after the leagues on end of brown. The plants were immaculately kept, yet Jeld felt none of the disdain such frivolous gardens invoked in him in Tovar. Here, this was a treasure worthy of any cost.

"A fighter," Tejani whispered, shaking her head.

He gave Tejani a sheepish look. It's not as if he'd lied to her, just reframed the truth a bit. He considered revealing he could actually manipulate people's perception and emotions, but thought better of it. These skills would better serve him in secret if he had any hope of finding this elusive inquisitor training. Reframe. Withhold. Enough truth for the day.

"It's not entirely untrue," he said.

"Why did I ever believe you? You're so small."

"That's what swords are for. I didn't say I was a wrestler. I really did fight an inquisitor. And I did train with Handan Tovaine. I'm not bad."

She smiled a sad smile. "Your life has been rich."

"Rich?" Jeld scoffed.

Rich with blood, maybe. What he wouldn't give for a simple life. Operating a mill, perhaps. He started to speak but trailed off. Would he really trade it all away for a simple life? If it meant bringing back Niya, then without question. Still, Lira, the theater, the palace...even the swell of joy he still felt from a warm loaf of bread in hand, were those not all fruits of the trials he'd faced?

In any case, the thought of working a mill years on end was somehow terrifying. His idea of a simple life would at least be on the road. And with people he loved. Was she always alone there? Despite the long journey together, they'd shared little of substance about their lives.

"Rich," Jeld said again. He frowned and shook his head as if weighing the word. "Maybe. But what you had with the mill was nice too, right? Stability. Peace. Challenging, with all the crafting and engineering you've told me is required to keep the thing running."

Tejani fell silent as the water trickled beneath them. Cool air rose off the little stream and Jeld realized it was not nearly as hot in here despite the baking sun outside. Even these last days in the mountains had been as hot as any summer day he'd ever seen in Avandria, but not here. Could the stream be cooling this place?

They passed time rotating between walking loops around the courtyard and settling into the chairs the woman at the front desk had indicated. Only a handful of visitors came as they waited, most delivering messages and a few known parties being admitted. The courtyard and thus the building itself grew dark as they waited. The trio of workers shuttered the windows, lit several candelabras, and turned some wheel upon a wall that set the stream water steaming. Jeld and Tejani were nearly finished with yet another slow lap around the place when the woman who had gone to contact Sinwo returned and approached.

"We have received word from Master Sinwo. I cannot admit you. The master—"

Tejani laughed bitterly, eyes flashing between fury and sadness. Jeld actually felt a great weight lift, realizing only then just how afraid he'd been. Still, if they were not admitted he should still sneak in and snoop, and that might prove even more dangerous than hiding in plain sight. At least it would give him an excuse to test some ideas he'd been contemplating for how to exploit Kelthid's bag.

"*The master* wishes to meet you and decide for himself," the woman continued impatiently.

Jeld swallowed, the weight he now recognized as fear returning twice over. *Master Sinwo.* Names rarely made their way into song and legend while still they lived, but not so of Master Sinwo. He would not be easily impressed.

"We'd be honored for the chance," Tejani stammered. "When would he see us?"

"This night," the woman said. "It may be some time before he is available. You may wait here." And she walked off without another word.

"Well, this should be interesting," Jeld said.

Tejani took a breath and nodded. Her bitterness had faded. Now she just looked nervous, perhaps wondering how in dreams she could repeat her little feat of magic?

"We wait," she said.

Time dragged on and their laps slowed until they did not stand again from their chairs. The three at the desk retired and were replaced by two more young men who silently studied at the station to low lamplight. Jeld and Tejani had long since quieted and they were sharing some trail food when a thought occurred to Jeld.

"You told that lady who you really are, didn't you? I thought I heard it."

"I don't see how I could be admitted otherwise," Tejani said through a big yawn. "That *Corr* name of yours will be fine for a westerner, though, I'm sure."

"But if you're supposed to have been hanged, your lawmen could track you here, couldn't they?"

Tejani stiffened in her chair. "Oh, there is little chance of that. Something tells me the citadel does not readily share its records."

Jeld nodded, but as he met her eyes, her guilt was unmistakable. She flinched away, as if recalling Jeld's talent and meaning to block it.

"I don't much care if you've done some crime you're not proud of," Jeld said. "Believe me, I understand."

"I did no crime!" she snapped, then an abrupt sob escaped her and she covered her mouth.

No crime... Yes, that much seemed true. But for what then did she feel guilty? He examined her aura even as she flinched away, her eyes shut tightly as if to ward off his scrutiny. There was something else there. Shame? How could she feel such guilt over a crime she didn't commit? Some easterner pride? Well to hell with those sensibilities if it brought shame for being hanged for—

Jeld's breath caught. Tejani's eyes shot wide open on seeing the realization upon Jeld's face, then she deflated, lip trembling.

"It was you..." Jeld breathed.

Her eyes squeezed shut, a tear pinching free and streaming down her cheek. She said nothing for a long, terrible silence. Finally, she spoke.

"I failed at everything I ever tried. All my parents ever wanted was for me to excel in university. Like every parent in Ishdalar. But I wasn't good enough. This happens to many, but I was *smart*. It was just this *peshjot* scrambled mind!" She rapped the side of her head half a dozen times at the last. "I cannot focus, cannot think!"

"Hey, it's nothing."

"You do not understand our ways. It is the ultimate shame. But it is not why..." Her voice broke and she clenched her jaw to still a quivering lip. "I went on to do the same to my daughters. The same pressure, and now they have no love for me. How could I—" She broke into anguished sobs.

"You can't blame yourself. It's like you said, just the way of this place. You can't expect yourself to—"

"No! I can hate this place, this way, but I can *blame* only myself! I know this now, but it is too late. It is too late."

Idols, what to say to that? What would Director Sammel say? Or Prishner Walson. Or his Sayer mentor across the flickering fire, his every word always sounding like some ancient proverb. Even Krayo would offer something, in his own stoic way.

"It's… done," Jeld said. "Make the rest of your life matter. Help someone. Teach someone not to make the same mistake. The citadel here if we're lucky. An apprentice at your mill? A coin to a beggar? Or at least let yourself enjoy something."

Tejani shook her head, not bothering to wipe her tears. "I shouldn't have any time left. I should have died on that rope, but I didn't even have the courage to die."

"Ah but you had the courage to live," a voice came from behind.

They both spun to find an ancient, frail man in a dark blue evening robe standing behind them. He had an ornate wooden cane in one hand, though he didn't seem to be leaning on it.

Tejani jumped to her feet, wiping her eyes. "I'm—I—oh forgive me." Face a deep red, she hurried toward the entrance.

"Won't you stay for a moment?" the man called after her in a soft, shaky voice. "Give an old man an evening's conversation?"

Tejani stopped, slowly turning back to them.

"Thank you, Tejani. Ah, Corr would you…"

The old man gestured at moving one of the chairs to face the others. Jeld obliged, rearranging all three for better conversation.

The old man, presumably Master Sinwo, sat with a grunt. "Come now, sit."

Jeld and Tejani did as bidden.

"So, you two wish to join the citadel. We typically buy eggs to sell chickens, you know. Best way to ensure quality." He looked perfectly comfortable with a long silence before shrugging his brow. "So, tell me, how did two very different chickens end up journeying together to my citadel?"

"We met in the halls," Jeld answered, Tejani shooting him a cautionary look.

Master Sinwo blinked. "In the... Incredible. The probability... I've yet to hear of two people meeting there since the Idols. Visits there are so brief, you must have been in the same hall. Tell me, which was it?"

"Vincet's library," Tejani answered.

Master Sinwo laughed, then leaned back in his chair and turned to Tejani. "You see? The silly tests in university are indeed a poor measure of intellect, then. And of wisdom. And a still worse measure of potential. Of *perfection.*"

His wrinkled cheeks rose in a gleeful smile. "Look at what you can achieve when you bring your thoughts into focus!"

"I don't know how I did it, Master," Tejani said.

"Yes, this *scrambled mind*, you say. The healers have written of similar afflictions. Thoughts moving in too many directions. But you know what I see? I see a mind honed through a lifetime of struggling, compensating. The strongest muscles are those which have been ripped the most times. I once knew a blind man who could see using clicks of his tongue."

Tejani started to protest, but Master Sinwo raised a knobby hand. "Did you not come here to convince me? Must I now convince you? Stay your worries. I have many ideas for how we can achieve this."

The master turned to Jeld without waiting for Tejani's answer. "You, though... I have not produced one with your particular talent. These sorts of skills rarely blossom, if they are even real. No, forgive me, but I'm afraid I cannot admit you."

The magnitude of disappointment Jeld felt surprised him even more than the rejection itself. The old man had seemed genuinely interested just moments before, unless it had all been directed at Tejani. Something about it didn't add up. He sensed none of the skepticism Master Sinwo had eluded to. And was that exhilaration? Anticipation?

It brought to mind High Priest Naelis at the council table as his trap was closing around Jeld and Prince Dralor.

Jeld almost chose an arrogant smile and quip, but this was not Krayo he was dealing with. The old master wanted talent, not confidence. Raw skill, not cleverness. He wanted to be awed. He wanted to find the most beautiful stone to collect and polish to perfection.

"You are not as skeptical as you let on," Jeld said, staring deep beyond Sinwo's eyes. "You know I can do this, and you *are* interested. You are excited. You thirst for it like a collector finding a treasure. You hunger for the possibilities like a dog for meat."

When Jeld pulled back from the depths, he found Master Sinwo staring gravely back. He began to doubt his approach, even his read, then Master Sinwo laughed and clapped his bony hands.

"Wonderful!" Master Sinwo wheezed between laughs. "Oh, yes. Yes, you're quite right. Very well then, I invite you both. You do know that all students pay a debt for their education here? You will be no different."

It seemed to Jeld that any fee should be reduced considerably, given they both were already Idolic. Felt a bit like paying for a ferry after swimming the river, but he nodded. No matter. He didn't plan to stick around for the tab after his mission here was done. Tejani, though...

"A small price to pay," Tejani said.

"Very good," Master Sinwo said. "You met Kleshtal there earlier, at the desk. Return to her tomorrow morning and she'll see you settled. You will not be treated like young new recruits. You will have your own rooms adjacent to the dormitories. You'll be invited to join in some of the common exercises, but I will tailor your training."

"You honor us, Master," Tejani said.

The old master used his cane to rise. "You honor the citadel. Now, rest. I'm afraid our training can be quite rigorous."

Chapter Seventeen

J eld drew a card from a stack upon the desk. A three. Across the desk, an eastern trainer a few years his senior drew a card from the same pile, reading it carefully so Jeld couldn't see. Jeld stared past the card into the eyes of the trainer, then deeper until he was swimming through the man's aura, or it through him, searching. *Three*, he silently chanted in his mind to frame and focus his search. His task was to determine whether their cards matched. Master Sinwo and he both knew he could read feelings, and even intentions to a degree, but this tested his ability to read precise details of a person's thoughts.

It was not the least bit hard to believe that three weeks had passed already at the citadel. His body had quickly adapted to the physical training despite the withering journey to Delvarad, and he'd had worse food. It was the numbing mental training that made the days drag. That, and the routine. The captivity. He felt like a caged animal. A school child. Not only was he surrounded largely by people younger than him, he was entirely beholden to the rhythm of the citadel. From dawn to dusk. The tides of Sinwo.

A pulse of frustration—not his own—jarred him from the task. He looked out over the dozens of students with training swords in the sporting hall. Beyond them, Tejani sat pinching her temples at a desk in an alcove just like the one in which Jeld sat. She looked over, and the moment their eyes met, the frustration boomed. Jeld felt his own flare up to echo it, glad for the company.

The trainer cleared his throat and Jeld renewed his focus. He searched for something, *anything* like a three in the maelstrom that was the mind of the trainer. He found something he thought he recognized from the last time the trainer had ended up revealing a three. It was probably nothing, maybe a coincidental feeling if anything at all, but he nodded and the trainer flipped his card around to reveal the number two.

Jeld suppressed any reaction as was the strict protocol. The trainer collected the cards without reading Jeld's, placed them carefully atop a hundred other spent cards in a small box, and made some marks on a paper. He drew another card, and so the afternoon continued.

Several bells later, when the sporting hall had long since emptied, Jeld was again deep in the trainer's thoughts when they suddenly shifted. He opened his eyes to find Master Sinwo dismissing the trainer, then taking his seat. His usual attendant—a squat, stoney-faced fellow—stood nearby with his back to them. The old master pulled the used cards out of the box and began flipping through them, glancing at the trainer's notes after reviewing each pair.

"Not good, I know," Jeld said. "I think it just works better with feelings." He considered his ability to predict where his opponents would place their attacks. "Maybe just more general thoughts? Intentions? Numbers are just so... shallow."

Master Sinwo frowned. "And yet by the end of the session you were matching nearly half of the attempts." He turned the trainer's notes around for Jeld to see.

"These... aren't right. No, even the last. It says he had a matching three, but he had a two."

Master Sinwo pulled the top two cards from the pile and revealed a two and a five. "You are correct. Even so, he wrote down that it was a match."

"But—I don't... I don't understand."

"This test was not about your ability to sense thoughts. Well, not *only* that. You *changed* his thoughts, Corr." A smile stretched across Sinwo's wrinkled face and a silent laugh built before finally wheezing out. "You changed them!"

Jeld did not need to feign surprise. Never before had he read anyone with such precision. That, and Sinwo had seen right through him.

"You knew this was possible?" Jeld asked.

"I suspected it. I noticed that when you fight, your opponent reacts to feints that you don't even appear to make. It was only logical that you were somehow able to manipulate their perceptions. This test proves it!"

Sinwo's excitement was palpable. Jeld wondered what possibilities might be running through the man's head. This talent could certainly prove useful in a game of cards, but he doubted the fiendish old master had games in mind. He would not be thinking of what such powers could do today, but what they might one day become. What if a king could simply force an enemy to surrender? Could he drive a person insane? Or calm a student's scrambled thoughts?

Master Sinwo broke his hungry stare and waved the trainer back over. He proceeded to devise a training by which Jeld would read a word or phrase from a card and attempt to convey it to the trainer.

Jeld spent the rest of the afternoon and a good bit of the evening completely failing to achieve this even once. Finally given leave, Jeld shared a meal with Tejani, then ventured with her to the third floor of the library. There, they sat upon their usual balcony off the third floor and sat looking out into the mountains.

"This is pointless," Jeld said, pulling at the long leather belt atop his white blouse. "I can't just send someone a word. It's about amplifying expectations. Or latent thoughts. Not just completely inventing new thoughts. It probably worked with the cards because there were only five options. They were expecting one of them."

Tejani seemed to consider this. "Is expecting words any different than expecting numbers? If five was possible, why not ten? Or a hundred, or a thousand? And then, is that not enough words to convey basic thoughts?"

Jeld frowned contemplatively. "I just don't think it fits. It's not what I do."

Tejani shrugged and went to the rail. Leaning against it, she took a deep breath and her shoulders eased. Jeld followed her and looked out at the jagged, rocky mountains. To the west, only partially visible beyond the city wall from their height, was an expanse of blackened rubble. Charred husks of once great structures stood frozen in time.

If more than rubble had remained

Beneath the fires of Khapar

The words of "Fires of Khapar" echoed through his mind. Such death, dealt by one of the very gods the west worshiped. Perhaps it was for the best that they were gone. And yet, the one who provoked such destruction by killing the Mother was said to have been sent from Khapar. From the Citadel even, under the very tutelage of the man now training Jeld.

"How are things going for you?" Jeld asked.

"Well enough." Tejani's eyes grew distant. "I can see the trail almost always, now. The trees passing by, never ending. It reminds me of when I would come ashore after a day fishing on my father's canoe. I would feel the rise and fall of the water still all night."

"Is it... helping?"

"It might be working a little. When my thoughts wander, I let them turn off the path, fading to whispers, and I stay my course. Somewhat, anyway."

Jeld rubbed his tired eyes. "Well, that's something. I can't believe he makes you do it in the sporting hall, though. Couldn't he at least let you perfect it somewhere else first?"

"Mm. That would be nice. Well, what is it you say? Trial by fire?"

Looking out over the remnants of the destruction Tovados had wrought, Jeld grunted.

"It is probably for the best," Tejani said. "All that, and the tutoring I give... Well, keeping my mind busy is for the best."

"You can't blame yourself forever."

Tejani didn't answer.

"Alright, even if you can blame *that* Tejani you can't blame *this* Tejani," Jeld said. "If you learned from what she did, you are no longer her. You are someone new. Regret it, sure. But learn and move on."

Tejani was silent for a long while then spoke. "Would that not render morality obsolete, were we able to dismiss the actions of each passing day? Mm, no... no, change is the key. So long as we change, then. Yes... wise. Wise beyond your years."

She took a breath and rolled her shoulders. "Enough of that. Any luck with your... search?"

Jeld shook his head and clenched the stone parapet. "Nothing." He looked up suddenly. "Why, did you find something?"

"No. I fear we have exhausted our search. Perhaps some of the best fighters are just given to your high priest to serve as these inquisitors?"

Jeld's gaze strayed from the rubble to a group of young trainees playing with a ball beneath the street lamps in the pristine grounds below.

"No," he said. "The inquisitors are more than just fighters with robes. They are far worse. Inhuman."

"Mm. Yes, perhaps so."

Jeld sighed. He'd been a fool to trust the word of an inquisitor, even one with a knife at her throat. Krayo had once told him extraction only worked if the subject thought they had a hope of living, or at least deferring pain, and Jeld doubted he'd been advertising anything but death. Besides, as highly trained as inquisitors were, it seemed likely they prepared for such situations to protect their secrets.

"We should get dinner before they run out of food," Tejani said.

Jeld rapped the parapet with his clenched fist and followed her back inside. They were halfway to the stairwell when Jeld froze, only his eyes flicking in thought.

"What is it?" Tejani whispered.

Jeld looked around the room then pulled her into a dark aisle between bookshelves.

"Food," Jeld hissed. "If Sinwo is training inquisitors in secret, they must be getting fed. We just need to follow the food."

Tejani cocked her head at Jeld, looking concerned. "Jeld… there is nothing to find here. If Sinwo is producing these inquisitors, it is not inside the Citadel. Perhaps we could examine the accounting records? Maybe they will reveal another program somewhere?"

Jeld started to protest then let out a breath and nodded. They walked to the dining hall, finding it mostly empty, typical for so late in the evening. Only two other small groups remained before emptied plates, as well as the stoic custodian, who was cleaning tables.

"Yes, being a miller is a big part of me," Tejani was saying as she chewed. "As were my studies before, but I spent more years being a mother than I spent at either of those. I have—Corr!"

Jeld's eyes flicked from the door leading to the kitchen, landing back on Tejani and finding her glaring at him.

"Sorry, what?" Jeld asked.

She narrowed her brow. "You're still thinking about the food thing."

Jeld smiled sheepishly and started to talk, but the custodian slapped a rag down on a nearby table and started scrubbing. He took the opportunity to stuff his mouth with some spiced beans, waiting in awkward silence as the man worked his way down the table.

"What happens to all the extra food?" Jeld asked.

At first the custodian seemed to assume the question was not for him, but when Tejani did not answer, he looked up to Jeld.

"Hmm? You need more food?" the custodian asked, his accent almost indecipherable.

"No, I mean... extra food is... thrown away? Goes to garbage?"

"Ah. No. Ah... give? Give away. In city."

"In the city..." Jeld echoed as the custodian walked off. "That's good, I was worried it would be wasted"

Jeld looked to Tejani, inviting her take with a little half shrug, but she only shook her head. It would hardly make sense to buy food from the city only to deliver it back out to the city. Even so, Jeld finished his meal quickly and excused himself.

Tejani gave Jeld a suspicious look. "Good luck. Be careful"

Jeld bid her goodnight and left the dining hall. It was almost fully dark outside now, the tall street lamps glowing brightly. He circled to the back of the dining hall, finding a small covered wagon pulled by a single horse parked beside a rear door. The custodian's wagon, no mistaking. The man was a fixture of the citadel, always at one task or another, and his wagon never far off.

Jeld slunk into the shadows between some bushes and waited. It was not long before the door opened and the custodian appeared pulling a cart. He loaded several crates into the wagon then took up the reins and gave them a rap. Jeld bit his lip as he weighed his next move, then jumped up and raced after it on silent feet, eyes fixed on the custodian through the narrow gap beneath the cover.

He climbed into the wagon, crawling toward a low wall beneath the gap. His shoulder struck something and a crate crashed down beside him. He dove, back thumping against the low wall, and froze as he felt the custodian's gaze sweep past him. Jeld didn't so much as breathe, despite his aching lungs. A quick, fruitless, stupid ending to the whole charade. Unless he felt like killing the man, but he didn't.

There was an unconcerned grunt and the scrutiny faded, Jeld's held breath blowing out with it. He quickly detached his bag from the inside of his shirt and, ignoring a stab of fear from the last time he'd done this, climbed into the bag. Careful not to pull the bag in after him, he reached a hand back out of the bag, grabbed its edge with two fingers and walked the rest along the bed of the wagon like a spider dragging its prey. To his amazement it worked as he'd hoped, if a bit slower and more awkward. Peering out through the bag, he walked it behind a flap of excess canvas from the cover, and he waited.

The wagon stopped at what Jeld took to be the gate, a few muffled words exchanged before it set into motion again. Jeld poked his head out and around the canvas to peer out the back, indeed finding the wall of the citadel now behind. He continued to watch, a head floating atop a leather bag, as the wagon wound its way through the city, until finally it came to a stop in an alleyway. He ducked back into the bag, listening as crates scraped across the bed of the wagon, then silence.

Chancing a look, he found the custodian hauling two stacked crates through some door. The crates were large, too large for such a modestly sized man to be carrying like that if they were full of food. Granted, the custodian could be stronger than he appeared given his constant laboring, but even so Jeld couldn't keep from pulling himself halfway from the bag and prying at the top of one of the remaining crates. Empty.

Footsteps. Jeld pressed the crate closed, then pulled himself back into the bag just as a shadow grew from within the doorway. In the darkness of the void beneath the halls, he quickly changed into his travel clothes as the custodian unloaded. The wagon started off before he was done. With a silent curse, Jeld frantically tugged his second boot on, grabbed his shirt, and reached a hand through the bag. He crawled his hand up the back of the wagon, again dragging the bag after him between two fingers, and jumped down to the dusty ground.

Jeld waited until the rumbling wagon wheels faded into the distance, then climbed from the bag. The building the custodian had visited was nondescript. He tried the door. Locked, but it gave way quickly. He pocketed his picks and peered inside. A sparse room. Just crates. A few shelves with more crates. He snooped at the crates. Empty, empty. More empty. Just a warehouse of empty crates. Hardly following the food.

With a frown, he left and started back toward the citadel. Most likely just returning crates from a daily food purchase, Jeld considered. If that were the case though, where was this *donation* of excess food the custodian had spoken of? He'd just have to keep a better eye on the kitchens and try again to follow the *actual* food. Plans settled, his thoughts turned again to how he might find Lira should this fool's errand turn out how he expected.

Back at the citadel, he scaled the wall and snuck to his bed, a rare private room afforded him given his status as one of the few trainees already Idolic. The next day he put on a good enough show of being ill to be excused from training and spent the day staking out the dining hall under the guise of reading on a bench. He'd discovered nothing of value by dinner, but remained as the sun fell for what he was certain would be a futile repeat of the prior night. Tejani was seated beside him, having also stopped by several times to check on him throughout the day.

"Maybe there just was not any food left over yesterday," Jeld said, eyes on the back door.

"Maybe," Tejani said unconvincingly.

Time dragged on and still the custodian did not appear. Jeld opened his senses. Master Sinwo's regimen had explored both range, indirect line of sight, and sensing someone's location, and indeed he was able to discern a single person was inside near where the tables would be.

"You sense him?" Tejani said quietly.

"Someone. Him, I think. He's moving back into the kitchen now. Probably gathering the food."

Tejani said nothing, but Jeld felt her skepticism and concern pulse beside him. Probably gathering the empty crates, more like. Maybe her thoughts, maybe his own. Jeld tracked the custodian's aura to what he thought was probably the kitchen area, but it grew distorted, out of focus somehow. Jeld's eyes clenched in concentration as he tried to make sense of it.

"What is it?" Tejani said.

"I'm just having trouble. Maybe he's just getting too far, or—"

Instead of trying to merge the fuzzy aura into focus, Jeld pulled it apart. Once, then again. Three auras now, not one.

"There are three people in there now," Jeld whispered. "It was just the one before, I'm sure of it."

"Students come late for dinner?"

"Maybe? I didn't see them coming. Doesn't the custodian usually lock the door after he cleans?"

"Perhaps he forgot."

This time it was Jeld's turn to be unconvinced. He scrutinized the three auras. One was unmistakably the one he'd been following, the custodian. This was confirmed when the door opened and the custodian emerged with his cart of crates. The others, still inside, were almost indistinguishable from one another, both… cold. Sharp, like frosted glass. He'd felt their kind before, too many times. *Inquisitors.*

"Inquisitors," he breathed.

"Jeld, we don't—"

"It's them."

The two new auras began to move toward the door, then through it, yet nobody else emerged. They continued, as if strolling invisibly across the grounds. Idols help Avandria if the inquisitors had somehow gained the ability to hide in plain sight, Jeld thought, until suddenly he understood.

"They're underground," he said. "That's where Sinwo has been hiding them. Probably the same way he survived the fires and hid from the Warrior." He jumped up. "Wait here."

Jeld hurried after them, trailing behind and staying out of sight despite the ground separating them. They led him in a generally straight path deeper into the citadel. After a while they neared the very wall of the citadel, then continued past it. Jeld looked around to be sure nobody was watching, then climbed up the wall. Arms wrapped over the top, he pulled himself up enough to see over it. There, he watched as the auras continued away, deep beneath the scorched rubble of the old citadel.

Chapter Eighteen

J eld carefully placed another step between blackened fragments of stone. The jagged top of a charred wall at his back was barely distinguishable from the starless sky above. He must have been picking his way through this fell place for at least two bells, though the final night bell had long since rung. His hope of finding a better way into whatever complex lurked below was dwindling, at least for tonight. Perhaps whatever passage the custodian had used beneath the kitchen would have to do.

Stopping once again, Jeld listened for any signs of company. He resisted the urge to reach out with his Idolic sense, clamping his walls shut tight. If the inquisitor had been telling the truth about the citadel, what she'd said about their ability to track his power was probably true also. So, he steadied his breath and listened. No bugs here. No birds. Just sand and debris hissing along the stones with the faint breeze.

The whispering wind could almost be a voice. He'd found on the road and city alike that if you listened hard enough, you could hear pretty well whatever you wanted. Or, whatever you feared. So it was that he paid the wind's whispers little attention until suddenly there was no mistaking it. A voice.

He froze as it drew closer. Then footsteps, many footsteps. He shrunk into a dark corner, fighting to keep his sense shut. It was every bit as difficult as trying not to smell something, but he managed and they passed by without incident. The rare voices and soft steps faded back into the breeze, but not before Jeld was following after them, sure as the east is dusty that he should be running the opposite direction.

The rare scuttle of gravel, hushed voice, or glimpse of a shadowy figure led Jeld deeper still into the wreckage. It wasn't long before they stopped somewhere ahead, a voice rising up from the darkness. Jeld crept into the husk of a building, picked his way up the jagged remnants of steps, and wedged himself under a fallen wall to peer out toward the voices.

Shadows filled a clearing that might have been the remains of a small stadium. They formed two groups, the first with darker robes, black maybe and so short they could only be children. The second were taller, some perhaps fully grown, with gray robes. One other stood before them all in a robe that must have been white by day. Words took shape over the rustling of ash and pounding of Jeld's heart. A woman's voice.

"When you venture from this place one day to serve the Wise One, the air will not hold this sour scent of ash. The stones beneath your feet will not be black. But you must not forget the end days. You must not forget that in the end, they sacrificed themselves to save those who had hurt them most."

The one at the front shifted into a fighting stance, movements as smooth as flowing water, then suddenly punched. The others followed, sleeves of their robes cracking like whips.

"We bear their burden, though it rend our very souls. There is no price too high to stop the destruction that follows should we fail. You will abhor your actions." She threw an elbow, the others mirroring her to another chorus of cracks. "You will hate yourself." A high knee, then a kick. "You will *be* hated. But we must not break. We must feel only duty. We will bear this burden."

The preaching went on. Brainwashing, really. Indoctrination. Jeld found himself feeling sorry for the inquisitors. They really stood no chance against this incessant poison pumped into their veins since they were young children. Despite his sympathy, a chill ran down his spine. Somehow it was worse that their every terrible deed was motivated not by emptiness nor malice, but by a twisted righteousness. They believed they were good. They believed they were saving the world.

Suddenly a shadow flashed before him. He flinched back but only collided with the stone surrounding him. There was a blur of motion, a flash of pain in his head. Somehow he was on his feet, a robed figure coming at him through the spinning darkness. He ducked the least blurry version of a staff flying toward him and charged, knife lashing out.

A sword came out of nowhere. Jeld jumped back and it sliced the knife from his grip. Better than slicing the hand from his wrist as had been intended, but not good. He kicked the new arrival in the shin, turned, and ran. Three strides, and something caught his ankle. He went down, wrist rolling painfully, head slamming into the edge of a stone brick. Jeld scrambled halfway to his feet but collapsed, face slapping against the char. He tried again and this time rough hands tugged him to his feet. His vision spun, nothing but black and gray, stone and stars. Figures. One or twenty.

Jeld might have been walking. Dragged, he was being dragged. He bucked and twisted, but the grips only tightened, his arms jerked up behind his back halfway to his neck. He clenched his eyes shut but his vision only swam worse, his foggy mind no better either. He retched.

A stupid idea, coming out here. Stupid to come to Khapar at all. He had to do something. Had to fight. Or a ploy—they were taking him alive, so perhaps some charade would be sufficient to get him free. But his mind was as dim as his vision.

They threw him to his knees. Jeld looked up to find a woman in a white robe looking down at him. She held a long wooden bo at her side in a way that somehow seemed to mean business, like a butcher might his cleaver. A good two dozen of the young inquisitor trainees in black and gray robes stood behind her.

In that instant of certain death, he didn't fear for the pain. Not for the image of blade cutting through his flesh into the vital bits. Not even for the end. He feared instead for what would befall his friends. What terrible fate these bastards would deliver to Lira. Would they torture him to find her, he wondered? Probably he didn't know anything more than them about that. Krayo though... would they extract his loyalties from Jeld? And the theater, the whole crew. No. No, it was escape or die.

Jeld glanced over his shoulder. Three inquisitors back there now. He'd never escape. Hardly having to act, he sagged to the ground, hand beneath him closing on a chunk of brick. Going for their leader would be the best way to get himself... the best way to help his friends.

His stomach twisted. His throat tightened. His breath came faster, pulse pounding in his ears. Now! Now or they'll take you alive! But he couldn't budge. Through clenched teeth he blew out breaths like a bull readying to charge. He tensed, fingers digging into the brick. Now! Now, dream it! Now!

Finally he sprung at the woman in white, swinging the brick at her pale face with all he had left. She was only just beginning to look surprised when there was a sharp crack, a flash of pain in Jeld's head, and then nothing.

***

Jeld's eyes eased open. It was still dark. Good, more time to sleep before Master Sinwo could torment him with more training. He closed his eyes. What had it been again? Ah, transmitting phrases. Or rather, failing to.

His head throbbed. Far from the first time pressing his power too far had done so. He pressed a hand to his temple and pain shot through his head as his fingers fell upon a sizable lump. How had that gotten there? Had he fallen? There was sparring, but he hadn't joined yesterday, had he? No, there'd been Sinwo's tricky number cards, then the silly phrase exercise. Dinner with Tejani as usual—actually, hadn't it been outside? Ah, following the food, yes, and then the auras underground, the inquisitors, and—

Suddenly it all came rushing back and he sat up, ignoring the pain in his head. The room was dark save for a faint flickering light coming from beyond a barred door. The walls were of stone—not bricks, but solid stone. He stood from a bench carved directly into the wall and went to the cell door.

In the small room he could see beyond, a man in a gray robe sat rigidly upon a low stool. His hair was closely cut like an inquisitor. A single candle burned by his side. The man's eyes flicked Jeld's way then back to the empty wall opposite him. Barely a man, Jeld realized. He put the trainee just a little shy of his own age, yet the zealotry somehow made him seem younger, like he was still a child heeding his mother's every call, believing her every word.

Jeld backed around the corner out of the trainee's view then reached for his bag. His hand closed on an unfamiliar collar and he looked down to find himself wearing a different tunic. He didn't know if he was happy to be alive or not, but damn did losing that bag hit him in the heart. He couldn't escape or pluck out a weapon. Worse, the idea of Naelis getting it. And he couldn't bloody well hope to convince the bastards he was just some lost student if they discovered Kelthid's bag on him.

Perhaps he wasn't entirely weaponless. There was his Idolic sense. But what was he to do, plant some silly phrase like *blue bird* or some useless number into the guard's mind? Make him sleepy, maybe, but that would hardly open the cell door. Devoid of a plan, he nonetheless opened his sense and stepped back to the cell door.

"This is part of the citadel, right?" Jeld said, feigning ignorance. "I'm a student too, so just tell Master Sinwo I'm here and he'll straighten this out."

The boy gave no sign of hearing Jeld, but something pulsed in his aura. Mistrust. Disbelief. Well, it seemed he spoke western common, anyway.

"I was just looking around, you know. I've been hearing stories of the fires since I was a little kid, and wanted to see the ruins. I didn't mean to cause trouble."

Still the guard said nothing. Jeld sank further into his character even as he crafted it.

"Saving everyone, isn't that what your teacher said? Helping? Y-you guys are good then, right? Won't you help me, then?"

Jeld felt a flicker of something like pity, even saw a fleeting hint of it upon the boy's face. As if that were a spark unto kindling, the boy's aura flared in a dozen places, humanity bursting free, but just as quickly it pulled back into the icy shell. Jeld found a lingering thread and, like crafting another character, he spun up a purest sympathy and stoked the thread with it.

"I'm sorry I intruded," Jeld said, voice cracking. "Please. Please, I—I'll ask Sinwo to dismiss me if I must. I'm a better farmer anyway, I just wanted to make a good wage so my brother would have a better life. Please, just talk to Master Sinwo. Please!"

Sweat beaded on the guard's brow. Jeld stoked the sympathy further, brushed away the conviction, plucked at countless nameless feelings to open the indoctrinated trainee's heart.

"Be quiet!" the boy suddenly yelled, turning to Jeld for the first time.

Eyes wide seemingly in surprise to his own reaction, the boy looked quickly away and his aura contracted to a tight, icy ball. Jeld frowned. He'd been foolish to suspect sympathy would get him anywhere. The boy had been brainwashed to think he was doing the right thing. In a way, Jeld had to convince him to do the *wrong* thing. No, he'd need more than sympathy. He needed to dismantle the whole system.

"Your training is supposed to be a secret, isn't it?" Jeld said. "You're afraid I'll tell someone, and you think it's acceptable to keep one person prisoner if it saves more people by keeping your secret, right? Because you think you can set the world right. Avoid some... destruction? That's what your training teaches, isn't it?

"Is this the world you want to preserve? A world where innocent people get imprisoned, or killed or whatever you want to do to me? Because to me, that sounds like a world worth destroying to get to something better."

Jeld felt something new pulse in the guard's aura. Regret? Yes, regret that this path was necessary. Jeld pulled at it.

"You think it's the only way. That's what they've taught you. That's what the people who *abduct children and brainwash them* have taught you. They have made you willing to imprison and kill innocent people at their whim, for some destruction they've taught you to believe will come if you misbehave."

Jeld waited as the words soaked in, waited as he crafted his next words and matched them to the notes he plucked on the future inquisitor's mind.

"Have you heard of the Sayers? They had similar beliefs. Or had similar conviction, at least. Their faith was weaponized by their leader. They were manipulated to do evil, then the same man discarded them when he had no further need of them. The man was High Priest Naelis, you know. That is who you are being farmed for. Why should this time be any different?"

The boy's aura went wild. Doubt, curiosity. So many questions. So much uncertainty. But he didn't even flinch, just dutifully staring ahead.

Jeld continued. "Even if it were true, even if you weren't just being manipulated for power, how far—"

The door opened. Master Sinwo entered. He waved the guard away and sat upon his stool, both hands leaning upon his cane in front of him. Though Jeld knew the old master must be behind this terrible program, he nonetheless felt a surge of hope knowing he was dealing with a thinking, feeling human. Master Sinwo couldn't have any reason for holding him beyond merely keeping this place secret. With that, Jeld framed his character.

Master Sinwo gave a sympathetic frown. "I'm sorry to see you like this, my boy. Truly, I am."

"What's this all about?" Jeld said, voice trembling. "Those... students, in the robes, they're supposed to be a secret? Well, I won't tell anyone. I won't tell anyone, so just let me go. Please."

Master Sinwo stared back and Jeld got the sinking feeling that the master could detect Jeld's subtle manipulation of his aura.

Sinwo sighed. He reached into his robe and pulled out Jeld's bag, still splayed open more like a flat piece of leather. Jeld fought to keep from showing a reaction as Master Sinwo eyed him. The old master pulled up the liner, revealing the black void, and dipped his fingertips inside.

"Kelthid's, wasn't it?" Sinwo said.

"What do you want of me?" Jeld asked.

"Me? If it were left to me, I would want only to keep training you. To test the limits of your abilities, and unlock your full potential. But it seems Naelis has been searching very hard for you, Arvin Emry."

Jeld's stomach sank. "He doesn't have to find out. I can be more valuable to you alive. You could keep the bag for yourself, train me still and sell me off."

"I don't sell people!" Sinwo snapped. "We sell services, jointly." He sniffed and recovered his calm demeanor. "Regardless, it isn't so simple. High Acolyte Chontri found the bag before I had even heard of your capture. I'm afraid she has already sent word to Naelis."

Jeld shook his head as the reality of his situation sunk in. "I don't suppose you'd let me go before they take me."

Master Sinwo gave a sad smile. "In truth he wants the bag more than he wants you. But I don't think he would take kindly to my letting you free."

"You must see that this is wrong," Jeld said. "Naelis, the inquisitor. It's all wrong."

Sinwo's eyes drifted up, up toward the rubble above. "I've seen the destruction just one of the Idols could cause. Naelis came to me after. After the Idols had ascended. Vincet had told him that the power would soon spread, so he asked for my help building a force to police it. He thought, standing amidst the ashes, that I would see it his way. In truth, I only agreed because I was hungry to see how far these foretold powers could go.

He shook his head. "Incredible specimens, the Idols were. Truly incredible. Fires or not, I only wish we could have seen what they might have become given more time."

"Naelis killed them," Jeld said. "He killed the Idols."

"What?" Sinwo chuckled. "No, he—"

Jeld rattled the door. "He killed them! It's true."

"No. Impossible. He loved Vincet."

"It was Vincet who ordered it done. He didn't trust anyone being so powerful. He even fabricated the whole idea of ascending to fight Discord, just to give their sacrifice meaning. They didn't ascend, they're dead."

Master Sinwo searched for truth in Jeld's eyes, the single candle dancing in his own. "They were so beautiful... So irreplaceable."

"This is all wrong, Master. It's not too late to fix this."

Master Sinwo seemed to consider this, then his eyes fell closed. "It is too late, I'm afraid. Much too late." He stood and faced Jeld. "I'm sorry, Corr. Arvin. Whoever you are, I'm sorry. Another great waste."

Master Sinwo turned purposefully away and started for the door, cane clacking along beside him.

"Wait," Jeld said, both hands grasping the bars. "Wait! You are better than this, I feel it!"

Sinwo stopped in the doorway at Jeld's words. The old master kept his feelings close, his mind tight and shielded, but Jeld plucked furiously at what sympathy and guilt and doubt he could get hold of.

Finally Sinwo turned, a look of wonder upon his face. "That's you, isn't it? You are manipulating my mind even now, are you not?"

"Perhaps it is your conscience."

Master Sinwo gave a sad smile. "Such potential. Such waste." He stuffed Jeld's bag back into his robe. "Don't speak of this bag to the students. Perhaps I can at least keep it out of Naelis's hands, somehow."

Shaking his head, Master Sinwo turned and left the room. Jeld sagged against the bars, turned, and slid down to the cold stone. The young inquisitor trainee returned and reclaimed his stool a while later, but Jeld remained still, silent.

Chapter Nineteen

J eld licked his bowl clean and set it on the bench beside him. He was well enough fed, but somehow being confined to a cell made one savor every crumb. Perhaps a precaution in case the food should stop coming, or perhaps being treated like an animal simply made one an animal. He could sense his usual guard starting bantae by the steadying of his aura. Jeld walked to the cell door and began a poor imitation of the guard's bantae exercises.

"Like this?" Jeld said, his eyes closed.

Of course, his guard did not answer, nor had he spoken a single word since his initial lapse the day before. Jeld's efforts to manipulate him had thus far proven futile. Well, perhaps if he poked the right spot enough times he might pierce the boy's armor.

"I never got to say goodbye," Jeld said, again pulling at his guard's emotions. "Never got to tell her I loved her. I won't ever see her again, will I? You're going to kill me, aren't you?"

Jeld shifted his stance awkwardly. "All because I peeked at your little meeting. Whatever you people are, you're evil. I don't care what you say about protecting this or that."

How to convey the foolishness of defining morality in such cold, mathematical terms? Killing one innocent to save a thousand? Actually, that didn't seem so wrong. But it wasn't so simple. Everything the bastards did involved lesser evils instead of finding better solutions.

Ways not to kill the one. Not only that, it wasn't trading one for a thousand, but rather trading one on the off chance of some mythical destruction being real.

"Okay, so say murdering some kid is all it takes to save the world. What makes you so sure it works? What makes you sure you are right? Some old book? Some old story?"

Jeld played at losing his balance a little as he copied his guard's strike. "There are many different books out there, you know. Different stories, religions. If you'd been brainwashed since birth to believe some other story, don't you think you'd be just as sure about that one?"

"Maybe you got lucky and were born in the right cult," Jeld said, wincing at the last. "The right religion. But even so, how do you know any given evil act is necessary? And how many evil acts before it's these acts that are destroying the world?"

Jeld stopped his bantae and leaned against the wall. Where had all that come from? He was beginning to sound like Lira. Too much time spent reading books in the Halls. He glanced through the bars and found his guard looking troubled, his usually flowing bantae jarring. Jeld searched the guard's aura and his shoulders sagged. Just as usual. Sympathetic but unmoving.

"Why are you even in here?" Jeld almost yelled in frustration. "Afraid I'll sneak out through the solid stone?"

Jeld habitually tugged at his collar where he could normally access his bag, then shook the cell door. He paced away but suddenly froze, then returned to the door.

"They're hardening you. You're the decent one, aren't you? Resisting during your puppy kicking training, right?"

The inquisitor trainee froze mid-maneuver, his eyes shooting open.

"Be proud," Jeld said softly. "You are not the failure. You are the only one who passed the test. You didn't break."

The guard closed his eyes, took a deep breath, and resumed his bantae.

"They're killing you. No, worse. They're hollowing you out. They won't stop until you are dead inside, then they'll use what's left to do terrible things. To murder. To enslave and kill by the thousands like the prince's—like the tower at Tovar. To destroy Avandria."

Tears joined sweat streaming down the guard's face as Jeld tore at his mind. Even closed, the trainee's eyes were haunted. Anguished. But still the boy continued his exercises, even as his hands shook.

Jeld fought back tears of his own. Tears for his tormented guard—the price of touching minds—and tears of frustration. *Dreams* but the boy was strong. Too strong even to let himself walk free of the fire consuming him. There had to be another way, but what? This was his only weapon in this damned cell.

Jeld blew out a breath. He'd get out of this, and when he did, he'd need to know what to do next. He needed to know more about where he was, and how to find his way out.

"So, clouds are red?" Jeld asked, his sense wide open.

The guard didn't flinch, but Jeld felt his reaction and calibrated his expectations accordingly.

"Or clouds are white and gray?" Jeld said next. A flash of something different this time. Truth. Affirmation. "Okay. And, we're underground, aren't we?"

Jeld continued his interrogation for a long while, even after his guard had lain down upon his thin mattress. By the end he'd gained a fair understanding of the vast underground compound he was imprisoned in. It felt like progress, if only a little, despite being no closer to actually getting out of his cell.

Jeld made use of his chamber pot then laid down upon his bench.

"Night time, then?" Jeld asked, to no outward response. "Right, well, goodnight to you as well."

It took a long while before the tormented guard fell asleep, and longer still before finally Jeld too was taken by dreams.

Jeld awoke with a start. He strained his ears for any sign of what had disturbed him, but heard only the flickering of the candle and the steady—no, erratic breathing of the guard. The guard gave a small groan. Dreaming, Jeld realized. A wave of terror struck him then, and he corrected his assessment. A *nightmare*.

With only a moment's hesitation, he swam into his guard's mind, searching for what haunted him. He went deeper and deeper, but the meaning evaded him. There was only emotion, raw and meaningless. He pressed harder, wrapped himself in the aura, wearing it like a character so he might understand it. Something took shape. A feeling, or a thought, or a word. Empty? A picture... The door of Jeld's cell, hanging open, the inside... empty.

The young trainee was terrified Jeld would escape. With this knowledge so many unknowns in the aura took new shapes, held new meaning. In the once meaningless terror he found terror of retribution from the boy's master, yet also dread of failure itself, the rebuke from his peers, and from himself.

Even as Jeld felt a swell of sympathy for his guard, he stared hungrily like a wolf at the beating vein of an exposed neck. He could use this, *amplify* this. Only, to what end? To drive the man insane? Even then, Jeld would still be stuck here. Perhaps to make him truly believe Jeld had escaped? Then the guard would just run and fetch—

Jeld's eyes widened. His guard would not be quick to fetch help. He was too afraid of failure. He would inspect the cell first at least, but would he open it? The more Jeld considered the idea, the more ridiculous it sounded, but what did it cost him to try?

Diving deeper still into the guard's mind, Jeld stoked the fear. *He's escaped. The cell is empty. He's gone. They'll kill you. They'll ridicule you. You aren't good enough. You failed. Empty. He's gone. He's gone.*

Jeld thickened the paint on the inquisitor's vision of the empty cell, wove it into the fear itself, formed the image in pristine clarity and burned it into the boy's mind. The slumbering guard whimpered and moaned, breath frantic. Pressing himself to the wall, Jeld tugged at the guard's fear in a sudden spike.

The guard cried out and Jeld felt him come awake. There was a long silence save for the guard's panting, then Jeld heard the rustle of clothing and tap of footsteps. The sound of the guard's breath catching came from what sounded like the cell door. A terrible long stretch of silence, Jeld clenching his eyes shut, clinging to the image of the empty cell like aching lungs to breath beneath the water.

A sob. A curse. Another silence. Another curse. Finally, the scratch of a key and turn of a lock. Jeld forced his clenched eyes open a slit, pouring his every ounce of will into holding the image in the guard's mind. The trainee stepped into the cell to stand directly beside Jeld, then walked deeper inside.

Taking a slow breath, Jeld slowly bent and picked up his chamber pot. He eased from the wall, slunk after the guard, and swung. The trainee spun and a hand shot up to block, but it was too late. The chamber pot cracked against the side of his head and he folded to the ground.

Jeld stared down at the fallen guard, and laughed. It had worked. It had actually worked. But, the euphoria quickly gave way to panic at the escape ahead. Jeld collected the trainee's dagger and pressed it to his throat. Clothes. He'd need those, and they'd serve him better not covered in blood. He set the knife aside and stripped his guard's clothing off. Finished, he again pressed the knife to the boy's throat.

He couldn't shake the memory of the guard's fear, and his suppressed sympathy. Jeld had felt it all like it had been his own. The curse of his gift. The kid wasn't broken yet, not entirely. He was still a shadow of the child they'd taken to mold. Probably the strongest among them, to have deserved this duty.

Jeld cursed and tucked the dagger away. Gray robe donned, he walked from the cell, a small step closer to freedom. When he closed the door, his eyes fell upon the sprawled guard beyond. Idiocy, leaving an enemy alive behind him. Idiocy. But, he turned the lock, pocketed the key, and turned his back. Probably he'd be dead before the bastard woke up anyway.

Jeld raised his hood and walked out of the room with the confident, intentional steps he'd observed from the inquisitors and their trainees alike. He emerged into pure darkness save for a faint glow in the distance, which he started toward. Suddenly something struck his head and he ducked, senses flung wide. A rock. Just a low, rocky cave ceiling. Hands held before him, he continued in a crouch.

After a while his eyes adjusted somewhat. He was on a narrow path of polished flat stone. To either side of the path, the stone was jagged like a natural cave floor, as was the stone overhead. Jeld followed the path toward the light at its end.

The cave opened into a vast chamber filled with numerous stone buildings like a small city. These were not carved like the tunnel, but rather built in the mountain's hollow. Among more ordinary structures was an intricate circular structure. Perhaps the very arena the inquisitors trained to kill. Only a handful of torches were interspersed across the vast space, their light doing little to fill it. A web of passages narrow and broad opened out from the chamber walls.

Jeld caught movement amidst the buildings and spotted two robed figures. They disappeared from view, emerging a short time later at the edge of the chamber before passing into one of the side passages to the right.

Ducking out into the chamber, Jeld crept along the wall over the uneven stone toward the left. He'd gleaned during his interrogation that this was the proper direction, but *dreams* there were so many passages. He peered down a low, natural opening, but scurried past, certain Sinwo wouldn't have tolerated ducking on any main thoroughfare after all his years here. The next passage was broader with a leveled path running into it. Inside was a long building like a barracks, stone with a plank roof like many of the others.

What sounded like a snore echoed down the passage. That had to settle some old idiom, didn't it? Inquisitors *do* snore. Jeld's breath caught as his probing sense caught dozens inside the building. Dozens of inquisitors. A chill ran down the chill already on his spine. Trapped in a cave full of inquisitors.

He started at faint voices. From the main chamber. A faint glow between buildings, moving closer. He winced at the barracks full of inquisitor trainees before hurrying on silent feet into the passage and slipping into a small crack in the wall. Two trainees in gray robes passed right by him and went inside the barracks. A short while later, they or two others emerged and passed by again, disappearing back into the underground city.

Jeld shivered and snuck to the next opening. It was more like a hallway, a comfortable height with smooth walls and a floor etched to look like tiles. Seemed before that he'd damn near mapped the whole place out. Now, less so. He glanced ahead to the next passages, cursed, and hurried into the hallway.

The floor sloped uphill, a good sign. He quickened his pace, steps silent. The faint light behind him faded until he was hurrying through almost complete darkness, hands again outstretched before him. He came to a twisting stairwell and followed it up, then into another hall. A sliver of light took shape ahead, and at last he came to a door of iron bars and thick planks.

He closed his eyes and reached out. People above him, it seemed. And below, back in the main chamber, perhaps. Beyond the door though… no, it seemed not. In any case, better than staying in this hell hive, so he gave the door a gentle push. It didn't budge. A pull, but nothing again. Unsurprising, but hardly comforting. If it was the right door though…

His hand found a lock in the darkness. He blew out a breath. Almost didn't even want to try it, for fear of it not working. What then? But, of course that would hardly get him anywhere. He produced the key for his cell, blew out another breath, and turned the key. The lock gave with a wondrous little clang. Fresh mountain air rushed in as he pulled the door open. It might have been paradise, never mind the blackened wasteland before him. He climbed a pile of rubble, spotted the wall of Khapar in the distance against the starry sky, and crept toward it.

The momentary exhilaration of freedom gave way to heart-thumping terror as he hurried away. Only a small dagger for a weapon. No place to go, with Sinwo on Naelis's side. No bag. He winced at the last. Never mind it. Hardly useful if he was dead. Still, the loss tore at him even as he fled. Every shadow was an inquisitor, every hiss of the wind a whisper. Then he sensed something behind. Another phantom, probably. Then it seemed to move off to the side. No, not move, it was a second. People. Inquisitors. Then another ahead, and another. All around.

Something struck the stone at his feet. A short, metal bar. He jumped aside as a second flew past and struck a wall where he'd been standing. Abandoning caution, Jeld ran, weaving and vaulting through and over the ruins. Glimpses of gray and black robes flickered in and out of view all around. He ran faster still.

A figure in gray burst out from a corner right in front of him. Jeld's dagger was out—catching a sword before he'd even thought to draw it. The attacker pulled back his sword and swiped again. Jeld dodged, slipped inside his assailant's guard, and stuck his dagger up through an armpit. Giving his dagger a twist, he pulled it free and ran.

Then another was upon Jeld, a black robe wielding two knives. Jeld dodged the first, caught the wrist bearing the second. He lashed out toward an exposed neck, but hesitated. That wrist... it was so thin. The black robe, short stature. Just children. Jeld turned his dagger and struck the back of the young trainee's head with the hilt.

Jeld cried out as something bit into his arm. He spun. Another black robe, a thin, bloody sword in hand. Jeld dodged two more thrusts, drew out his attacker's blade with a low feint, and slashed him across the hand. The trainee's sword fell and Jeld slammed his fist into the kid's jaw.

Jeld shouldered past, but a gray robe and another black robe were there. Black Robe's blade shot out. Jeld deflected, hesitated again, winced as his kindness earned a shallow gash down his cheek. He parried a second strike, feinted with the best projection his frantic mind could manage, and drove his dagger through Gray's shoulder.

Jeld fell back, froze, and spun. He got his arm up just in time for a bo to crack against it. An explosion of pain and his dagger fell from his numb grip. He staggered back, foot catching something, and went down, bloody cheek slapping against the sooty stone.

He rolled, a sword clicking against the stone where he'd been, only to find High Acolyte Chontri standing over him once again. Beside her, still dressed only in underclothes, was the young trainee Jeld had hit with a chamber pot. Jeld cursed himself a fool. No kindness goes unpunished.

He scrambled to his feet, but weapons leveled all around him. Two gray robes, two black, the trainer in white, and his cell guard, who had acquired a short sword. Jeld's eyes fixed on Naelis's acolyte. Was she an inquisitor? He thought not, but she certainly knew how to swing a bo. It hardly mattered. Too many.

"Who are you?" Chontri asked.

"You know who I am," Jeld said.

The bo cracked against Jeld's back. He cried out and rolled onto his side.

"Who!" the woman spat.

"Arvin Emry," Jeld groaned.

"Who sent you?"

"No—" Jeld broke into a fit of coughing. "Nobody."

The bo came down onto one of his fingers with a crunch. He screamed, spilling over onto his back.

"Nobody sent me! I came on my own!"

Again the woman swung. Jeld rolled, grabbed the woman's leg, and bit. She shrieked, then her bo came down again. Pain exploded in Jeld's temple. Everything went white. His mind spun, just a haze. He was holding something. Biting something? A taste in his mouth. Blood. He was fighting. Dreams if he knew why, or who, but damned if he was going to let go. He sunk his teeth deeper still. Blood welled through his teeth into his mouth. Someone shrieked louder. Chontri. High Acolyte Chontri, that's who he was fighting.

Kicks knocked the wind from Jeld. Grips clamped upon his legs and arms and tugged at him, but still he clung to the woman, nails too now digging into her leg. She fell. Jeld released his bite and clawed his way toward the woman's throat, but he was dragged off. Then the grips were gone and he was free. Open air rushed past. Then he crashed hard into a pile of rubble with a cry.

High Acolyte Chontri scrambled to her feet. "Enough of Sinwo's games!" she roared. "Kill h—"

Gasps and cries rose up from the group. Jeld managed to turn his head and found his former cell guard standing over High Acolyte Chontri's still form, his eyes wide and sword bloody.

"Y-you killed her!" a black robe shouted.

"What have you done, Fhide!" a gray robe girl said, knuckles tight around one of those throwing bars.

"It was all lies," Fhide breathed, eyes wide. "The coming destruction. The terrible things they say we must do." He turned to the girl. "We can do better!"

The others had all turned from Jeld to face Fhide. Jeld knew it was his chance to flee. He tried to rise, tried to crawl, tried to do anything, but he had nothing left. He sagged against the stones.

"You've gone mad," the gray robe girl said venomously, changing her grip on her throwing bars.

"No! Think! Think for yourself, this is all wrong! Why should we believe darkness is light just because a woman who enslaved us said to believe?"

"She warned us of this," another gray robe with two knives said. "Some will not be strong enough to bear the burden. To do what must be done no matter the cost."

"You can't see… She has been poisoning us since childhood. You must look past it."

"No," said the gray robe with knives, turning to Jeld. "I think it was this boy who poisoned you."

Jeld's eyes fell upon his fallen dagger. He took a breath and dragged himself toward it. His uncooperative fingers slowly wrapped around the end of the hilt. Still lying on the ground, he lifted the dagger up before him pitifully as the gray robe stalked closer. Behind him, another trainee struck the sword from Fhide's grip.

In a whirl of gray robes, the one with knives kicked the dagger from Jeld's hand. He stared down at Jeld, and Jeld wondered—back to the cell? That didn't seem half bad, now that he'd been beaten, stabbed, and had his finger broken. But the trainee's face hardened, and the knives flashed down toward Jeld.

"Enough!" a voice boomed, eastern accent thick even in the single word.

Jeld opened his eyes, looking past a dagger frozen before his face to a figure in white standing atop a broken wall. The figure's face was shrouded in shadows beneath a raised hood.

"Enough of this," the cloaked figure said. A woman's voice. "Your friend Fhide is quite right. You have progressed far enough to be granted some hard truths. And you'll not murder the intruder. He is High Priest Naelis's prize."

"But..." the gray robe girl began, "Fhide killed High Acolyte—"

"Good! If any of you try to harm Naelis's prize, I'll ask him to do the same to you. The acolyte did her duty. The final step in your training is always breaking free. Without free thought, you are more danger to this world than boon."

"But who are—"

"You will be told what you are meant to know," the woman scolded. "In time."

Jeld struggled to one knee, then climbed to his feet against what looked to have once been a statue. His broken finger was agony, the stab wound in his arm burning. Not as deep as he'd feared, it seemed, but it bled and hurt plenty. Every bit of him hurt, really. He pushed it aside, tried to focus his battered head. Didn't stand a chance of escaping. Like a limping doe surrounded by wolves, but if they were obligated to take him alive now, well, why not try. He began to backpedal, but froze as the newcomer lowered her hood. It was Tejani.

"Back inside, all of you," Tejani ordered, going to Jeld's side. "I will see this one sent off toward our high priest, and return here shortly to put things in order. My congratulations to you all for reaching this milestone. Now, off you go."

"He's dangerous," a boy in black robes said.

"I am dangerous," Tejani said icily.

A tad overdramatic, Jeld thought, but it had the desired effect. The boy said nothing further, nor did any of the others. Many bloodied and battered, they stalked back toward the door with limited glances.

"Tell Fhide to stay," Jeld whispered to Tejani.

"You," Tejani called. "Fhide. With me."

A muttering rose from the others but they melted into the ruins, leaving Fhide standing alone in the darkness with his former prisoner and the strange new master. Jeld picked up the dagger he'd taken from Fhide, eyed the young inquisitor in the making, then tucked it away.

"Come on!" Jeld said, limping toward the city wall as fast as he could manage. "Before they change their minds. We'll circle and go into the city for now. The citadel won't be safe. Sinwo is behind all of this."

"You were right," Tejani breathed, following Jeld.

They both turned to find Fhide unmoving, a sword in his hand, staring at Tejani.

"Oh, she's a friend," Jeld said. "And... thank you, Fhide. I knew there was good in you, but I didn't think you'd, well, come around."

"She is not a master," Fhide said.

"No, she's not. A small lie. Your training is not entirely wrong. Sometimes you must do what is necessary. But you do what feels right, not brainwashing."

Fhide's eyes flickered in thought.

Jeld grit his teeth. No time for this. "Now, come on. I will share more when there is time."

Fhide returned an unnerving stare, like a black eyed snake deciding if you were food or not, before finally following. Jeld's anxiety faded at least a little as the distance grew between them and the other inquisitor trainees. He fell in beside Tejani, looking over at her. Didn't look much like a powerful acolyte of Naelis now. Just, Tejani, in a cheap looking white robe.

"How?" Jeld asked.

"You did this in many of the stories you told me," Tejani said. "Act with confidence. And you told me of the zealotry. I know something about it already from the universities, too. So, I became a master. Plus, I'm a mother. I know how to get a bunch of nasty kids to behave."

After many backward glances into the shadows, they finally reached the city wall and circled toward the gates. They soon found their path cut off by a steep rock fall spilling down toward the floor of the gulch below. They picked their way across it, Fhide catching Jeld twice as he slipped on the loose stones, then descended a steep but stable slope to the bottom.

Jeld collapsed onto the water-smoothed stones. "Let's go," he panted. Wincing, his eyes fell closed and did not reopen. "Need to move. Need to... move."

Jeld opened his eyes what seemed a moment later, squinting at something bright. He blinked, eyes adjusting, and realized it was the sky. Light clouds spotted an otherwise blue sky, the sun not yet visible above the surrounding mountains.

"Hungry? Sorry, no meal on the fire like our last trip," Tejani's voice came.

Jeld turned, wincing at the pain in his ribs, his head, his arm, his hand. Everywhere, really. Stiff and aching like one big bruise. He felt every bit as if he'd been beaten by a gang of evil children, locked in a cage for a while, then beaten by more evil children.

Tejani was holding out a stick of jerky to him. Fhide sat beside her, staring at Jeld. He had a sizable lump on the side of his head where Jeld had struck him with a chamber pot. Jeld accepted the jerky and took a bite. He stiffened at a jolt of pain, discovering a loose tooth with his tongue. The other side of his mouth felt alright, and he managed to bite off a piece.

"Sorry about the head," Jeld said to Fhide before his gaze returned to the bright sky. "I don't remember settling in for the night. We shouldn't have stopped out here."

Tejani smiled. "Not settled. You more... fell over."

Jeld pulled off the robe he'd stolen from Fhide and looked himself over. Someone had bandaged his arm. Tejani, judging by the white swash of cloth and the matching tear in her robe. His finger was black and blue around a makeshift splint, and he was covered in bruises and cuts, stiff from the swelling.

He struggled to his feet and tossed Fhide the robe. "Thanks for the nap. Ready?"

They continued through the gulch and out into a broader valley at the foot of the plateau bearing Khapar.

"Master Sinwo could be watching for our arrival," Tejani said.

"Suppose he'd know to send riders after us if we didn't arrive anyway, then. Regardless, we need supplies, maybe a few days' rest."

Jeld gestured to Tejani to hold back from Fhide, who was leading a ways ahead.

"I'm not leaving until Master Sinwo is dead," Jeld whispered. "And until I've brought down that whole place."

"The citadel?" Tejani asked, eyes widening.

"No. The caves."

"Ah." Tejani looked only slightly less concerned. "How?"

"Not sure yet. If you can become the leader of a cult of Idolic murderers, I figure I'll manage somehow."

Tejani smiled. Ahead, Fhide slowed and they rejoined him. Jeld felt a stab of guilt as he eyed their ever-vexed companion.

"I truly am sorry," Jeld said. "Not just for the chamber pot, but for everything."

Fhide seemed to withdraw within himself. At first Jeld thought he was fighting back tears or even anger, but no, he was merely uncomfortable. Jeld wondered if the inquisitor trainee had ever before been treated like a person, or been given an apology.

"Your gift," Fhide said finally. "You touch minds?"

"Yes, Something like that. Read emotions, mostly, but... pull on them too."

"But the cell..."

Jeld squinted ahead at what looked to be the road rising to the gates of Khapar. "Ah. Yes, that's new."

"Your cell was empty. You made me see this?"

"What?" Tejani gasped. "You did it?"

"It's all related," Jeld said. "I just played to your fears. And before that, tried to make you more receptive to me. I'm sorry."

"You only helped me hear the truth," Fhide said.

"I hope so. I don't know everything, but I do know Naelis is evil."

Fhide's eyes grew distant, then he nodded. "Yes."

They reached the road and passed into the city. They bought a room above the pub they'd gathered gossip from on first reaching

Khapar so many days before. There, they spent the day resting, gathering supplies, and plotting, with certain details left unsaid in Fhide's presence. All were settling in for the night when a knocking sounded at the door.

Jeld's hand moved to a sword they'd purchased at the market. Fhide turned to Tejani for instruction. The knocking came again and Jeld stood.

"Go away," Jeld barked like a regular.

"You have a visitor, Arvin Emry," a muffled voice said through the door.

Jeld exchanged a look with Tejani, then waved Fhide toward the side of the door. He reached out with his sense and found two presences, one unmistakable. He opened the door and there stood Master Sinwo, his usual attendee at his side.

Tejani gasped, and Fhide nearly tripped over himself trying to both bow and assume a fighting stance.

"Corr!" Master Sinwo laughed joyously. "You did it, then! Wonderful, just wonderful." He nodded to the others in turn. "Tejani. Fhide. We must talk."

Again Fhide looked to Tejani, who in turn glanced at Jeld. Jeld narrowed his gaze at the old master. Somehow the idea of killing Sinwo felt wrong despite the man's deeds, like chopping down an ancient tree. Well, he didn't have to decide now. He pulled the door wider and stepped aside. Sinwo waved for his attendant to stay outside then entered, one light tap of his cane after another.

Master Sinwo fell into the chair Jeld had been occupying and bid them sit with a nod. They did, Fhide only after an impatient wave from Tejani.

"A most impressive little operation from a most odd trio," Master Sinwo said. "And quite a predicament this leaves me in. Ah, but never mind that. Tell me, Corr, I'd hear of your achievement directly from you."

"This program ends now," Jeld said.

Master Sinwo's smile faded. "I have long considered our last conversation." He eyed Fhide and Tejani, then turned back to Jeld. "Vincet's betrayal, you know this to be true?"

"From his own diary."

Sinwo nodded, then sighed. "Then we must do as you say. And as Naelis is already trying to kill you, perhaps I shall blame you for it."

"You agree? Where was all this when you were condemning me to die down there!" Jeld's hand clenched around the grip of his sword. "I should just k—"

"Now, now. I had not yet fully made up my mind, but I did not condemn you to death. You achieved a level of psychological manipulation not seen since Kelthid lived, the leader of the inquisitor program is dead, and you are quite alive. I would say things have gone quite swimmingly for you."

Jeld huffed. "You can't be serious?" He pulled aside his collar to show the bandage wrapping the stab wound on his upper arm, then waved his splinted finger. "Would you like to take credit also for the beating I took while Chontri interrogated—"

Jeld's eyes widened, then flicked about as his thoughts churned. "She didn't know who I was. You didn't tell her..."

"Nor Naelis," Master Sinwo said.

Jeld shook his head. "It was a test..."

"For the most part. Your capture was not my doing, but I made the best of it."

Jeld stared at Sinwo, for the first time seeing the depth of the old master's obsessions. He stood and leveled a sword at Master Sinwo.

The old man's breath caught and he shifted in his chair. Surprise looked very out of place on him.

"End the inquisitors," Jeld said icily. "Save what few you can. The youngest, maybe. Do what you must with the rest. Do it, or I will return, and I will kill you."

Surprised maybe, but if Master Sinwo was scared, he didn't show it. In fact, he looked proud. Gleeful, even. Jeld had half a mind to at least hit him out of principle.

"Yes, I think you will," he said finally. "I will see it done."

Sinwo dug in his robe and produced Jeld's bag. He rubbed its smooth leather, then sighed and held it out to Jeld. "Keep it safe. I fear Naelis's obsession with it is more than academic. He sees power there, somehow."

Jeld took his bag, a wave of relief washing over him.

"You go to kill him now?" Sinwo asked. "It would save us both a great deal of trouble."

Jeld lowered his sword. "Easier said than done, thanks to your inquisitors. But I don't mean to tell you my whereabouts."

Master Sinwo frowned, managing at least to look a little ashamed. "I understand." He cleared his throat. "Well, in case you happen to be returning to your allies in the west, you should know there's been unsettling news."

Jeld's stomach twisted. "Go on."

"There was a battle. Havaral betrayed Princess Liraelle. Her army was massacred."

Jeld went still. "And Lira? The princess?"

"Not seen since. Maybe fallen. Maybe escaped. Some fear... taken."

Jeld's gaze fell. So much in those words. Joy—she'd made it out of Glendmill alive. Anguish—she was gone again, mission or worse. A swell of pride—she'd gotten her army. She'd lost it.

Tejani wrapped an arm around him. "I will go with you."

With him where? She was right that he would search for Lira, of course, no matter how slim the chance. Probably better she was killed than captured by Naelis. Did that make it wrong to still hope for the capture? Whatever the case, he'd search. Whatever the case, Naelis had to die.

Jeld forced a smile, but shook his head. "You are kind. But no, I think you wish to stay. Finish here. Whatever comes of your training, I think you have a place here."

Tejani pursed her lips, then gave a nod.

Jeld turned to Fhide. "Will you stay and help with the others like you? They may respond better to one of their own. Or you can come with me, if you want."

Fhide considered a moment. "I will stay."

"There will be... difficult choices, for some of the trainees."

"We do what must be done."

Jeld frowned, but nodded, his mind on Tovar. "Yes. We do."

CHAPTER TWENTY

Even a week away from Fallstival, signs, doors, and no few folk were decorated in the Fallstival colors. Jeld couldn't help but feel a hint of nostalgia, though it brought more melancholy than anything else. It had been three days since he'd arrived in Tovar, and each day had seen him passing by the theater by chance. He ached to rejoin his family there, but that would only put them at risk.

At the surface level, the city seemed to have regained its vibrance. It was cleaner, far more so than Jeld had ever seen before, and busy as well. People no longer looked down, no longer scuttled like rats, and Jeld couldn't have been more irritated by it. He hadn't known what bothered him more, that Naelis's methods had worked, or that the people might love him for it.

But it wasn't long before he saw through it. Through the heads held high. Through the city's sparkle. It was all shallow, fake, like a facade in one of Director Sammel's plays. Some knew it, just characters in the show. Others, a tension. An anxiety that came with being lucky enough to have landed on the right side of the wall. Of living beneath a cloud of oppression, even if it wasn't now raining. Of course, there were the few whose spines were held straight not by such worries, but by faith in Naelis at worst, or at best an easy disregard for those on the receiving end of injustice.

Jeld's gaze lingered on a girl with dark hair and blue eyes beneath the green hood of the Mother. It wasn't Lira of course. It never was, nor would it ever be, but always he looked despite himself. He tore his eyes away from the girl. Focus. Focus on the real search, and that meant getting in with the resistance, either to find her, or avenge her.

Thus far he'd managed only to scare off the few supposed resistance fighters he'd tracked down. So, just the day before, he'd changed course. He needed to make himself *useful* to this resistance if he had any hope of gaining their trust, and nothing made one more useful than information.

Jeld circled past a crowd in a small public square. Atop a small stone platform at the gathering's center, two priests in red bearing long daggers flanked a bearded man in travel clothes. Two watchmen with red swatches over one shoulder held several shackled prisoners behind the platform. Jeld wrestled a scowl from his face.

"Bear witness! Bear witness!" called one of the priests. "Jaim was once lost, but embracing Vincet's wisdom has saved him! Bear witness!"

The bearded man spoke next. "For... for many years I—I traded my life away, one drink at a time. But then I opened my heart to Vincet, and my ear to... his wisdom. I want for nothing now. I thirst only for water, and to pass on his blessings. Vincet is merciful. Our high king is merciful. Thank—oh, thank you!"

He stepped off the platform then glanced back over his shoulder. One of the red priests waved him off, and the man hurried through the crowd, people laying hands on him as he passed. Then the watchmen shoved another man onto the platform, this one white faced and shaking.

"Bear witness! Bear witness!" a priest called again. "There is mercy in life. But so too is there mercy in death. Mercy for those carrying the burden. Mercy for those who would wear the scars."

The prisoner on the platform cried out and began to sob. The anguish shot through Jeld and he gasped. He shouldn't have felt anything, tight as he'd been keeping his walls, but so strong was the man's anguish that it was like trying not to hear a loud noise. He clenched them tighter still.

Jeld hurried from the square, far too aware of what the priests would do next. Reborn, the red priests called their order. Another cult of Naelis's like the Sayers before them, only this one was not some obscure and ridiculed sect hijacked by Naelis, but the Crown's own. This one did not preach purity for goodness sake, but rather under threat of execution.

He turned down a narrow alley he knew to offer a good changing spot. A nook at its end was mostly shielded from view and well cloaked in the long shadows of the evening sun. He pulled a watchman's uniform out of his bag through his collar and donned it. He waited until ninth bell to give the outgoing watch shift ample time to get drunk, then emerged a watchman. Then he made his way to a tavern, above which hung a sign of a lantern dangling from a halberd. Once called the Dangling Lantern, the watchmen referred to the place now only as Dangle's.

Jeld groaned as he sunk into a chair at one of the many tables packed with watchmen. Hanging his head, he pinched between his eyes.

"Jeppy," a man greeted.

Yenny was the watchman's name, and it was no accident Jeld had sat beside the loose lipped old watchman.

Jeld feigned surprise. "Oh. Hey. Sorry, it's been a day."

"Ain't it always," Yenny said, then threw back his tankard, holding up a finger to bid Jeld wait, and finally wiping his gray beard with a sleeve. "Mm! And now we've got the high king doing this blazin' parade next week? As if we weren't busy enough, right?"

Jeld grunted his agreement and looked about the room. "That why it's so rowdy in here today?"

"Didn't ya hear? We finally got one. Really high up, I hear. And he broke!"

"Oh yeah? Got some names, then?"

"More than names. There's to be a meeting at the old brewhouse tomorrow. We'll snag a good lot, I'm told, and a good lot more leads from them. Might bring the whole bleedin' resistance down."

Jeld took two drinks from a serving girl, passing one to his fellow watchman and giving the girl two copper pebs. "Hope Naelis had the sense to keep the parade up the hill someplace?"

Yenny shook his head. "If only. Straight down the ave from hilltop, a quick stop at the north temple, then it's on down to Riverside."

"*Khapar*," Jeld cursed. "Can't keep a rotten shoe safe there. What's the route?"

"It's not half as bad as it used to be around there, but yeah. It's, ah... south on Shambley, down Kingsway, onto Docksbound, south on Riverfront. Loop back around at the square there."

"Not bad," Jeld said. "You on the route, then?"

"Jeppy boy, we'll damn near all of us be on the route."

Jeld grunted his agreement. "Well, at least we got that broken resistance leader to celebrate."

They raised their glasses and drank to that. Jeld excused himself after just one drink, citing a date. In truth, he replaced his watch uniform with his old courier getup, penned a few letters for his next task, and made for the old brewhouse Yenny had mentioned.

Jeld found the place at the back of a quiet little square just as he'd recalled. Resisting the urge to feel for people inside, he marched right up to the door and knocked. Best to look purposeful. Just a courier. Nobody answered and he knocked again. Still nothing, so he gave it a push, to no avail.

He turned, looking about as if checking he had the right place, then made his way down an alley to the side door. Another knock, another tug, then a click as his picks found their mark. It was completely dark inside, a good sign it was vacant given the relatively early hour, but no guarantee. Jeld slipped inside, closing the door silently behind him. He waited in the darkness, listening.

It was only then, standing in the darkness, that Jeld remembered he was supposed to be making contact, not sneaking about. Old habits. How quickly they took over. Only a small part of his years, yet a huge part of his life. Of him. As much as all his years on the road somehow.

Well, now that he'd intruded it seemed silly to call out a hello. So, he produced his lamp and sparker. Sparks flitted a hundred pictures of the room in the blink of a squinting eye, then light stretched out around him as the lamp caught. Everything was pale, scratched old wood. The floors, walls, two long rows of barrels, and a row of shelves, all looking almost to have been cut from the very same tree and scarred by the same time.

Upon a desk he found a ledger with recent accountings. They'd turned exclusively to small beers by the look of things, no doubt part of Naelis's new laws against harder drinks. Not such a bad law, actually. Of course, his father probably would merely have drunk more to compensate. Still, that would have kept him in the pub longer, so, a good law indeed.

Completing his search of the lower level, he searched several rooms upstairs but found nothing of note. He muttered a curse as he descended the stairs. Another day wasted, not a single step closer to Lira. He had half a mind to march straight to the theater, caution aside, and see what Krayo knew. Probably knew plenty. But no, best keep them safe. He'd return to the brewhouse tomorrow and try again. Back at the entrance, he blew out his lamp, tucked it away, and pulled the door open.

Figures stood silhouetted in the doorway. Jeld jumped back, throwing the door closed, but a hand caught it and the figures pressed in. One in the back uncovered a lamp. There were three of them.

"Wait!" Jeld said, backing toward a row of barrels. "I'm on your—"

"Resist, resist, resist!" one shouted, the others joining in.

One of them lunged forward and grabbed at Jeld with a big open hand. Jeld jumped aside. Forcing his hand from the hilt of his knife, Jeld instead punched the man in the chin. This seemed barely to bother the fellow, who came at him again without pause. He tensed to jump one way, but the second man was there, leaping at him. His heel scraped against the wooden floor as he turned his weight and vaulted over a row of barrels, the men crashed into each other.

"I know who you are," Jeld said, breath quick and heart pounding. "I'm on your side. I can help."

The third man was circling behind.

"Naelis will be in a parade next week," Jeld said quickly. "On Falls-day. I know the route."

Across the row of barrels, the closest one hesitated, but it was gone just as fast. "Lies!"

"Please, we can—"

Just then, shouts came from the doorway. "Drop your weapons! Lay down or I'll lay you down, rats!"

"Down! Get down!" another voice called.

Watchmen stormed inside. Two, three, four. *Eight.* Eight watchmen, swords drawn. They charged in a tight formation toward the resistance fighter bearing the lamp. The fighter drew a knife as the two leading watchmen raised their swords to strike.

"Khapar," Jeld cursed, mostly at himself for even thinking of anything other than flight, but he was already vaulting back over the barrels. Pulling a sword from his collar, he darted past the resistance fighter and slashed through the flank of the lead watchman. A second turned his attack toward Jeld, who danced back and punched the lamp out of the resistance fighter's hand. With a bright flash suddenly they were in darkness, only a hint of light from the cracked doorway.

Madness all around. Clatters, shouts, screams. By the sound of things, the watch formation had dissolved, the melee spreading all around. Backing toward the wall, Jeld reached out with his Idolic sense, Inquisitors be damned. Just chaos, a storm of emotion and thought, no better than the mess of noise. He focused, and individual auras took shape, but friend and foe were the same tangle of fear and shock.

"Resist, resist, resist!" Jeld shouted.

Pride swelled in three of the auras, and Jeld smiled as he crept toward one of the others. A board creaked beneath his feet and the smile vanished as he jumped backward. The tip of a blade sliced across his cheek. Jeld chased it with his own sword, finding meat and bone. Then came the sound of a sword clattering to the ground. Terror and agony slammed against Jeld's sense, chilled him, froze him. He steeled himself and slammed his sword down with a wet crunch, the presence flickering out like a candle.

Jeld started toward where three watchmen seemed to be sneaking up on a resistance fighter. The floor creaked as the resistance fighter stalked toward him.

"Easy," Jeld whispered. "It's me. Three behind you."

To Jeld's surprise, the fighter stopped. With that, Jeld darted around him and into the fray. Images of attacks flashed in his mind, blades slashing and piercing, kicks, grabs. His sword struck something soft. A scream. Jeld jumped back, crashed into something—the barrels—and went down. Rapid footsteps. Jeld rolled, felt his way behind the other barrels, and came back to his feet, crouching low.

"It's me, you blazin' tit!" someone yowled.

Jeld stalked back in and slashed hamstrings, stabbed a man through the back, cut a throat. Tears and blood streamed down his face as he and his blade flicked in and out of the fray, until only three auras remained. Three frantic breaths, made louder for their efforts to be silent.

With a twist of his sparker, again Jeld lit his lamp. Blood and bodies littered the floor. Jeld counted eight dead watchmen before turning his attention to the resistance fighters. They had somehow managed to stay together and were huddled in a corner by two dead watchmen, knives at the ready. One was skinny and bearded, another cleanly shaven with huge forearms. The third, a short and heavyset man with no neck, was bleeding heavily from one of his arms. All were staring at Jeld.

"Still think I'm a watchman?" Jeld asked, desperate to make light of the horrors.

"Who are you?" the skinny one asked.

"I just want to help."

The man with the forearms cinched a bandage on his friend's injured arm.

"Easy!" the injured man said, wincing. "Alright, you. Help us to our room. Out the front. They always post more men at the back. On raids, at least."

Jeld obliged and soon was walking the dark streets behind the three men. No watchmen had awaited them outside. Between the frequent backward glances of the trio, Jeld snuck a fresh shirt from his bag and donned it over the bloody one. After a hushed exchange, they led him to a nondescript inn. Jeld looked on as they paid for a room at the bar, gathering his new friends didn't trust him enough to reveal their true dwellings. Good, he didn't want to work with idiots.

The skinny man shut the door of the room behind them. "Now who in dreams are you?" he blurted. "How did you kill all those watchmen?"

"I can fight," Jeld affirmed. "Now look, I need to talk to a leader about this parade. With the route, we can set up an ambush. We can end Naelis. But you'll need me."

"Just give us the route," said the injured one, sitting on a bed and reworking his bandage. "You're good at fighting in the dark. We're good at ambushes."

"I need to help."

"If you really wanted him dead you wouldn't care who did it."

"It's not that," Jeld said quickly, though it probably was that. "He'll be surrounded by inquisitors. I can help."

"You can fight inquisitors?" said the skinny one, still by the door.

Big Forearms sat in a chair, broad shoulders stooping "No. Nobody can fight them."

"But he—"

"It doesn't matter," No Neck said. "We ambush, not fight. Look, the captains wouldn't put a newcomer on something this big. Too many lives at risk."

"Let me meet with your captain," Jeld said. "He can decide. I doubt he'd be pleased to hear you turned away a guy who could kill eight watchmen in the dark."

"Six. But no, he wouldn't be. Tell me, where did you get the route? We knew about Naelis in the parade, but not the route."

Jeld hesitated.

The man smiled. "You don't trust us either."

"It's more than trust, it's just... protecting secrets, for both our sake."

The short man gave a short laugh. "So you *do* understand." He rubbed the back of his head. "Look, give me the route, and I'll figure out a role for you. No meeting a captain, not involved in planning, not turning the knife, but involved. Take it or leave it."

Jeld frowned. They'd have a better chance at Naelis if they let him in. And oh, to at least *be there* to watch Naelis bleed out his last. But, with the route and a bit of luck, they'd probably manage. Naelis's death would be more than enough.

"Do you have any intelligence on Princess Liraelle?" Jeld asked. "Does Naelis have her, or...?"

"Hmm? The princess? No, still thought to have been killed in the battle near Plemenol when Havaral turned."

Jeld nodded distantly, took a breath, then nodded more firmly and extended his hand. "Alright. Deal."

The squat man twisted his uninjured arm over and gave Jeld a firm shake with his plump little paw.

"Right," the man said. "I'll set up a letter drop for you so I can get you the details in... say, three days. Now, let's have the route."

Jeld pulled a slip of paper from his pocket, gave the three of them another look, and handed it over. "You'd better make this count."

The short one detailed how they'd reach Jeld with orders, then they exchanged pleasantries before Jeld bid them farewell. The night dragged on as Jeld watched the front and side doors of the inn from a dark alley. He spotted what looked to be the skinny one exiting with a larger group, but lost him after a few blocks. Frustrated as he was as he made his way back to his room at another inn, he couldn't shake a smile at their having managed to lose him.

***

Jeld pressed through the colorful crowd parading down Hillside. The ground was an icy slush beneath Jeld's feet where the crowds had stomped away the snows that blanketed the ground earlier that evening. Still the snow fell, bright in the countless warmly lit windows throughout the city, to land upon the heads and shoulders of the dense crowd as if upon a thick forest canopy.

Already looping back toward Hillside, the front of the parade had slipped ahead once again, and once again Jeld squeezed into an alley to pull ahead. Jeld cursed the resistance fighters as he pressed through the still crowded alley. That afternoon he'd checked the letter drop that should have contained his orders, but found it empty. Empty, as it had been the dozen odd times he'd checked over the last few days. He could appreciate a good lie, but damn that chubby, neckless little man.

Jeld cut back onto the main route and climbed up onto a brick window sill as the parade approached. A company of knights in gleaming plate led the procession. Jeld winced again at the perhaps thirty red priests walking behind them, a desecration of the Fallsday he remembered. The King's Guard followed, a small group of knights in gleaming crimson armor and white capes. Behind them rode a full twenty inquisitors. Jeld shivered, shutting his mind tight.

The inquisitor at the front turned his head to reveal a long scar running down his face. A memory flashed in Jeld's mind. An inquisitor, staring from the distance, blood running from a deep gash across his eye. The gates of Tovar slamming shut behind him, Dralor left for dead. The same inquisitor who would later injure Benam on their flight toward Delvarad.

A tightness gripped Jeld's chest. Sweat prickled under his collar despite the chill. Any moment one of the inquisitors would turn and lock a cold gaze upon him. The ambush would be blown, and he'd be on the run. Captured. Dead, maybe, or back into his bag. He clenched his mind shut tighter still.

Then he could see High Priest Naelis through the crowd. He wore a jovial smile and fur-lined white robe, looking every bit the part of a wise and kindly old priest-king. Jeld's glare deepened. From the front he wouldn't be far from striking distance. A couple steps and a jump would close the distance. His heart pounded faster. He could do it, he told himself. He could end Naelis. Protect Lira, if still she lived. Avenge her, if she didn't. Avenge Avandria. Set the world right.

His eyes flicked back to the inquisitors. No, he mustn't forget their speed. Perhaps he could slip past one, if only for a blink, but never so many. And were he to fail, it would spoil whatever the resistance was planning, though it was looking increasingly likely they'd decided against it too.

His thoughts drifted back to the last time he'd stood beside the Fallsday parade wishing death upon the Crown. Prince Dralor, that time. Raf had saved him, then. He wondered then after Raf. Perhaps he'd have to stop by her candle shop soon.

Suddenly Naelis's carriage and the entire procession stopped. A moment later, cries rose up from the crowd ahead, then watchmen burst from two tall buildings on either side of the street. Bloodied men were shuffled out at sword point, maybe four, though it was tough to see through the crowd. They carried broken bows.

They were rounded up at the front of Naelis's carriage. The old high priest himself carefully stood atop the bench with the help of two inquisitors flanking him. He held up a hand and incredibly the massive crowd fell silent.

"Wickedness does not stop even on Fallsday. But, most importantly, nor does kindness." He turned to the captured men. "You who would murder, who would put an arrow through my heart as if again through the mother herself anew, who would end peace and fling this kingdom back into war... you will be spared a traitor's death this Fallsday. We all have darkness, but together our light shines brightest!"

The crowd cheered. The would-be assassins were marched off by a sizable contingent of watchmen, and the parade continued along. Within a block, the crowd was quieting. After two, there might never have been any disturbance at all. Like Jeld had not just had his hopes completely shattered.

Jeld stepped down from his vantage and stared past it all as his thoughts spun. They'd failed. They'd turned him away, and they'd failed for it. Only, the watch hadn't merely stopped the operation, it seemed they must have known about it. The resistance was compromised, then? There seemed no other explanation. And had he been as involved as he had wished, he'd be among those being marched to whatever Naelis's mercy looked like.

Compromised. The resistance, the only thing left to at least buzz in Naelis's ears, and it was crumbling. Well, he'd bleedin' do it himself, then, and he'd do more than buzz. He had the bag. Getting into the palace would be trivial with his little hand crawly trick. Probably he could make it all the way into Naelis's chamber if he took his time with it. But did Naelis keep inquisitors in his chambers? And was it worth the risk that he might be delivering the bag Naelis sought straight to him?

When Jeld came to, he found himself walking the still busy streets of Midtown. The parade had ended but thinner crowds continued the tradition of snaking through the city. Jeld walked on with them, even sharing a smile with a pretty girl with a green hood and an unstrung bow upon her back. He hoped the festivities would raise his spirits. He wasn't dead, couldn't he just move on and live a life?

Alas, it was not long before he slipped away and returned to his room. He wasn't halfway back before he'd resolved what to do next. He stopped at an inn and penned a note. Give him thirty loyal men, fighters, and he'd get them inside the palace to kill Naelis. But this time, he'd settle for nothing less than talking to the man in charge. He folded it and marked the corner with a line of ink, then handed it to the young barkeep as the squat resistance fighter had instructed.

Between check-ins with this barkeep for an answer, he spent much of the next week frequenting the watch pub, Dangle's, though he wasn't too sure what he was even looking for. Perhaps some vulnerability in palace security, or another tidbit to ingratiate him to the resistance—or what was left of it.

Days later, he sat down at the bar and stared past its scratched surface. It wasn't until he reached for his long untouched drink that he found a letter waiting for him. He glanced to the barkeep, finding the man cleaning tankards with his back turned. Jeld forced himself to move slowly as he opened the letter, then read.

They wanted to meet him! He read on. Sit on a bench beneath the statue of the Mother in Fletcher's Market. Someone in a purple cap would join him, then lead him to a meeting. At last bell. Last bell!

Slapping a coin atop the bar, he jumped from his seat and ran out the door. Sweat was dripping down his forehead by the time he reached the square. He spotted the statue, then the bench beneath it. After a lap around the square to observe, he finally sat as instructed.

Jeld looked from face to face, hat to hat as he waited. The last bell chimed. A woman sat beside him. No purple hat, just a barmaid's apron sticking out from beneath a heavy winter coat. She looked not much older than Jeld, thin with short hair and big brown eyes. After a while, Jeld shot an annoyed look her way only to find she had donned a purple cap.

Ignoring him, she rose and walked off toward the edge of the square. Jeld waited a good professional time before following after her with a well-practiced disinterest. He thought he might have caught her glancing back through her dark hair as he tailed her through the streets, but if so it was impressive discretion.

Jeld followed her into a tavern, then immediately out the rear door and back into the night. He found her waiting just outside, where she took his hand and led him into another inn. Upstairs, she knocked on a door. It swung open. There were two men sitting just inside, swords in their laps. A thin black curtain had been draped across the back of the room, a man's boots visible beneath it.

The woman waved Jeld inside but he hesitated. The curtain was probably transparent from up close. Smart, actually. He had usually bagged heads for such arrangements, but that prevented one from seeing the visitor's face too, not to mention being highly suspicious when seen by others. He was again reminded he was dealing with professionals, but suddenly he wasn't so sure that was for the best.

Well, there was nothing for it now. He entered and the door closed behind him. A look over his shoulder told him the girl had remained outside. He faced the black curtain and a heavy silence ensued.

"Thank you for seeing me," Jeld said. "We share a common goal, and I'm certain I have a lot to offer."

At first there came no answer, then the man spoke in a voice rich with authority. "Leave me with him."

The two guards shuffled uneasily.

"Do not fear," the man told his guards. "Now, go."

Exchanging a look, the guards departed, leaving Jeld alone with the man behind the curtain.

"Arvin Emry," the man breathed.

Jeld's eyes went wide. The man stepped around the curtain, and Jeld found himself staring slack-jawed at Prince Dralor Tovados.

Chapter Twenty-One

Despite having been reunited with his friends for two days, Jeld couldn't suppress a stupid smile as he looked about the theater den. In large part he was surprised by how little everything seemed to have changed. Everything in its place. Everyone still there, except for the pretty, young Tabe, who had gone chasing stardom.

There was a slightly different feel to the place, though. It had always been a safe haven for Jeld, a place to be warm and protected no matter the danger. But now, that danger had cast its shadow even here. Dimmed its flame, if only a little. Ewan had lost a hand in service to the resistance. The others too did their parts on that bigger stage. It was still the place Jeld knew and loved, but so too was it a battlefield tent full of beloved comrades.

"Did you say you *ordered* him?" Yelana asked.

Jeld shrugged sheepishly. "Threatened, maybe?"

Yelana gasped and fell speechless. On the cushy chair beside her, Alal laughed and shook her.

"You don't know Master Sinwo, he —he's not a man to be threatened!" Yelana said, actually sounding afraid. Either her accent had thinned, or Jeld's time in the east had accustomed him to it. Her beauty on the other hand had not diminished in the least.

"No, *you* don't know Jeld the inquisitor slayer," Hawss said. He'd grown taller, still handsome with eyes like a hawk and a crooked smile.

Jeld glanced at Cass in the chair beside Hawss for her inevitable grimace and was surprised to find her grinning.

"He doesn't care about some old robe," Hawss continued. "Everyone's always thinking old people are so special, but all they've done is not died for longer." He turned to Director Sammel. "Begging your pardon, sir."

Cass finally shook her head. Director Sammel only smiled, his eyes quickly returning to Jeld. Something about the kindly old director's gaze said he was looking back to the broken, ragged urchin he'd discovered lurking the theater walls like a rat. Jeld smiled, nodded, and turned away to stop the tears welling in his eyes.

Gruff old Erol grunted. "Boy is single-handedly taking down the inquisitors, and we're here doing propaganda shows for Naelis."

Evelyn waved the comment aside. "Erol, dear. You know we do more than our share."

Ewan leaned back and crossed his legs, then spoke in his theatrical voice. "I happen to think doing Naelis's shows makes our *off stage* work all the more sweet."

Jeld found himself watching Roba as she conversed with Erol. He wondered what Fen's last moments must have been like. A slow, tortuous gut wound? Something faster, like a blade through the heart? Even the quick death of a cut throat though... those moments helplessly watching your own lifeblood spurt out... And that damned thing people did, putting a hand over their gaping neck as if to hold the blood in. He pictured Fen doing it and felt his stomach twist. Roba began to turn toward Jeld and he quickly looked down before she might glimpse his thoughts.

Only then did he recall Master Edlin's lute in his idle hands. He rubbed its wood, strummed the strings lightly, then lost himself in a song. Eyes closed, the music poured from him. He kept his walls tight for fear of attracting inquisitors, not reading nor touching the minds around him, but he already knew these minds.

The lute sang to Roba's loss, and Ewan's. Of the shadow cast through their home, and the troupe's heroism and sacrifice. The music spoke of home and family, of arms open no matter the years between. He thought again of Fen, and wondered if Lira had been there with him at the end, if he'd watched her die, or she him. Again he saw fingers clasping at a cut throat, red spilling out between them, only this time it was Lira's hand. Lira's desperate eyes. Lira's paling face, Lira's wet, choking starved breaths.

Abruptly the notes soured and Jeld stopped. Blinking, he looked up to find everyone staring at him.

"Beautiful," Director Sammel breathed.

Master Edlin wiped his eyes. "I don't know that you hit a single note properly, but yes, beautiful nonetheless. You've come a long way."

"Lot of time to practice when I was stuck in a bag," Jeld answered.

"Yet another reason to always carry a lute with you."

"Actually I... borrowed Kelthid's."

Edlin gaped. "Kelthid's... the Traveler's lute?"

Jeld followed Roba's gaze to the hallway. Krayo Rusrivon stood there, just as he had when summoning Lira and him so long ago to plot the botched escape that would lead eventually to Lira's death.

"A word, Jeld?" Krayo asked.

Jeld gave another look to his companions, who all watched him still. He stood and joined Krayo, following him up the stairs to his office. The wall of windows overlooking the warehouse were shuttered for the winter and a small fire burned in a modest fireplace. A huge smile stretched across Ement's broad jaw as Jeld entered, and he patted an empty seat between him and Prince Dralor.

Dralor nodded to Jeld. The two had caught up at length on their reunion. The prince, it turns out, had become effectively the leader of the resistance. Krayo would not object to this classification, though in truth it was he who enabled it all. Dralor had told of his rescue by a fledgling resistance, his captivity in the prison camp, and a stay at some farm. Though he'd been elusive with details on the last, the pain in the prince's eyes was unmistakable.

Krayo took a breath, no doubt to get to business, but interrupted himself with a rare smile at Jeld. With nothing more said on the matter of Jeld's return, he began.

"They have another of our captains," Krayo said.

Ement straightened. "Another! That's three in as many weeks. Who is it?"

"Tolastha," Dralor said, eyes darting.

"There were many people captured in the parade," Jeld said. "Maybe someone gave a lead?"

"We cut those threads," Krayo said. "They won't lead to anyone anymore."

Dralor nodded. "Different cells, too. Different chains, even. Just as with the last captain."

"Same arm, though," Krayo said. "Do you think..."

"No, not Aarosh," Dralor said sharply. "More likely a coincidence. Pick any three captains and there's decent odds they're under Aarosh. Plus he takes on high risk missions, more likely to have issues."

"Dralor, we—"

"A message drop," Dralor interrupted. "The captains of those cells were communicating through a common drop. If it was compromised..."

Krayo frowned. "It shouldn't be shared. Not at that level."

"No, it shouldn't be. But that's what we scrapped together after cutting too many threads. I'll look into it. Maybe we can use this to feed bad intel if we're careful."

Krayo pursed his lips, then nodded. "I was hoping Jeld could wade into this."

"We could use the help," Dralor said, turning to Jeld. "And you want this?"

"Best start making myself useful," Jeld said. "Seems I'll finally be settling in."

They went on to discuss the details of Jeld's investigation, then a number of resistance matters. Dralor excused himself as the conversation moved to Krayo's other business. When they were finished, Erol gave Jeld a painful pat on the shoulder then retired, leaving Jeld and Krayo in the quiet office.

"So much has changed, and yet so little," Krayo said, leaning back in his chair.

Jeld's gaze fell. "It doesn't feel right just moving on when... others cannot."

"Why do anything at all, knowing we all meet the same end? It's all pointless, isn't it?"

Jeld blinked. "You truly believe that?"

Krayo frowned. "Not... entirely. I might agree there is no true purpose, but I can think of nothing worse than wasting this senseless existence doing nothing."

Jeld bit his lip. Krayo was not typically one to cite philosophy and abstract concepts, nor was he among the few Jeld cared to open up to. Still, he was glad for the companionship.

"And you choose to do this?" Jeld asked. "Vie for power and coin, own a theater, fund a resistance to your own boss? Why not walk away with your money, get yourself a nice plot of land and a fancy house somewhere. Servants, all that."

Krayo met his gaze. "To have no impact on the world? No control of it? To simply exist? No... to me that is worse than death. But I understand how some might find it appealing."

"Helping the resistance, that's about control too, then?"

"Somewhat, yes. Control. Decency."

Jeld bit his lip. "How can you help Naelis at the same time, though? All you do on the council, I mean. The trade, the logistics, all that."

"I think he'd do just as well without me. What I gain for the resistance far outweighs what I give Naelis." Krayo's eyes narrowed. "I'll dig the man's well, and one day, when he's most thirsty, I intend to shit in it."

"Ah..." Jeld said.

Krayo cleared his throat. "What of you? Will you be spending your unpaid wages on a mansion and a servant?"

Jeld considered. Was that what he desired? Did he not constantly dream of returning to his childhood trade and wagoning the open roads? Of crackling campfires, the chirp of crickets and frogs? The creak, rattle, and rock of the wagon beneath him? And yet, were he to achieve this dream, would he not inevitably heed the call of chaos and abandon it all? Maybe not if he had Lira at his side, but without her...

"I want to want that," Jeld said. "Another day, perhaps."

"Perhaps," Krayo said, himself looking distant. "I know this empire I've built is meaningless. Just a silly obsession. But I do hope to see it live on."

"It's not meaningless. Not anymore."

Krayo nodded, then took a breath. "Jeld, I'd like you to learn the business. Not just the covert stuff you already know, but the whole of the business. Trade, accounting, negotiation... proper business. And the guild management."

Jeld shifted uneasily in his chair. "Krayo, are you..."

"Fine. Fine, yes, I'm fine. Just planning for the future, and glad to have you back. In trades, a master might spend an entire lifetime training an apprentice. Business is no different, yet I'm well behind schedule. You may not know business, but having the right head for all this is more important."

"I'm... not sure, I really don't have a mind for... well, money. None at all, actually."

"And you think I do?"

"Ah... yes?"

Krayo smiled. "I care about strength. Survival. Independence, control. Winning too, petty as that is. Money is just the weapon. And the shield. And while Naelis lives, every coin you gain is one you can use against him. If there is something about the world or life you want to change, coin is the most powerful tool."

"It's a fine metaphor, but—"

"The power to give a street boy a chance."

Jeld wasn't sure if Krayo was going for a guilt trip or genuinely suggesting he might want to help fellow urchins, but more than likely both. Idols, between stopping people like Naelis and helping the forgotten, coin would indeed prove a vital weapon. He nodded to Krayo.

"Excellent," Krayo said stoically. "Do as you will for Dralor, I know there will be no keeping you from the resistance. Join me as you have time. We can formalize something later."

Jeld was surprised to find himself feeling pleased with the arrangement. Maybe it was the purpose he'd needed. Maybe merely the distraction he'd needed. He gave a half smile and nodded again.

"Thank you," he said.

Krayo held up a hand. "Wasn't it Vincet who said something about all acts being selfish?"

"I go away for a little while and now you're a philosopher?"

Krayo actually laughed, then spoke as Jeld reached the door. "Off to check on the captain situation?"

"Best not wait until tomorrow."

Krayo held his gaze. "You think it's Aarosh."

"I suppose it could just as easily be the message drop, but having never met this guy, yeah that's where I'll start."

Krayo frowned and was silent for a moment. "Do what you must."

Jeld nodded. "Good night."

***

The night sky was starless and the ground freshly blanketed in snow as Jeld made his way west to lower Hillside. He wore topper finery compliments of the theater prop room. Erol trailed just a step behind, dressed the part of a watchman. Together they stopped outside the door of an establishment. The sign beside the door was an intricately painted portrait of a man in a humorously large hat.

Erol looked to Jeld, who shrugged, then pounded on the door. Nobody answered, and he knocked louder.

"Oh open up!" Jeld yelled. "You want us to have a healthy relationship, do you not?"

The words could mean many things. The best kinds of words, those. Maybe just the words of an impatient topper keen to get his portrait done. Maybe a knock on the wrong door. Or, maybe an associate of those owed a favor come knocking.

The door opened. A tall, thin man with sloped shoulders stood in the doorway. He wore a white apron over a fine blue tunic, and looked back and forth between Jeld and Erol.

"Not sleeping after all?" Jeld said in a haughty toppertongue. "I'd hate to think you were trying to ignore me."

He pressed inside. Portraits lined the walls and filled several displays and easels about the studio. One canvas was lit by several candles, its paint still gleaming wet. It was a picture of a woman, eyes filled with pride and love turned down toward a half drawn child in her arms.

Jeld's resolve weakened, but he held character. Frowning distastefully, he inspected several portraits before settling into a high-backed chair at one of the easels. Forcing himself not to look back, Jeld heard the door shut a moment later.

"I'm sorry," Aarosh said. "I didn't know it was... you."

"Well, that's settled. Are you alone here?"

"Yes."

"Fine. Now, sit. I have need of you."

Aarosh took a few steps toward a nearby chair but hesitated. "This was... supposed to be settled."

"The more you cooperate, the faster it will be settled. Sit."

Aarosh glanced back to Erol looming just a step behind, then sat. "What of my family?"

"What of them," Jeld said.

"Are they... safe?"

"On the word of the Crown."

Aarosh shuffled uneasily. "Yes... but... you said last time that they would be released."

Ahh, and there it was already. Compromised and in the Crown's pocket.

"And they will be!" Jeld snapped, then took a breath and straightened his fancy tunic. "Let's not allow anything to change that. Now, we need more intelligence. What haven't you told me?"

"Nothing! Everything, I've told you everything."

"I want the whole chain, up and down, as far as it will go. Every last person."

"I've said all I know," Aarosh said, almost in tears. "I gave you the captains that I could. I gave you the drops that I knew. I even gave you the higher-up that I alone have. Nobody else even knows their higher up! You don't understand, there are many protections in place. Failsafes, disconnects, all manner of measures to ensure one person cannot bring down the resistance."

Jeld sighed a genuine sigh, but not for the reason his character might. He looked over to Erol then sighed again and waved Aarosh toward a door. Krayo would want him to do what must be done, but he'd rather Erol didn't see him like that. Erol had seen things. Been through much. He'd understand, but ever after his eyes would whisper, *murderer.*

"In there," Jeld said. "I'd speak with you in private on a sensitive matter."

Erol straightened. "Sir, I can't leave you to—"

"Enough. I'm confident our friend won't do anything foolish enough to endanger his family. Now, come."

Aarosh eyed Jeld, then set his jaw and went into the room. Jeld followed, meeting Erol's gaze as he closed the door. The room beyond looked to serve many purposes, with a desk, shelf of painting supplies, and a small bed. Jeld stopped mid step as he spotted a well-loved stuffed rabbit upon the bed, but he recovered and came to stand before Aarosh. Jeld noted a knife on the desk, and the slight step Aarosh took toward it.

"How could you turn against us?" Jeld said, dropping his topper accent.

Jeld felt little of the anger in his accusation. Of course the man would break to protect whatever small child had once snuggled the little toy rabbit upon the bed there. But Jeld needed the anger. He *needed* the anger to do what must be done.

Aarosh blinked, halting his discreet backpedaling toward the knife. "You're one of us..."

"Do you know how many will die because of this? How much it has cost us? Do you know what happens if we don't succeed?" Jeld's voice fell to a sharp whisper, his anger finally catching fire. "You are the reason the parade operation failed."

The words struck Aarosh like a blow. "They got it from a drop I gave them. Or... the higher up I gave. I never meant—I never told them about the plan. I never *knew* the plan."

"He'd be dead if not for you! He'd be dead!" Jeld's voice cracked at the last. He drew his long knife and took a step toward Aarosh.

"Please! I—I never wanted this. I am with you. I had no choice! They had my little girl! My little girl!"

Jeld's anger wavered. "I'm sorry. I... understand. I too am only doing what must be done." He took another step closer.

Aarosh's terror gave way to a sad resignation. The resistance captain swallowed hard and squared his slight shoulders.

"Wait," Aarosh said. "There is something you must know. The enemy has been monitoring the drops, and I think they found the source. I'm not sure how high they chased it, but I suspect they are close to the top. You must warn the others. Warn the leaders, whoever they are. Find them before the Crown does."

Meeting Aarosh's eyes despite his best efforts, Jeld nodded his thanks and took a final step into striking distance. Aarosh's legs struck the little bed and he stumbled to sit upon it. Jeld's eyes flicked to the little bunny upon the bed, then to his knife. *Do what you must*, Krayo had said.

He was no stranger to necessary evils, only... was it truly necessary? If this captain had no further information to divulge to the enemy, what danger was there in letting him live? Why kill him, if not for retribution? And retribution for what? Was it truly treachery to choose one's family over one's cause?

Jeld sheathed his knife. "Where are they keeping your family?"

***

Two days passed before Jeld had Aarosh's family free and the lot of them in a safehouse. To protect the family from reprisal, Jeld never told those at the safehouse who they were, but he'd been transparent with Krayo. While not pleased, his boss was also not overly displeased.

Another few weeks passed, with Jeld spending most of his time supporting Dralor's struggling resistance and learning the business with Krayo. The mood at the theater darkened every day, with each bringing a new host of captured members and compromised cells. What little time remained Jeld spent helping the theater crew run their shows, a time he cherished.

Jeld was seated on the bed in his old low-ender room, fiddling with his lute. Beside him lay an abandoned book on business by none other than Olind Emry, his would-be uncle from his time spying in the palace of Tovar. His eyes were heavy, but the sooner he slept, the faster the next day and all its pains would be upon him. Operationalizing new message drops and closing down compromised cells were not especially trying beyond the long hours, but to always be on the defensive weighed heavily. And to see the resistance endure blow after blow, loss after loss.

At first he was glad for the rare opportunity to strike at the Crown, taking out watch leaders or the rare topper, but these began to mar his spirit like black scars. He finally fell asleep, dreams haunted by Naelis being ever out of reach, Lira bleeding out on a battlefield, and the faces of his murdered enemies.

Krayo was already in his office with Dralor and Erol the next morning when Jeld entered with dreary eyes.

"There's been a letter from the Isles," Dralor said as Jeld sat.

"The Isles?" Jeld asked. "Does Queen Alaesh wish to trade finally?"

"It is not from Alaesh Ghallad. It is unsigned, but we think it could be Liraelle."

Jeld's breath caught.

Krayo held up a letter. "Whoever it was, they wrote to me. It seems they have convinced the Isles to open their arms to refugees of Naelis's terrors. And she—whoever it might be—wishes my aid in establishing secure communications and logistics to enable this."

"Why do you think it's her?" Jeld said, shaking his head. He snatched the letter and began to read.

"You'll see it's all very discreetly written, but the person thanked me for the aid in freeing their former *guild leader* and securing transportation of their *goods* to Delvarad. And of their trade deal between Havaral and Caldemoor nearly bankrupting them. All this before it goes on to an invitation from the Isles and bid for our assistance, equally disguised but clear enough. I can think of no other it might be from."

"She wishes to help the kingdom, but no longer seeks to control it," Dralor said distantly.

Jeld just shook his head for a time, then out burst a breath of laughter. She was alive. *Idols*, she was alive! He had to go to her. He'd make arrangements that very day, and ride out at dawn.

"Won't that be suspicious?" Erol said. "A bunch of people flocking to the Isles? Surely that would just invite Naelis to respond."

Dralor frowned in consideration. "It is not unheard of. Caerghallad did the same thing after the Vanishing Wars. They are proud of their neutrality and charity, but honestly I think they also like provoking us with their superiority."

Jeld looked at Krayo, the snake oddly quiet. "You're displeased. You wish me to stay."

"My mind is elsewhere," Krayo said. "It's..." He wrapped his fingers on the desk then sighed. "Dralor and I have decided to end most of our resistance efforts."

Erol whistled.

"What!" Jeld said. "No, you can't. You can't just give the city to Naelis."

"The city belongs to Naelis now, whether we like it or not. The network was compromised. Dralor cut the last of the main chains loose this morning. We'll retain just a few of our smaller cells, only the best. Do some good still, but not directly oppose."

Jeld turned to Dralor. "But... everything we discussed. Giving Naelis what he deserves. Saving the kingdom!"

Dralor pursed his lips. "We're now getting as many good people killed as we are saving. We'll follow Lira's lead, focus on aid, but nothing more."

Jeld's heart sank for just a moment before his mind returned to Lira.

"I know you'll be leaving, Jeld," Krayo said, then nodded to Dralor.

"We'll gather what's left of our network and their families," Dralor said. "Then you and I will lead them to the Isles."

Chapter Twenty-Two

Dressed the part of a young noble, Jeld brought his mount to a stop atop another rolling hill and looked back over his shoulder. His convoy stretched across the grassy countryside below. Dralor rode at Jeld's side in watch garb with the crimson bracers of a captain, looking instead at the path ahead.

"Riders," Dralor said.

Jeld turned his horse and followed Dralor's gaze to a cloud of dust working its way toward them from the side of a distant hill.

"Our scouts?" Dralor asked, squinting. "Damn old eyes."

"I think so," Jeld said. "Yeah. It's them."

Their scouts were incredible. Unstoppable. Ghosts. Part of the wild. Jeld tried to join them whenever he could, but Dralor usually insisted he was too important to risk. Hardly important, Jeld thought, but he obeyed more than not.

Five weeks had passed since the letter Jeld hoped was truly from Lira, and three since they'd departed Tovar. Dralor and Krayo had gathered up a shocking two hundred people, two-thirds men and the rest women and children. With well-counterfeited orders to establish a new labor camp, and no few watch uniforms, they'd made their way north. They had passed Plemenol just three days prior and sent scouts ahead to the small town of Olth in their path.

Jeld turned at the sound of a familiar bark and smiled. Erol rode beside another man who, like Erol, was dressed the part of a watchman. The old spearman gestured firmly out to their flank, rapped the man's chest with his fist, then patted his shoulder and rode toward the front.

"What's the hold up?" Erol asked as he approached.

"Waiting for the scouts," Dralor said. "Everything well back there?"

Erol grunted. "Doing better than any civilians I've ever moved. They're tough. Been through a lot."

"Our watchmen are looking more like the real thing every day," Jeld said. "This is quite the perfect job for you, Erol. You get to be a soldier and an acting coach at the same time."

Erol didn't answer, and they all turned their attention to the approaching scouts. At the front rode a handsome young man with a chiseled jaw and thick neck. Annik was his name. Next came Torral, a small man with quick eyes and only a few wispy hairs upon his chin. To hear Krayo tell it, this seemingly innocuous Torral fellow was as good as they came, a snake by word or fang. This made Jeld uneasy, for even he could see little more than a simple if capable soldier. Annik stepped his horse aside to let Torral approach Dralor.

"I suggest a halt, sir," Torral said. "Some trouble in Olth we best discuss before we near."

Erol was off raising the halt signal before Dralor could finish the nod directed his way. Dralor, Jeld, and the scouts rode back toward the center of the convoy, as Jeld had learned was standard military protocol. There they dismounted to stretch their legs whilst sharing the news, as their would-be watchmen made a show of securing the prisoners for any prying eyes.

"It seems a gang of ruffians has plagued the town since the Bloody Cross," Torral said, referring to Lord Annend Cross's betrayal of Lira. "Nearly a hundred of them in the town, and as many again about the region. They seem to have a deal with the local governor priest and carry out a good lot of his enforcement. Reckon we'd be fine with our numbers and orders, but maybe best to just skirt the town."

Annik glanced to Torral, who gave an approving nod. "Red bastard doesn't do a thing but run tellings about purity while this gang taxes the townsfolk to their teeth. Anyone who doesn't attend the tellings or speaks against their beliefs is jailed or worse. Priest gives this gang free rein of those trouble folk too. Free rein of their women, even!"

When Dralor did not respond, Jeld looked over to find him distant.

"Best turn east at the juncture?" Jeld suggested. "Quicken our pace and we should have a fair gap between us and Olth before sunset." Jeld looked to Dralor.

"No," Dralor said finally. "We cannot just leave these people."

Jeld cleared his throat. "Our people are counting on us to see them safely to the Isles. We'll fight Naelis another day, perhaps." In truth, Jeld just wanted to get to Lira.

"To dreams with Naelis! Save the people, as Liraelle would."

"Will you reclaim every city between here and the Isles?" Jeld posed. "How much is too much risk to those we have already saved?" True enough, but again his mind was mostly on Lira.

Dralor seemed to consider this, then bared his teeth. He paced away a few steps then turned. "East then, as you said. We'll bypass Olth."

"Beggin your pardon, sir," said an old but sturdy man leading his horse, "but to dreams with safety."

"No, Jeld is right," Dralor said. "We cannot risk it. Even if we succeed here, we'd be attracting far too much attention. It wouldn't end well."

"Maybe," the man said flatly. "Or we'd save a town from rape and pillage and get on our way all the same."

Dralor shook his head, at a loss. He couldn't shake the thought of all the women and children in their convoy being dragged to the prison tower, many of them having been sprung from the very place.

"The Mother won't look kindly on us if we leave them," a younger man said.

"Aye," said a rough looking woman, grasping a sword at her hip.

"No," Dralor said firmly. "Enough. Too risky. We—"

"Ask," the woman interrupted. "Ask our people if they want to risk it or not. You can't decide how we'll live our lives, nor how we'll spend our blood."

"Here, here!" the old man said. "Who died and made you king, anyway? They need us."

Dralor's eyes fell for a time, then he looked up with a spark in him that Jeld had not seen since he'd spied the prince walking with his brother the night he was murdered.

"As you wish," he told the woman. "Go take a count of volunteers and report back to me."

Dralor turned something short of a glare upon Jeld, seeming to dare him to object. But Jeld only nodded. It was the right thing to do. His conscience would thank him later. If he didn't get all their people killed, anyway.

One hundred and forty. That was the count when the woman returned. Nearly all the able bodied men, and no few women. Satisfied, Dralor sent the non-combatants around the town under a small escort, then marched his force toward Olth.

Jeld and Dralor plotted as they rode. They dismissed a direct assault. Might have slight numbers, but they were hardly a trained force. Trickling in and executing as many as possible by night had appeal, but in reality they'd manage little more than to stumble around an unknown town in the dark with little sense of their enemy. Arming the locals was another option, as was a longer term infiltration, but they had little appetite for anything drawn out. They settled on drawing out the enemy, and so as the sun set they turned off the road to set up camp while Jeld ventured alone into the town against Dralor's better judgment.

***

Jeld burst into a half packed pub, panting and wild eyed. His hair was matted and wet with sweat, his watch uniform stained with blood and dirt. In Tovar, people would have cried out, probably run off. Here though, the rough folk merely watched.

"There's a—there's a mob coming!" Jeld raved, panting. "Killed my squad. Where can I find the local guard? The governor? Your priest?"

Silence. A few chuckles. Heavy stares.

"They attack at dawn, dream you all! Help me or they'll take the town!"

More silence. Several hands eased closer to blades. Then a point jawed young man jumped to his feet and drew a short sword. His lip was set like a resentful child denied candy. Not altogether the most intimidating opponent, but sharp metal cut all the same, and Jeld didn't figure the other two dozen swords would keep their clothes on even if he came out on top. He took a step backward.

"Sit, boy," came a raspy voice. A greasy man with a thick beard kicked out a chair at a table with five other men. "Join us, watchman."

Jeld eased toward the greasy man, eyes fixed on Pointy, who sat with a scowl. "You can direct me to the authorities?"

"The Red One has... *deputized* many of us to maintain order. Now, name's Ghare. Tell me more about this situation, my friend."

Jeld looked around the room again then sat. "A mob, outside the city. Farmers and the like. Said they wanted to take back the city. From the Red One, no doubt. Captured just me and my sarge. Murdered all the rest."

Jeld shuddered then rubbed his wrists, which were ringed with red as if from bindings. Another of the many uses for shoe polish. He suppressed a smile as the man seemed to notice the markings.

"What brings a watch patrol to Olth?" Ghare asked.

"Not to Olth, only passing by. Orders to patrol, keep bandits at bay."

"Got away, eh?"

"Slipped their knots. Not a guard in sight. None awake, anyway. Whole camp was abed resting for their attack."

The man looked to his companions, receiving only a range of shrugs and frowns.

"Did nobody hear me?" Jeld said. "Let us make preparations! We don't want to be sleeping when they attack!"

As Jeld cast his words, so too did he weave into the men's auras an image of Ghare leading a group of riders into an encampment and butchering a slumbering army. The men shifted in their chairs. Mouths opened and closed with not a word spoken. Eyes went to the Ghare.

"Kill 'em while they sleep instead, then?" said another man.

He looked so ordinary, his delivery so nonchalant despite the murderous words. The hairs on Jeld's neck rose up.

"I swear, that's always your plan, Paet," Ghare said, the group erupting with laughter. "But I admit, I had the same thought. Figure we could maybe hold them off here, but it wouldn't be pretty."

Surprised at how easy that had been, Jeld turned his attention next to making it inconvenient to also murder him.

"Not a bad idea," Jeld said. "I can show you right to their camp." He let his chin quiver. "What would you have of the watch for avenging my squad? Are you being paid by the Red One? The watch has paid mercenaries good sums, I don't doubt we could arrange something for your service."

Many perked up at this, all looking again to Ghare.

"That would be welcome," Ghare said. "We volunteer our time, but that does little to put food on our plates, swords in our scabbards, or roofs over our heads. We survive on the good will of the locals."

The thug might actually do quite well on stage, but to Jeld's keen eye the lies were sickening. Jeld squeezed Ghare's arm and gave the man a firm nod as a tear slid down his cheek. The apparent leader of the ruffians gave a smile like a fox invited to guard the chickens, then jumped up from his chair.

"Assemble the men in the market," Ghare shouted. When nobody moved, he booted a chair between a seated man's legs and sent the man toppling over. "Go wake everyone up! Let's put these farmers back in their place!"

The bar cleared out. Jeld followed Ghare to the market, then sat atop his mount beneath the stars as men trickled in. They were a nervous lot, probably not accustomed to people actually fighting back. Good, just bullies. Still, they had numbers, and most in Dralor's lot were no better equipped. Jeld's thoughts drifted to the women and children they'd sent away, traveling through the night to grow their distance. He wondered what would become of them should he and his compatriots fail.

Clouds blew in over the stars, rain began to fall, and still men gathered. While himself lacking in military experience, Jeld was certain mustering troops was supposed to be faster than the changing of weather. In any case, he was as glad as he was wet when finally a short man in mail ordered the march. Ghare clapped Jeld on the arm, and the pair rode out through the gate at the front of the small army.

Jeld set a slow pace for the men on foot, a good half of the force. The group was quiet as they made their way through the night toward what Jeld hoped would be more massacre than fight. Rain fell lightly but steadily, clinking on the odd piece of armor. Hooves and boots sucked in the mud. The darkness was nearly absolute save for the faint shape of the road.

"How much farther?" Ghare whispered after a good while.

"Not far," Jeld said, heart beginning to race. "I remember rounding this curve here. They're just off the next after that."

"You... sure?"

Was he sure? Damned if it wasn't the darkest blazin' night he could remember. He squinted into the darkness.

"Yeah, next one. They turned off right at the inside of the curve. Figure we should cut in from the side, work our way down the draw there. Just in case they have a guard posted where they turned off."

"You said there were no guards..."

"Probably isn't, but I snuck out the back so can't say for sure they didn't post someone on this side. If they have a single guard, that'd be the spot, their tracks being there and all."

Ghare grunted something like agreement and they continued on until Jeld reined in his horse and pointed just off the curving road ahead. Jeld felt Ghare's gaze on him and fought back a panic, but Ghare only signaled the halt. Behind them, the shuffle of feet and wet slap of hooves faded like a whisper into the distance as the order cascaded down the line, until they stood in near complete silence. Jeld drew his sword.

"Hold it," Ghare whispered.

Jeld's heart skipped a beat. "Yeah?"

"Wait here."

Ghare rode back down the line, leaving Jeld sweating in the darkness. Wait here while I get people to put swords in you? Wait here while I piss? So many kinds of waiting that Jeld didn't care for. He returned with the short man who had ordered their departure from Olth, and pointed toward where Jeld had indicated. The man rubbed the whiskered chin beneath his flushed cheeks, then looked at Jeld.

"There?" he asked, pointing. "How far?"

Jeld nodded. "Few hundred strides down a draw there, aye."

"How are they arranged?"

Jeld gestured haphazardly. "Just strewn about, really. It's no army. You'll see their fires still, probably."

"Fifty?" More chin rubbing. It was not so much fat, more puffy like a horse's lips. He turned to Ghare. "Best put them down. Put down one rebellion, stave off a dozen."

Jeld had read something like it in a book once. Best he could recall, it had been about kings ruling, not about thugs killing farmers. The little man headed off toward the rear without another word. Seemed he hadn't read the chapter on leading from the front, though Jeld too found that idea a bit disagreeable.

"We go," Ghare said. "Come, show me the way."

Pulse beating in his ear, Jeld pressed into the woods, a small army following at his back like long shadows. Sticks cracked and the occasional hushed cry or curse sounded from behind, but all in all the group was quieter than Jeld had hoped. He hadn't exactly discussed a signal with Dralor, only that Jeld should take care not to be caught in the ambush himself when the time came. Yet here he stood in the front, indistinguishable from the enemy in the darkness.

When Jeld could again see the distant campfires through the trees, he stopped and drew his sword as noisily as possible, wincing in anticipation of an arrow through his neck. Ghare stopped beside Jeld and blew out a nervous breath.

"Should be easy enough," Ghare said, as much to himself.

Jeld frowned. Easy enough to be the first one killed if he didn't get out of the lead, anyway. Didn't suppose a sudden cramp would be convincing. A bout of battle shock, frozen by fear as the rest streamed past? Couldn't blow the ambush. So close to saving a whole lot of people. A whole town. What did it say about him that he wouldn't risk anything to help them?

Ghare widened the line as more men filled in, blew out another breath, and ordered the advance. The forms of tents and cots took shape in the shadows, the fires growing from distant lights to flickering flames through the trees. Jeld slowed his pace and men slowly streamed past. He caught a glimpse of Ghare turning toward him just before disappearing from view.

Jeld veered to the edges of their line, then slunk into the shadows. He circled wider around the campsite, watching as the silhouettes of the gang passed before the campfires. Hoofbeats sped, battle cries rose up, and they descended upon the camp. Then the twang of bowstrings and hiss of arrows filled the air. The battle cries turned to screams, many cutting short as more arrows flew. He could make out Dralor's voice over it all, calling out orders loud and sure.

He dismounted and tied his frightened horse to a tree. Competent a rider as he was, he didn't know the least bit about mounted combat. Granted, he also didn't know much about fighting a mounted opponent on foot either. Still, it felt good to be afoot. The shadows welcomed him readily now as he stalked back the way they'd come.

A rider burst from the darkness ahead, one of Ghare's in full flight. Jeld jumped aside, but suddenly a sword slammed into the rider's chest and sent him toppling. One of Dralor's men, riding off toward another fleeing thug. Terror and agony beat against Jeld and he almost missed one of the gang charging at him from the campsite, sword held high. So much for stealth.

The man seemed to recognize Jeld in his watch uniform and his sword lowered. "Let's get out of here!"

Jeld nodded to the man, let him pass, then spun and stuck him through the back. The man went down, already still. Jeld tried to pull his blade free but it wouldn't budge. Caught a dreamin' rib. The contents of his stomach rose up as he pressed a boot to the man's shoulder like some piece of meat.

Then another man was upon him, a wiry fellow with paper skin and a giant sword. Jeld's blade pulled free with a sound like a boot from mud and met the other's to a jarring crash. Then another with a blond beard, shield, and short sword lunged at him. Jeld jumped back just in time and the attack whooshed past. Handan's drills took over with another parry, with circling to keep the enemy in one another's way, with strong footing, easy balance, and a low slash at the leg of Shield Guy. The man cried out and fell back.

It was time enough for Jeld to gather his wits, and the two attackers' thoughts snapped into clarity. He ducked a two handed blow from Big Sword. The bent attacker with the bloody leg came up with a roar and swung a blow at Jeld's head. Jeld saw it coming, leaned aside as the blade came down, and hacked the same injured leg. Blond Beard cried out again and toppled to the ground.

The giant sword hissed from behind. The big blade cut through the air beside Jeld, just where he'd projected himself to the wiry foe. It bit deep into the ground, a spray of mud and rocks and sticks spattering Jeld's face as he turned, then speared the man through the neck.

More cries. Voices approaching, silhouettes before the campfires taking shape.

"Here!" shouted the man Jeld had cut across the legs. "Here! Help! He's—"

Jeld's knee crunched into Blond Beard's throat. Jeld turned to the approaching men. "Help! He's alive!"

Two men fled past without a word. Two others came to Jeld's aid, hefting the man with the crushed throat up between them. The man's mouth moved with barely a choked whisper, bulging bloodshot eyes fixed on Jeld as he was dragged away. As Jeld followed the lot of them and raised his sword.

The suffocating man's panic beat against Jeld. The horror of the whole thing. Screams of men and horses below. The death. The killing. His sword in the other man's rib. His knee against this one's neck.

Jeld lowered his sword and slunk into the shadows between two trees as the others pressed ahead, the man with the blond beard staring back. Stupid. The kind of stupid that cost a man later, and cost a lot. Rapers too, hadn't the scouts said? Robbers, too.

He raised his sword. Killing them was the right thing to do. The necessary thing. Not a necessary evil, a necessary good. But he didn't move. Just stood there as they began to disappear into brush and shadow. Then a rider slammed into them, blade flashing a line of reflected firelight.

Jeld stared at the still forms left in the rider's wake. Probably for the best. The necessary got done, and not by him. Then he set off running toward the already quieting sounds of battle.

The fighting was done and the campsite relatively quiet by the time Jeld reached it. He rejoined Dralor as the black prince was ordering riders out to pursue those who had fled. His orders were nearly whispers now, but no less commanding than his roars during the short battle. Secure a perimeter. Tend their wounded. Retrieve their dead. Prepare a pyre.

It wasn't long before the pyre was kindling to life. Jeld watched as Dralor stared grimly into the flames. They'd lost only four. Four too many, Dralor's eyes seemed to say. Four people they were supposed to be saving. Four people they'd promised to protect. The others all watched in somber awe.

Weary as all were, they heeded Dralor's orders to move while the flames still burned tall, and made their way back to the town of Olth. They were greeted by the sound of commotion. Riding inside, they found perhaps thirty men and women standing over several bodies. People were standing outside their homes all down the streets.

"Caught some runaways for ya," a red haired woman said. Her eyes narrowed. "You aren't farmers..." She glanced at Jeld. "And you're that watchman from the pub!"

Suddenly she kicked a dead man in the ribs and glared at Dralor. "If you think you can take the place of those bastards and keep this town—"

"Though you'd be foolish in these times to believe me, we came only to help," Dralor said. "But you need not trust me, we will be leaving. Are there others in this town you would be rid of?"

"We've dealt with them. There may be a few others, but we'll handle them after the priest."

Dralor's eyes widened. "Where? Where is the priest!"

The woman gave a perplexed look. "Hiding in his temple as usual, if they haven't managed to take his head off yet. Why? What do you care?"

Before Dralor could answer, Jeld kicked his mount into motion and was racing toward the temple, Dralor close behind. Axes lay discarded in the street outside the temple. The doors of the temple stood open, one marred by a broad, jagged hole. Three men emerged dragging a man in a red robe by both legs and one arm.

"Please, no! Please, it was all them, not me! There was nothing I could do! Do not let their darkness dim your light! Light their darkness! Light their darkness!"

He screamed as they dragged him to his feet, then toward a platform with a chain and executioner's block. A gathering crowd jeered. How many heads of Olth townsfolk had been removed under the priest's watch, Jeld wondered. Even if none, how many women had been abused or livelihoods broken under his governorship?

"Stop!" Dralor shouted, but nobody heeded him.

Dralor charged his horse into the middle of the ruckus. He reared his mount and let loose a booming shout.

"Enough!"

The crowd fell silent.

"Now you'd help the Red One?" a voice called.

The red haired girl ran huffing into the street. "Dreamin' right we won't trust you!"

"If you kill that priest, Naelis will raze this town!"

Jeld positioned his horse between Dralor and an angry looking man with an ax who was easing closer.

"He deserves it!" an old man shouted. "He has to die for all he's done!"

"Don't trade an enemy you know for one you don't! Your vengeance will get your loved ones killed!"

The red haired women seemed to hesitate. Murmurs rose up from the crowd. Then suddenly, a stocky man who'd been among those dragging the priest pulled a sword.

"No!" Dralor yelled, but it was too late.

The sword pierced into the priest's back. The priest cried out and fell to his knees. The sword seemed to catch and the attacker kicked the priest onto his chest then jammed the sword deep. The priest's back arched, limbs jerking, then he slackened.

Dralor fell silent, just shaking his head. The stocky man spat at the priest, then eyed Dralor as he walked off, leaving the sword protruding from the priest's back. A few cheers rose up from the crowd, but they died away to silence. Dralor slowly wheeled his horse and plodded back toward the gate.

"At dawn we will march for a new life in the Isles," Dralor boomed, not turning. "Any who join us will be welcomed."

Jeld followed, the rest of their men falling in behind them. Dralor's deep melancholy pressed against Jeld like a dark weight. They made camp just outside the city.

When they woke, three hundred townsfolk of Olth awaited them.

Chapter Twenty-Three

A gull leapt from the scarred railing of the ship, squawking as it soared into a gray sky. Jeld watched it fly over the sea between the rocky, moss-topped islands ahead to either side, landing on one of the three other ships packed with refugees. He stumbled as they slid down the back of a wave, then his budding sea legs regained their rhythm. Dralor stood leaning on the rail at his side. Sailors hurried about their work upon the deck behind them. The rowers' calls came steadily from below.

Their captain, Crais, had the wheel himself now and spoke quietly with his usual helmsman as the crew more or less ran itself. Crais was a skinny, deeply tanned fellow with shaggy blond hair and squinty eyes. Erol worked at coiling a pile of rope nearby, ever busy, while Krayo's man Torral lounged in a hammock, looking not the least bit guilty for it.

Dralor tensed and Jeld followed his gaze to another island coming into view. Its coastline was a sheer rocky cliffside.

"It's that one, isn't it?" Jeld asked again, certain this time.

"Yes," Dralor said in a hushed voice.

Jeld searched the vacant cliffs, as if he'd find Lira just standing there waving. Would Benam be there? And Fen? Could all three have been so lucky to have survived the massacre? No, he had to prepare himself for bad news. Maybe she wasn't even here. Maybe the letter and all its vagaries weren't from here. Maybe—

He chided himself for again forgetting his friends so easily. Nonetheless his thoughts drifted back to Lira. To her fingers intertwined with his, her—

"You love her," Dralor said. "Not just some princess fancy."

"I loved her before I knew she was a princess," Jeld said, still searching the cliffs as more and more came into view from behind another island.

"Remember we cannot be certain she's... the one who wrote Krayo."

Jeld's gaze followed a short wall running atop the cliffs. It grew to fill a narrow gap as the cliffs descended sharply to the sea.

"I know," Jeld said, nonetheless searching still for Lira.

Jeld let out a breath and forced himself to look away. Dralor's knuckles were white upon the rail. Jeld glanced over at him.

"You fear she will not be pleased to see you."

Dralor gave a single humorless chuckle. "Would that she were merely *not pleased.*"

"You're not wrong, but she will forgive you."

Dralor turned away from Caerghallad. "No, I think not."

He started to speak but pursed his lips and fell silent. Jeld knew his thoughts, even with his sense again locked away tight. Dralor had taken her father. Taken Benam, Handan. Taken her home. Taken her blazing kingdom, for that matter. No, forgiveness would not come easy. Maybe he was right that it wouldn't come at all.

Jeld bit his lip, then looked out to sea. "My sister died fighting off your watchmen when they took our shop. I nearly died on the streets. I... hated you. Even tried to kill you during the Fallsday parade, but someone stopped me. But none of that matters now. That isn't you.

You're a good man, and if someone as broken as me can forgive you, then you can be damn sure Lira will."

Dralor's eyes darted, brimmed with tears, fell, closed. Then they opened, and he gave Jeld a nod.

"You cannot make light by putting out darkness." Jeld said softly. "It's something I heard, once. From a Sayer, actually. It means... I suppose it just means we must do good. Ah I don't know, don't even know why I said it."

"I like it."

Nodding more resolutely, Dralor said nothing further as they drew closer to the wall. There was a pass in the wall, like any city gate, only stretching across the sea. They passed through it, and suddenly they were not in some uninhabited island wilderness, but a bustling port. A harbor packed with ships filled the wall's embrace like a lake. Broad docks with no few fishermen stretched before city blocks packed with shops. The buildings were modest, but made up for it in number. Children played upon a small beach, three partially built ships up the sandy slope behind them.

"Let her run!" came the captain's order.

The rowers let off and they coasted perfectly into positions beside the pier with only the tiniest bump. A dockhand caught and secured their lines, and soon Jeld was following Dralor across a gangway amidst others of the crew. Dralor had ordered the other refugees to stay back until they'd sorted things out. That, and they'd agreed it best if the others didn't know about Lira just yet, assuming she was here. Only the red haired woman from Olth joined them, having established herself as the closest thing to the leader of the refugees of Olth.

A fair crowd had gathered at the influx of refugees. Front and center among them at the end of the gangway was a striking man in something like a long skirt, with a billowy white shirt that stood out from the crowd in its cleanliness.

"Good Avandrians!" the man greeted them with the typical long vowels and doubly long o's of the islander brogue, though not nearly so pronounced as a fellow Jeld once shared a cell with. He waved them ahead and fell in step beside them. "Queen Alaesh Ghallad welcomes you."

Lira's face was everywhere as Jeld followed the man down the dock. A higher walk ran above at street level. More faces. Jeld's gaze passed over someone on the walk above, then backtracked. A young woman, in the simple homespun like all the rest, brown hair and blue eyes. He smiled a sad smile and walked on. Another face, another phantom.

"Thank you," Dralor answered. "You, your people, and your queen are most gracious. But please, we ask nothing more than your open doors."

"Blessed be those the winds bring," the man said. "It is our way to do more than just open our doors to the wind. We embrace it. And anyway, it is best for us all to see you properly rooted."

The apparent official exchanged a fond greeting with a fisherman then continued. "But, please, this is for you and the queen to discuss. I am Mraisic. I will help you settle your people in the coming weeks. First, let me show you to your lodging. The queen is like to treat with you tonight."

A boy pushed his cart of oysters from their path. A woman with a bundle of fish draped over one shoulder eyed them curiously. A pack of laughing children nearly ran into Mraisic, who grumbled, flashed Dralor a guilty smile, and patted one of them on the head. A young woman up on the higher walk was pushing through the crowd, keeping pace. Brown hair, blue eyes, homespun. Familiar. Yes, the same girl he'd glimpsed before, actually. Curious. For a people who supposedly welcomed strangers, they didn't seem too accustomed to having them around.

Jeld tripped a bit on a raised board, catching someone's arm to keep from falling.

"Sorry," Jeld said. "Didn't mean—" He turned back to the upper dock, searching, suddenly out of breath. She was gone. Silly, anyway. Just another—

The girl squeezed out from between two people and stopped against the rail. She squinted, blinked, squinted again, then the color drained from her face. She staggered backward, a hand to her face.

Jeld froze, though he did not know it. The world around him fell away, even his own body forgotten as he finally saw through the pessimism he'd emplaced to protect himself. As his heart swelled. Then he was running, and she too, eyes barely leaving one another, finding each other again each time anyone came between them.

Jeld turned up a narrow ramp, forced to slow behind an elderly couple walking arm in arm. From the top, Lira smiled through them and Jeld back at her, the joy finally breaking his shock. Finally the couple reached the top and Jeld darted past. And there was Lira, standing before him. He froze, staring into her eyes, afraid to move as if it would wake him from a dream. Then it didn't matter, nothing else mattered, and they ran into each other's arms.

Jeld's fingertips buried in her hair. He breathed a laugh, a sob. Lira pulled him closer, her cheek against his, and he could have just died happy that very moment.

"I thought you were gone!" Lira cried.

She pulled back and looked upon him. Tears flowed down her face from reddened eyes. Their foreheads pressing together, Jeld wiped her tears. Then, cupping her cheeks, he kissed her, and she him.

"You're alive," Lira breathed as they kissed, voice cracking.

"You're alive," Jeld echoed.

Then Jeld just held her tightly again, eyes closing until something caught his attention. A flash of fury. Behind Lira, a man with thinning hair, broad shoulders, and a short beard was glaring at Jeld. General Handan Tovaine, unmistakable at second glance despite the new hair warming his chin. Jeld's shock and joy at the general's return did war with embarrassment, and his hold on Lira slackened before it dawned on him that the general was not glaring at him. Jeld spun to find Dralor at the end of the general's glare.

Lira spotted him next, eyes going wide. She ran into Dralor's arms. That embrace melted a thousand fears from Dralor and he stood wide eyed in her arms before embracing her. His eyes fell closed, squeezing tears from them.

Jeld took the opportunity to greet the general, who offered a firm shake and a kindly smile. Then Jeld saw Benam and damned if he didn't hug the old knight, grinning like a fool as he looked between the trio. Then his grin fell away. Fen, then. It had to be someone, he supposed, but that hardly made it any easier.

"I am sorry, Handan," Dralor said. "Truly sorry."

"You betrayed me," Handan said. "You betrayed Avandria."

"Yes," Dralor said, the absolution of Lira's embrace fading already.

"This is not the man who betrayed you," Benam whispered, searching Dralor.

Handan shook his head, then gave Jeld a nod and stalked off.

Dralor stared after Handan, Benam placing a hand upon his shoulder.

"We'll talk somewhere more private," Dralor said, eyeing Mraisic. "First, there are many with us who would be settled."

Lira nodded, giving Jeld a quick smile before business and scorn for Dralor took over. "Mraisic has made preparations." She turned to him. "Would you, please?"

He bowed, and led them to a modest office where he enlisted a number of dockhands. They spent the whole of the afternoon and evening settling the refugees into various shelters, from a warehouse by the shipyard, to an encampment in a beautiful moss-covered field outside the city proper. Still others were housed in the homes of willing locals. Lira did not hesitate to lend her sweat to the task. Jeld often found himself standing idle watching her, and they would share smiles before returning to their tasks. Handan too returned to aid the refugees of Tovar and Olth, speaking not another word to Dralor.

They retired exhausted to one of the adjoined stone buildings forming a ring around a small central keep of sorts. These quarters and keep alike were simple, the people of Caerghallad seemingly a modest folk in most things. Lira and Jeld sat pressed against one another in a small sofa beside the fire, Jeld's lute laying upon his chest. Benam and Dralor were seated at a table nearby, as was a page boy Lira called Wess. Handan had gone to train after the bulk of their tales were told, listening most intently as Dralor told of his time in the prison. According to Lira, he rarely trained so late.

"Sinwo said it was all about the bag?" Benam asked, more relaxed in his chair than Jeld had ever seen him.

The old knight seemed distant, numb even, since Jeld's revelation that Naelis helped murder the Idols, and that Jeld had sat before The One himself.

"It's powerful," Jeld said. "One could move an army by pigeon, in theory."

Benam hummed something like agreement. "Yes. His want will be for power of one sort or another." He shook his head and mused distantly. "The power to sit amongst gods, perhaps."

"It felt more a curse than a power to me."

"Much of what Dralor desires is a curse to the rest of us," Benam said.

The door creaked open. Jeld turned, hand raising to greet Handan, and found himself waving instead at Fen. Older. More muscled, somehow. Darker, somehow, and not his skin. But, it was Fen all the same. Jeld's mouth fell open. He looked around at the others, as if to check whether they too had seen a ghost.

Fen beamed, some of that darkness melting away. "Little prince. Heard you were back. Sorry I couldn't get away sooner." He reached out his broad arms for a hug, but Jeld sat transfixed. Fen laughed and pulled Jeld up into a hug. "It's good to see you too. I—Jeld? You alright?"

"You're alive," Jeld said, shaking his head.

"Well yeah I'm alive. Didn't they tell you?" Fen unwound Jeld with an arm around his shoulder and looked around the room accusingly. "Did nobody think it was worth mentioning?"

"I—I didn't know you thought otherwise," Lira said.

Jeld thawed and patted Fen on the back. "I just... I couldn't bring myself to ask."

"How could the Halls have felt like a curse?" Wess blurted. "The One, the magic... it sounds incredible."

Jeld gave Fen another pat, waved him to a chair, and returned to his own seat beside Lira. He considered Wess's words, mind wandering back to that place.

"I suppose much of what unsettled me I did not bother to tell," Jeld said, plucking a few notes. "I guess being trapped anywhere is no adventure. I couldn't get to you all. Then there's the timelessness. No sleep. No hunger. Never-ending hallways. Never-ending voids. Voices. Ghosts."

Jeld trailed off, the whole room falling silent with him.

"You never have to sleep?" Wess said, shattering the silence, and the melancholy for that matter. Even Dralor laughed a breath.

Jeld caught Fen up on his journey, and Fen on his. The fire popped and crackled. Lira's fingers were intertwined with Jeld's again, and his heart was full.

"Isn't this damned queen supposed to see us?" Dralor blurted after a while, rubbing between his eyes.

The door opened and Handan entered, a simple longsword held in one hand.

"Keeping up on your training, Arv—Jeld?" Handan asked as he gathered a change of clothes from a small trunk.

"Not enough. Though I did enjoy my regular Bantae in the Warrior's Hall." His fingers plucked that rustic yet cozy, powerful feel of Tovados's great hall.

"Oh!" Jeld said, then hefted Handan's immense sword from his bag as Wesslund looked on with wonder.

Never before had Jeld seen such joy on Handan's face. The general took the sword with the awe of a mother holding her child for the first time.

"How?" Handan breathed.

Jeld's thoughts returned to his final days in the palace. It had been a simple enough matter to take the sword in those chaotic days after the king fell. Suddenly Jeld recalled something that had only recently stopped haunting him. Lira still didn't know he'd set the fire. The diversion that let Naelis kill her father.

Lira cocked her head at Jeld. He managed a weak smile before looking quickly away.

"I took it not long after you... left," Jeld said, Handan glaring anew at Dralor. "Easy with a magic bag and a penchant for lies." The last he said with another guilty look at Lira.

Handan sat upon the floor and began polishing his sword, his sweaty clothing forgotten. The conversation turned next to the matter of how to set up a network to aid refugees, which Krayo had extensively primed Dralor on. This went on at considerable length despite the hour until Benam abruptly interrupted Dralor.

"This isn't right," Benam said, staring into the fire.

"What," Dralor said through clenched teeth.

"We can't just ignore the problem. Sure this aid is noble, but we're... we're saving one chicken from the wolf. It's not enough."

"Did you not sneak around the prison tower lending aid?"

"That was much different. There was nothing more I could do. Liraelle, I know you—"

"No!" Lira roared. "I will send no more to die for a blazing hat and chair! I went against my better judgment before and now thousands are dead."

Everyone fell quiet, then a whisper came from Benam's lips.

"What did you say?" Lira hissed.

"Cowardice," Benam repeated. "Forgive me, but it's true. Far more will suffer should Naelis's reign continue. You know this. It's not lives you're unwilling to risk, it's your guilt."

Lira shook her head in disbelief, managing only a breathy huff, then another. "You think I don't care whether my people live or die?"

"I didn't say that. I said you'd think it right to risk them for greater good were it not your own conscience at stake."

Lira fell silent, sinking in the chair beside Jeld. Jeld wanted to put a hand on her back, but stopped himself. All friends here, but she was a princess after all.

"It's not some simple trade, it's a *gamble*," she said. "And a bad one at that! I would sacrifice much to give Avandria peace, but I will not burn half of it to the ground for some dreamer's folly."

She looked around the room like an animal hungry for a fight, but none came. Benam soon retired, and Jeld was himself yawning when the Mraisic entered. The queen would see them in the morning instead, he informed them. Welcome news for the lot of them, and all save Lira were asleep shortly thereafter.

The next morning they were awakened by one of Mraisic's counterparts, who escorted them to the royal dining. A long row of doors stood open to a balcony, the sound of the ocean washing in with the morning light. Queen Alaesh Ghallad sat across a table of rough stone that looked to have been simply plucked from the cliffsides below. She was a squat woman with graying black hair, little by way of a neck, and crow's feet at her eyes that said she smiled often. She wasn't smiling now.

"The general had the excuse of having been following orders those years past, at least," the queen said, spreading on her toast a fish paste that Jeld found nauseating. "Now who shows up but the man giving the orders."

Beneath the table, Dralor's fist clenched. If he had to explain one more time that he no longer—

Queen Alaesh waved a thick-fingered hand. "Never mind it, never mind it. You'll find no grudges in the Isles." She took a bite, Jeld's stomach turning. "How fare your people, then? Do they want for anything?"

Though the queen looked to Dralor, the once-king turned pointedly to Lira and said nothing.

"They are settling in wonderfully," Lira answered. "Never have I met a more gracious host, both queen and nation."

"You'll not find hunger in the Isles either," the queen said.

Between the pickled fish paste and the apparently pristine altruism, Jeld could almost gag. He'd seen goodness a time or two, but it still raised his hackles. The queen glanced down at her spread then back to Jeld.

"I'm certain Tovar sits upon the sea, does it not? Have your people not yet discovered there are fish in it?"

Jeld smiled. "We have, Your Highness. It's the pickling we don't care to discover yet."

The queen grunted, then chuckled, the lines at her eyes finally puckering. The exchange was just enough to loosen Jeld's lips.

"Do you not worry that taking in so many Avandrians might invite conflict with Naelis?" Jeld asked.

The queen's chewing paused for a fleeting moment. "I suppose it might. But then, is my taking these people not cheaper for him than building prisons for them?"

"He doesn't build prisons to be rid of people, Your Highness," Benam said. "He builds them to punish."

"Then the jagged rocks of our cliffs welcome him."

"He will, you know," Lira said softly.

The queen took a draft of her drink and leaned back in her chair, shoulders slumping a little. "Yes, I think he will."

Jeld frowned. She knew Naelis would attack, and still she took them in. Maybe she just figured refugees made good soldiers?

Queen Alaesh straightened. "Let us hope he thinks better of it. We welcome all, but I have no mind for the squabbles of Avandria."

"We *must* make ready, then," Benam said. "We must fight."

"Benam!" Lira snapped, the room falling silent. "We will absolutely not revisit this!"

"You spoke of not gambling lives. Would you have the Isles just hand over their city, then? Or should they fight?"

"Has the Isles been twice defeated and reduced to some beggar with a crown!"

"Not yet," Benam said pointedly.

Lira's fury faltered as Benam's words sunk in. *Not yet.* What could she do, though? What had she left to sacrifice? And *who*?

"Enough, now," the queen said calmly. "I'll not have any Avandrian squabbling around my dinner table, either." She raised her tankard. "Now, drink with me and tell me a tale of your land."

They did. Benam told of the Vanishing Wars. Fen, at the queen's insistence, of a simple night by the fire with his father, and Dralor of his childhood with Loris. When finally they parted, Lira, Jeld, and Fen joined Dralor making rounds to check on their people, then split off to simply walk the town. They had sweet rolls at the docks, shopped the market, and even caught two fish with a line from Jeld's bag. Roba's absence was not unnoticed, yet for nearly two bells it was almost as if their lives were normal again.

Fen departed afterward to the shipyard, where he'd been volunteering with a master shipbuilder simply to learn how ships were constructed. Jeld and Lira shared a smile, their hands found one another, and they descended to the beach. Shoes dangling from their free hands, they walked with their toes in the fine sand, cool waves coursing over them before sliding back out to sea.

Jeld looked over at their intertwined fingers, then to Lira, and just stared with wonder. It had always been easy to dismiss any notion of the Idols watching over him, but damned if this didn't make him wonder. To find such a gem as his ilk was never meant to so much as glimpse. To cross the world and find her again. She looked over and met his gaze, eyes smiling warmly. And to be loved back....

After a time they settled onto the drier sand to look out at the sea and the beautiful neighboring islands. Both watched a young boy at play with equal interest as they spoke of times behind and little of those ahead. Their sand-filled shoes carried them next out of the city proper to one of the refugee encampments not far off the bluffs. Afterwards, they walked the slopes where ancient stone peeked out from luscious green moss, still hand in hand.

Under the shade of a small tree, beside a trickling stream that ran over the moss itself, they shared another kiss, then fell into one another's arms with a tender clumsiness. The sun was just beginning its journey back down toward the sea when finally they untangled from one another. They started picking their way back along a craggy hillside, sharing grins and no few laughs.

"What do you think?" Lira asked, stopping before a large boulder and turning with a distant look upon her face.

"Hm? Ah... I—well, good? I—I love you."

Lira beamed and pressed her body against his with a long kiss.

"I love you too," she said, alight at her own words for a moment. "But that isn't what I meant." She started up the boulder. "About the kingdom. About Naelis. About... war."

Jeld followed as he considered his words. "You are the only thing I've ever wanted more than seeing Naelis fall. Now that I have you, I want only to be with you." He blushed. "I mean, to just, you know, buy sweet rolls, take walks, sit by a fire. Cook meals. To wake up with you, and know I'll do the same the very next."

Jeld crested the boulder and Lira took his hands in hers.

"Yes. Yes, but isn't that all anyone could want? And could anyone at all have it if nobody will fight for it?"

"It's not as if Naelis will destroy every corner of the world."

"Queen Alaesh thinks Naelis will come. Will we flee, then? Or pose as townsfolk, hope to avoid the front lines then live under Naelis's rule?"

"There will always be wars to fight, as long as Hearth lights the northern sky."

"There would be far fewer if I sat the throne," Lira said.

"I... don't know that it warrants much thought, Lira. I don't see that we have much of a choice at this point unless it'd ease your conscience to kill a few hundred faithful idiots and probably get yourself hanged before you give in. You have no army, right? Warrinton and Odsgaard, maybe? No more Delvarad, and little hope of anyone—"

"Yes," Lira interrupted. "Yes, I know. There's little left."

They quieted and walked on.

Three days passed much the same, with Jeld waking up beside Lira on each to look upon her when she stirred. On the evening of the third day, when they gathered in the great room of their allotted apartments to dine, Lira was exceedingly quiet. Near the end of the meal she set her mug on the stone table and looked up to speak, finding everyone already looking at her.

She smiled, but it quickly fell away. "My friends. I'm afraid I have erred. We cannot sit idly, in luxury or rags, while our kingdom is ravaged. This is not about who wears the crown, but rather about the people. About civilization. A victory for Naelis could mean losing a thousand years of progress. A thousand years of suffering by millions, all because of our unwillingness to risk a handful of lives."

"No!" Jeld yelled, coming to his feet. "Lira, no. You had the right of it before. Help where you can. Save those we can. But don't... don't do this. It won't work, it will only—"

"While we breathe, we fight. Not for us, but for those who can't."

"I felt much the same not long ago. But there is little we can do," Dralor said.

"A leader must know when to fight, when to flee, when to surrender," Handan offered in agreement.

It was Fen who spoke next, his voice somber. "She's right."

Fen said nothing further, but he didn't need to. Everyone knew his hatred for war and what it made of men, and a silence came over the group. The fire crackled.

"I don't mean to lead a reckless charge into battle," Lira said, voice hushed. "We will form a resistance across Avandria. Armies cannot move without roads, cannot eat without supplies, and cannot fight what they cannot see. We will exploit these. There will be a time for proper battle, and so too will we call upon Odsgaard and Warrinton when the time comes, but only then. And when it comes, they will not fight alone. We will also build an army here. The queen has already agreed."

Jeld looked from face to face helplessly. Benam might as well have been watching the rising sun. The rest were more conflicted if not downright disapproving, yet still there was a pride throughout that Jeld could only shake his head at. Even Fen, who had spoken in her favor, did not look pleased. How could he be, as much as he'd spoken of foolhardy young going pridefully to war, and foolhardy Jeld for that matter.

"I'm truly sorry to call upon you all when you've already given so much," Lira said. "Know that if any of you wish to leave my service, you'll do so with only great honor."

Jeld watched as she turned to each in turn, and each gave their nod. Then she turned to him. He could only shake his head in shock. In betrayal! His fantasy of a lifetime of days together like these shattered. Just fantasy. He'd been foolish to think he'd found peace. To think he'd be allowed it. Or that he deserved it, for that matter.

He looked around the room again, and *dreams* if he didn't feel a swell of pride. Excitement, even. How easily one forgets starvation and the terror of battle, but could he ever forget the guilt—envy even, *dream it*—were he to abstain while they fought?

He looked back to Lira. She offered no puppy dog eyes. Her lips were a line, shaky with effort. Jeld smiled a little. Trying not to influence him? Bless her but she was no actor. But Jeld's smile fell away. That wasn't it at all. She was conflicted, of course. Wanting him to join her, but afraid of what may come of it. What probably *would* come of it.

Jeld sighed. There was nothing for it now, he supposed. Nothing but to support her, and if he was lucky, to put something sharp through Naelis. With another sigh, he nodded.

"Thank you," Lira said, eyes on Jeld before sharing the words with the others. "Now, we'll write to Krayo for his aid in our resistance efforts. Queen Alaesh will put out a call for refugees under a humanitarian guise. Handan and Dralor will lead our training efforts. I will—"

"I will not allow a traitor to command a single man in my army," Handan said. "Mistakes can be forgiven, but this, Liraelle? I gave *everything* to the kingdom, and he betrayed it!"

"We cannot afford to squabble amongst ourselves. Dralor is—"

"I'm sorry, Princess, but no. There is nothing more important in war than trust, as you well know."

"*General!* Surely you would not compare him to Annend." Lira looked between them, a tired breath escaping her lips. "Please, I need you both."

Handan bit his lip, fighting to keep his bearing. "I do not think the comparison is so far—"

"It's alright, Liraelle," Dralor said, holding up a hand. "It's alright. He's right. I must not be involved. It would not serve your cause well were you found to be working with the *Black Prince.*"

Lira's shoulders fell. "Uncle..."

Dralor turned to Handan. "Let me serve in your army. Just enlist like any common man. I know trust is no less important for any man in service. I know the only favor you owe me is a cell. But allow me this. Please."

Handan stared back gravely. His frown deepened, then finally he nodded. Dralor's eyes fell shut, a great weight leaving him. He looked like he'd been granted some great boon rather than being stripped of rank and cast to a grueling and likely bloody fate.

Lira looked back and forth between them, whatever weight Dralor shed taking up residence upon her shoulders. "Very well." Then she turned to Jeld. "Jeld. Benam. Fen...I—I ask that you travel east."

Jeld's world fell away. War at her side was together all the same. This, though...

Benam cleared his throat. "Liraelle, surely I can be of better use in your council."

"Would that there were two of you. I need you out there. Recruiting, liaising, building our network. You are known, and trusted. You are a strong sword, skilled in politicking, and you know war more than you like. There is no task that needs your hand more than this. And you make a good pot of beans."

Fen patted Benam on the shoulder, then gave Lira a somber nod before she turned back to Jeld.

"There's no other way," Lira said, almost pleadingly. "Nobody else can do it, and we'll all be killed if we do nothing. I'm sorry. There's truly nothing I want more than—"

"I understand," Jeld said, and he did.

Lira gave a sad, grateful smile, then steeled herself. "You three must travel first to Havaral. There are many refugees and a strong underground we may be able to bring to our cause. We'll need captains and others we can trust in the city to move so many people to the Isles. They won't be as noticed in so large a city."

Jeld shared a look with Benam and Fen, and when he turned back to Lira, found her staring distantly.

"They say the people don't know what my grandfather did, you know. He has them thinking it was Naelis's doing. The people of Havaral have a long history of allegiance to the Cross line, if they could see past his lies I don't think they'd stand for it. Maybe they can't take the city, but more might join our cause."

Jeld weighed the thought. "Reasonable. We can spread the truth while we're there."

Lira nodded. "And remove him, Jeld. Make every last person in Havaral know of his betrayal, and remove him. Whatever else the outcome, it will occupy Naelis for a time."

"You... wish me to remove your grandfather," Jeld said.

"I wish you to kill him."

Chapter Twenty-Four

"Damned Reborn have cleaned the character out of this place," Torral said over his shoulder to Jeld.

They were walking up a narrow street lined with towering buildings, some four full stories tall. While Tovar was a good deal bigger, Havaral was far denser, everything packed over the decades into its original, towering black walls. The crowds were thicker than Tovar's too, and while there was none of the filth or blatant crime Tovar's riverside had once displayed, Jeld saw plenty of character still.

"Looks pretty seedy to me," Jeld said.

Torral scoffed. "You should have seen it before. Worse than Riverside, if ya know it."

This question pleased Jeld. At least Krayo had kept Jeld's life secret from Torral. Seemed only fair, considering Krayo had never so much as hinted at Torral's existence. Jeld found himself wondering how many others Krayo had promised his legacy to.

"Over here," the scrappy little man said, making a turn up another narrow street.

It wasn't that Torral was smaller than Jeld, just that most men two or three decades older put on a certain thickness in limb or belly, but not Torral. Jeld had learned little of the man during the journey to the Isles, and still less on the trek to Havaral.

They'd stopped at three towns on the way south, and Torral had known people in each, like minded folk who took well enough to their proposals. It was the farmers in little villages and homesteads who had been easiest to bring aboard, and wouldn't you know it, Torral had acquaintances in those too.

Jeld eyed the countless windows above as he followed Torral. Torral had come this way earlier to meet a woman he knew while Jeld and the others had attended to other business. This woman, Senach, was reportedly a contact of Krayo's and had been quite wealthy from trade until Lord Annend's wealth tax. Dubbed by Annend as his "Shared Light" tax, and by those with coin as "robbery," the tax conveniently excluded those of high birth, which this Senach was not, leaving her to other opportunistic pursuits.

They entered an undeniably seedy tavern. There was a decent amount of seemingly sober merriment, cards and tonics and simple chatter. The ban on harder drink was holding well enough if the lack of heads on tables, brawls, and general rowdiness were any indication. They went up a staircase, then through one of several doors into a small apartment, two men and a woman passing from the room without a word as they entered.

At the back of the apartment, Torral slid aside a panel Jeld had taken for an ordinary wall. Beyond was a makeshift tavern complete with a little bar and hodgepodge of mismatched tables. This one appeared far less sober. A burly guard raised an eyebrow at Torral and Jeld.

"What now?" the guard asked.

"We need to see her," Torral said.

"Not happening. Boss said you could do the bar, though."

"On the house?" Torral asked.

"No."

"Right. Well, look. We have something she seemed very interested in."

The big man folded his arms. "She don't want much these days."

Torral held out his open palm, two silver royals atop it. "I promise you she will wish to hear our proposal, and if she finds you delayed such an opportunity I worry she may be upset."

Eyes on the coins, the guard frowned, then took them. "Alright. This way."

The guard waved another man over to take his place and led them back out into the apartment, then into another a few doors down. This one had a family inside taking a meal, but they didn't so much as look up as the guard led them through. He opened a trapdoor under a rug and led them down a set of steps into a dark room.

Jeld's eyes began to adjust. There were just a few candles about the room. Two long rows of low benches faced a small cleared space at the front of the room. There was something on the wall behind it... the tree of the Mother. It was simple, just painted in white, with the lines of the wall boards showing plainly through it. Jeld turned about and found the others upon the remaining walls. The open hand of the Craftsman, eye of the Wiseman, sword of Tovados, and Kelthid's lute. Above them all, a white ring was painted upon the ceiling.

A woman was seated upon the front bench, a short-haired man in a black robe beside her. Jeld's breath caught. A prishner. Not some Reborn red priest, but a real prishner. Jeld felt a swell of hope, the reaction catching him off guard.

The door closed behind them, the guard standing before it. Turning, the woman sighed visibly then whispered something to the prishner and came to them. The black hair upon her head was pulled back haphazardly, several loose strands hanging down around dark, tired eyes.

"Was I not clear?" said the woman, presumably Senach. "I have no interest in heroics. And now you bring another to this place?"

"This is my associate," Torral said. "And actually I believe you said you weren't interested *unless* we had the lord of Havaral's bloody head in a sack."

Senach looked them up and down then gave an expectant shrug of her eyebrows as if to say, "Well?"

Jeld cleared his throat and glanced at the prishner, then the guard. Senach got the meaning and dismissed both. At this, Jeld held up a finger.

"A moment, please," Jeld said. He climbed the steps back into the apartment. He reached into his collar before noticing the family was there, still working at their meal. He'd forgotten about them. The hallway, then. There, he took his bag from his shirt, pulled the liner fully free, then set it upon the floor.

"Come out," Jeld hissed. "Quickly."

Two tanned arms with white hair emerged and Benam pulled himself through, grunting with effort. Next came two hands tightly bound in rope, along with muffled cries. They wrestled back through twice before Benam and Jeld were able to pull the man through. Fen emerged behind him with a firm grip on the back of his shirt.

The bound man was old but not frail, with a short, neatly kept gray goatee and a mess of thinned hair going every which way other than over the bald head it usually covered. The first thing he did upon coming to his feet was fix said hair, the second was look about, and the third was set his jaw primly despite the muzzle tied through his mouth.

Replacing his bag, Jeld led the way back toward the temple. This time the family at the dining table did look up at Lord Annend's muffled complaints as Fen and Benam pulled him through their home, though none appeared particularly concerned. Not your typical family. Not your typical place.

Down the steps, and back into the dim temple. When finally Jeld could see Senach's face, he found not surprise upon it, but rather the skepticism of a magic show patron. She eyed all the newcomers in turn before scrutinizing Annend. Jeld spotted a flicker of recognition, but it was gone just as fast.

"It's not bloody," she said.

"True enough," Torral answered. "You are dealing with amateurs, remember."

Lord Annend tried to speak, but Senach interrupted. "It changes little."

Torral shrugged. "Suit yourself."

He drew his knife, Annend's eyes widening, but Torral only started sawing at the bindings.

"Perhaps another price," Senach said, her feigned disinterest cracking.

Torral kept sawing. "Wish I could."

"You can."

"Naw, just the one we discussed. Not my choice."

Her eyes narrowed. "Who? Krayo still?"

"Of course not," Torral said with little effort to sound convincing.

Suddenly a thought struck Jeld. "You're like him, you know," he told Senach. "Like Krayo. You like coin well enough, but you like the game even more."

"I have money!" Lord Annend seemed to say through his muzzle.

Jeld silenced him with a look, then carried on. "I'd wager you weren't even one to sit for a prishner's telling until you weren't allowed to anymore. Now you've got your own temple."

"It drives good business."

"Maybe," Jeld said dismissively. "Help us. You want a con? There's none greater. Con the one behind all this. Annend is just a pawn."

Annend nodded fervently at this. "Juss a hawn!" he affirmed.

Jeld elbowed Annend. "Save Avandria while you're at it, if it pleases you. Or, just see your enemies crumble."

He pushed Lord Annend at Senach, who caught him as he stumbled, again fixing his hair as he recovered. Her lip folded back in a snarl before she buried it behind a stoic mask.

"Annend Cross..." Senach said. "You robbed me of everything. You robbed this city, and of far more than coin. Do you feel no remorse for letting these priests lob heads off your people freely? For taking their religion, their drink, their freedom? For throwing your own people in death camps!"

She pushed Lord Annend onto the bench. The old lord shouted something through his muzzle.

"What's that?" she asked. "Naelis? Let me guess, Naelis made you do it? Did you instead consider defeating him alongside your granddaughter instead of *killing her and massacring her army!*"

Jeld felt a flash of fury from behind despite his shielded mind. Benam stood behind him glaring at Annend. Of course! He'd been there that day. His father had been there...

Senach pulled a dagger from her boot. Annend screamed and tried to stand but Senach pushed him back onto the bench. He turned and tried to say something. *Benam. Benam,* he seemed to say. The old knight, ever calm, ever peaceful, ever good, returned a haunted gaze, then turned without a word and walked from the room.

Jeld turned back toward a pained cry. Senach had her dagger plunged to the hilt into Annend's shoulder. She leaned to stare directly into Annend's eyes as he continued to scream.

"She was sixteen," she said through her teeth, voice breaking and eyes shimmering. "*Sixteen!* Sixteen years I raised her, and they took her head like it was nothing. I don't think they felt a thing. It was just... like chopping a vegetable. Just nothing to them."

Annend's screams seemed to try turning into words.

"Yes, I suppose you want to tell me you had no say in it," Senach said. "Let's hear it then." She cut the muzzle free, nicking his cheek twice.

"I didn't! It's true, I am nothing! It's all Naelis's people. They don't even let me attend council meetings!"

Senach shook her head. "I don't doubt that. But you did this to yourself. Your cowardice did this to all of us."

"No, no I did this to save the city from another war!"

"You had another chance!" Senach spat. "You had another chance after you learned what Naelis truly was, and instead of fighting for your people you murdered your own granddaughter!"

"Please, no, I never—I have information! Naelis is massing to move on Warrinton. He's massing in secret, and the east—"

"You took my girl!" Senach screamed.

She pulled her dagger free and reached it back to strike.

"Wait!" Jeld shouted. "We need to know—"

Senach plunged her blade into the lord of Havaral's heart. Lord Annend let loose a terrible cry nearly as chilling as the horror in his eyes. He spilled over backward as if scrambling from his wound and stared down at the dagger protruding from his chest.

Jeld ran over to him. "Tell me more of Naelis's plan! When? From where? What armies? What of the east?"

Lord Annend looked up to Jeld almost pleadingly. His lips moved wordlessly, a pained groan, then he was still. Senach staggered backward. Her chest rose and fell. A shaky hand went to her mouth and she sobbed a short breath. Somehow Jeld knew it wasn't for regret, nor disgust, nor horror. Nothing like that. No, she was just realizing that the one thing she'd lived for—vengeance—could not bring her daughter back.

Jeld sat upon one of the benches and stared at the Traveler's lute painted upon the wall, his mind returning to the day he'd met Lira as Annend bled out nearby. Could she ever look at him the same way, or would she just see the man who killed her grandfather? Her orders or not, wasn't that something that would stain a person? He hadn't been the one to strike the man down, at least.

"I'll help you," Senach said after a time, doing nothing to wipe the tears from her face.

Jeld nodded slowly then stood. "Torral, would you settle the terms? I must be off to Warrinton."

CHAPTER TWENTY-FIVE

Dralor started awake at the sound of the taskmaster's call. He looked about frantically as dread gripped his racing heart. He was not on a bunk, but rather a bedroll atop rocks just thick enough to keep him mostly off the mud. Three dozen others in various states of waking were situated much the same. A low makeshift stone wall surrounded them, a thatched roof overhead with a small gap between two showing a light rain outside. There was no stink of death, only the stink of life.

The icy grip on his heart eased. Not a death camp. Not a taskmaster. Not another day in the quarry, not more executions, nor ash in the air, nor the gaunt, shambling, walking dead.

"Up, C Troop! Move, Crauul!" their troop leader barked, kicking the foot of an unmoving man down the line.

Dralor eyed their leader while digging his boots out from beneath his blanket. Corporal Davit. Young, brawny, and handsome. He was among those who had joined them in Olth, his father a smith now supporting the effort. Davit was a good kid, ambitious enough to work their troop reasonably hard, though naive enough to do it for the wrong reasons.

The corporal kicked another laggard then came to Dralor and stopped mid bark as Dralor looked up at him. It wasn't a mean look, at least not intentionally. Not the glare of an aged man who didn't care to be bossed around by young pups. Maybe just the look of a man you don't bark at. Davit cleared his throat, gave a quick nod, and moved on down the line kicking any boots still pointed skyward.

Dralor rushed to fasten his boots. Some people slept in theirs. Not a bad idea when an attack—or an angry sergeant simulating one—was imminent, but otherwise it was just a sure way to get foot rot. Boots donned, Dralor began the daily trial of loading his pack. Why were they issued packs that couldn't fit the very items they were issued to hold? At least, not without folding, rolling, puzzling, stuffing, and ultimately a bout or three of wrestling.

"Up, Lans! Up, or... you'll move bricks all night!" Davit yelled.

Their young corporal kicked the boot of the only man still lying down. Lans was his name. A sturdy fellow, tough, distant, and just insubordinate enough to have not been beaten. He was a former soldier to be sure, solid with a blade and comfortable in the field.

Looking over his pack as he wrestled it closed, Dralor fought the urge to drag the man out of his bedroll. But no, he wasn't in charge. It would not do him well to stand out, nor would it be doing Davit any favors to suggest he couldn't handle it on his own. So instead he took his anger out on his pack, managing to stuff in the last of his possessions with his fist.

After receiving another kick, Lans finally rose and began to dress and pack, not sparing a look for Davit. Lowering his glare, Dralor set to rolling his bedding up. He hurried to catch up with those youngsters who either slept fully dressed or merely moved faster in the morning than an old prince.

Dralor had gained a new appreciation for just how much time these simple, soldierly tasks occupied. He'd spent a great deal of his time soldiering, but always had men minding his gear—polishing his boots, wrestling his packs, and the like. Then there were the watch shifts, kitchen details, shit trench digging, and countless other duties.

Of course, leadership was a different kind of busy. A different kind of stress. While soldiers enjoyed their rare moments between duties or suffered their late shifts, often Dralor had poured over maps, prepared orders, letters, logistics plans. And in the rare respite, there was no escaping the weight of command. Now here he was, his only concern trying not to be the last one ready to march. Different indeed.

In short order they were marching through the fine mist upon a muddy road through the mossy craglands. They set a fast pace, with many envious glances to the several other troops of men they'd already passed. Some had already stopped for some training or another. Dralor did not dwell much on that, though. Nor did he dwell on the sore, strap-bitten shoulders, aching back, nor blistered feet. As with his days on Eshal's farm, the labor proved a welcome outlet. A distraction at times, though it was not so easy to leave his darker days behind while actively training to confront them.

Dralor futilely wiped rain and sweat from his eyes with a drenched sleeve and marched on. It felt good to be working toward something. Toward absolution. Yes, be it in death or victory, he marched toward absolution.

"Get back in there, Keply!" came Davit's shout.

"Leave 'em," Lans grumbled a few rows back. "Fat bastard is no soldier."

"Let's go, Kep! Stay with me!"

Just off the road, Davit led a fat, altogether soft looking man toward the front of the formation. Keply's every heavy step looked to come only at great effort. A painful, rolling shamble, but the steps kept coming, Cheeks a hot red and fuzzy chin dripping, Keply chased Davit to the front, where their troop leader deposited him before running back down the line giving encouraging shouts and slurs. As soon as he was out of sight the line slowed behind Keply, thanklessly grateful for it.

"Gonna get us killed," Lans said. "Like carrying a casualty into battle instead of out. Dead weight."

Cheeks billowing with his quick breaths, Dralor watched Keply through the bobbing heads in front of him. He had once personally removed a man from duty for making the uniform look bad, and signed off on countless other such removals. War was unforgiving, and indeed an army could not afford to slow down for the sake of a few who couldn't stop stuffing their own gullets.

Still, that was battle, not training. They would hardly remove a strong farm boy from training for poor swordplay before adequate instruction. No, this was more about the stigma of being fat than it was about being slow.

The sun climbed behind a gray haze. They came to a stop in one of their usual training sites, a rocky, flat hilltop with an astounding view and plenty of stones to teach one the importance of not tripping in a swordfight. They wordlessly established a perimeter, and waited. Another soldier skill Dralor gained a new respect for, but found himself lacking utterly.

Dralor's knees ached and legs shook as he knelt beside a boulder. He glanced to his either side, searching through boulders bald and mossy. He spotted his closest comrades, both sprawled on the ground, propped up against their packs and facing not out toward any imagined enemy but inward, toward their troop leader. Strong on concealment, but hardly securing anything.

Dralor sighed, looked about to ensure Davit wasn't watching, then sprawled onto his back.

"Rings!" Davit's voice came before Dralor could even let out his breath.

Dralor groaned, detangled from his pack straps, and struggled to his feet. His troop gathered in a flat area within the perimeter and formed into two concentric circles. Each man paired with one in the other ring, and Davit called for the first bout to begin. Training swords clacked, curses and cries marred the serene countryside, and after a short round, Davit called for a switch. The inner circle rotated and they began again with their next opponent.

It was the fourth round, Dralor's grip already aching, when he heard Keply's cry and the unmistakable clang and rattle of a dropped sword upon the stony ground. Dralor parried an attack and chanced a look, finding Keply on his back a few bouts away, bleeding head against a jagged stone. Lans stood over him, shaking his head.

A blade hissed toward Dralor. He leaned back and it narrowly flew past. Dralor's opponent grinned at him. A wiry fellow, lean but tough, with red hair and buggy eyes. Carredine was his name. A ruined farmer, he'd joined them from one of the small towns Jeld and company had recruited from on their way to Havaral.

"Keep lookin' over there," Carredine said. "I can almost take you when ya ain't looking,"

Dralor grunted. Probably could have already, but like most, Carredine had the good sense to hold back a bit, both to conserve strength and to keep from injuring comrades. Of course, Dralor probably could have killed him a long time ago if he hadn't been more focused on Keply's fight than his own.

He circled his opponent, trading a few blows along the way, until he could see Keply's bout just over Carredine's shoulder. Keply had managed to reach his sword and was lumbering to his feet, pressing two plump hands to his knee to rise. Lans had not pursued, just shaking his head. Beyond Keply's clumsily raised sword, his eyes were wide and his open mouth twitching.

Lans curled his lip in disgust and stalked forward. Keply swung his sword, Lans casually sidestepped it, and Lans cracked him across the ribs with his wooden blade. Keply cried out and swung again. Lans raised his sword high in a two-handed grip and brought it down hard against Keply's sword hand. Keply shrieked and dropped his sword again, cowering behind his upraised hands.

Dralor did not hear his own pleas to not get involved, to lay low. He did not feel Carredine's sword rapping across his back. Nostrils flaring, jaw set, and head cocked, he stormed toward Lans. Lans turned before Dralor reached him, smirked, then swung at Keply's backside.

Dralor's sword shot out, knocking the blow aside as he advanced without pause. Lans' exaggerated disinterest broke in a flicker of surprise, then he glared and puffed out his chest.

Lans advanced as if to push his chest against Dralor's "You'd better-"

Dralor punched Lans squarely in the nose. Lans staggered backward and fell onto his ass. To the bastard's credit, he kept hold of his sword. Dralor grabbed it, twisted it free, then took a handful of Lans' beard and pulled him over backward. He dragged Lans out of the ring of soldiers, the stunned man obliging just enough to keep some tension off his beard and keep his footing.

"Del!" Davit's voice came from behind. "Enough, Del!"

Dralor heard Davit's shout and knew the sense of it, but the damage was done, and he had unfinished business. He slammed Lans down over a stone, craning his neck by the beard, and raised his sword. Thick with tears from his beaten nose, Lans' eyes widened. He flinched away as Dralor's sword came down, then crashed against the stone beside his neck.

"The next time you turn on your own, I'll have your head," Dralor said icily, then turned sharply and started back toward the rings.

"He'll—he'll get us all killed," Lans said from behind, voice small.

Dralor stopped, chest rising and falling fast. Keep walking, he told himself. Just keep walking. But instead he turned.

"Why are you here?" he shouted. "To disrespect your leadership? To maim your comrades?"

"Because soldiers need an army, and I'd bleed the Mother before I'd join Naelis's."

"You're as good as serving Naelis."

"We're better off without that fat oaf. He's a disgrace! This is no army anyway. Naelis might as well—"

"Then make it an army!" Dralor roared. "Make him a soldier!"

Dralor turned and stormed past Davit, who stepped aside and gaped after him, as did the entire troop.

"With me," Dralor said as he passed Keply, continuing to a relatively clear area outside the rings. When he turned, Keply was standing before him at attention.

"Switch your feet," Dralor said, looking him over. "Now, bend your knees. No, just a little. Bring the point of your sword above your fist, you've no control with it out there. Now, stop staring at my sword. Watch my body."

"Alright, C Troop!" Davit shouted at the gawking recruits. "Rotate and begin!"

Dralor continued his instruction and the drills resumed. After a while he sent Keply to rejoin the others, and followed suit. This went on long past when their fingers would have quit working just weeks before. The shadows cast by the many peculiar standing stones strewn about turned then stretched across the mossy ground. Next came formations and battle drills. Finally, aching from blows and numb with fatigue, they began their march back.

C Troop was silent save for the beat and squelch of their steps upon stone and mud. Davit allowed an easier pace than the march in, though it was not slow. When finally they reached camp, most of the other soldiers were already sitting around cookfires, grooming, or sleeping. The usual bitter and envious grumbles as Dralor's troop waddled on rubbery legs through the camp were different somehow. As lounging troops jeered, C Troop postures seemed only to straighten. Pride, Dralor realized. They were proud.

Dralor washed, changed into his one other uniform, and joined his troops at their fire. The men fell silent when he sat, and Dralor kept his gaze in the fire as he ate. Twice men tried to spark conversation with mention of their swordplay drills, but none pressed when Dralor responded only with murmured acknowledgments or nods. Lans was quieter than usual, and turned in quite early.

Tired as they were, their numbers dwindled quickly as the ever-present island gloom darkened to a thick black. Soon the only evidence of the gloom was the missing stars, and the rising embers of the fire disappearing too soon. Dralor's thoughts were distant when a voice stirred him.

"You've led men," Davit said, sitting nearby.

Dralor met his gaze then looked away.

"Where was this the whole time?" Davit asked. "I knew it, though. I knew it."

Dralor shook his head. "Never mind it."

"Tell me your story. Best to know your men."

Dralor looked at Davit. The kid sounded curious, but more so he sounded as always as if he were reading from a script on leadership. Well, he'd get things figured out soon enough. For a moment, Dralor almost smiled, until he recalled what would harden the kid. Only battle. Blood. Loss.

"They're a good troop," Davit said, "but it's hard to find the right balance of discipline and, you know, keeping them liking you."

"You don't need them to like you, you need them to respect you," Dralor said despite himself.

"Yeah. Yeah, that's what they say. Maybe easier when you're... older. Or more experienced."

"No, always. You don't want them to hate you, but respect is the key. This can be respect for your experience, or your skill, yes, but also respect for your values, your rank, your authority. Even your discipline."

"Firm rule. Hard consequences." Davit supplied.

"No, no. Well, to a degree, yes, but not only that. Armies running on fear alone will break eventually. Rule of law is important, but respect is not fear."

Davit fell silent. Dralor bit his lip. Enough, just turn back to the fire. The kid would learn soon enough.

"You're doing well," Dralor blurted despite himself. "But look, you march around like a child playing soldier. Like you are playing a part, or you are on some quest for glory. War is not glorious. Leadership is not a costume. And these are not young, summer recruits. They know we train for killing and death. Do not discount their sacrifice."

Davit shifted uneasily then cleared his throat. "I see."

"You are very capable. Captain Heath selected you for good reason."

In truth, Dralor wasn't convinced Davit was the best choice, but in the absence of many experienced candidates he could make some sense. Davit could be trusted to work the men hard, and his puppy dog loyalty would make him easy enough for a commander to wrangle.

"Right. Thanks," the young troop leader said sulkily.

"Leadership is your most powerful weapon—the troop's most powerful weapon. Would you train men in swordplay but not subject your own leadership to instruction?"

Davit sagged a little, then straightened. "No. No, you're right."

"Good. You'll do this troop well." Enough! Enough before any more questions. Dralor stood. "Good night, Corporal."

Dralor made his way to their makeshift barracks, carefully picked his way through his slumbering comrades, and turned in for the night. The next morning Davit woke them with the news they'd have the day off, compliments of Captain Heath. In town, Dralor slipped away from his troop as they made for a pub, but they were quick to recover him despite his protests. So too did they manage to put a drink in his hand.

"Dreams no, I'm too old for that shit," Erol said, having wandered over from where his own troop was gathered. "Corporal will do fine. Gotta keep up, but glad to spend more time barking at my men than training."

"It's a good position for you."

Erol took a drink and grunted his agreement. "Authority without too much of the responsibility. Just enough to shield the men from some of the stupid."

"What do you make of this Heath fellow?"

"Good as any officer. Said he served under Prince Dralor."

Beside them, a sturdy fellow with a short, ear to ear beard across his chin groaned. Lalow was his name, one of the Islers who had joined their ranks.

"Long ago, mind you," Erol added dismissively.

Lalow shrugged. "Suppose there's few better to have reared him for war. Tovaine maybe, and we've got him now, too."

"Glad to be on the same side as *that* man," said Carredine, the bug-eyed fellow Dralor had fought during drills.

"Aye," said Lalow. "Though I heard it took just two of Naelis's inquisitors to take him down."

Dralor's gaze fell to the scratched tabletop.

Carredine spat. "Oh sure, catchin' him by surprise. Then what happened in Delvarad, eh? Took down two in a fair fight, didn't he?"

Lalow swallowed a mouthful of ale. "Ah! True there, true—"

A chorus of cries came from across the room, then the pub fell silent save for one man yelling.

"If I was in C Troop I'd have put him on a spit by now!" came the shouting, to laughter and raised mugs.

Dralor stood and searched through the crowd. The man making the ruckus was fairly young, somewhat tall, and had arms as thick as thighs. He stood with one of those stony arms around a red-faced Keply seated at a table.

"Maybe they keep ya around to block arrows, eh?"

Keply grabbed the soldier's arm and pulled him nearly to the ground before the man slipped free. Coming to his feet, Keply swung at the man, but where beneath his girth he might be strong, he was not fast. The big man dodged it and gave Keply a solid blow on the cheek. Keply showed no sign of noticing. He grabbed at the man, then took a fist to the nose with a crunch. This time he felt it, crying out and staggering back. Lalow pursued, reached way back, and threw his weight behind a big white-knuckled fist.

Suddenly Lans was there. He caught the other man's arm and headbutted him straight in the face. Before the man could do anything more than give a stupid look, Lans punched him in the gut then laid him out with a hook to the jaw. He sat Keply down and slid the unconscious man's drink in front of him.

"Crauul," he said, patting Keply on the shoulder. With that, he sat beside Keply and swept a challenging glare over the pub.

Dralor found Davit staring his way through the waking merriment. Their gazes met for a long moment, then Dralor gave a nod and turned his attention back to his men.

CHAPTER TWENTY-SIX

"Hyah!" Jeld shouted, slapping the reins.

Hooves thundered upon the dirt as he raced down a hill, and not just the four of his own mount. He glanced over his shoulder. Only four riders visible now, but gaining, and the rest would be close behind. He ducked a branch from one of the many pines covering the foothills and searched the way ahead. *Dreams*, where was that road?

Another glance behind. He could nearly see the whites of their eyes now, and still they gained. Beneath him, his horse's breath was rapid, its once drenched and lathered coat now nearly dry. The ground leveled off, then began climbing anew. He fought to keep his mount pointed up the hill, eyeing the thickening trees to either side. Slim chance of hiding from an army, though, and unwise to risk his mount's ankles when his pursuers had so many more ankles to gamble with.

His mount shook its head violently and slowed. Jeld kicked its flanks and managed to wrench its head straight, but it only slowed more. Cursing, Jeld let it turn and with another kick it sped into the treeline. That settled that, then.

"Hyah!" Jeld urged, kicking and slapping the reins.

His mount picked up speed, at this point probably more from falling down the hill than anything else. He pressed into a thicket until his pursuers were out of sight, then leapt off his horse. His feet slammed to the ground, legs wobbling as he raced to keep from falling. He slowed, slammed into a tree, and scrambled around behind it. There he froze, back pressed to the tree, heart thudding and breathless. Three riders pounded past, then a fourth. He stole a look around the tree then barely ducked back around in time as another half dozen men thundered by.

With another quick peek, he turned and ran up the hill. Stiff from the saddle, his legs obeyed little better than his poor horse had, but they loosened up and soon trees were flashing by to either side. The occasional beat of hooves racing to the south came from behind, but he didn't slow. He quickened his already reckless pace down the other side of the hill, immediately rolling his ankle. He cursed, but it wasn't a bad one, and after a few awkward strides favoring it he was accelerating again.

Everything fell quiet after a time save for his own huffing breath, pounding heart, and scraping steps upon the dry sunward hillside. A moment later, more hoofbeats came from the south where he'd misdirected his pursuers, growing louder. Drawing closer. He finally spotted the road down below, hope swelling for a fleeting moment before realizing it did him no good now. Not without a horse. Probably would have done no good with his tired horse either.

Jeld raced toward another thicket pinched between this hill and the next, strides so wide he was more falling than running. A glance behind. They hadn't appeared over the hill yet. There was still time. Still time. But then they appeared at the crest of the hill. One pointed his way, then they raced toward him.

Panic pierced Jeld like a blade. The bag. Had it come to that? Into the *blazing* bag again? Leave Lira again when she needed him most? Leave Renae and Warrinton to fall to Naelis's advance without warning? Then with horror he realized he hadn't needed to pull it in behind him, he could have just hid inside and left the bag concealed somewhere when he'd broken away from them before. Well, there was nothing for it now.

He freed his Idolic sense and reached back toward his pursuers. At least twelve of them now, and a sense of more further behind. He needed something to use. What did they want? Him, of course, but leading them off in pursuit of a phantom on foot would not distract them for long. There was something... an anxiety despite their dominant position. He drank it in, let it settle into his mind as if the fear were his own until he could almost see it—a Warrinton patrol, charging like death up the hill toward them. They were worried about a patrol. Jeld sank his teeth into the idea, poured his will into the perception until he could feel the very ground shaking underfoot.

Behind, one pursuer reined in so suddenly that he spilled from his horse. Another fled. The remaining six slowed or even stopped, but all of them shook it off and took up the chase again. Cursing, Jeld fought to sharpen the illusion as he raced for cover, but he couldn't hold it. It faltered. He let his tired legs flop to a stop, huffing for breath. Then he drew his sword, and turned.

To a man, Naelis's soldiers cried out, wheeled hard, and charged back up the hill. Armored riders in Warrinton blue were suddenly charging past Jeld—real riders, not some illusion. They caught up to Naelis's exhausted men and dispatched them with brutal efficiency. One raised his hands in surrender and received a sword through his chest for his trouble. Another lying in dirt with his leg twisted at an odd angle pleaded for mercy until a blade hacked the top of his head off. This was Jeld's introduction to the men of Warrinton.

Horses tied off, they searched the bodies then moseyed back over toward Jeld. None said so much as a word to him as they set to cleaning the blood from their weapons, others passing around a sack of jerky.

Jeld might have thought he was invisible if not for a few brief glances in his direction.

"Anyway, as I was saying," a big bearded man began, "The stars gotta be pretty far away to stay so still when we move, ya know?"

"They do move, ya twat," said an older man with a scar across his face. "Pass across the sky every night, then back to the start during the day while we can't see them."

"Oan didn't say they don't move," said a third, younger man. "He's talking about how—you know, how you've got to turn to track a tree as you walk by it."

"Not so for a star," said the bearded man, Oan. "Or the moon, even."

This went on as a lean, cleanly shaven man with a touch of gray in his pale hair rode down from the hilltop where he'd been scouting. He noticed Jeld, swept an exasperated glare about his men, then sighed and approached on foot. The helm under his arm was more ornate than those of the others, and he had a pin as if for a cape on the shoulder of his cuirass, though it bore no cape.

"What have you done to earn such a send-off?" the man asked.

"I impersonated a messenger from Naelis and delivered fake orders to withdraw," Jeld said.

The man laughed, then stopped when Jeld kept a straight face. "You're serious."

"It worked well enough on their front. Wager they're packed up and moving by now."

Laughter from the others.

"I knew he was alright, Captain, seeing as the enemy wanted him dead," said the man with the scar.

The bearded man who'd gone on about the stars frowned at Jeld. "You were discovered, though."

"Yes, well. The commander of that army they've got hiding to the south apparently caught on faster than I'd hoped."

The now jovial chatter died.

"Army to the south?" the captain asked.

"That's why I came. To warn you. Something about the east, too. They are involved somehow, but that's less clear. Please, we need to get word to your commanders immediately."

The captain's eyes narrowed. "How did you come by this information?"

Jeld considered his options. "That's probably best left for your lord's ears only. Please, we need to hurry."

"You won't be coming near our lord's ear if you don't answer the question!" barked the older one.

"You wouldn't have much reason to grant me audience if you got everything out of me, either."

"If your goal is truly to warn him, what's it matter whether he sees you or hears it from us?" the captain asked.

"There's more than this warning," Jeld said, trying his damnedest to keep his irritation from showing. "And your lord would not be pleased were it shared with anyone but him."

The captain eyed him for a time before speaking. "Surely you can see how—"

"Start talking or I'll have your balls," the older one said boredly, not looking up from slicing an apple with a sharp knife.

Jeld looked between them, then sighed. "You asked how I learned Naelis was moving on Warrinton. Fine. Lord Annend Cross told me."

"The traitor entrusted you with this? Or you overheard this? You are a spy, then?"

"He did not tell me willingly. I tortured him."

Never mind that it was the woman Senach who had done it. The soldiers, many of whom had casually eased closer to the conversation, fell silent.

The captain shook his head. "How..."

"A knife," Jeld said quickly.

"No, no. How did you get to him? Who do you serve?"

"The answer to those questions, I promise you, is for the lord of Warrinton, and he alone. Or Renae Warrin, if it pleases you. He is a good friend of mine."

The older one's eyes flicked to the captain, who finally sighed. With that they were soon headed east. Jeld hurried closely behind on foot until they happened upon a horse from one of their dispatched enemies. The mountains towered higher and sharpened with each crested hill. They were not the massive snow-capped peaks of the north, but they were plenty tall and far more jagged. The party came to a road, following it alongside the foot of the mountains and past a guard tower before turning up a pass aglow with the low western sun behind them.

Warrinton greeted them with a sheer wall across the full of the pass. A massive drawbridge lay open over a moat cut in the rocky ground. A gate of thick iron bars sealed the whole of the gap. Soldiers atop the battlements greeted Jeld's escort with familiarity and others below opened a smaller wicket gate, which they passed through. The captain dismissed all but three of his men, sending all the horses with them, then led Jeld inward on foot.

The first thing to strike Jeld about the city was the amalgamation of eastern and western architecture. Intricate and colorful tile mosaics, tiled roofs, fine columns, plentiful narrow archways. He remembered hearing that Warrinton had first belonged to the easterners, but never stopped to consider what that meant for its architecture. He looked back at the gate, still imposing in the growing distance, and wondered how the west had managed to conquer it. Second to strike Jeld was the sheer number of soldiers here. Almost every other person about the city had on a sharp Warrinton uniform and a sword at the hip.

Jeld walked between his escorts, or perhaps captors, to a complex at the heart of the city. There, the captain began an unenviable journey through what seemed the full of the Warrinton chain of command. Eventually Jeld found himself in the keep itself, standing with the captain and the bearded stargazer outside a broad set of double doors carved in the intricate eastern fashion. Two knights stood guard, dressed in the customary dull gray armor, with light blue petticoats spilling out over their legs.

A while later the doors opened and a hodgepodge of people from robed women to grizzled military men exited. A man who looked more soldier than chancellor despite the ceremonial staff in his hand waved them inward.

"Captain Geraud," he announced, sharply but not making a show of things.

Jeld followed the captain, *Geraud*, inside. Beyond a dozen tiled archways was a vast chamber dominated by empty stands and an intricate throne. A council table was rather tucked aside in a separate room between the first archways, two men seated in conversation. The first was an elderly fellow with a tutor's robe and bent posture to match. The second a handsome, muscular, grim-faced man in a sharp military jacket. Renae, Jeld realized after far too long. A man now, more so than Jeld could have imagined. He wondered if he himself had changed so much in so little time.

Captain Geraud stopped before the table and bowed his head. "My lord."

Jeld eyed the old man. It seemed Lord Terich Warrin was a more meek and academic sort than his reputation suggested. Then Jeld's eyes widened before settling on Renae. Could it be that his young friend was now the lord of Warrinton?

"What's this I hear of an army?" Renae said. "Is this the messenger?" He squinted at Jeld, then his eyes widened. "Arvin?"

Jeld smiled, shaking of his surprise. "It's good to see you."

Renae shook his head as if to clear it. "I'd... heard you were dead. Or, missing? Received a letter from—"

"Er," Jeld interrupted, glancing at the others, "I wonder if..."

"Yes, fine. Forgive me, Cathius, I'll send a message in a bit," Renae said to the tutor, then turned to the others. "Excuse us, please."

"My lord," the captain said with a bow. He gave Jeld another look as he made his way to the door, closing it behind the old tutor when finally he'd made it through.

"Well, this is unexpected," Renae said, clearing his throat.

"Before we catch up, Naelis has an army massing near—"

"Sutherwood."

"And—"

"And you fear the east is stirring. Yes, your message was relayed."

"Right," Jeld said. He shifted uneasily. Renae was looking at him like a stranger. No, like a hostile.

"I've taken some measures," Renae said. "More on that later. Sit, won't you?"

Jeld pursed his lips, then shrugged his eyebrows and sat across from Renae.

"Who are you?" Renae asked with a piercing stare. "And don't say Arvin Emry."

It was a knife in Jeld's gut. Far from the reunion he'd anticipated. Hardly surprising in retrospect, though, having deceived his friend as such. Still, the friendship had been as real as anything about him, hadn't it? Jeld looked away, steeled himself, and spoke.

"My real name is Jeld. Just a street kid, really. Wound up working as a spy, and that's where I met you. You were truly my friend though, Renae."

"A hole or two in that story, wouldn't you say?" Renae said.

Jeld gave a humorless smile. "I sheltered in a theater. Got to be a pretty good actor, I guess. Lent itself well to spying."

"Who were you spying for?"

A heavy silence stretched for a few painful breaths, then Jeld shook his head. "I shouldn't. People with the best interests of the kingdom, though."

Renae frowned and looked away with feigned disinterest.

"But that's not why I'm here. I'm no spy anymore, Renae. I'm here for Lira."

Renae stiffened but did not look up.

"She's alive. She's building a sort of resistance across all of Avandria. Unconventional warfare, I think the books would call it. She'll... need a proper army though, too."

Renae was deep in thought for a long while, then finally spoke. "You read a book?"

Jeld opened his mouth to explain, then Renae looked up and gave a devious grin.

"Proud?" Jeld asked.

Suddenly they were just old friends again. Jeld caught Renae up on the less sensitive areas of his journey. Renae told of his father's passing, his ascendance to the throne, and his conflicts with Naelis's armies. The candles upon the table were burning low and a hearty meal well picked over when Jeld's mind finally returned to business.

"You've heard nothing of an eastern attack?" Jeld asked.

"They always attack," Renae said, plucking a grape from a vine.

"An army, Renae. Not a patrol. Not marauders. You've heard nothing?"

Renae ate his grape and plucked another, frowning all the while. "It's been quieter than usual. Some rumors. One of our patrols did not return."

"An army to the east. An army to the west. What do you mean to do?"

Renae grabbed his goblet and just stared at it for a while before answering. "I mean to defend Warrinton."

"Common wisdom is that when you're surrounded, you charge an enemy. I doubt that applies when you're in a castle, though."

"No, I don't suppose it does."

Jeld refilled his plate with a tasty stew of beans, appetite insatiable after his frenzied journey from the Isles. He was thankful for the time chewing bought him, but there was no delicate way to put it.

"March west," he said. "Not to battle, but to the Isles. Join Lira."

"Abandon Warrinton?" Renae scoffed. "I am not some military unit to be repositioned, I'm the lord of this city! I'll not hand my people over to Naelis, you know what that would mean for them. And I'll damn well not lose Warrinton after just weeks when my father protected it for decades!"

"Give it to the east. That'll keep Naelis busy. Then it'll be him caught between enemies."

"I won't abandon my people."

"Renae, how long can Warrinton last between the two? Two *kingdoms*. Warrinton will fall, but your army doesn't have to. You can likely evacuate a fair lot of your people, too. Don't just wait here to die."

"We can hold," Renae said.

"Do you truly think so? On two fronts? Even if they just lay siege… you'll be completely cut off. Maybe you have stores, but you can only delay so long."

"*If* there is an eastern army. *If* they are allied! *If* we can't hold! *If—*"

A servant entered and Renae bit off his words. The servant placed a tray with tea onto the table, a log into the fire, then quietly departed.

Renae continued more calmly. "Ishdalar would not help Naelis. He's a bigger threat than Warrinton."

"If Naelis offered them Warrinton?" Jeld asked. "What reason would they have to refuse that?"

"He wouldn't. Naelis wants more, not less. And the east is a bigger threat than I am. Handing over the only thing standing between the east and Avandria would be foolish."

Jeld frowned. "I suppose when you are in a meat grinder it hardly matters why."

He poured some tea, dumped in twice as much milk, and was drizzling a third spoon of honey when he looked up to find Renae's eyebrow raised.

"I never did like tea," Jeld said, sliding the tray to Renae. "Even in Tovar I loaded it up."

"It was a good thing you were playing the part of a lowly commoner."

Jeld smiled, but it gave way to a grave look. "Move half your army west. In secret. You can't make use of so many in the city anyway. If I'm wrong about the east, or if it seems you might hold, then no harm done. It's a sound tactical move anyway."

Renae set his jaw as he took his tea. "And if you're right, abandon the rest in Warrinton and march to your princess?"

"Seems a preferable contingency to slaughter. But only a contingency. I hardly see any reason not to position men to assault an enemy's flank. I'd wager you've already done it to a degree, so just... do it more."

The flames flickered with a sound like a hung bed sheet flapping in the wind. A servant entered and made to close the windows, but Renae turned him away and went to one of the windows. Renae stood there in silence, looking out over his city.

"Very well," Renae said after a while. "Commoner spy or not, you have a point. But I don't mean to abandon Warrinton should it..."

"You owe me no answer now," Jeld offered.

Renae turned and narrowed his eyes at Jeld. "Arvin would have a smug look on his face. Probably have his feet on my table. Was that all an act?"

Jeld's eyes fell to the table. Had it been an act? Or was *this* the act? He wasn't sure. But then, wasn't it normal to adapt one's behavior to others when needed? Was that false, or empathetic?

"I'm not sure," Jeld said. "Maybe smug better suits trivialities like the tantrums of Calane Demerious. Not the fate of cities and kingdoms."

Renae let out a slow breath and nodded, then sent one of the guards from outside to fetch his general. The conversation turned to such trivialities and their time in Tovar until the door opened. In came a grizzled, rigid fellow with a deeply lined and closely shaved face. Like Renae, he wore a military coat.

"General Shelsid," Renae began, "we must reposition—"

"It's true, My Lord," the general interrupted. "A massive host to the east, and they're on the move."

Chapter Twenty-Seven

A cool mountain breeze blew through Jeld's hair as he stared out past the walls of Warrinton into the darkness beyond. Had the scouts not given warning, he might not have noticed the writhing, shadowy mass drawing ever nearer, but he'd have heard it still. The army of Ishdalar sounded like a churning sea, not a single voice to be heard from the disciplined force, just the steady beat of twenty thousand feet.

The east. The term had always seemed little more than a direction before, even as he'd traveled Ishdalar. A land, a people, sure, but only that. Now, standing here at the eastern edge of Avandria and staring at the encroaching tide, it seemed a force. *The east.*

With a final rumble like the sigh of some great beast, the army fell silent. Jeld squinted through the darkness. Nothing now. Perhaps that bit of roughness there atop the usually barren landscape, or maybe he only imagined it. He turned and joined Renae at the opposite balcony. Another army stretched across the valley to the west, this one already still and unmistakable with its countless torches in a line like a wildfire. Renae's own troops, repositioned under cover of darkness over the nights prior as Renae had agreed, would be out there somewhere in the deep woods to their north.

A cold fear gripped Jeld's racing heart. He was no stranger to danger, but typically he'd always approached it on his terms. Usually it was him sneaking through the darkness, or at least behind the veil of some character, not just standing dumbly between two armies. His little acting, sensing, or other tricks would do him little good while being ground up like meat with the rest of them.

"Damn," Renae breathed. "Damn."

Jeld watched as Renae once again turned his attention to their defenses. The eastern and western battlements were packed with archers. Swordsmen filled the northern and southern battlements and spilled from the bases of the many towers awaiting breachers. Crossbowmen were staged near the eastern and western portcullises, ready to greet whatever sorry lot made it through the outer gate.

Despite his rising nerves and prior doubts, Jeld nonetheless wondered whether he actually favored Renae's odds. Warrinton would never survive an extended siege, but a battle... Idols, he didn't envy the brave or stupid bastards making ready to throw themselves against these walls. Still, given enough men...

"Come on, bastards," Renae said through clenched teeth. "Come on! What are you waiting for!"

At that, a horn blared to the west, then a hundred more in a piercing wail. Even on the highest tower surrounded by stone and a friendly army, a panic rose up in Jeld at that terrible dissonance. A single booming voice thundered something lost to the night, battle cries rose up over the horns in a great roar, and the ground shook as they charged. Jeld spun to the east, finding them still and silent, at least. Then their dark mass shifted and rushed toward them.

Jeld's skin crawled. He longed to find some shadow to slip into, to descend the northern or southern wall and slip into the wilderness, even to just become some old commoner who might simply welcome and bow before a new master. Instead he stood shoulder to shoulder with the target of the two armies, Lord Renae Warrin, and watched death close its jaws around them.

As suddenly as the charge had begun, Naelis's army stopped, the attack horns still wailing. Not long after, the eastern army too stopped.

"What the dreams are they doing," Renae cursed, looking from one army to the next.

Finally the horns quieted and left them in an ear-ringing silence.

"Maybe testing us?" Jeld offered. "Trying to spring any traps before stepping in them?"

"No," Renae breathed. "They're afraid to commit…"

Jeld hummed his disagreement. "That was too organized a halt. Not some hesitant soldiers. And why march all this way just to—"

"No, not scared to fight. Afraid to commit forces before the other. You saw the Ishdali advance at the west's signal. Then the west stopped, yet they kept their horns blaring."

"Naelis's forces were trying to get the east to engage…"

Renae nodded, eyes fixed on Naelis's army. "Probably want to pick up the scraps after we and the east have killed one another."

Jeld looked back and forth between the two armies. Maybe there was hope. Maybe the distrust between Naelis and the east would be enough to keep them both at bay.

"Perhaps it's good you didn't abandon your city like I'd suggested…" Jeld said, earning a slap on the arm.

Jeld smiled. Renae hit him again, then once more before Jeld turned to him.

"Alright already!" Jeld said. "I—"

"Look," Renae hissed.

A single torch had been lit at the head of the eastern army. A mounted figure was holding something overhead. Jeld couldn't make out what it was, then it flashed white in the light of the torch. A flag. A white flag.

The figure slowly started forward, perhaps half a dozen others following on foot. They stopped just out of bowshot, then shouted up as if directly to Renae.

"I would treat with the lord of Warrinton!"

It was a woman's voice, loud and thickly accented. Her words echoed in the night then faded to a palpable silence. Jeld looked over at Renae, then elbowed him. Renae ignored this, eyes darting from side to side in thought, then finally he shouted back.

"Warrinton welcomes you!"

Jeld grimaced. Not only at the cliche response, but the danger of welcoming an enemy.

"Not worried it's a trick?" Jeld asked.

"If they wanted to attack, they could have. If Naelis betrayed them, we could have an ally in this."

Renae stopped at the top of the stairs, took a breath, set his shoulders, and descended the stairs a confident lord. Jeld followed.

"See her in," Renae ordered a commander as he and Jeld emerged onto the northern battlements. "Through the wicket, mind you, and be ready to seal it. And admit her attendants. See them to the council table. Under guard, but show respect."

"Yes, my lord," the man said with a bow, then hurried off.

"Stand down!" came the commander's calls. Others echoed the order into the distance, falling pikes and bows and a collective sigh flowing with it.

Jeld followed Renae down another set of stairs then through countless soldiers standing ready to reinforce either front. Most bowed at least a little as they passed, one pretending not to notice until a grizzled superior elbowed him. Passing through the doors of the great hall, Jeld sat at his lordly friend's side. The old tutor, Cathius, was already at the table.

"A most interesting turn of events, my lord," Cathius said with an almost excited academic interest.

Renae hummed his agreement. "Naelis's army tried to lure the east into attacking first."

"Yes, that seems the logical conclusion. This assumes they were collaborating to begin with. Of course, it's also possible they were never allied, and now each is faced with two hostile armies."

"Either way, they do not like each other," Jeld said. "This is good news for us."

Cathius eyed Jeld. The old tutor had not taken warmly to him. Perhaps leery of an outsider with his lord's ear, or maybe jealous for it. His narrow gaze suggested the former.

"Yes," Cathius said finally. "I quite agree."

A short while later the doors opened. They stood as General Shelsid entered with a squad of soldiers. At their center was the eastern envoy. Her skin was the typical pale gray, her hair dark with a tail of sorts bent to spill back over her face. Perhaps fifty of age, her face lined and serious. Two men in loose clothing of purple silk stood with her, heads slightly bowed.

"Please, sit," Renae said, taking his seat. "Forgive my haste, but there are two armies threatening my city."

Jeld reclaimed his seat beside the lord negotiating for the future of the kingdom, shrugging at another sharp look from Cathius. The eastern envoy slowly approached, an icy gaze on the tiled archway as she passed beneath it.

"Beautiful, is it not?" she mused, turning to inspect an intricate pattern etched into a pillar.

"It is," Renae said. "And had Ishdalar not tried to invade Avandria, you might still have it."

Her eyes flicked to Renae, and such was the venom in them that Jeld thought she might hiss.

"Invade? Invade the land you drove our people from?"

"It was scarcely populated. You have your own kingdom, we have ours."

"Kingdom," she scoffed. "*Barbarians.* Fighting for your crown year after year. Your civilization has not advanced in a hundred years."

"Our nations are free, not slaves like yours. Freedom is not easy, but it's worth fighting for."

The envoy bit her lip, then forced a smile. "Forgive me. Warrinton still holds a dear spot in our histories, and to see the Ishdali architecture..."

Renae blew out his anger. "No, it is I who must apologize. I've not been a gracious host. Please, sit. Let us start anew."

The effort with which she maintained her smile seemed at least to lessen a little. One of her attendants pulled her chair out for her and she sat across the large table from Renae. General Shelsid and Cathius sat at either side of the table.

Renae placed his hands upon the table. "Now, I am Renae Warrin, lord of Warrinton. This is my top commander, General Shelsid. Tutor Cathius, leader of my council. And my trusted advisor, Sir—Jeld."

"Well met," the woman said. "I am Atek Chjesh Sarvati. High Voice Sarvati, I think you people would say it."

"Good. Now, pray start by telling me what in dreams you and Naelis are doing?"

She seemed to consider her words. "Your new ruler offered us your city."

Tutor Cathius clicked his tongue. "A most generous offer. Why do you suppose he favored ceding a city to a hostile empire over leaving it in the hands of an isolated, vulnerable enemy?"

"We all know your priest's intention."

"You knew he would betray you, yet you came anyway," Renae said.

"Yes."

A long silence followed. General Shelsid's eyes flicked between Renae and the envoy.

"What are your intentions, Chjesh?" Renae said flatly.

A smile touched her thin lips. "Good. This is the key to effective negotiation. Our intention is simple. We want Warrinton."

Tutor Cathius hummed, Renae frowned, and the doors opened. Several of Renae's servants entered with trays of food held ponderously overhead then began setting the table.

"Ah," Renae said. "It so happens that I have the same intention. Shall we split it then?"

One of High Voice Sarvati's servants began filling a plate for her, the other remaining at an unobtrusive distance.

Sarvati frowned at a skewer of meat and set it aside. "You are surrounded. It matters not whether we and Naelis are allied, you will be sieged or conquered. Surrender now and I'll see your people spared. Or join me in defeating Naelis, and you'll be rewarded."

General Shelsid slammed his fists against the table. "Outrageous! Better we—"

Renae silenced him with a raised hand. The general's mouth twitched but he managed to keep it shut.

"Perhaps I simply bend my knee to Naelis and we destroy you together," Renae said.

"I think you do not wish to do that," Sarvati said.

"Keep my city. Keep my kingdom. Destroy one enemy. I'll get over it."

The doors opened again. This time a commotion there drew Jeld's gaze from the envoy. Warrinton soldiers entered again, this time escorting a goateed man in armor embellished with dark yellow, a red priest at his side. The armored man was immediately familiar, but despite the coloring of Harborstone, it took a moment before Jeld recognized him.

"Lord Telestor Carsidge, Lord of Harborstone," announced the chancellor from the doorway.

Renae blinked. "Lord Carsidge..."

Lord Carsidge forced a frown and gave a curt nod. "Renae. I'm sorry we must meet like..."

Carsidge trailed off as his gaze fell upon Jeld. He squinted, then glanced at Renae. When he looked back to Jeld, he blinked. The resemblance was still there, but it was a different man. The cheeks were too hollow, the eyelids too heavy, the mouth too... slack. Just a trick of the light, maybe. Hadn't the last time he'd seen the Emry boy been with Renae? Yes, just an associated memory, then.

"Please, sit," Renae said cordially, then turned a glare upon the red priest. "You, too."

Carsidge eyed Sarvati suspiciously then sat near Cathius with his priest. The young priest sat rigidly, looking from face to face with that obnoxious smile of the righteous faithful.

"We were just talking about *intentions,* Lord Carsidge," said Sarvati.

"Were you," Carsidge said.

"Let me guess," Tutor Cathius said with a breathy laugh, "you want Warrinton?"

"It does not please me to be on different sides. Know that at least, but High Priest Naelis is our ruler now, and Avandria must stop squabbling."

Renae seethed. "Squabble? Defend! While you cower to these wicked priests!"

"*Your intentions*, Lord of Harborstone," the high voice pressed.

Lord Carsidge eyed her then turned back to Renae. "I don't want Warrinton. High Priest Naelis does not wish to *take* Warrinton. Just pledge fealty, and this ends! You keep your city. We keep Avandria, and instead of spilling the blood of our men, we join our armies this very day."

Jeld perked up at this. So many ways to pledge fealty then massacre Carsidge's army. Meet tricks with tricks. But he could hardly share that with Renae here. He glanced to his friend while still maintaining his persona. *Dreams* but Renae looked to actually be considering it! Jeld had to protest. Had to stop it.

He sat suddenly forward in his chair and made to speak, then froze. He didn't need to stop anything. Not now. Better to let the deal unfold. He could get Renae on board afterwards, in private. Everyone was staring at him, Cathius outright studying him. Jeld grinned and waved the thought off.

"He cannot be trusted!" High Voice Sarvati said, a foreign panic suddenly showing through her icy front. "He meant to lure us into war and see your city destroyed! What will he do to you once your gates are lowered? Once your people sleep?"

"I did no such thing to you," Lord Carsidge said, looking quickly away and busying himself with filling a plate.

"What compelled you to feign a charge at our walls, pray tell?" Tutor Cathius asked. "Or did you have a change of heart, perhaps?"

Telestor Carsidge cleared his throat. "As I said, I'd rather not see Warrinton destroyed if we can bring things to order peacefully."

Jeld followed her venomous glare as it swept from Carsidge to Renae and felt her panic rise. It was all there in Renae's eyes. He would care little even whether Carsidge would betray and depose him. Even subjecting his people to the evils of the red priests would pale in comparison to the prospect of his lifelong foreign enemy occupying his city. His *father's* city.

High Voice Sarvati's nostrils flared, but she took a deep breath and closed her eyes. When she reopened them she had regained most of her composure.

"A moment please. I must prepare a message to my people or they will be attacking soon, I'm afraid."

General Shelsid laughed humorlessly, throwing his hands in the air.

"We did not expect three party negotiations. And you understand we could not be certain I would return. You should think on this more anyway, before you so readily make a deal with this demon, Naelis."

"My lord," General Shelsid began, "Are you sure that's—"

Sarvati laughed, taking writing supplies from one of her servants. "Afraid I will order an attack, General? Would you like to read it first?"

"Write your letter," Renae said, looking less optimistic than he had a moment before. "A brief recess, then. I'd consult with my council. You have the room, and my men can see you to the privy if you require it."

Renae swept a look over his people and hurried from the room. Jeld, Shelsid, and Cathius followed him into the hall.

"Watch them," Renae said, sending two guards into the council room.

He led them into a nearby room down the hall. Tutor Cathius sat at a more modest table inside, Jeld perched upon it, and the general poked irritably at a low fire.

"Let's hear it," Renae said, pacing. "But I won't surrender the city to the east. Not while there's any chance."

"Surrender to Naelis," Jeld said, savoring the shock upon Renae's face.

"I didn't think I'd hear that from you. But, I'm considering it."

"If he'll fight the east, let them kill each other then finish them off and take Warrinton back. If not, you can—"

Renae groaned.

"What? They both tried the same thing against you. Did you need a more honorable way to kill your enemies?"

"He's right," General Shelsid said, throwing a log into the fire. "Fair fights will not hold Warrinton. Naelis and Annend Cross did worse to Princess Liraelle."

"They would likely not see it coming from you," Tutor Cathius mused.

"And if Carsidge suspects our ruse as we did theirs? If Carsidge's first order of business is executing enough of our leaders to kill any such chance of betrayal?"

"Negotiate better terms," Jeld said. "Keep them out of the city."

"He's not a fool," Shelsid said. "He won't take foolish terms. And the moment fighting breaks out between you, the east will attack. Or when half of us are dead. Either way, they won't risk Naelis's men securing it."

"We should simply defend the city," Cathius said. "No need for alliances with toothy animals. They are no longer allied."

Renae considered. "Neither can risk an engagement with us or the other will attack."

Tutor Cathius nodded. "And if they should just encircle us, well, it will buy us time."

"Time for what," the general stated more than asked.

"A new plan," Cathius supplied. "Evacuations. A turn of events, perhaps. Time brings opportunities."

"And if it doesn't?" General Shelsid asked, then dismissed the question with a grunt. "We could always surrender then. Perhaps the same deal will still stand."

Jeld watched his old friend. It made sense enough. He would have preferred that Renae simply abandon Warrinton and march west to join Lira's army, but he didn't suppose that was worth bringing up again.

"We hold, then," Renae said, eyes distant, unblinking.

"Ah, my lord," Tutor Cathius said. "There is the matter of how we message as much. If I may, I suggest you make it *quite clear* that you won't be allying yourself with either of them, so as to avoid the other party waging an attack."

Renae frowned thoughtfully. "Right. Fine." He went to the door then turned back to them. "Let's get to it then, before one or more armies attack."

Sarvati's attendants were being escorted toward the privy as Jeld trailed the others from the room. In the great hall, Renae and the others rejoined Sarvati at the table. Lord Carsidge was absent.

"You got your letter off, then?" Renae asked.

"Yes."

Renae tapped his fingers on the table, eyes distant. "You'd be wise to leave my city be, you know," he said after a long silence. "You know I've no mind to encroach on your empire, so why not let me guard it?"

High Voice Sarvati frowned, then shook her head. "It matters not whether I trust you. Warrinton will be ours, and I cannot let your priest have it."

Jeld's friend gave a slight, weak nod, He looked so tired. So defeated. His face was flushed, bags under his heavy eyes and a sheen of sweat upon his forehead.

"What is your decision, Lord of Warrinton?"

"Let us wait for Lord Carsidge," Renae said, glancing at the door.

Silence stretched on as they waited for the lord of Harborstone to return. Finally the doors opened, but it was only Sarvati's servants returning.

"Tea," the high voice ordered at once without looking back.

One of her attendants produced a box from a sack slung upon his back, sprinkled some dried leaves into her cup, and poured hot water over them from a kettle left by Renae's servants. Sarvati took up the cup and breathed in the steam for a good while before looking up to Renae. She took a sip then cradled her cup in both hands.

"Jathice," she said to the others, who all watched her. "Tenil petals, infused with Ketaketa fruit."

She turned to her attendants, who had already started drifting back against the wall behind her. "More for our hosts, and this Lord of Harborstone."

Jeld watched as the attendant brewed four more helpings. He'd be damned if he was going to drink anything they served him. He eyed the attendants as each took up two cups and circled either side of the table toward them. Their tension beat against Jeld as one circled the table toward Shelsid and the other toward Cathius. Up to something, or nervous at least. Of course, their high voice was probably the sort to execute servants who spilled tea. Difficult to say whilst maintaining his little character for Carsidge. Surely the others wouldn't be stupid enough to drink it anyway, offensive or not.

"None for me," Jeld blurted, all eyes jerking to him. "Wouldn't do to put tea on top of that brew we had earlier, right my lord?" He smiled and patted his belly. "I traveled Ishdalar once, and *oof* that combination set me bubbling like crauul spit."

The utter confusion upon Sarvati's face was enough to convince Jeld he'd somehow misjudged the situation, but a sheepish look had only half formed upon his face when there came the sound of a sharp breath, a thud, and the rattle of dishes. The servant nearest Tutor Cathius jerked the old man's bloody, limp face from the table by his hair and slammed it down again. Across the table, the other servant was pinning General Shelsid's bleeding face to the table, the general snarling and fighting to break free.

Without a thought, Jeld was on his feet charging across the table toward the general. In the span of a few steps, the servant kicked the chair out from beneath General Shelsid, slammed his head against the ground twice, then spun and raised an arm as Jeld's sword came down. The blow should have cleaved straight through the arm and into the easterner's head, but instead it scraped to a stop with a metallic shriek. The easterner seized on the moment of surprise, grabbing Jeld's wrist and twisting until the sword clattered to the ground.

Jeld's hand flashed into his collar but the easterner caught that arm too. Jeld slammed his forehead into the man's face, but the attacker kept his grip and wrenched Jeld's arm behind his back. They spun and for a moment Jeld could see Renae. His friend seemed to be faring better, sword still in hand. Just then though the attacker slapped Renae's lunge aside with his wrist and disarmed him, just as the other had done to Jeld.

This was all Jeld could glimpse though before he stomped on the attackers foot and threw himself backward against the table. He landed upon the easterner and pulled an arm free, but the damned sticky easterner grabbed him around the neck and pulled him tight, legs too closing around Jeld.

Jeld tucked his chin and reached again for a knife in the bag at his collar, but the easterner rolled atop him, pinning his arms to his chest atop the table. Gritting his teeth, Jeld fought his fingers toward the bag and strained to keep the arm around his neck at bay. Face pressed sideways against the table, his eyes fell again upon Renae.

His friend was in much the same position, screaming as the other easterner pulled his head back with two fingers in his eye, then clamped an arm around his neck. Renae's eyes bulged as the choke tightened, then they flicked to Jeld, the panic piercing. At the far side of the table, Sarvati had come to her feet, but looked almost paralyzed at the conflict.

The arm around Jeld's neck pressed deeper. Jeld's breath was rapid, his heart pounding, his every muscle tensed to hold whatever speck of freedom keeping the blood pumping through his neck. He reached back to claw for eyes, but his attacker's face was down and tight against Jeld's shoulder. Damn! Damn if this was the end. Damn!

He inched his hand toward his bag as he fought for breath. His hand reached the collar. Reached the bag. Reached the stone rim within. He felt the knife against the back of his hand, but couldn't turn his hand to grasp it. His vision began to blur. The tips of his fingers brushed something. His sparker, maybe. Then a rope. A rope! He grabbed at it, pinched a fiber of it between two fingers, reeled it in. Finally his hand closed around it.

Now if he could just turn to face his attacker. He bucked. Rocked. Squirmed. Darkness crept in at the edges of his vision. Face red and eyes bulging with effort and death, he blasted the man with an image of Renae charging, sword raised high. He felt the man's face lift off of his shoulder to look, but it wasn't enough. The easterner's legs were wrapped too tight for him to turn.

Face ground into the table, mouth full of blood from his own teeth cutting into his cheeks, Jeld's eyes landed upon Renae. His friend had managed to turn at least, but now his easterner had a forearm across his neck in a front choke, Renae pressing feebly at his face.

Jeld slammed the back of his head into his attacker's face, rolled the both of them onto their sides, and tugged the rope. With a *click*, a *thwick*, and a hollow *thud*, a crossbow bolt punched into the chest of the easterner atop Renae.

In all this though, there was no give in the grip around Jeld's neck. Instead, in the jarring it had claimed what miniscule space had been allowing just enough blood to Jeld's head. He thrashed and kicked and pulled. His head seemed to swell, his vision darkened, and then nothing.

CHAPTER TWENTY-EIGHT

Next Jeld knew, Renae was slapping his cheek. Harder than was necessary, he couldn't help but consider. A sharp crash and they both looked toward the door. A servant stood frozen there, a shattered tray of desserts at his feet.

"Get me soldiers!" Renae shouted. "Stop that woman!"

Sarvati was gone, the still half-unconscious Jeld realized. The servant remained frozen for a moment before blinking and racing off. Renae inspected Tutor Cathius. His shoulders sagged and he gently laid the old tutor back onto the table. Jeld staggered to his feet as Renae crossed to Shelsid upon the floor.

"He's alive," Renae said.

Renae rolled the general onto his side and blood began to drain from his mouth. Renae froze and Jeld followed his gaze to the still form of Lord Carsidge under the table they'd been sitting at. A dozen or so soldiers arrived just moments later, two of them dragging High Voice Sarvati. At their front was the burly bearded one who'd been so keen on the stars. Oan, wasn't it?

"Someone fetch a surgeon for Shelsid!" Renae ordered. "Send word to Commander—"

"My lord," Oan interrupted. "The northeast and southeast towers have been lost. Word is several commanders have been killed. There's—"

"What? Lost—how?"

"Fire, my lord. They're ablaze."

"How…"

Renae turned to Sarvati, but before he could speak, shouts erupted from somewhere outside, then a blare of horns.

"You two stay with the general. The rest of you, with me!" he said, storming off. "And bring her!"

Jeld followed Renae and the soldiers from the great room. The shouts grew louder, their steps faster until they were running down the hall toward a chorus of screams. Battle cries, cries of pain, of panic, all blended together. Then the clashing of steel joined. They burst from the outer door and into the night, the deafening sound of battle crashing against them.

Men ran every which way, pushing past with little regard or awareness for rank. Where the northeast tower should have been, a blaze of fire stretched high above like the clouds themselves were afire. To the southeast was a glow of orange beneath plumes of black smoke curling into the air. Jeld, Renae, and their detachment of soldiers pressed through the chaos toward the northern battlements. When they arrived at the base of the tower, a stern-faced commander with a thick gray mustache and short gray hair was barking orders at a mounted messenger.

"What in dreams is going on, Nathin?" Renae shouted.

"My lord! Crisn wants reinforcements to the east, but I don't see what they can do with more men when the battlements are inaccessible and the gates are packed with men already. And damned Vines is already calling for more pikemen for all the ladders hitting the west wall! I've sent what we can, and repositioned—"

"They've both attacked," Renae breathed. He rounded on High Voice Sarvati. "You did this!"

She sneered back. "You were never going to side with us."

"No, but I wouldn't have given it to Naelis."

"You would have fallen eventually, and we won't let Naelis take it."

Renae shook his head, then turned back to the commander. "General Shelsid is wounded. You're in charge, Nathin. Make them both pay for every step."

Renae left his escort and the high voice, secured horses for him and Jeld, and together they sped toward the eastern gate. Instead, they came to the beginnings of a makeshift barrier between buildings where the road spilled into the open square by the gate. Beyond it, bodies littered the ground amidst shattered boulders. A man screamed and splattered to the ground from above. Jeld looked up to find the battlements now entirely undefended.

"Commander Crisn!" Renae shouted.

He rode up to a middle-aged commander atop a white horse. The man had a bit of a gut, thick sideburns, and a square jaw.

"Archers have been repositioned atop these buildings," the commander said quickly and without preamble. "This barrier extends from north to south wall, or should by now. Others closer in are being readied should we need to fall back again."

Jeld started as a boulder crashed into a building to one side. Fragments hailed down upon them, someone nearby going down screaming as a brick took him in the shoulder. In response, Warrinton's archers loosed a thousand arrows from the rooftops. The arrows arced high into the sky, then came down just beyond the wall to more screams.

"We can't defend the outer gate so well," Renae said, "but I suppose we've still got an advantage."

An easterner crested the battlements, took no fewer than twenty arrows before he could raise his shield, and tumbled to splatter atop a boulder in the graveyard below. Warrinton men burst into laughter until another man appeared atop the battlements, then fifty more all at once. This time most managed to get their huge shields in position, and a row of archers began to form behind them. Cries from the archers above thickened as more and more enemies returned fire.

Several soldiers pointing at something caught Jeld's attention, and that's when he saw the inner gate begin to lift. Jeld knew losing the battlements was devastating, but only then did he realize the full extent of it. They had the gatehouse. They controlled the gate.

Just then there came a horrible rumbling. Not the gate, but from behind. Jeld wheeled his horse and hurried to the end of the block, where he peered down the long road cutting through the city. The northern tower was an inferno stretching high into the sky. Renae reached Jeld's side just as the tower seemed to shift with another rumble, then it was falling.

Jeld could only watch as the blazing tower spilled with an unsettling quiet into the city. Then came the deafening crash that shook the ground beneath them. A plume of fire splashed into the sky. A gust of hot wind swept over Jeld and the others, then ash and smoke. It did not pass. This was the color of the new hell that was the battle for Warrinton.

Another crash, another spray of rubble from above, and more screams. The orange glow in the sky grew. Brighter, even through the smoke. Closer. Then, charging out of the smoke, easterners descended upon them with curved blades held high.

"Tell Nathin to send everything he can!" Renae shouted to a mounted soldier as steel clashed. "And send word to our men on Carsidge's northern flank, hit them hard."

"Wait!" Jeld said, coughing from the smoke. "Renae, save them—"

"No!" Renae barked as soldiers rushed past toward their line.

"Your city is surrounded! It's breached, it's—it's on fire!"

"Which is why we must save it!"

Renae turned toward the messenger but Jeld caught his shoulder. Renae jerked it free and shot him a venomous snarl.

"How many times have you told me to use my head instead of my heart?" Jeld asked. "Which one are you using?"

Renae's fury waned, if only a little.

"The city is lost, whether you or your father would have it," Jeld said. "Your assault might buy time, but your people will all be killed, and the city they die for will be gone anyway."

Jeld fought his reins and gave his horse a pat. "Save what you can, Renae. Evacuate your army, surrender the city while it's still standing. And *join Lira* to take back Avandria."

Renae spun his horse about, perhaps taking in the devastation, or maybe just too angry to hold still.

"Damn it!" he roared, then turned back to the messenger. "Give Nathin the order to evacuate. And do not hit their flank. You hear? Keep our men in Sutherwood. Have them prepare for movement, and for refugees."

The soldier glanced at Jeld.

"Go!" Renae barked, and off the soldier rode.

Renae wheeled his horse and raced back to Crisn, Jeld in tow. "I'm evacuating the city. The longer you hold, the more lives you save."

"What?" Crisn shouted. He barked at a sergeant, pointed him to the south, then turned back to Renae. "You can't be serious! Your father—"

"My father didn't fight two armies and a burning city! Now hold the line, the city is counting on you!"

Crisn's nostrils flared, his jaw set tight.

"Soldiers will be the priority," Renae said. "We will take anyone who makes it out, but the soldiers are more likely to be put to the sword, and we'll need them most to take back Warrinton when the time comes."

Shaking his head, Crisn looked about as if to identify some clever alternative, but all he could have seen was death and fire.

Renae continued. "Prepare fallback positions toward the north gate. We'll get your men out when we can."

Crisn frowned, took a few breaths, then straightened his posture and pressed a fist to his chest. "We'll hold."

Without delay, the commander turned and rejoined the battle. Renae drew his sword and followed.

"What in dreams are you doing?" Jeld asked.

"What needs doing," Renae said without slowing.

"I didn't realize your army needed a dead leader!"

"How well do you think that line will hold when they hear of the evacuation and see their lord fleeing?"

"You have nearly half your army out—"

Renae turned sharply to Jeld. "Then we shall get the other half!"

And with that he rode off, Jeld following as ever. They followed the screams and battle cries to the front line. The men had formed a shield wall, others standing behind it jabbing spears through and over it. Enemies slammed against it, blades and spears piercing through, men falling and others taking their place.

Jeld had the sudden urge to flee. To cower. To cry. To scream. It hit him like a brick to the face, consumed him, paralyzed him. His eyes flicked over the dead, the wet steel, the burning and ashen sky. But it wasn't his terror, he realized, not his alone, at least. It was theirs, an entire army, his own terror welcoming it, sucking it down into his heart like a siphon.

Jeld fought it back, empowered by the knowledge that it wasn't his. The sort of strength one got on realizing he was dreaming. He had control. He could beat this. He battered it back, disentangled his own thoughts from the maelstrom of battle rage and fear and agony. His mind slammed shut and he blinked, looking about at the hellscape with only his own fear.

Renae paced his horse, looking anxious to do something to help, but his sword would do little good behind the shield wall, and Jeld hoped it stayed that way. Busy as the soldiers were with their violence, though, Jeld saw them take notice. He saw men point. He saw shoulders straighten, jaws set. The panic beating against his mind diminished, if only a little.

The battle raged, the orange glow in the sky growing steadily. More boulders sent stone and men shattering upon the ground. Jeld's eyes burned in the ash and dust, sweat and horrors. Men staggered back from the line bloody, others running wide-eyed past them to take their places.

Then suddenly—no enemies. Just gone. No ringing of steel, no battle cries, just the wails of the wounded and dying. Just the distant screams of the burning, and the anguished survivors.

"Make ready!" Renae shouted, riding up and down the line. "They are massing! Hold the line!"

"We should reinforce the line," Renae said, riding up to Crisn.

"No, my lord," the commander said. "We don't know where they will hit. Better to keep reserves ready. I've got most working on the barrier for now, anyway."

Renae didn't argue, just stared out into the haze. Jeld watched Renae from a bit of a distance before himself gazing into the smoke and dust. He stayed there even as Renae dismounted and joined a group of men dragging a tangle of what might once have been part of a wagon through the line and atop the sparse barrier. This done, Renae moved on to the next task, whether to assist or merely distract himself Jeld didn't know.

The more Jeld stared into the void, the more the swirls of smoke could almost be easterners massing under cover. Sometimes an archer from above with the same idea would loose an arrow, but always it just hissed out into the haze without a cry, setting the shape swirling to nothing but smoke.

Renae was back atop his horse beside Jeld when another lone arrow shot out from above. Again nothing, just a—

A scream pierced through the smoke, then a battle cry. Then thousands. A cloud of arrows slammed into their line, men dropping and shields bristling with them. An army burst through the smoke and crashed into the shield wall before it could reset. A wedge of easterners pressed through and reinforcements swarmed, pressing it back and filling the gap.

One easterner spilled through somehow, stopping dumb in front of Renae's horse as if he'd never expected to actually make it through. Renae kicked his horse forward and cleaved the easterner through the shoulder, cheers rising up all around.

"Behind!" several voices called.

Jeld's horse reared and suddenly he was on his back, gasping for air. A hoof narrowly missed his head, then a blade flashed down toward him. Steel rang and half a head fell to the ground beside him. Hands pulled him onto his feet, and then he was just one tooth on two meat grinders coming together.

He ducked a blade with what miniscule freedom the line offered him and stabbed someone through the neck. Another easterner slammed into Jeld while his blade was still stuck in the other's neck.

Jeld headbutted him, then tried to throw a punch but his arm was stuck on someone else.

"Forward! Push!" a strong voice came. It didn't matter whose. Jeld was thrust forward, shoulder to shoulder with the men of Warrinton. The easterner against him went down, clawing at Jeld's neck, his side, his leg, and then the line went over him. There was another in his place. Jeld's sword came down on the armored shoulder of the next to take his place, to little effect. It suddenly occurred to Jeld that he might be the only person in the entire battle who wasn't wearing any armor, then the easterner thrust a sword at him.

A shield came down right in front of Jeld, then more all around. Someone pulled him back and stepped in front of him, shield in one hand, spear in the other flashing out and taking the easterner in the neck. Suddenly a full shield wall fronted their line, and Jeld and the others were just weight behind it.

"Fall back!" came the voice again, and this time Jeld turned to see it came from Renae, still atop his horse. "Back to the next barrier! Northwest! Northwest!"

They slowly surrendered ground as they fought. They held each intersection until their men from the line could be evacuated, often fighting on two, sometimes three fronts where the line had broken.

"Back? Are you mad!" shouted one captain. "We can hold!"

"The city is gone," Renae said. "But our army can fight another day. Now fall back, Captain!"

That was all Jeld heard of it before another breach hit them from an alley and again his world was reduced to his sweaty grip upon the hilt of his sword and the battle crazed faces of his enemies. He wondered even as he stuck a man through the arm whether he looked just as crazed to them. More likely he just looked like a man pissing himself in terror. That's how he felt, anyway. A coward.

Wasn't there supposed to be some battle instinct that took over? Some animalistic rage or whatnot? Where was his? No armor didn't help matters. Plenty of sword training, but shit lot of good that did him here. He was a mover, hadn't Master Inado said? A mover, not a striker. Well, couldn't do either here. Might as well be a pig with a sword strapped to him.

The last enemy of that wave fell. Jeld wanted nothing more than to fight his way free of the press, allies or not, but instead found himself shuffling with them in retreat. A tide of civilians thickened, slowing them almost as much as the enemy. Soon the soldiers were the minority and all were intermixed. The hard folk of Warrinton bore weapons, even some of the children looking just as ready to use them. Looking less like a scared, sword-strapped pig than he did. Some, anyway.

Jeld turned a corner and a wave of heat slammed against him. A wall of fire, tall as any once-standing city tower, cut across the road ahead. Jeld stopped, an arm raised fruitlessly before his face. He tried to turn, but men spilled out around the corner, pressing those in front forward, pressing Jeld toward the inferno.

"West! West, damn it! Turn west!" came a call from somewhere, but might as well ask the leaves to stop the wind blowing.

More pressed around the corner, pressed Jeld toward the inferno. The heat grew, burned even from the distance. Jeld spotted an alleyway and shoved his way toward it. He was far from the only one. The whole mob pushed, clawed, punched their way toward it before it could pass.

It was more than halfway past now. Almost in reach. Almost, but it was passing too quickly. Had to hurry. He pushed past someone and more or less dove for the alley, but someone else pulled him back. His head was in, then it wasn't. The heat searing his back, Jeld grabbed the edge of the alley wall, but his hand slipped free, and the tide took him toward the flames.

Then it stopped, and Jeld was handily pushed into the alley. Armies were funny that way, as were caravans of refugees, in Jeld's experience. One moment you're digging in heels to keep from crashing into someone, the next you're running your ass off to catch up. Took time for change to propagate through the masses. And it couldn't have come sooner.

By the time they reached the second defensive line, the East was again absent. After they'd consolidated, Commander Crisn ordered further withdrawal and they reached the final line without contact still. They were at the edge of the northern square, another hodgepodge of furniture, doors, wagon parts, and everything else imaginable stacked at the many roads leading into it. The north gate stood open, a river of people pressing through it.

Jeld distanced himself from the soldiers manning the defenses and the archers climbing to the rooftops above. The others were far better equipped for that, in armor, strength, or spirit. He spotted Renae, still atop his horse. Hard at work as ever, despite a deep defeat growing ever more prominent with each retreat.

Well, it hardly made sense to wait here. Jeld pressed into the river of evacuees. Behind him, a boy barely past walking was crying. A girl held his hand, a sword in her other. Tears carved a path through ash staining her face, but her jaw was set strong. Frowning, Jeld let them pass. He looked over his shoulder to an older man carrying a baby. With a sigh Jeld trudged back to the barrier. Not *too* close to it, but close enough. Renae was there, showing a flicker of a grin at Jeld's approach.

"We won't be fighting Naelis another day if we let all the civilians out but get all the soldiers killed in here," Jeld said.

"Good lot of them made it through before we got here. And we've got more doing ladders to the west a bit."

"Well, it won't be easy marching with all these folk either."

"Perhaps not. I suppose you'd prefer to just let them burn or be killed by the Ishdali?"

Jeld frowned. It would be more practical, certainly. "No. I suppose not."

Jeld turned back to the east. The orange glows to either side were like two suns rising, yet the sky otherwise remained black with smoke. Archers stood behind the barriers, in windows, on rooftops. A shield wall was formed behind them, and reinforcements readied en masse all around. Men, women, and children of Warrinton emerged from the smoke one after the next, the men atop the barrier helping them over into their perimeter.

A young girl climbing down the barrier tripped on table leg or wagon spoke or whatever else, fell, and tripped again, sinking to her waist in the tangle. Jeld ran over and took the child's arm. Still the girl struggled, so Jeld waded into the pile, lifted her up, and set her closer to the bottom. She tripped again, then made it down to flat, if rubble strewn, ground.

Then she turned and reached out a little hand to Jeld, who was still knee deep. For a moment Jeld thought the girl meant to help him, then realized maybe she just wanted to hold his hand. Both sweet. Both dreamin' tragic. Jeld smiled and it nearly squeezed tears from his eyes.

"Go," Jeld said. "Get out of this place."

But the girl only stared at him with wide, sad eyes.

"Run!" Jeld shouted, heart wrenching.

The girl flinched back, turned, glanced back once, then finally ran off toward the gate. Jeld had the mind to lie down and die, but instead he climbed free of the rubbish pile and hurried from the line. He took cover behind what he hoped was a sturdy building, doing his best not to feel or look guilty for it. The flow of evacuees slowed until each trickling in might be the East and spears would rise. But the East didn't come.

"They're holding Naelis back," Renae said, dismounting beside Jeld. "Just spoke with Commander Vines. Damn well might have held to the east too had we stayed."

"Holding ashes," Jeld said. "Or becoming ashes."

Renae didn't argue, though he didn't look convinced, or pleased anyway. And what was on Jeld's mind was not likely to lift his spirits any.

Jeld shook his head at himself, then spoke. "You should open the western gate."

Renae looked sharply over to him, then softened as if he must have misheard. "What's that?"

"You should open the western gate. Let them fight it out. Weaken one another. If the East just takes the city, fewer will die."

"I won't—" Renae objected, then fell silent.

Jeld watched him. Won't what? Let the west in? Lose Warrinton? Hardly worse than handing Warrinton to its mortal enemy. Renae knew, but still he did not speak for a few long breaths.

"Not just more enemy deaths, but fewer of our own. Our enemies will be less able to pursue if they must contend for the city."

Renae was silent again for a time, then remounted and rode over to Crisn and Nathin. Jeld expected a heated exchange, but the shouted protests were halfhearted and quickly turned to sagging shoulders before the commanders rode off at a gallop.

Still no sign of the Ishdali by the time their western forces arrived, adding to the crowds before the gates. With the wall abandoned, Naelis's army would not be long behind. Finally the masses began to thin, but the thickening smoke more than made up for it. Jeld could barely see their line now. Lot of good the archers would be doing, then.

Even so, it was the sound of a bowstring Jeld heard first, before the shouts that followed. Jeld's heart raced as the same hell began anew. Battle cries, a chorus of hissing arrows like stormwinds through a forest, and the ring of steel.

More hissing arrows, this time growing louder not softer. Closer. They scraped along the side of the building Jeld hid behind, dropping countless braver men standing in the open. Jeld shivered and turned to the gate. The crowd before it had diminished significantly, but what remained was in a panic, pushing like a herd of cattle against the northern wall. As best as he could see through the smoke, the lines seemed to be holding, at least. Just a little more time.

Then, cries of alarm over the steadier rhythm of battle and death. A building at the eastern edge of the square was suddenly ablaze. Men fled a section of the defenses beside it and easterners spilled into the square, immediately flanking the men at the next section and letting more of their comrades through. A few blinks, and enemies were everywhere. An open melee.

Jeld pressed himself against the wall. Just then though, an arrow splintered against the stone beside him. Probably some Warrinton archer who needed a lesson on marksmanship. But then, two soldiers fighting easterners fell with arrows in their backs. That's when Jeld saw archers in Harborstone yellow atop the wall to the north and west, behind them.

"Archers!" Jeld shouted, pointing.

Suddenly easterners were upon him. He cut the first down before he'd so much as thought to move. The second had a spear though, as well as the sense to keep Jeld at a distance. The spear flicked down and Jeld barely dodged, showed the easterner a move to the left, then darted in and cut the man's hands off at the wrists. Man screamed, spear fell.

Jeld wound up a blow but someone slammed into him. He fell, landing hard on his side, blade skittering away as pain shot through his arm. An easterner stood over him, blade already coming down. Jeld rolled and the blade bit through his sleeve and rang against the cobblestones.

Jeld kicked a knee, rolled again, and came to his feet. Blood splattered against his face. The easterner folded to the ground, the side of his head caved in. Sword gleaming wet, Renae rode past and cut down another easterner. Then Renae cried out, grabbing at an arrow in his shoulder. Jeld ran to him

"Get down, they'll target you!" Jeld said, tugging at Renae.

"Get off of me!" Renae said, face twisted in pain. "I can't lead if I—"

"If you're dead!"

Jeld pulled Renae from the saddle. A rider reined in beside them and Jeld blinked at the sight of General Shelsid. His face was bloody, purple, and knobbly, but otherwise he looked considerably more alive than when they'd left him.

"Get to the gate, Renae!" the general ordered sharply.

The stampede before the gate was dwindling, but there had to be a couple thousand still. Even bovine civility had gone, killed by arrow and steel, stone and flame. Now, they fought one another outright.

"Damn the gate!" Renae said.

"Your army out there needs its lord. Go!"

The general gave a wave and four men grabbed Renae, two of them begging his pardon. They dragged him into the crowd, clearing a path with waving swords. Jeld had a mind to jump to his friend's aid despite fully supporting his extraction. Instead, he settled for accompanying his friend, glancing back at General Shelsid through the already closing crowd and thickening smoke. The general stared after them, looking every bit like he'd cast Renae into the fire instead of spared him from it, but he soon returned to barking orders.

"Get your hands off me!" Renae shouted. "That's an order from your lord! I'll have your damned head for this, soldier! Let go! Let me go!"

Renae's shouts turned to shrieks, shrieks to sobs, then a terrible silence as the crowd carried them through the gate.

CHAPTER TWENTY-NINE

The flames of a small campfire flickered in Jeld's vacant eyes. He was sitting against a wagon, a familiar comfort in that at least. A long gash upon his temple glowed red, his hair was matted, clothes ragged. He had acquired a few pieces of light leather armor from the many who would no longer be needing any, for all the good it had done them.

Three weeks had passed since Warrinton fell. Three merciless weeks of Naelis's forces nipping at their heels. Three weeks of daily battles, nightly fortifying. Of constant death, and constant struggle to keep the infirm moving.

A glimmer in the sky caught Jeld's eye and he looked up to the great star Hearth. He raised his hand and measured the distance from the star to the Wise One's eye, though he cared not one bit when dawn would come. He was not present, but back with Lira, showing her how it was done. His cheek was beside hers, hand upon hers, counting the fingers until dawn.

His father had taught him that trick. Funny, he'd learned plenty from the bastard. Mostly from his neglect, but a few proper teachings. Probably he'd be dead a few times over if not for those hard lessons. The callouses on his morals, the mistrust in his blood. And sure, the ways of the outdoors.

Jeld's tired eyes blinked slowly as he stared into the flames. So tired. It all blurred together. That afternoon's battles. Yesterday's. Tomorrow's. Even a coward could be numbed to it, to wonder if it wouldn't just be easier if the sword struck home next time instead of some other.

There was a second bedroll near his, the young girl he'd helped from the debris pile in Warrinton fast asleep upon it. When Lira seemed too distant, and the odds of this retreat too long, the girl gave him something to keep breathing for, at least. For reasons lost on Jeld, she'd taken to him, and he meant to keep her safe.

Jeld's gaze found its way from the girl back into the flames, and he blinked another slow, tired blink.

Daytime now. Cries of battle from behind, probably the rear guard engaged. The crazed roars of the frenzied. Screams of the dying. Arrows hissing, steel ringing. There were dozens of carts just in view at that very moment, all pulled by refugees who looked little healthier than those in the carts. A family was trying to free one of them from a muddy rut. Upon the cart was a soldier with a bandaged leg, and the young girl from Warrinton.

Jeld cursed and ran to the stuck cart. He joined a woman and an old man tugging on the handles, and when it didn't budge he went around behind and pressed his back to it. Veins bulged in his neck and his legs burned as he pushed, but his feet only slid across the ground. The sounds of battle were drawing closer, loud now. He heaved. Again. Again. Again, and finally the cart slipped free, Jeld falling onto his rear as it rolled away.

Jeld scrambled to his feet just as enemy cavalry burst from the treeline behind. Six of them, which meant more nearby. Damn. Not the first time they'd hit their flanks, but only rarely so deep behind their lines. A pair of spearmen fell first, one of them stomped for his heroism and the other cut down by the next rider. Another rider hurtled straight towards the people Jeld had aided.

Jeld charged to meet him. He formed the image of himself jumping to the rider's other side and pressed it into the man's thoughts. The rider turned and swung his sword at nothing but air as Jeld sliced him across the leg. Another cavalryman took down two more soldiers then trampled a woman holding a spear. He turned to another and charged.

"Hey! Piss face!" Jeld shouted, waving his sword.

The rider turned. Not Jeld's favorite insult, but it did the trick. With a kick to the big mount, the rider charged.

Jeld tried to conjure some feint but couldn't piece anything together before the man was upon him. He jumped aside and got his sword up just as the rider's swept toward him. Steel rang. The force of it shot pain through his arm and sent him tumbling to the ground. Somewhere amidst the fall, the ground tore his sword from numb fingers.

He climbed to his feet. Where was his sword? Just dirt. Shrubs. Carts. People. There! He dove, grabbed his sword, rolled to his feet with a swing of the blade. But the rider was on the ground, an arrow protruding from his chest. The injured soldier in the cart Jeld had freed was already nocking another arrow. They did not share a look, a nod, a moment, just moved on. This was war, after all. There was no time nor reason for such gestures.

Jeld froze. There was a rumbling. Hoofbeats, from the south. A full troop of cavalry charged down a hillside toward the road. Toward their column. He cursed. They had their own troops aplenty, but not here. A handful of spearmen took up the defensive. Jeld had other thoughts. He turned to flee into the treeline, then jumped aside as another rider burst from it. Then dozens more, all in Warrinton blue.

Easily twice the enemy's number, the riders of Warrinton charged up the hillside to meet the enemy. Naelis's force turned and fled, the Warrinton riders pursuing. It seemed the men afoot should break into cheers, but this was war, after all, and far from the end of it. Just another day of not quite dying.

Jeld stared after them, eyes on the battles of yesterday, and tomorrow, then went to tend the wounded.

Jeld started as his brothy beans burned his hand through his old bowl. He adjusted his grip and gazed through its steam into the flames of the campfire. He took a sip and his eyes flicked over to the young girl sitting upon a thin blanket close by, an empty bowl at her side. Jeld looked again down into his bowl, let out a breath, and poured a good splash of it into hers.

The girl met his gaze. It was barely the same girl he'd first glimpsed in Warrinton. Even then she'd been traumatized, probably had just lost her family, but there was life in that suffering. She'd been bleeding, so to speak, and now she'd bled out. Jeld nodded to her, and she stared back for a time before taking up the bowl and turning to the fire.

A deep anger rose up in Jeld as he watched the poor girl. It was good to feel something at least, but damned if he could do nothing. Damned if they would fight so hard each day, endure such torture each day, only to be chipped away at like some carcass. Damned if monsters could do evil and not have to answer to it. And damned if gods could let it happen. His mind turned to that glowing thing of light in the Halls. The One... either all powerful, or benevolent, but not both. Not both, if such monsters can exist, and such children can suffer.

"Can we not take a stand?" Jeld said abruptly, voice loud in the night.

He glanced over to Crisn. The commander had been talking to Renae, Jeld only just realized. Crisn's thick sideburns roiled atop jaws clenched in annoyance. At Renae's prompting, Crisn cleared his throat, swallowed some irritation, and answered.

"We could, of course. But you know why we haven't, and our situation hasn't changed. They'd likely dig in, and we'd be forced to either kill ourselves against their defenses, or retreat again. Or maybe they don't dig in, just meet us on the field, trade blows to the last man."

Crisn sipped his own beans from a wooden bowl he'd whittled, then shook his head. "I'd take the chance were it for some great final victory. Were it to give our side the war. But the truth is we're much too far from victory to make such trades. Say we won, and hobbled to your princess with a handful of men. What would we have gained but a fraction of Naelis's army defeated?"

"At the cost of half of hers," Renae said, coming to his feet. He let out a breath, then stalked off down the line into the darkness, waving off two guards who made to follow.

"And what of the crossing?" Jeld asked Commander Crisn. "If they're still upon us when we reach the river, what then?"

Crisn was silent for a long moment. "You will have your stand, then, if only while others cross. Better to save what we can than to color the river red for naught."

Jeld could think of nothing else to say, only nodding to the commander. The young girl lay down now, her eyes open and staring into the flames. He watched her until a hushed voice in the night caught his attention. He stood, the little girl at once tensing and looking his way. Offering her a reassuring little wave, Jeld followed the whispers.

He passed person after person lying upon the ground, lucky if they had a thin blanket to their name. Lucky how little rain the valley got this time of year, if you could call such folk lucky. The nights were made to feel cooler by the hot days, cold enough without the misery of being wet. These people were luckier than those who had been killed in Warrinton, anyway. Those crushed by boulders, impaled by arrows or steel. Stomped and squished in the mass exodus. Burned alive. The families of the lucky ones.

A wagon took shape in the darkness, then a person, and another seated. Renae, standing over High Voice Sarvati, who sat chained to the wagon.

"What will they do to my people?" Renae asked.

"Who can say?" Sarvati answered in her accented voice. "We must wait and—"

"The Voice can bleedin' say now!" Renae snapped.

"There are many Voices. Three High Voices. We are ambassadors. Envoys, but we do not make the decisions. This is for the Seven."

"You aren't deciding. You know your people, so tell me what they will do."

"I can't know what—"

"Damn it! What they're *likely* to do!"

Jeld's breath was loud in the darkness as a silence stretched, then Sarvati spoke again.

"Ishdali are a practical people. We do not like to waste good resources. Soldiers will be enslaved. Some tradesmen as well. Most others will be expelled."

"Not killed?" Renae's voice came.

"That might be practical, but we are not so barbaric. Not unless the Seven thought their release would pose a great threat."

Renae fell silent. Jeld made his way back to his bedroll and laid upon it. A moment later, he felt the little girl's back press against his. He still didn't know her name. Jeld closed his eyes, but soon found himself once again staring into the flames.

More cries of death and battle madness. More digging. More walking. More scars. Jeld's hair was longer, his breath steaming in the colder mountain air. His bloody feet lay upon his boots beside the fire. His eyes glistened, thinning cheeks stained with tears as he stared down into his cup of beans. They had long since cooled, a good lot of them remaining. He forced himself to take a sip, chin quivering as his eyes flicked down past the bowl to the empty bedroll beside his.

His lute found its way into his hands at some point, the first time since... well before Warrinton, anyway. The strings wept. There was just so much, and not a spare thought for the river crossing that should be occupying his mind. Warrinton, war, defeat, this miserable retreat. And older pains, losses he thought he'd made peace with. But above all, the girl.

It was so unfair, not only that one so young should be killed, but that she had to suffer so terribly only to be killed anyway. Couldn't she have just died among the first and been spared such pain!

"I didn't know you played," Renae said quietly. "Couldn't you play something a bit more... uplifting, though? Idols, these people are broken enough."

Jeld looked about in the dim light of the stars and campfires as far as the eye could see. People had gathered around him, some sitting nearby, others just gleaming eyes and shapes in the distance. Others, he sensed. So many others, listening from afar. Few slept yet, what with the crossing ahead, and the east not a stone's throw behind. He eyed Renae, then looked back down to the neck of his lute.

"I don't think we can fool people with a few songs," he said.

"Not *fool*, just... a distraction. Something to enjoy."

"It doesn't work that way. Like Fallstival melancholy. Nothing hurts like joy when the spirits are already down. They need to feel this, Renae."

Jeld opened his mind to the countless others all around him. They were almost a single entity in their mourning, their misery, their agony, their hopelessness. Together, though. There was something to that. Pain together…

Jeld began to play, not masking their woeful melody, not fueling it, but embracing it, warming it with this togetherness. No joy. Not sunshine melting away the whole of winter. Just the slightest touch of a warm breeze. A single blade of green grass reaching up through the snow. Hundreds, thousands of people, all with him now. Their spirits did not soar, but they began to heal, if only a little.

The girl's blanket was clutched against Jeld's chest when he awoke with a start after a restless night. First light glowed a deep blue in the still dark sky.   He craned an ear. No battle, just a stirring army.

They were quickly up and moving. Might be inundated with wounded, young, and old, but they were orderly and efficient. These were people of Warrinton, after all. Still, they'd readied far faster than usual this day. The crossing at last. Their advanced party would already be arriving, digging in for the inevitable attack. If they weren't all dead, anyway.

Already they'd passed where the river forked. They marched now with the nearest, a good ways off at times but usually close enough to hear the water's song. The music should have promised fresh water to drink, fish to eat, and a bath, but instead it spoke only of the coming death. It was a narrow, but deep and turbulent bastard, plenty of river to either kill them or slow them enough to let Naelis's army do the honors. The scouts assured them they'd reach the crossing before the sun was halfway through its descent.

Jeld eyed the woodline nervously as he walked along the dirt road. The sun was not far from center sky now, and still no attack. Perhaps they simply hadn't caught up yet. They could be waiting for the crossing, but the military minds had all been certain the east would attack before Renae's men had a chance to dig in there.

"Where are the bastards?" Crisn said, riding back from the front. "We could have given Vines the full guard to start digging in with."

"Then they'd have attacked," Jeld joked.

Crisn grunted. The commander's gut had thinned a bit on the difficult journey, as had his mistrust over Jeld's sudden and unexplained inclusion and authority. A bit. Jeld had grown to like the man well enough. Sideburns aside, he put on little pretense. He knew his business, had the respect of the men, and got things done.

"Scouts," Crisn cursed. "Where are our rear scouts? They should have returned by now."

Again Jeld scanned the trees. They'd lost a few scouts thus far, plenty others delayed at times by terrain or other circumstance, but this had been a simple enough mission. Should nearly have been able to just look over their shoulders.

"Probably just delayed. Wanted to get a good look," Jeld said, but he knew what it must mean. They'd been killed by an enemy force already moving along their flank.

"Good look at what, *Delvarad?*"

Jeld forced a smile. His heart thudded in his chest, eyes darting. His screaming feet at times took his mind off it, if only a little. Even his shoulders began to ache a bit, despite his pack being merely stuffed with lighter objects so he didn't look too lazy, with everything else in Kelthid's bag. Scouts really must be dead, though, the worry nagged. Cursing, Jeld marched on.

The sun was near to mid sky when Renae rode up from the rear to join Jeld and Crisn.

"They've fallen behind," Renae said. "Trees blocking the way, best the scouts could tell from—"

"Damnable scouts," Crisn cut in sharply. "We expressly ordered a focus on speed today, not—"

"No. They didn't do it. Not that they'd admit to, anyway."

"How far behind?" Jeld asked.

"They've been quick to clear our blockages before," Commander Crisn said. "I doubt it will buy much."

"A fair distance, actually," Renae said. "Apparently the enemy was stopped for a full bell or two before the scouts sent a runner back. We won't know anything further until more scouts return with an update. For all we know they've advanced a strike force and move upon us even now. We must be ready."

Jeld's shadow turned east as he marched on, wincing with each step as blisters ground against boots. Jeld was riding near the front of the column just behind a small forward guard now. It was nice at the front. No dust. No horse shit. No mud, though that had rarely been a problem. A more steady pace too, free from the countless stops caused by every little hiccup propagating like a wave back through the column. There was still the chance of ambush, but thus far the enemy had hit their front only once.

A banging in the distance grew louder as the sun continued its descent. The clacking of axes, shovels, picks. The road, if it could still be called that, turned east. Jeld's breath caught as he spotted a man off the road just before the bend, then exhaled, hand falling from his hilt. It was just their top scout, a stern faced man named Tolm. Tolm casually waved them straight into the grove behind him, as if he were pointing out a place to piss rather than directing an army.

Jeld took a breath and followed their forward guard into the grove. The sounds of the defenses being constructed grew louder. They hiked up a slight draw, the smell of pine thickening, then passed a barrier to either side of the road. Men were sharpening logs and digging a trench to ward off cavalry.

Beyond, the horizon fell away and the river lay just below at the foot of the decline. It glimmered in the sun, flowing slow and shallow over a wide stretch of stones. Damned if it wasn't a pretty sight. Never mind glimmer and all that, it was shallow! Far shallower than the veritable sea he'd been expecting, anyway. Beautiful as it was though, a black dread crept into Jeld's heart. A proper battle was near at hand.

A shovel was Jeld's weapon of choice for the laborious evening to follow. He could be Renae's man absolved of responsibility again another day. During the battle, most likely, at least enough to keep himself out of the line. For now, Warrinton needed shovelers, and he didn't much mind. He'd never signed up to be some noble's right hand man, anyway. Didn't get paid enough for that.

Jeld shoveled on as the endless herd of refugees streamed their way across the river, those in wait joining the soldiers in their preparations. A group of men in the middle of the river were working at righting a wagon that had lost a wheel and toppled onto its side.

Jeld threw down his shovel and stretched his aching back. When the enemy did arrive, he'd barely be able to lift a sword. He glanced warily behind. Everyone was quiet, labor notwithstanding. The air was thick with tension. Dread. Worry. Fatigue. Perhaps it was time to cast aside his shovel and don a lute. Better yet, time to cross the river. Didn't get paid enough for battle either.

On the hillside, Renae had a hand on a young officer's shoulder, pointing at some odd thing or another and moving on with his rounds. Jeld sighed and gave up on the idea of crossing just yet. He winced as he picked up his shovel again, gave Renae another look, then threw it down and jogged toward his friend. If it wasn't time to cross, perhaps it was at least time he replaced the heavy shovel with the much lighter burden of the Lord of Warrinton's proximity.

Just then two riders came galloping down the hillside to Renae. Scouts, ragged and tanned. Crisn reached him next, and finally Jeld just as the scouts departed.

"They've been quick to clear our blockages before," Crisn was saying, "how could—"

"Cattle..." Renae mused. "In the road. A damn lot of it, they said, and blocked in by the felled trees."

"Cattle?" Crisn tried, rubbing the beard that had begun filling the space between his chops. "Must've turned on from that little road we passed?"

The commander looked at Jeld for affirmation or explanation, a gesture that should have both amused and amazed Jeld coming from Crisn, but he could only shake his head and shrug.

"Apparently they've barely moved all day," Renae said, then chuckled, still looking very much in shock.

Jeld blinked. All day...

"We can make it," Renae breathed, looking over at the crossing. "Two more to cross, but they say this is the bigger of them. We can make it."

Jeld felt a great weight release him, but he clung to it. Optimism had no place here. Only fear could keep him safe from disappointment, and from complacency.

Shouts rose up and Jeld turned. There was a commotion in the middle of the river, two men on horseback, riding the wrong way. Renae and Jeld shared a look, then hurried behind Crisn toward the sprawling river. Jeld squinted up at the larger of the men, then quickened his steps until he was jogging. He stopped in the knee deep water only when the face came fully into focus.

"Fen!" Jeld called.

"Little prince!" Fendrith called in his soft voice, a big smile upon his face.

Suddenly the worrying weight was gone, and this time Jeld didn't care. At least, until his eyes fell upon a stranger beside Fen and he realized Benam should be standing there.

"Benam's fine," Fen said, Jeld's smile returning. "Come on, I'm not hugging you until it won't get my boots wet."

Fen made good on his promise at the bank, climbing from his horse and embracing Jeld as Renae and Crisn looked on impatiently.

"Fen, this is my friend Renae Warrin," Jeld said. "Lord of Warrinton."

Renae pursed his lips and Jeld winced. Lord of Warrinton no longer.

Jeld cleared his throat and hurried along. "And Commander Crisn, commander of—"

"General," Renae interrupted. "*General* Crisn."

Jeld nodded, smiling as Crisn blinked in surprise. "Very well. *General* Crisn, leader of the armies of Warrinton."

"Well met, my lord, General," Fen said, surveying their defenses. "No enemy yet? It worked, then? How far back are they?"

Crisn wiped a prideful eye. "The cattle, that was you?"

The man beside Fen suddenly laughed uproariously. He was nearly as tall as Fen, solid but thinner than Jeld's broad-shouldered friend. Older too, somewhere near middle years, with a thick head of short hair. Ruggedly handsome all around, in the long unbathed sort of way.

"I knew old Barty would make it work!" the man said, clucking another laugh. "What'd I tell ya? What'd I tell ya!"

"You told me," Fen affirmed. "This is Rudy Lowbrook. We've had to move quickly with our arrangements and recruitment, and Rudy has been—"

"Oh don't act like I'm doin' ya any favors! It's I should be thankin' you for fighting those bastards."

Renae took a step forward and extended his hand. "Even so, I owe you great thanks."

Rudy clasped Renae's hand and gave a big, unceremonious shake. "Sure, sure, lord sir."

Renae cleared his throat. "Your cattle expertise proved remarkably effective."

"Oh I'm no cattle expert, lord sir. Just a wagoner who's been stuck behind them on the road a time or twenty."

Jeld perked up at this. A wagoner, and with all the social graces of his father.

"We've got a blazing river to cross," Crisn snapped as the man prattled on. "And an enemy just a day behind. You've got supplies? More men? An encampment?"

"No army," Fen said. "A handful of capable locals ready to continue harassing Naelis's men. But Odsgaard has a small force in Kjael, just ten days' ride."

Jeld watched Fen with wonder. Always before his friend had seemed simply to exist. To follow, wherever the currents took him. This man though... this man traveled the hostile lands amidst war. This man liaised with lords. This man raised armies, or resistance at least. Perhaps Fen had changed. Or, perhaps he had always known what he wanted, and Jeld had never thought to ask.

"A northern army, here?" Renae asked. "How many? Why?"

"Eight hundred. Most of their army remains to the west. King Ralegus said if a thousand northerners can't defend against ten thousand southerners in the mountains, they don't deserve the mountains."

"King?"

Fen shrugged.

"You were in Odsgaard?" Jeld said, puzzling through the days and distances.

"Hmm?" Fen said, hugging a raised knee to stretch his leg. "Oh. No, Ralegus is there. In Kjael."

Renae turned to where the people of Warrinton were wading, riding, towing their way across the river, then to the thousands crafting or manning their defenses. He grew distant, quiet. The others all watched him. Finally he turned to Crisn.

"What say you we hurry the crossing along and make for Kjael?"

Crisn nodded, following Renae's gaze to their people, hard at work. "I say aye, my lord. Establish defenses on the other side just in case, and ride at first light."

Renae nodded, Crisn saluted, and off the general rode to make it so.

CHAPTER THIRTY

J eld looked down into the mead swishing in his raised tankard. He couldn't smell the stuff without conjuring up thoughts of his father. Usually kept him from touching drink, but *dreams* if he was going to let Quintem control him. Not tonight.

He took a big swig and slapped his mug back onto the table, one with the sound of countless others, amidst a chorus of song, cheers, laughter, stories. He was at a long table packed with big, hairy men who would most definitely not call the fuzz upon his face a beard. The narrow hall around them was all wood and fire. Torches, heavy iron chandeliers, roaring fireplaces. People everywhere. It was in all ways a model of the Warrior's great hall on a smaller scale. Yet, filled with northerners and men of Warrinton sharing drink, food, and song, it was even more grand.

"Cattle!" King Ralegus howled, slapping Renae on the back. "Bested by cattle!"

Beside Jeld, Renae winced and shot him an exasperated look. By now Jeld was certain his friend would have quite a bruise, but there was nothing for it. Beyond Ralegus sat Queen Dahled, sturdy and gray. To Jeld's other side sat the chieftain of Kjael, a young blond boy of perhaps thirteen. Fen, Benam, and Crisn sat across the table, surrounded on either side by more northmen.

Jeld took a charred pig's rib from the table and sank his teeth into the juicy meat. He washed it down with a swig of mead, took another few wondrous bites, and repeated this process until the table bore a pile of bones, and his head a foggy buzz.

Renae scooted his own drink away, looking a little bleary-eyed. "You don't mean..."

"You're damn right I mean," Ralegus barked. "It's hit Tovar now or sit back and let him dig in first. Good half of the lot that chased you off is heading back to Warrinton, but the rest toward the crossing at Erlundane. Don't wager it's back to Tovar from there, not with your lot about. No, they'll take Delvarad."

Renae glanced at Jeld, then back to Ralegus. "We're to join Princess Liraelle, not get ourselves killed. Even if we beat them to Delvarad, we'd have to face them to reach Tovar. By then Havaral, Caldemoor, and Tovar forces could well converge."

Ralegus sat back in his chair and rubbed his gray beard. "I wouldn't count on Havaral. Even with the better part of my army pulling back from their border, I'll keep the fear in them. Caldemoor more likely, and Tovar certainly. They'll have numbers, but not too bad. And your militias pecking at them won't make travel easy, nor supplies."

"We could write to Lira," Sir Benam said. "Perhaps she can meet us at Tovar with ships."

Ralegus smiled. "Never heard you do anything but object to war. Not in a long while, anyway."

"There are more poor reasons for war than there are good reasons," Benam said, looking down into his tankard of water. "But this is just. This is necessary, Ralegus."

"Maybe you're accustomed to having to convince people. Not me. I'll end that priest." He stood, raised his mug, and bellowed at the top of his lungs. "Odsgaard will end the bastard priest!"

To the last northerner, even the chieftan child, and no few folk of Warrinton, men raised their mugs or fists and boomed their agreement. Ralegus drank, then sat down laughing, others returning to their conversations as if there had been no interruption.

"You're right, of course," Renae said over the ensuing music. "Better to attack now and risk missing the opportunity than to wait until there isn't one."

Jeld bit his lip. True enough, but all he could think about was Lira getting word of her overzealous army's slaughter. Or worse, not getting word while rushing to her death at Tovar. True all the same, though. His eyes flicked up to find lords, kings, generals, all staring at him, and almost laughed at the absurdity.

"All we'd gain by waiting is winter and enemies," Renae said.

"War is all risks," added Ralegus, taking a bite from a sausage held in his big fist. "Can't be outright stupid, but you've gotta take your chances. Got to be bold when your enemy expects you to be cautious."

Jeld's eyes fell closed. It wasn't just about Lira. It was how many might die by his mere nod. Oh he was through fussing over whether it was worth it. Naelis had to be stopped, not despite the people but *for* the people, but damned if he wanted to be the one to condemn them. Just like Lira. Shaking his head, eyes still closed, he nodded.

"We're doing the right thing," Benam's voice came after a while.

Jeld opened his eyes. The others had all broken into other conversations. Benam sat watching him from across the table, looking entirely too calm.

"Let me guess, you have faith?" Jeld said.

Benam straightened. "I didn't mean that. I know you don't like to hear such things."

Jeld managed a slight smile and shrugged. "It's fine. I suppose you've been right so far, eh?"

Benam frowned. "I don't think of it that way. It doesn't matter what happens now, only that everything will come to pass."

"Meaning you could be the last man alive and you'd still believe."

Eyes bright, Benam nodded.

Jeld looked out over the men at song and drink. He thought of the little girl from Warrinton. Of the inquisitors, the prison, Cobb, Niya.

"No decent god would allow these men to die. This whole world of... No, no it doesn't make sense."

"Who can say? Maybe The One is not all powerful. Maybe he has a plan, a path, and we must walk it. Or, maybe he is opposed."

"Discord " Jeld scoffed. "I told you it was a lie."

"Yes. But there is much we don't know."

They were quiet for a time.

"You sat before him," Benam finally said. "You alone, of every person alive. So, what say you?"

What say him indeed? That he'd shied away from The One's touch? That it had hardly seemed particularly busy saving the world? That he put little faith in anyone whose divine plan includes killing his sister?

He took a deep breath. "I think you're right that there is much we don't know."

Benam forced a sad smile and nodded.

"Warrin says you play?" Ralegus's booming voice came.

"Hmm?" Jeld said, finding Ralegus looking his way. "Oh. Only just learning."

"Bah. Play."

Jeld started to shake his head but stopped and sighed. There was little point arguing with the king of the north. He pulled his lute from his shoulder and tested the strings.

"Hah! There's a good lad. Give us a song to remember." He stood and raised his tankard to the room again. "Tonight, we drink! Tomorrow, we wish we hadn't. And in three days, we march on Delvarad!"

The room burst into cheers. Not much feeling the enthusiasm, Jeld nonetheless took it all in and fed the hall of warriors the song it needed.

Sweat dripped from the edge of Jeld's red cap as he hurried after a servant down the barren stone halls of the keep of Delvarad. Other servants, nobles, and soldiers alike melted quickly from their path at the sight of Jeld's red robes. While setting a brisk pace, Jeld's sweat was not born of this, nor of nerves, nor of the painstaking efforts not to trip on his untailored robe. The sweat was his character's, this red priest fresh in town and rushing to meet his counterpart at the aviary.

Jeld followed the servant up a spiraling staircase. They passed a door, then another, and finally entered the next. He tripped on his robe passing from the stairwell and his nerves exploded from behind the veil of his character.

Dreams. Dreams, what was he doing? He was no assassin. He'd done his share of sneaking. His share of killing, even, but not like this. It had been self defense. Battle. Vengeance, even. Necessary, but never so... premeditated.

The servant led him down a dark, stone hallway. Narrow windows lined the way, the night lending only faint lines of light from the city or stars above. Sweat continued to bead and trickle—his own sweat now. At the end of the hall they passed through two sets of doors into the aviary. It was clearly the tip of a tower, a rounded room with a high pointed ceiling. There were several cages large enough to walk into, each marked with a city name and containing several birds. There were other smaller cages as well, and a writing desk. No other red priests present yet.

Jeld dismissed the servant with a nod and sat at the desk. His pulse beat in his ear, mind on murder. Damn. He took a breath. This was a red priest he meant to kill, not a child! Not an innocent. Far, far from that. With that, and one of Director Sammel's character audits, his nerves eased. He shuffled aside a few odd letters, tucked one in particular into his collar, then plucked up a thin strip of blank paper, readied a pen, and set to writing.

The door creaked open. Jeld's heart thudded, pen halting. He shoved himself deeper behind his character and the pen resumed as a fat old red priest stepped inside.

"There you are," Jeld said, some slow, cool voice that was not his own. A bit of Benam's calm, slow faith in that voice, even.

"Yes, here I am," the red priest said with unmasked irritation. "And there are you. Now *who* are you, and what's this all about?"

"Yes yes, ample time for pleasantries after we've got the bird off," Jeld said, pen scratching. Then the pen stopped and he looked up. "I assume you still haven't sent word?"

"Well!" the priest huffed. "Thank Vincet himself you've come bearing this wisdom. I hadn't thought to send a letter from my aviary!"

Jeld eyed the priest, then continued writing. "So you've already informed the high priest of Delvarad's impending collapse, then."

"Of course I sent—collapse? Delvarad will do no such thing, I'm charged with—"

"What did you report, then? A small force keen to bleed itself against your walls?"

"I told his royal eminence we'd handle this little squabble!" The priest raised his chins and straightened his robes. "Now, who—"

Jeld slammed his pen to the desk. "Squabble! The whole damn north is nigh beating at our gate!" He stood and started toward the cage labeled Tovar. "I'm sending for aid at once, and you can bet I've made note of your idiocy!"

"Why!" the priest hissed, words choked with fury. "I'll not be spoken to—you'll see the inside of a cell is what you'll do, pup!"

Jeld pulled the cage open and the priest slammed it closed with a meaty hand.

"Sit down!" the priest bellowed. "Sit! I want to know just who—"

Jeld spun and sunk his knife to the hilt into the fat priest's chest. The priest sucked in a sharp breath and staggered backward, crashing against another cage door. Clutching his chest, he looked past the bloody blade in Jeld's grip to meet his eyes, opened his mouth as if to speak, then collapsed. Laying upon the floor, head propped up against the bars of the cage and mouth moving like a caught fish, he stared with wide eyes at the darker red spreading across his robes.

Jeld barred the door, and when he turned back, the priest was still. As he emerged from behind his character, he found not an ounce of sympathy emerging with it. Good. Red bastards. He wiped his knife on a clean patch of the priest's robes and sheathed it. There was a spot of blood on the back of his hand, and he wiped it too but managed only to smear it. His pulse began to thump in his ear, his breath quickening.

Closing his eyes, Jeld found the panic and started pushing it away, wrapping himself in a character who wouldn't spare a thought for what he'd done, or rather what he'd become. His knee brushed a bloody fold of the priest's robe, leaving a smear upon his own, and he spilled over backward, scrambling back against a cage. He clenched his eyes shut and retreated farther, sculpted his cold assassin until it was real, until it was him, and he only watched from afar.

When he opened his eyes the panic was gone. The blood on his knee was just a day's work. A bit of dirt from working the fields.

He stood and finished penning his note. Fear not, Tovar, they had dispatched the small force, and all was quiet again about Delvarad. Their defenses were strong, numbers bolstered by recruitment sweeps throughout the countryside. There were reports of a Warrinton force having crossed back over the northern Kline presumably to retake their homeland. Many reports, in fact.

Jeld pulled out the letter he'd pocketed, gave it a good look, then copied the signature onto his own letter. Rolling it up, he looked about at a loss. Truth be told, he hadn't ever even witnessed the process of sending a bird. Still, the premise seemed simple enough. He found a little leather tube in a desk drawer, managing to stuff the note in after a few more attempts at rolling it tight. Picking up a bird was not so much harder, to his surprise. The simple looking little pigeon barely moved as he strapped the little leather tube to its leg, gently pecking his hand once as he worked at tightening it. He carried it to a window and off it went. Generally south, at least.

He scooped up the other two birds in the Tovar cage and frowned down at them. "Sorry," he said, then sighed, then smashed their heads against the stone wall. Those in the other cages he settled for setting free, hoping he wouldn't regret it.

That done, Jeld tidied the room a bit, shoved the priest into a dark, shitty corner in one of the cages, and was soon walking the city streets. He was a messenger now. A cold assassin playing the part of a messenger, anyway. The city was abuzz with soldiers preparing defenses, tradesmen seizing the final moments before battle to produce a last arrow, craft a last shield, hone a last edge. Much of the citizenry had been enlisted by whip or watchful taskmasters to aid in the preparations, though they didn't look to be moving particularly fast.

It didn't take long to follow rank and rabble to a command post, a shop near the wall with a banner posted at its door. A few young officers mingled nearby. An armored knight was hurrying out, helm under one arm.

Jeld walked past the place, stuffing the aviary keys into a cracked brick wall a few blocks away. He rubbed his hands along the dirty bricks and smeared the muck across his face, his neck, his pants. He spilled his waterskin down the front of his shirt as he was halfway across the street, panted as if with exhaustion as he kicked a leg over a horse tied beside the road, and a moment later was riding as fast as the crowded streets would allow back toward the makeshift command post.

Those milling about before the place parted readily as he jumped down then hurried past. He barged inside, stumbled, and came to a stop bent and panting. A quick take showed three in the room, one old, one big, one young.

"What—" one of them started, but Jeld cut in breathlessly.

"Enemy to—the west. Thousands. Took most—the scouts down. Thousands."

Jeld staggered back against a wall, leaning his head back, eyes mostly closing.

"West?" the old one said. A commander, with golden insignias on either side of his collar, and one sleeve covered in golden embroidery. "Not possible."

"The northmen that were hitting Havaral, maybe," the big one said. Another commander, if less decorated. "No surprise there. Makes sense they'd join this lot."

"No bloody surprise? You've prepared for it, then?"

The big one said nothing.

"How far," the senior commander demanded of Jeld.

Jeld straightened. "Not far. On you before the sun if they hold their pace."

"Thousands…" the young lieutenant said.

"*Idols,*" their leader cursed. He was silent for a moment, the others watching him intently, then turned to the lieutenant. "Fine. Wentz, order the reserves to the western wall. Thin the northern ranks to muster a new reserve, say one in five."

The lieutenant settled in his chair and set to preparing a pen.

"No, go yourself," the old commander said impatiently. "I'll not have the orders questioned or not read. And spread this news broadly, best all were prepared. Quick now, go!"

The lieutenant hurried to the door, hurried back to retrieve his coat, and finally was out the door.

The senior commander paced quickly just a few steps then flung himself into his chair, slamming his fist against the desk. "Idols, what a mess. We need to send word to the keep. They'll need to get a bird out for Tovar. Best case, we'll need reinforcement soon."

"Aye, sir. I'll update them," the other said. "Then we'd best get outside. Should have contact on the north wall any moment. There's—"

He looked up sharply at the sound of Jeld barring the door. Jeld drew his sword and started backing from the door, crouching in a defensive stance as if enemies might burst through at any moment.

"What in dreams are you doing, son?" the fat one said.

"They'll be here soon," Jeld said in a panic. "They almost had me out there. I was the only one that lived. The only one. Only one…"

"Easy, son. Easy. In battle, you've got to keep your head or else they'll take it off."

A chair creaked and Jeld felt the man approaching. A hand patted his shoulder.

"Go rest upstairs there, why don't you?" the fat voice came.

"Rest when the enemy is dead!" the older one snapped. "Now raise that bar and get the hell out of my command post!"

Jeld turned and slashed the fat one across the throat. As the first spurt of blood was still shooting toward the ceiling, Jeld dashed toward the other officer. The old commander nearly fell over backward in surprise. He recovered quickly though and reached across the table for his sword.

Jeld's blade came down just as the commander's hand closed on the grip, bloody stump raising up as if it bore the sword. This time the commander fell over proper this time, loosing a quavering groan like he'd seen death itself. Then death came down across his temple and he was silent.

A thud from behind and Jeld spun. The fat commander was on his knees, eyes going empty. His head rolled back and he crashed to the ground, knocking over a table with a loud racket. Jeld froze in the ensuing silence, then footsteps thudded above and voices echoed down the stairs.

Jeld cursed. It was unlike like him to infiltrate a place he hadn't scouted, but then, there had hardly been time for that. His eyes darted as he considered his next move, and a moment later he was racing to the stairs.

"Help!" he shrieked. "Enemy! Enemy!"

Three men rushed down toward him, swords drawn. Two uniformed officers, and another in full armor moving slower at the back. Jeld turned, swung his sword toward an enemy that was not there, then ran up the stairs.

"Help! They killed the commander!"

Jeld squeezed past the two uniforms, then the armored one, defying all instincts to keep the enemies distant. It needn't last long, though. He turned and booted the armored man square in the back. The knight went down in a crash and tangle of steel. The other men both turned. One took the full brunt of the knight's fall, going down hard. The other took a hit behind the knees and went down all the same.

The knight lay rolling and grimacing when Jeld reached the bottom and put a sword through his neck. One of the soldiers lay still beside him, face bloody from the fall. The other had already retrieved his sword and was coming to his feet. This one spun just as Jeld's blade flashed at him. Steel rang. It was a fast reaction for anyone, never mind having just fallen down stairs. Jeld jumped backward as the man retaliated with a practiced lunge.

Jeld feinted to the right, backpedaled, then darted in and slashed at the man's exposed leg when his guard opened. The soldier cried out and pushed Jeld back with a heavy swing. Done being clever, Jeld pressed in. Steel rang once, twice, and again, then he circled faster than the man could limp around and took him in the side. Another cry, but the sword came around still. Jeld turned it with a touch and landed another stab through the shoulder, then finished with another through the heart.

The remaining soldier was moving now, blinking fog from his eyes and grimacing. Jeld saw now that his leg was twisted at an odd angle. With another blink the man's eyes widened and he pressed himself back into the corner pitifully.

"P-please," the man stammered, wincing as he pressed himself upright. "Please. I've got kids. I'm no threat here. Please. Please."

Jeld stood over him, horror and mercy pressing through cracks in his character. He managed a half step forward but stopped. The man had to die. He'd scream. He'd share what happened here, blow the whole thing about another army. Probably he'd kill Jeld when his back was turned first, though he wouldn't be moving quick with that twisted leg. No, he had to die, and now.

Someone pounded on the door. Again, the door shaking with the blow. A spike of something like fear and resolve pulsed suddenly and he turned just as the man upon the ground swung a blade toward his ankles. Jeld jumped the blow at the last second, his blade piercing through the man's eye before he landed.

Jeld blinked down at the man until the door burst open in a splintering crash. In an instant, Jeld formed the image of the room as he'd found it. No blood spattering the ceiling and covering the floor. No bodies strewn about. No killer by the stairwell, even. He slammed it indelicately into the minds of the four soldiers in the doorway. To a man they seemed to hesitate, then one of them blinked hard.

"Hold it!" the shout came, but Jeld was already taking the steps two at a time.

At the top he turned up a second staircase, then darted out into a hallway, peering into room after room for some escape. There, an open window facing the alleyway behind the building. He slid to a stop and darted into the room, closing then barring the door behind him.

He ran to the window, peering outside and feeling along the outer wall for a handhold. The bricks were cleanly laid, not enough of a gap even for his practiced grip. A rope, then. He frantically reached into his bag for it, then an idea struck him and he ripped the entire bag from his collar instead.

Banging at the door now. Jeld pressed his arms into the bag. Boards cracked behind him. A plank broke off, then the door burst open and men spilled into the room. Jeld grabbed the rim inside the bag, swallowed hard, and jumped not into the bag but right out the window.

Jeld pulled himself up, down, whatever, into the bag. He felt the wind against his legs as he sailed, tumbled through the air, top half in darkness. The bone shattering ground must be close now, but his mind was mostly on the darkness constricting around him. Don't let the bag get pulled in after him, caught on a boot or blown by the wind. Then he was through.

He turned back toward the little window of light. Spinning sky, buildings. Cobblestones, shooting toward him, bigger, faster, faster, then they were upon him. He flinched away. When he opened his eyes, he was looking up at the still sky.

Jeld blew a breath out, reached through the bag, and crawled his hand along the ground, towing the bag like a hermit crab its shell. He worked his way into a dark corner, retrieved his hand, and spilled onto his back in the void, eyes closed and panting hard.

Blood spurted from the fat commander's neck. Jeld's sword plunged through a soldier's eye. Another's shoulder. The Knight's neck. The red priest's. Stabs of the horror, pain, sorrow of the dying. Of the murdered.

Jeld opened his eyes but everything was just as black and the flashes of thick blood and death continued just the same. He turned the bag to let in a spot of light and set to changing his clothes.

He emerged a while later in a soldier's light armor and a carpenter's bag over one shoulder. The sounds of battle raged all around. Not yet the clash of steel, but the twang of arrows loosing, the tap or wet thud of incoming arrows landing, men screaming and shouting orders.

Jeld pressed through a big gaggle of reserves, brushed past a handsy sergeant looking for able bodies with a show of his tool bag, and helped some men move a barrel of oil up the steps to the battlements. So thick with people were the battlements that Jeld could almost have been pressing through the Fallstival crowds back in Tovar, if not for the arrows, death, and boiling pots of oil.

Jeld hurried along the battlements, wincing with each crenel he darted past. Seemed like he'd come too far to get dropped by a chance arrow, but he hardly considered himself on good terms with luck.

There was only a single guard posted directly outside the gatehouse. Young, almost resembling a boy in his father's uniform, and looking plainly battle shocked. Jeld stopped before him and casually nodded to his tool bag.

"What?" the young guard said, wide eyed as if Jeld were a surgeon come to take a limb.

"Engineer," Jeld said sharply.

The soldier looked around fearfully. "Yeah?"

"Commander said you were sent word, no? I'm supposed to inspect the gate. Some worry it wasn't secured properly."

"N-no, no, nobody told me. I thought—"

"Probably one of the poor bastards bleeding out back there. Just takes a blink of bad luck, ya know. But, can't worry about that stuff. Now, open the damn door before the northerners open the gate and eat our dreamin' hearts."

The soldier stared open-mouthed at Jeld for a few blinks then fumbled for a key and opened the door. Jeld went inside and turned back to the guard.

"Now get the door locked back up. And don't wait for me, I'll go out the other side."

"Okay. Okay," the soldier breathed, more consoling himself than agreeing, but he closed and locked the door all the same.

Jeld let out a breath and crossed the small stone room to the gate lift mechanism at its center. With several ropes, pulleys, gears, and the like, it was more or less as Fen had described, only far more daunting in person. He started at the sound of the lock turning over from behind. The door he'd come through opened and the young soldier rushed in, closing and locking the door behind him with trembling hands.

"I can't," the soldier panted, back pressed to the door. "Can't. I can't."

Jeld's heart sank even as his hand found the grip of his sword. He started to patch the cracks in his character where sympathy shone through, but slapped the effort away. It was better he did the deed himself. Better to feel it than to not. No. No, there had to be a better way.

Jeld let his hand fall away from his sword and smiled. "Can't what, stop yourself from helping me? Probably the most important job in the defense, ya know."

The soldier blinked.

Jeld winked. "I'll be sure to let your sergeant know you were vital to securing the city, if he comes asking."

The soldier managed a twitch of a smile.

"Lock that back up, would you?" Jeld said. "Don't want to make this easy on the bastards."

The soldier remained frozen a moment then spun and worked frantically at the lock. Finally it turned over.

Jeld nodded. "Good. How many other keys out there?"

"Keys... j-just one other. With the guard at the other door. Maybe more somewhere else."

Jeld went to the other door, probed at it a bit with picks to explore the mechanisms, then dropped three iron marbles into it.

"For the best," Jeld said over the sound of barked orders and dying men. "Beats the enemy taking it from him and raising this here gate. Now, how much do you know about gates?"

"N-nothing." He looked as if he wanted to say something, then finally did. "Used a well plenty back home, if that's..."

Jeld nodded along to whatever the kid was saying as he looked over the gate mechanism. The ropes were disengaged from the counter-weight pulleys, just as Fen had predicted.

"Sure, sure," Jeld said. "Alright, quick now, pull these ropes onto those pulleys there. I'm going to see about these pins."

Spotting the two thick metal pins proved easy enough. Fen was again correct that the pins wouldn't budge, and that the defenders had not been so kind as to keep any sledgehammers nearby during an assault. So, he played at ducking into a supply chest while digging for the sledgehammer he'd staged in Kelthid's bag.

"Name's Corr," Jeld called behind him. "Yours?"

"Carey," the soldier said through clenched teeth as he fought a rope into place. "Like this?"

Jeld peered back over his shoulder. "Perfect."

"These connect to the counterweights, don't they?" came Carey's voice.

Not an idiot, this boy. No, the idiots were the calm ones. The roaring ones. The brave. In war, the wise could be found nursing self inflicted wounds in the infirmary, or hiding in gatehouses.

"Good," Jeld called back. "Yes, but if we rig this up properly we can use them to double the weight of the door instead of offsetting it."

Was that possible? Seemed logical enough, anyway. Jeld turned with a sledgehammer in hand and knocked the first locking pin free in three blows. He could feel the soldier's confusion as he set to work on the remaining pin. More of a battle than the first, but it clattered to the floor soon enough. The soldier was staring at him when he turned, but quickly resumed working the final rope, which appeared not to be budging.

"Snagged down there," Jeld said, kneeling at the soldier's feet and working at a tangle. "Hold on."

"What were those pins?"

Jeld cursed to himself. "Lock pins. They don't work with this counterweight trick."

Again Carey's confusion pressed down at him. More now, though. Scrutiny. Doubt. Skepticism. Meanwhile, the roar of battle grew louder. Not just arrows now, but an army.

"Are you sure? How does—"

"Do you want this dreamin' gate to stay closed or not! They'll be at it any blink." Jeld cleared the tangle. "There. Try now."

Carey grabbed the rope but hesitated, eyes tracing it through the contraption. He shook his head. "Sorry, I just don't—"

Carey sucked in air as Jeld's knife pierced up into his chest. Jeld shoved him back, forced the rope into place, and scrambled away until his back struck the stone wall. Carey toppled onto his side, looking slowly from his bloody shirt to Jeld, realization dawning on him. He knew he was dying. Knew it was the end. Jeld could see it all. Feel it all. How he'd never again feed the animals at his father's side back at the farm. Never hear another of his mother's stories, or fish with her by the brook. Never laugh with his sister. Never—

Jeld clenched the walls of his sense shut tightly. "Sorry," he managed, sliding down until he sat behind his knees like a beggar. "I'm sorry. I'm sorry."

The young soldier pressed a hand to his chest and it came away drenched with thick, dark blood. He let out a horrified sob and his head lolled to the stone floor. Staring at Jeld, his mouth opened and closed but no words came out.

"I'm sorry. I'm—"

Jeld's stomach twisted. He pinched his eyes closed, not daring to look, wishing, hoping desperately it had only been some dream. He peeled his eyes open, and the soldier, Carey, was staring at him. Jeld cried out, pressing himself back against the stone. He flinched away, but again whether by guilt or some morbid curiosity he looked again. Carey stared still, but past now, eyes vacant. Gone.

Jeld gave something like a sob and pressed himself harder still into the corner. He reached desperately for the cold assassin and it came readily. The panicked anguish sharply vanished. Only silence. No pain. No guilt. Nothing. Nothing.

No, there was something still. That small part of himself he always retained to keep from losing himself to his characters. It was calling out, muted, distant. This wasn't right, this hiding. Always hiding. The voice was screaming. He ripped the costume off and the pain returned, terrible and sweet all the same. But there was another costume. He mentally ripped that off too, but again there was another.

He had to be free of them. Had to find himself beneath. He tore at them with his every will, one, then the next, then the next, until he just sat curled in a ball staring at the dead boy, tears streaming down his cheeks. Still tainted by his characters. Still not finding himself, as battle fell upon Delvarad in full, and with it the horror of the dying all around.

Jeld sucked in a breath. Benam knelt beside him, a hand on his shoulder. He was still in the gatehouse, pressed into the corner. The gate had been raised up through the slot in the floor. It was quiet all around, save for subdued voices coming in through the open door. Jeld almost mistook the man standing in the doorway for a common soldier, but it was Torral. Krayo's man gave something like a nod then left, closing the door behind him.

Jeld's eyes flicked to where the young soldier, Carey, had lay staring at him. Benam's cloak lay over the body, now. Just a dark, unmoving mound.

"I'm sure there was no other way," Benam said.

Jeld didn't answer. There probably wasn't a better way. Knock the boy out? Gag him and tie him up? What if mercy only got him killed and the gate couldn't be opened? It had to be done, but that was only a small comfort. He just shook his head in silence.

Benam sat at his side with a groan. "You saved many lives today."

The words were precisely on target, the cloak over the soldier perhaps the greatest gift anyone could have given him, but Jeld could sense Benam's doubt. It wasn't insincerity, more like he was trying to convince himself. Perhaps, like Jeld, the old knight contemplated the unnerving similarity of his words to the inquisitors' talk of necessity.

"I know I'm probably not the best one to say as much," Benam continued. "I'd probably not have it in me to kill one person to save the entire world."

Jeld's eyes pinched closed again.

"Look, I'm not so sure that's a strength. A weakness, probably. I don't know where the line is drawn. Between necessary evil and evil. I know what side Naelis and his pursuit of salvation is on, and I know you're not on that side."

Jeld met Benam's blue eyes. He hadn't expected Benam's absolution to mean so much to him, but there it was.

"You've done right, Jeld. You've done right. Would that I could save so many lives."

"Your gift is to heal! Mine is—" Jeld laughed a bitter, humorless laugh. "To feel people's pain, and to kill despite it." He laughed again, almost a sob. "What sort of curse is that!"

"Not a curse. A curse would be to not feel it. To kill without remorse."

Jeld laughed another broken laugh. "Oh, I've got that too."

"And yet here you are. Not quite a cold killer, if you ask me."

Jeld bit his lip, straightened, and gave Benam a nod. Clearing his throat, he wiped his eyes. "Damn it! Pathetic. A lot of people have worse to cry about today."

Benam patted Jeld on the shoulder. "All in all it's been a good day. Sixty men lost."

"Sixty," Jeld breathed. "We expected hundreds, even with the gate."

"For some reason they had half their men on the western wall. Their command structure was broken. And the gate. They surrendered quickly."

Only the gate had been planned. The rest, just license of his foul art. Jeld shook his head. He forced his breath slower, steady, feeling Benam's calm presence. The weight began to fall away, if only a little.

"What other news?" Jeld asked quietly.

"The city is ours. My sister has been safely released. The others are in my father's council chamber, plotting our next move."

"*Your* council chamber now, isn't it?"

Benam frowned. "No, I think not. Tetchmira will make a far better lord. I'll be busy at Lira's side."

"Don't put that in writing just yet. You never know, after all this."

Benam brushed it off and went on updating him. If Tovar advanced fast enough to join with Caldemoor, or the force at Warrinton joined them, it would make for a tough next fight. Some held out hope that Lira would heed their call to sail on Tovar, and that doing so would draw more forces back to Tovar. Many ifs, but the orders were unchanged. March south, take out the enemy before they could combine forces, and join Lira in reclaiming Tovar.

"Torral arrived, you saw," Benam said. "Joined us just after we convened in the council room. Said he had something urgent to discuss with you."

Jeld took an easy breath and stood. Extending a hand to Benam, he pulled the old knight to his feet, gave him a nod, then bid him lead the way with a wave.

"Let's rejoin the others," Jeld said.

With one last look back to the still form of the young guard beneath Benam's cloak, Jeld followed Benam from the gatehouse.

CHAPTER THIRTY-ONE

Jeld stood atop a hilltop overlooking the morning's work in the valley below. Countless of their own lay dead, few of the enemy's. Men on both sides were digging graves, picking over bodies. Kill one another, then clean up the mess together. It felt oddly transactional. Impersonal, like a man dressing after lying with a woman.

Torral stood with Jeld, the little rat-fox of a man squinting in the morning sun. Havaral's ships filled the river behind the army of Caldemoor and the small contingent from Tovar, some coming, others returning likely for more men. Their predawn charge at one army had quickly ended in a bloody predawn retreat from two. Nobody had seen it coming, and Ralegus was still livid at his oversight.

"Well?" Torral asked.

Jeld sighed, Benam's forgiving words from the gatehouse running through his mind, then nodded.

Torral clicked his tongue. "Right. We'd both best be off, then. See you there at dawn."

With that, Torral plodded off down the hill toward the battlefield. Jeld stared after him a moment before walking back over to where he'd left Fen just out of earshot. Fen was sitting against a big rock now, arms upon his raised knees.

"What was that about?" Fen said, eyes not leaving the bloody battlefield.

"Nothing," Jeld lied. "Just some snooping about. Are you alright?"

"Better off than all of them, anyway." Fen waved a hand down at the graveyard below.

"I'm sorry," Jeld said, sitting on the ground beside his friend. "I never meant to get you involved in all this... death. You're too good for it."

"It's not that. It's not the killing, Jeld. It's that the killing doesn't bother me anymore. Not like it should, anyway."

Fen finally turned to face Jeld. His eyes were bloodshot and filled with tears. "I told you when we first met that I'd promised my da' I'd get out before I went cold."

"Fen, you can't blame yourself—"

"I promised him! It's all he ever wanted, and look at me? I'm just like the rest."

"No, Fen," Jeld said, recalling Benam's words. "I think your da' was worried about the sort that are down there checking pockets or already playing cards, not the ones sitting on mountain tops crying about losing their humanity."

Fen snorted, looked to the battlefield, then back at Jeld and nodded. "Thanks. Go on, I'll catch up."

Jeld gave his big friend a pat on the shoulder, failed to think of anything more to say, and left for the command tent. Renae, Ralegus, Benam, and Crisn were all standing around a map table inside when he arrived. Even the indomitable king of the north showed a chink in his resolve as they pored over their plans, if only a little. Two knights and a uniformed officer stood talking at the other end of the tent.

Jeld went to the table and surveyed the map. The only changes since he'd stepped out were more chits on the river, and more on the riverbank. More enemy ships, more enemy soldiers. All the more justification for his plan with Torral, but no more likely to sell it.

He opened his mouth to speak but only closed it again. Looking over each of his unlikely comrades, he considered their reactions. Always his gaze settled on Benam. Damn.

Jeld cleared his throat. "I've some news."

Everyone fell silent, the anxiety in the room palpable. It was only then that the implications of his plan's potential failure occurred to him. They'd be massacred. Lira would arrive in Tovar only to be swiftly routed. It would be the end, and it would be entirely his fault. It was a chance, anyway. A better chance than doing nothing, though? Probably. Probably.

"Good news, actually," Jeld lied, a growing trend that day. "I've just got word that the enemy's numbers are far less than they'd seemed. Closer to ten thousand, not twenty. We should advance."

"What?" Renae scoffed. "Our scouts are no fools. What's this, then?"

Jeld's eyes flicked again to Benam, masking the look by brushing at his shoulder. "Torral. He—"

A collective groan filled the tent, coming even from the other three officers.

"He has people inside, you know," Jeld continued. "Says the enemy is using dummies, repositioning troops, and the like. Says they've got little more than what we can see from the hill."

"Half?" Crisn breathed, shaking his head. "No, that can't be…"

"*Idols*, but this is no way to operate!" Renae cursed. "This *Torral*, these scouts—no, *spies* reporting to you. And who the blazes are y—"

Renae bit his lip and looked as if the words he were chewing were still very much alive and trying to come out. But he didn't need to finish, Jeld knew. Who the blazes was he. Some wagoner boy meddling in the business of lords and kings.

"Not my choice," Jeld said flatly. "Not my secrets." Of course, if they were, he'd be no more likely to reveal them.

"Yes, yes," Renae said bitterly. "This other that you and Benam serve."

Benam straightened. "I do *not* serve him. I serve Liraelle Tovados."

"Yes, well, you know him. You hold this secret."

"And do you think me a worthy judge of character?"

Jeld didn't think Benam looked altogether convinced at his own words, but Renae seemed not to notice.

"Enough," Ralegus said in his booming voice. "I didn't march my people into these bloody lowlands to bicker with you. Now, are we in agreement that the enemy has only ten thousand? We trust this Torral?"

Maybe trust was not the best choice of words, but nobody objected.

"Good," Ralegus said. "Now, we're back to nearly two to one. Not great with an even bigger army to face at Tovar, a dug in enemy, and not a single reinforcement, but we'll not get a better chance. So, we advance, aye?"

There was no resounding assent as there was in the northern hall any time Ralegus so much as raised a tankard. Renae looked outright pained. General Crisn skeptical, to say the least. Benam... guilty. They tossed their heads around. Frowned. Muttered. Eventually, Crisn gave an aye, and the others followed.

"Alright then," Ralegus grunted. "I say we hit them in the middle of the night. Easy enough terrain, and they won't expect it."

"Agreed," Crisn said. "Perhaps we split our forces in half. Hit them on the flank after we've—"

"Er, actually," Jeld interjected, "it would be better to wait until closer to dawn. Just before, if you wish. Got some false orders, misdirection, and all that going. Should be well worth the wait."

Ralegus grinned and patted Jeld on the shoulder. "We'll hit them just before dawn, then."

***

Jeld could just make out four of the six ranks marching ahead, each man picking his way through the sparse wood. His horse snorted, breath steaming in the cool air with the turning season. Stars shone brightly still through the canopy overhead. The Wise One's eye was nigh upon Hearth, dawn near at hand.

Renae and Ralegus rode nearby. Northmen filled in the bulk of the army behind the ranks of spearmen, ready to terrorize any enemy unlucky enough to pierce through. That's assuming they didn't just dig and let Jeld and company kill themselves against their defenses. To the northeast, an army of five thousand more northmen marched at the end of their line in preparation to flank or enfold.

The men were quiet, so far as armies went. The night should offer some concealment, and their rush should keep the enemy defenses light, but they would not be surprising anyone. Any moment the arrows would fly. Any moment the dying would begin again. The killing, though Jeld didn't mean to get as intimate with the enemy as he had of late.

The One would keep them safe at least, Jeld thought mockingly. Then he recalled something else Benam had said. The One might not keep them safe, just that he would have his way in the end. So, he wouldn't necessarily be catching any arrows for Jeld. On the contrary, if Jeld were to take an arrow or fall and hit his head this very moment, it was The One's plan. His will. His hand. The same hand that had killed Niya and done or allowed untold evils.

The One would understand, then, Jeld thought, not mad this time but rather desperate. He would understand what it was to make trade-offs. To do what must be done. Not like the inquisitors, though. Not like the inquisitors, surely. Surely.

A single shout pierced the night and Jeld's heart alike. It seemed it might be followed by another, perhaps a few, but instead only silence. Not even the sound of Jeld's breath, as it was held. Only silence.

Then, all at once, the battle was upon them. Shields crashed together to the south. Shouts all around. Immediately ahead, a dozen men fell as a wave of arrows rained down. A single arrow stuck into the dirt just beside Jeld, who set his horse backing away and casually drifted behind a tree. Ralegus was barking orders, or something like it. He and Renae both sat tall and confident, and not behind trees.

A pair of northmen dragged a bloody, screaming Warrinton man from the front and set him not far from Jeld. Benam and another man set to bandaging a gaping cut upon his leg, then split up as a second man was laid nearby. At first Benam was slow and methodical, personal. By the tenth he was only frantically applying bandages and hacking off limbs, then only shouting orders to his small team of medics, including several women from Warrinton.

A youngster with a mangled arm was screaming madly and wrestling a medic woman holding a cleaver. Jeld waited impatiently for one of the others to come to the medic's aid, but always more casualties stole them away.

Cursing, Jeld dismounted, tied his horse behind his tree, and ran to the medic's aid.

"Hold him!" the woman said through grit teeth.

Jeld climbed onto the man's chest and a fist struck him in the jaw.

"No!" the man shrieked. "Don't! Don't!"

Jeld twisted the arm around, pinning it. The man bucked, tried to roll. Tried to bite, even, so Jeld tucked his head down onto the poor bastard's chest. Something flashed past him. Wet splashed against his face. The cleaver was there, where the man's arm had been. The man was limp now, breaths small, rapid. Then he screamed bloody murder. Then, sobbing.

Jeld looked over to the medic, but she only hastily tied a bandage over the man's stump and moved on to another casualty. Left with the amputee, now silent between breathless, wheezing sobs, Jeld backed away. He tripped over something. Another casualty. A big northerner, hands pressed to a wound on his thigh. Jeld stood frozen, watching as blood seeped around the man's fingers.

"How 'bout a bleedin' bandage?" the big man said.

Jeld took another step back, blinked, then bent over the man's wound. He peeled the bloody, shredded pant legs aside. Thick blood pulsed out from a deep gash. He grabbed a bandage from a case set amidst the medics, then two more, and set to affixing them.

The first bandage soaked through quickly. He cinched the second tight to a groan, a spot of red already growing upon it. Jeld's hands began to shake as he fumbled with the third. Small talk, Benam had said once. Calms the patient as much as it calms the medic. Well, easier said than done.

"Almost done," Jeld said, calmly as he could manage. He winced. Small talk, not a progress report! "They say northerners never get cold. That true?"

Jeld forced one end of the remaining bandage under the man's leg, brushed off some dirt it picked up along the way, and tied it over the already red bandage beneath. He stared at it, the raging war and world all around reduced to the white strip of cloth. A spot of red wicked through and Jeld's stomach went tight. It grew, grew. Then it stopped, just a spot still, little bigger than a coin.

"Hah!" Jeld laughed, looking up at the northman. This would be the high that drew Benam to healing. To save lives instead of taking them. And, while not likely among Benam's draws, to do so whilst avoiding the worst of the battle.

Jeld's smile fell away. The northman's head was lolled over, eyes staring down at Jeld, chest still. Jeld came to his feet, backing away again, hands trembling. There were others laying there, dead, dying, bleeding. A pair of men pushed past him from behind, dropping another with an arrow in his shoulder amidst the others. One of the medic women was looking at him, yelling something, but Jeld couldn't hear it, wouldn't hear it. He backed away faster.

"Quarter reserves southwest!" General Crisn's voice came.

Jeld turned to find the general riding up to King Ralegus and Renae.

"Their main body is there," Crisn said. "You're only hitting the edge of their line."

"Good," Ralegus said, turning to a northman riding at his side. "Wheel the forces to the northwest. Flank and encircle."

The other northman went one way, Crisn the other, leaving Jeld staring out toward the front. He could just make out the enemy now, the legendary legions of Tovar in their crimson armor and tall, curved shields.

"Idols let them break," Jeld whispered. They couldn't afford to trade man for man. Not if there was any chance of facing the full force of Tovar awaiting them to the south. As if in answer to Jeld's prayer, if indeed that's what it was, their line pressed forward.

Jeld followed as their army advanced. The first enemy he saw in full was the body of a heavily armored Tovar soldier. The head was cleaved almost in two, the body dangling over the top of a hasty barrier. Jeld steered his mount through a break in the defenses. Bodies littered the ground beyond, the better part of them wearing Tovar crimson, but there was no lack of their own dead.

"Hold!" Ralegus bellowed. Echoes of his call went up all around. A northman at his side blew three short blares of his horn, these too echoed throughout.

"Too thin..." Renae said.

Ralegus nodded. "No sign of Caldemoor or Havaral. They want us up there, to be sure." He scratched his beard. "Best slow our advance. Send more scouts out in all directions. Double the rear guard. Shorten our line a bit."

Renae nodded and they sent runners out with orders. A short while later the horn signaled a slow advance, and they were moving. The dark sky above showed a touch of deep blue now, the outlines of tree trunks and soldiers standing out from the shadows if only a little. No enemy still, though Jeld could hear the beat and cry of their retreat. Ralegus looked like he'd rather be facing off with a battle axe than wading through this lull.

They pressed on and still nothing as the dawn grew brighter, then hoofbeats. General Crisn led two other riders galloping up to Renae and Ralegus. Scouts. Jeld recognized one of them as Tolm, the sneaky bastard who liked to make hiding in plain sight look effortless. He didn't look so calm now as he approached.

Tolm reported in a low voice muffled in the hum of thousands of footfalls, hoofbeats, whispers, and the occasional cries of the dying now mostly left behind them. Jeld felt Renae's gaze upon him, then the once lord of Warrinton was riding off toward the front.

Jeld considered slinking away through the dim. To where, he wasn't certain. Anywhere he might not have to meet Renae's eyes, he supposed. Men were passing him by on either side, moving faster now as their leaders charged ahead. Escape would be so simple now. He needn't even flee, just stand there and let it all pass by. But, with a heavy breath, Jeld nudged his horse ahead, toward Renae.

A murmur rose up through the ranks and the army slowed to a stop at the edge of a vast encampment. Jeld continued ahead, ignoring the calls of a few soldiers behind him, and pressed into the camp. He passed a body fallen halfway in a bush, and another that looked like it had clawed its way through the dirt only to die in more. Then they were all over. Bodies, everywhere. Hundreds of them. Some still in their bedrolls, most not far off. Doubled over or twisted, many beside or in their own filth. One beside a still smoldering fire was charred black, as if he'd fallen in.

Jeld spotted Renae atop his horse beside the smoking remains of another campfire. Ralegus was there too, both of them staring out over the death. Jeld stopped not far from them, as close as his shame would allow. A body beside them lay on its side in a bedroll, gut clutched and agony still showing in vacant eyes. A young girl lay with one cheek to the dirt, bringing to mind the Warrinton girl who had clung to him for so many days before her death. A tear had cut a clean line through the dirt upon her face from eye to the ground, where it lay still upon a fallen leaf. Jeld couldn't look away. She'd been alive there, dying just like that with her face in the dirt.

Benam and Fen galloped up not long after. Benam's hand came up to his mouth in horror. Nobody spoke for the longest time. Even Ralegus was silent. Finally, Renae spoke without turning.

"This was you," Renae said. "Your plot with Torral."

Jeld said nothing. What was there to say?

"Poison," Benam whispered, voice shaking.

More silence.

"How could you do this?" Benam said finally. "I trusted you. I vouched for you! I—"

The guilt and shame almost toppled Jeld from his horse. *Yes, you supported me. You encouraged me. You told me to do what must be done.* But he couldn't put that on the old knight. Maybe he was a coward, but he could shoulder that at least.

A rider approached Ralegus and the group followed him up a hill. Jeld made no move to join them, but he didn't stop his horse when it followed on its own accord. The sky was a beautiful pink as they crested the hill. The full of the Havaral and Caldemoor armies filled the valley below, all dead.

"By the Mother," Benam whispered.

Krayo had done it, Jeld marveled as he looked out over the sea of death. He had dug, then shit in Naelis's well just as he'd said he would. *The power to influence the world,* he'd said. Well, this was influence aplenty. So many dead, and Jeld felt not an ounce of regret at his involvement. Shame, disgust, but not regret. He'd save Lira yet. He'd save Avandria. He'd stop Naelis.

"Evens things up a little more, anyway," Ralegus said to Jeld. "Tovar will be well supplied, and well dug in, but we might do this." He looked Jeld in the eye, then shrugged his brow and rode off, barking orders ahead of him.

Renae was staring at Jeld like he'd never seen him before, as if he were a dog that might bite, or a snake who already had. "You didn't think we'd allow it."

"No, I didn't think so."

Renae was silent for a long stretch. "I think I would have," he said finally, almost a whisper.

"Maybe. Maybe. Well, now you don't have to."

Renae turned to him and some of the familiarity had returned. He let out a heavy breath. "Well. That's that, then."

Not sure what to say, Jeld nodded. Renae lingered in silence for a few breaths, gave Jeld another nod, then wheeled his horse and was off. Fen sighed, more at himself than at Jeld, Jeld suspected. He punched Jeld on the shoulder then departed.

This left Jeld with only Benam. Benam had not moved since cresting the hill, staring still out into the valley. It was an odd juxtaposition, this radiant, serene sunrise above such devastation. That warm pink glow that whispered of hope and new beginnings, shining upon the backs of the slaughtered thousands.

Jeld made to talk but stopped short. What was there to say? That poison is not so different from jamming a sharp metal thing through someone's neck? That he had saved many lives, just as he had by killing the boy in the gatehouse back at Delvarad? That it was necessary?

None of that would do. And so, Jeld turned his horse, and headed back to rejoin their army.

Chapter Thirty-Two

Heart thumping in his chest, Jeld peered out through the narrow opening at the top of his bag. It was an especially dark night, nearly as dark as the void his body lay in below. Or above, whichever the case. Fat raindrops slapped against his face as he scanned around the muddy hoof print he was hiding in. Through the rain and darkness, Tovar was a faint spattering of lights stretching across the valley below.

Funny. Tovar had not been particularly kind to him, but it still felt odd to march against it. It had been a home, for all else, with plenty of good. Plenty of memories. Even the unkind ones, edges softened by time. But they weren't here to destroy it, much as it felt that way. They were here to save it.

Ahead and to the west, a small company of Naelis's men was huddled under tents and all manner of makeshift shelters. He could still make out the back of Naelis's line behind. Originally headed north to join their comrades, they'd all fallen back to Tovar after the poison incident. Jeld's own army would not be terribly far beyond, but behind the enemy lines he could not feel more alone.

Jeld made to reach his arm out the mouth of the bag but froze at a shout that could have been beside him. His own breath held tight, someone else let theirs out in a pleased sigh. Even over the rain Jeld heard the unmistakable trickle of a man pissing. After a moment there came the sucking of boots from mud, and Jeld slowly turned the bag to see the back of a man melting away into the darkness.

Jeld gave his cramping hands a last rub then reached one out of the bag and into the mud. Into the piss, probably, but never mind it. He slowly crawled his hand over the muddy ground, towing the bag behind him. He could hear the river now. As they'd predicted, the line and reserves had been thinnest here, with only a fool likely to squeeze his army between the enemy and a steep descent to the river.

He looked about for an ideal spot to begin. Could be the whole war came down to this choice. At the very least, many lives. Not easy, looking through a bag in the mud. Would that he could just walk about under some guise, but he'd learned the hard way that some inquisitors could detect that, and Tovar was likely to have plenty. There was no stand of trees. No depressions, no cover at all. The darkness would have to be enough. Darkness, confidence if questioned, and the chaos of war.

Switching aching hands, Jeld veered toward what seemed a vacant stretch overlooking the river. This blessed, abysmal rain was on their side at least. It was the thick, cold, miserable sort that could soak through anything, if not on the way down then splashing and puddling up below. Jeld's muddy hand led him down a bit of slope into a particularly swampy area. Mud spilled and splashed into the bag and onto his face, but Jeld pressed ahead eagerly. The best place to hide an army was the least comfortable spot. Crisn had told him that on their long flight west.

Jeld stopped right in the center of the muck. Short of camping in the very river, this seemed as uncomfortable a spot as could be found hereabouts. Certainly nobody would be wading into the worst of the mud to piss. With a final scan fully around, he withdrew his arm and climbed to his feet in the void within. A twist of his trusty sparker and his lamp flickered to life. He ever so carefully picked up the bag at his feet, shuddering at the thought of accidentally pulling in its twin on the outside, then located the first scratch upon the ground marking the way out.

Another shudder crawled down his spine as he peered out into nothingness, but there was no time for heeding such fears. Into the darkness he went, eyes searching desperately for each next mark as the last disappeared behind. He let out a breath as he reached the door. Then it was up the stairs, up the ladder, and through the trapdoor, which hung open already.

A hand reached down to help him up. He'd have preferred iron bars and stone rim over a hand that might drop him, but he took it anyway and emerged in the nexus, as he'd dubbed it. Ralegus's eyes were as wide as they'd been when Jeld had left him there, in the awesome center of the mythical Halls. Five hundred gaping northmen milled about, most dressed in the Tovarian uniforms they'd taken from the dead. Buttons and seams were comically stretched to, or beyond, their limits, beards far longer and fuller than typical southern fashion. The deception would not stand to any scrutiny, but with any luck they'd not look like a northern horde, hopefully sowing even more chaos when the fighting began.

"All set," Jeld said. "Sorry about the mud, but it should keep visitors to a minimum while we offload."

And offloading would be no quick task. More than two bells by their math, assuming the northmen moved as fast as hoped.

"Ralegus," Jeld urged when the big king of the north only kept looking about like a child.

"Right, right. Best get to it."

Jeld laid his bag open on the ground. As planned, one of Ralegus's men grabbed the edges of the bag with the express orders of preventing it from getting pulled into itself, caught on a boot or elbow or sword. The northmen lined up, Jeld and Ralegus exchanged a nod, and down Jeld climbed into the bag.

His hands slapping against cold mud, Jeld pulled himself up into the pissing cold rain. The darkness, the cold air, the wet, all were a terrible shock despite knowing what to expect, but the night was not young. Jeld turned and pulled the next man through, then that man helped the next, and so on. Ralegus came before long, for a moment getting stuck before three men pulled him through. After only a moment's shock, he set to arranging his men in something like a perimeter.

Standing in the mud beneath the heavy rains was miserable, but it was a damn lot better than sitting in it. Jeld could only pull his cloak tighter, arms crossed beneath it over a Tovar uniform with a bloody hole in the side, and wait. There were at times faint voices and occasional shadows of enemies out in the night, but otherwise one could almost forget he was standing in the middle of an enemy army.

"Mud," Ralegus chuckled in the quietest voice Jeld had ever heard from him. "Smart. Might as well be invisible."

"Hopefully it lasts," Jeld whispered. "A rider might not be so put off by it."

"Mm, yes. Well, a little luck, and some quiet swords should get us through."

More northmen silently filled in. It seemed to be going slower than expected, and the troubled look upon Ralegus's face suggested Jeld wasn't alone in thinking so. First Renae would feint to the west. That was their cue to hit the east from behind, ahead of Renae's main assault. If Renae struck the east before they did, reserves flooding the line would likely make quick work of their little infiltration force.

"Sure you don't have any more of that poison?" Ralegus posed.

"Could pour it right into the aqueduct, couldn't we?"

Ralegus grunted. "I don't think your queen would be pleased if you poisoned the whole of her city."

"No. No, she'd not be."

Jeld wondered where she might be now. Circling the sea toward Tovar, somewhere. Readying to attack this very moment, if luck favored them. Maybe still in the Isles, their messenger dead or Lira simply thinking better of their plan. Or she was long dead already, dispatched as Jeld and company trudged their way here or waited for five hundred burly northmen to unstick their big asses from his bag.

"When this is over, will you rejoin Avandria?" Jeld asked.

Ralegus rubbed his beard. "Doesn't make too much a difference really, with us fighting on the same side. But, it'd only be right. Gave my word to the girl's father."

"You're a good man," Jeld found himself saying, staring out into the night.

Ralegus grunted. "Maybe. But not a smart one, else I wouldn't be here."

Jeld grunted a chuckle back at the big northman. They fell silent as more and more northmen packed the mud behind them. Both set to their rounds time and time again, checking their perimeter, their men. The rain somehow began falling even harder, and the night only grew darker and colder with it.

Shouts from the line, then. From the west. Ralegus winced, glancing back at his men. A horn blared, first the low rumble of a northern animal horn, then, closer, the higher toots of Tovar's brass. Then cries of battle. Beating hooves. Suddenly a rider emerged from the darkness right in front of Jeld.

"On your feet!" the rider shouted. "Prepare to move west on my orders!"

Many hands went to weapons, but to Jeld's surprise nobody attacked the man.

The rider looked at the ground as his horse shuffled its feet in the mud. "And get out of this blazin' mud, you twits!"

Then off he rode, echoing his orders over the sounds of battle.

"How many left?" Ralegus asked as he pulled a northman from the Halls.

"Thirty, maybe," the man answered in his too-tight Tovar uniform.

Ralegus looked anxiously toward the west, though there was little to be seen. He looked on the verge of ordering the attack, but bit his lip and waited, joining in hurriedly plucking more wide-eyed northmen from Jeld's bag. Men and beasts ran past, heading west toward the fight. Naelis's men would be too smart to move *all* the reserves, but it was something.

"That's it," a northman said, climbing from the bag. "I'm the last."

Jeld picked up his bag, fixing it back to his shirt. Something caught his attention and he looked up to find everyone staring at him. He turned to Ralegus and their gazes followed. Ralegus grabbed Jeld by the shoulder and gave a firm shake, then turned to his men.

"You all know the drill," the king of the north said over the rains and chaos. "And no bleedin' battle cries! Now, on me!"

Then, Ralegus was marching to the north with a horde of northmen behind him, Jeld at his side. They came first to a gathering of perhaps a hundred archers, all on their feet and most stringing bows that had likely been packed away from the rain. Ralegus gave Jeld a look and they shared a nod.

Silent as the darkness, northmen encircled the archers then calmly walked into them. A grizzled, rough looking fellow among them stood up and sneered at Jeld. "Sorry, did we get in your bleedin' way? Couldn't—"

Jeld's sword came down into his neck and shoulder. Five hundred more swords followed suit. The whole thing lasted barely a few breaths. A handful of cries before it was done, hopefully lost in the rain and shuffle and budding battle. The northmen didn't pause to see if anyone had taken note, but moved on as if chopping brush from a path.

The back of the enemy line took shape in the darkness up at the crest of a hill just ahead. Three ranks, but loosely packed to cover the distance. Just enough to hold an enemy at bay until reinforcements could arrive.

Jeld's heart pounded. The plan seemed ridiculous now. No horn to signal they were in place so Renae could begin his attack in full. What if he was late, and it was their little force against the whole of Naelis's army? But already they were wading into the unsuspecting enemy.

A soldier of Tovar turned, letting out a breath at the sight of reinforcement. Then a thick necked reinforcement cleaved a sword through the side of his head. Cries rose up, cries fell. Jeld waited for a witness at the edge of their attack to raise the alarm, but little came. They moved down the line upon shocked and speechless soldiers like a grindstone upon butter, leaving a gaping hole in the line behind them. As the grindstone ground, Ralegus led watchmen circling back into the darkness then slamming into the back of it, over and over like a rolling wave.

At Ralegus's side, Jeld cut down an enemy as shocked as the last. He felt none of the cowardice of past battles, whether by darkness or hope or butchery. Another fell to his blade, then another. Beside him, Ralegus pulled his sword from a man's chest and beat another man once, twice, three times with the hilt of his weapon.

But the resistance at their front built like the air before a speeding arrow. Five men free of shock fought back, then twenty, then a hundred. No longer a massacre, but a battle proper, slowing the northmen to a near halt.

Ralegus ordered a larger flank, northmen disappearing into the darkness then smashing into the side of the enemy. Forward again, and another flank. Not a grindstone now, but the jaw of some great beast taking bite after bite from the enemy.

A sword flashed toward Jeld. He could only get his arm up in time and the blade slammed against his bracer, pain shooting up his arm. He fell back, tripped in mud, and scrambled to his feet. A northman pressed in where he'd been standing, and a blade slammed into the side of his head. The northman toppled. Another took his place, and Jeld charged in beside him.

The enemy pressed in tight from south and west alike, then enfolded them entirely. More northmen began to fall around Jeld. They were stopped cold now. Jeld's courage died as suddenly as that last northmen unlucky enough to take Jeld's place, leaving him with just the gripping fear he'd felt at the fall of Warrinton. He caught a blow overhead and backpedaled. A spear nicked his shoulder, a second shooting toward him from behind. A northman cut it aside, then himself took a spear in the face and fell, screaming.

Jeld turned to press into the safety of his allies, but found himself looking at an enemy spearman. Both froze for a blink, then the spearman swung, too close for a stab. Jeld slashed the spear aside, swung his sword, then grunted as the man tackled him. The air shot from Jeld's lungs as the spearman came down hard atop him.

A boot came down beside Jeld's head, then a red-haired northman, vacant blue eyes staring. Jeld tried to lift his sword but the soldier atop him pinned his arm. An armored wrist pressed against Jeld's throat. Jeld grabbed the knife from the soldier's belt and jammed it into the man's side. The soldier screamed but didn't let up. Jeld pulled the knife out and lashed out again. This time the soldier rolled off of him, Jeld's attack whooshing past. Back still in the mud, Jeld swung his sword over but it only struck the dead northman.

Then the ground rumbled, and Jeld rolled aside as a horse went charging past, then countless more with it. He climbed to his feet. An enemy lunged at him with gleaming steel. Jeld jumped backwards, made to parry, and a rider slammed into the man with a crunch. The rider charged past like the man had been little more than a leaf on the path, blue tabard flapping behind him. Warrinton blue.

Warrinton cavalry crashed through the enemy that had encircled Jeld and the northmen, but ahead the enemy line was now a spear of ten thousand men pressing against them. Jeld dodged an enemy spear and took the attacker's hand off, but ten more took his place as the enemy swelled forward.

Jeld fell back, tripped over a body, scrambled to his feet, tripped over another. Someone pulled Jeld to his feet, then a wall of Warrinton shields charged past and crashed against the enemy. Renae was among them, looking every bit the Lord of Warrinton. More Warrinton men spilled through the gap the northmen and Warrinton cavalry had opened, and more enemy rushed to meet them.

Just another battle of lines, Jeld thought as he fell back behind the new arrivals, panting and holding his sword with two hands to keep from dropping it. They'd merely turned the lines from north-south to east-west. And during their assault it had seemed they'd cleared half the line, but the river flowed not far behind them still.

"Lot of good that did," Jeld panted, coming up beside Ralegus.

"Mm? Wars are won with many small victories, and that weren't small."

Jeld looked around helplessly. Men pressed forward, then others fell back carrying the bloodied and broken. "When's that small victory coming?"

"Where were we before, lad? Fighting up a hill against a dug in enemy. We've made a fair fight of it. Or closer to, anyway."

Ralegus slapped Jeld on the shoulder, nearly knocking the sword from his tired grip, then started down the line. Sword held high, he bellowed some orders in northern. Others echoed it. Not orders, but a song. All up and down the line, intermixed now with the soldiers of Warrinton, northmen sang as they faced and dealt death.

When Jeld could again breathe and lift his sword, he took a few slow steps toward the front then stopped. Swords raised and fell, lines ebbed and flowed, The screams though, those were constant. Jeld slunk back instead. Gone was any illusion that he wasn't a coward, and he felt only a little shame for it. Enough, though, to once again hide behind the guise of searching for Renae.

Jeld caught the reins of a panicked horse, riderless and spattered with blood.

"I know," Jeld whispered, rubbing her head. "I know. Me too, girl."

The horse ceased its shuffling. Its eyes steadied, and it lowered its head. Poor beast, trusting him. Still, he climbed up and pressed north. He crested a low hill and crossed the defenses marking Tovar's original line, a trench now filled with bodies and the scraps of a wooden blockade behind it.

Thick clouds above glowed with dawn's first light. The battle was everywhere. There were no reserves anymore, just two tides pressing together until only one or neither was left. Renae was there atop his horse, sword in hand, half a dozen of his guard nearby. A battered Warrinton lieutenant charged past Jeld, yelling.

"My lord, Ralegus needs more men to the south! We're losing ground."

"That can't be, I was just there," Jeld said, hurrying after and stopping at Renae's side.

Renae noticed Jeld for the first time. Their eyes met and suddenly he looked so tired. He turned to another young officer nearby. "We can't let them get behind us. Go north and send down whatever you can. One in five, maybe. Tell Crisn, if you can find him. I'll see what I can gather here and head south."

The soldier saluted and sped off.

Renae turned back to the lieutenant. "Tell him we're working on it. Tell him to hold at all cost."

Renae sped off to the south without so much as a backward glance to Jeld, who followed behind Renae's entourage. He cut into a thick point in the line and jabbed his sword to the south.

"All of you, south, now! Reinforcement to the south! With me!"

The whole of Warrinton did not rise up as one with cheers and glory, but a fair lot heeded his call. More followed after, joining their comrades whether by guilt, glory, or the promise of a brief reprieve from butchery with a brief jaunt toward other butchery. Renae rode on, more calls, and more men answering, until the lord of Warrinton was racing south with a growing force at his back.

The river flowed to one side, the battle to the other, men hacking each other to pieces. The gap narrowed, curved toward the river, until only a thin force of northmen stretching to the very riverbank kept the enemy from folding in behind them. This time Jeld felt a bit more guilty as he slowed beside the river and let their men pass by.

Battered and exhausted northmen fell back as Renae's reinforcements slammed into the enemy. Spears from an enemy shieldwall flicked out and dozens fell beneath them, but the enemy broke. Renae led fifty armored knights charging on horseback through the gap, the foot soldiers and even many of the just-relieved northmen filling in as the enemy fell back under their renewed assault.

From atop his horse, Jeld looked on with a horrified fascination. A mist of splashing raindrops and spattering blood seemed to hover above the sea of screams and swords and death. Tovar stood behind it, well out of arrow range but close enough to make Jeld feel small.

Suddenly a soldier standing beside Jeld cried out. He fell to his knee, a hand around an arrow sticking from his shoulder. Bending low in his saddle, Jeld scanned the enemy ranks for archers but saw none. That meant little, though. Then he spun toward another cry behind him and his eyes went wide. A ship upon the river loomed in the darkness, archers cramming its deck. The black banner of Havaral flew atop its billowing sails. Beyond it, dozens more filled the river.

Jeld charged toward Renae, but others reached him first and Renae turned to the river. Jeld saw his friend's eyes widen in a moment that seemed to stretch on, then Renae was shouting and pointing. His words were lost even in the short distance, but the meaning was clear. *Fall back.*

Their men needed no urging, nor did Jeld. They fled north, enemy cutting at their rear and arrows from the ships raining death upon them. Jeld cursed with each jarring bound of his mount, then doubly as Renae stopped to wave men past. He crouched low, flinching this way and that as arrows zipped by to either side. Finally Renae was moving again, and Jeld with him.

The enemy spilled into Jeld's path, and suddenly he was plunged back into combat. Two went down under his mount before they knew what hit them. Jeld cut down another, then another before his horse reared as friend and foe pressed in on all sides. Barely staying in his saddle, Jeld wheeled his mount and pressed north, Renae cutting down an enemy and following at his side.

Ahead, another part of the line collapsed and more enemy closed in. Jeld veered east and that's when he saw another Havaral ship pulling up beside them, a hundred bows upon its deck loosing as one. Jeld could only make himself small as the arrows came down all around. Dozens of men fell screaming all around, a few of them Tovar's own.

Jeld glanced at Renae, finding his friend unscathed. Bloody, but no arrows protruding from him, anyway. The way ahead was narrowing. Damn but war was fickle. Behind, thousands of their men lagged, fending off the enemy as they made their retreat. Renae saw Jeld looking at the closing gap along the river.

"Go!" Renae shouted to him. "You can still make it." He turned and charged back to the south, waving others past with his sword.

Jeld looked north once more, cursed, then pulled alongside his friend. They shared a nod, then Jeld cowered behind the head of his poor fool horse as hundreds of bows atop the deck of the closest Havaral ship were drawn once again.

Suddenly the whole ship rocked. A moment later a deafening crack washed over the battlefield and the great bow of another ship pierced through the Havaral ship like a great arrow through its heart. The bow of this new ship was a great tidal wave. Above it flew the light gold banner of the Isles. Out upon the river, more ships rammed and besieged and bordered the Havaral feet. Behind them, countless longboats packed with men rowed toward the bank.

A cheer rose up from the mess of northern and Warrinton men, and less pleased cries from the other. Renae seized the moment, raising his sword and charging into the enemy. This time Jeld did not follow, but stared out over the river, searching their decks for Lira.

Chapter Thirty-Three

The first wave of the longboats had reached the bank, others close behind. Jeld rode toward them, the battle at his back, eyes searching. He spotted General Handan pacing like a big hungry lion in front of the gathering Islers in their dull gray armor. That boy, Wesslund, too. Then someone moved aside, and there was Lira in her gleaming armor.

Jeld slid from his saddle and watched her. He wanted to run to her, but for two things. First, and perhaps most importantly, his tired body simply couldn't. There could have been a pot of gold before him too, even a tub of warm soapy water, and a spear at his back, but he couldn't have gone any faster. The second reason, an apprehension he felt whenever he reunited with Lira. A feeling that something must go wrong. That she should recognize their whole... *thing* as farce. That she should recognize him for the fraud he was. The nobody he was. The killer he was. Or if none of that, recognize that a princess could, or must, do a whole lot better. But even so, he trudged toward her.

Handan stopped abruptly, sword coming up toward Jeld. Jeld's stomach dropped at the gesture despite the distance, but after a moment Handan lowered his sword and alerted Lira. She turned and stared. Just stared.

Jeld froze again. His heart was full yet his chest hollow as they looked toward one another for what seemed the longest time. Then she was running toward him and, body be damned, he was running too. They fell into one another's arms. Jeld held her, pulled her tight, felt her cheek against his. For a moment there might not be thousands of men butchering one another just up the hill. Everything else was gone, and there was only her. He tenderly took her face in his hands and kissed her, and she melted still more into him.

Then she pulled herself free, and was the princess at war once more. "What's the status?"

Jeld blinked. "I... ah—"

It was such an abrupt transition he could hardly think. Then a thought struck him. He wasn't the only person who wore two faces when the need arose. He smiled, then pushed it away.

"We turned their line to get them out of position. Tough fighting at the southern flank. Some boat problems, but you saw to that. We've got some momentum now, I think."

Renae rode up, pulling along the horse Jeld had carelessly discarded. "Your Grace. Good timing."

Lira almost gasped at the man Renae had become in their lengthy time apart, scratched, muddied, and bloodied no less.

"Lord Renae," she managed, then Benam and Fen were there too.

Benam wrapped her in a tight embrace. She clung to him like it was all that kept her afloat, then he stepped back and bowed. She hugged Fen next, relief plain upon her face.

"Fifteen hundred men," General Handan cut in, giving Benam a friendly squeeze. "The rest man the ships. Where do you want them? Center I'd say."

Renae considered. "That would be best, General."

The general turned and slapped Jeld's arm with the flat of his sword. "Don't let your guard down," he said, then was off helping some Islers pulling another ship ashore and arranging a perimeter.

Ralegus rode up, calling out ahead. "Your Grace, we—Handan? What in dreams are you doing standing around? Get out there!"

Jeld couldn't recall ever seeing him surprised, no less addressed that way, but there was both.

"Protecting the princess," Handan said. "All of this is for nothing if she catches an arrow."

Ralegus scoffed. "A *tree* can block an arrow, but only you can put a hole in the whole bleedin' army. Get out there, Handan. Take some bites."

Handan looked to Lira, who nodded. He straightened, face deadly serious, then walked off toward the fight. They got Lira and Fen horses and all took a nearby hill, Wesslund only staying behind at her pointed insistence.

"Idols," Lira breathed as they crested the small hill.

By the look of the deafening, grisly scene below, Naelis's army had regained its footing. The Warrinton men had re-formed a tight wall and were holding well against a push from the enemy. Jeld thought he could make out General Crisn below in the midst of it.

"How did you know to come down the river?" Jeld asked Lira.

"Queen Alaesh never much liked the idea of assaulting Tovar. Even as a distraction, boats fare poorly against walls. When we saw Havaral's fleet missing, we had a hunch what they were about, and that the river might be high enough to do the same."

Jeld shook his head. Luck, then. Disgusting how often things came down to chance. He looked back over the battlefield. Handan was nearing the fight, each step inevitable, fearless. Every battered soldier he passed followed, a new army massing in his wake.

A blur of his great sword and the first enemy fell. Three more on a backswing. He stepped into the gap and in a blink a full arc of enemies surrounding him fell. His men pressed in, protecting his flanks as Handan Tovaine came alive delivering death unto the enemy.

Behind, hundreds of Islers had massed and headed now for the battle, countless more boats still heading toward the riverbank.

"*Idols...*" Jeld breathed as he watched Handan work.

It was like watching a seasoned farmer reap grass. Effortless, smooth. Only on closer inspection did the comparison break down—these were not single broad sweeps knocking down the enemy army, but countless precise strokes. He was fast, sure, and strong beyond measure, but more than anything he was perfect. His body was everywhere it needed to be and nowhere it shouldn't. His blade was an artist's brush, delivering the smallest strokes in all the right places.

"He's overextending," Jeld said.

Ralegus laughed. "Watch."

Their wedge pressed in deeper, Handan melting the enemy at its front, friendlies filling in behind them. When it seemed the enemy must surely envelop them, Handan began to circle, circle until they'd fully encircled a huge swath of the enemy line.

"There are two ways to take a bite from the enemy," Ralegus said as Handan's men pressed in. "The first is to let the enemy overextend, then surround them. The second is to press in as Handan has done, then close around them."

"What's to keep the enemy from biting you when you press in?" Jeld asked.

"Handan," Ralegus said, eyes fixed on the battle.

It was not long before the bite was swallowed, and the point of the spear was pressing into the next section of the enemy. Then something caught Jeld's eye. Riders, moving up through the enemy toward Handan. Knights, by the gleam of their armor in the sun. Not terribly many. Fifty, maybe.

Suddenly Fen gasped. "Inquisitors!"

Jeld looked closer. Not gleaming armor. White. They were wearing white robes.

"By the mother..." Benam breathed.

Without a word, Lira set off riding down the hill toward Handan.

Benam called after her. "Liraelle, you—"

"We have to warn him!" Lira shouted over her shoulder.

Jeld kicked his horse into pursuit, Benam with him, and the rest close behind.

"Go tell Crisn to compress the line," Ralegus shouted to one of his guards, then turned to another. "You, thin the southern line and bring more here."

The inquisitors cut into Lira's army south of Handan, enemy spilling in behind them. Most dismounted, swords and staves carving into their army. If Handan had been a reaper, they were an avalanche. A torrent of white spilling through Lira's army like death itself.

Lira pressed toward Handan. Men stared up at her in awe. Cheers began to go up around them, unaware of the white tide bearing down on them. She screamed for men to clear the way, to ready their flank, but in the chaos of battle they saw only a heroic charge. A beacon of light.

"Clear the bleedin' way!" boomed Ralegus, taking the lead. They did.

Handan was just ahead now. His sword flashed down and cut an armored man in half. It flashed again and took off a head in a splatter of blood. He dodged a spear, slapped aside a sword, blocked another and took off the arm holding it, all in a single moment.

"Handan, inquisitors!" Ralegus shouted. "Lots of them!"

Handan looked south and froze. The inquisitors were rapidly closing, cheers at Lira's arrival falling silent.

"Ready the line!" Handan shouted. "Lock ranks!"

"Lock ranks!" Renae and Ralegus echoed, men all around joining in their calls.

Their ranks swelled. Their formation tightened. They took a bit of ground even, orders or not. The inquisitors veered south, notably away from Handan, then struck. They didn't slam sloppily into the fray, but picked them apart like birds upon an ant hill. Men of war began dropping like they were children, picked off from behind shields, their attacks always one step behind the white monsters.

A group of armored Warrinton men got around one inquisitor as he faced a group of northmen, then the inquisitor went down to short-lived cheers before another took his place. The inquisitors pressed on. Still they hadn't veered toward Handan. Jeld had assumed they had been flanking him. Did they fear him? Did they not actually see him?

Handan charged into the side of the inquisitors. A cold faced inquisitor caught Handan's massive sword between two smaller blades. Handan spun his blade free and swung low toward the inquisitor's ankles. The inquisitor was only able to get one sword down in time. It wasn't enough. Handan's heavy swing cut through it. The inquisitor jumped, but Handan's blade had turned and was already sailing down from above. It cleaved through the inquisitor's shoulder and halfway down his chest.

Handan got in the path of another, and they traded blows, but the rest of the inquisitors only passed by, a sea of enemy pressing in with them. They weren't flanking Handan, but heading straight toward Lira.

"They're after you!" Jeld said. "They know it's over if you fall!"

Ralegus grabbed her reins.

"Stop it!" she barked, snatching the reins free. She raised her sword and reared her mount. "On me! Form ranks! On me!"

The breaking ranks solidified around her. More men heeded the call and thickened the formation. A mounted captain charged, waving his men in with him. They met the inquisitors head on. Not a moment later the heroic captain went down with a sword through the neck, and inquisitors carved through a dozen more without so much as slowing.

"Get her out of here!" Ralegus shouted to Benam, handing him Lira's reins then riding off rallying his men. "Hold the line!"

Renae gave Jeld a quick look, then rode off after Ralegus, echoing his call.

"No!" Lira pleaded, but they were gone.

Jeld could see the general still through the chaos, cutting his way toward them. Handan took down an inquisitor, but another was upon him. Others broke free and joined the push toward Lira.

"If you want this army to live, then live!" Benam chided, pushing her reins back at her.

With one more look behind, Lira slapped the reins and off they sped. No sooner, the inquisitors broke through, at least three on horseback charging after them. Jeld's heart raced with the thundering hoofbeats. Behind, the inquisitors were gaining, eyes menacing, hungry to serve their misguided justice. Jeld kicked, beat the reins, but his tired horse went no faster. Slowed, even, and the others seemed no better off. He had to do something. Had to stop them.

Jeld drew his sword with an aching hand and let free his Idolic sense. The horror and fury and agony of thousands hit him sharp as a brick to the face. He squinted his sense, reached for the inquisitors alone. There they were, creatures of ice and fire both. They were not fell things though. Not driven by evil, but by righteousness. A terrible, unblinking, unbending, and misguided zealotry. Pure faith. It was worse somehow. Worse than a predator killing for food. Worse than an evil killing for pleasure.

Jeld's breath huffed with each bounce. A panicked scream built up behind his clenched teeth. Four now, and gaining. There were trees not far ahead, as good a place as any for Lira and company to hide. They'd never make it though, not without something to slow the inquisitors down. Jeld blew out a breath and soothed his panic away. He found the pieces he needed to be. Maybe pieces of a costume, maybe pieces of himself. Then he slowed.

Jeld fussed with the reins as if trying to keep a faltering horse moving, and wrapped his mind around the lead inquisitor's presence. Not turning, he could feel the charging inquisitor draw his sword. He saw the picture forming in the inquisitor's mind, a quick flick lobbing off Jeld's head while riding past. The inquisitor's sword rose, then swung.

Jeld ducked at the last instant, the blade flashed past, Jeld's own shooting out. The inquisitor screamed, severed arm falling to the mud. Three more were closing fast. The two in back bore dual longswords, the one in the lead a huge greatsword, and a long scar down a familiar face. It was the one Dralor had saved them from as they'd fled the gates of Tovar.

This was the end, Jeld realized. He had no idea how to fight on horseback. Master Inado had called him more a mover than a striker, but atop a horse there was little moving to be done. Not against anyone, never mind three inquisitors, or the dozen more probably close behind.

Then the first was upon him. He raised his sword and threw a wave of panic out into the inquisitor, but Scar barely hesitated. Jeld's arm rattled and flashed with pain as the larger sword slammed against his. He barely got under the attack as it cut through his and swept overhead. Even as Jeld struggled with numb fingers to bring his blade back around, the second inquisitor reached him. A straight-jawed, almost handsome fellow if not for a terrible ambition in his eyes.

Jeld turned the first sword, ducked the second, kicked the bastard's poor horse in the nose, and Scar face was upon him again. The greatsword came down like it weighed no more than a child's toy. Jeld leaned left, but his horse moved him right. He raised his piddly blade and the greatsword slammed against it. Pain shot up Jeld's wrist, then his shoulder. Steel rang, then shrieked as the greatsword slid down Jeld's armored shoulder.

Handsome got his horse under control and kicked it rearing toward Jeld. The third was closing. Jeld started to form an image of himself just out of place, but the greatsword flashed toward him and his concentration shattered. He ducked this one, feinted a low stab and swung high. The inquisitor fell for it, but so fast was the inquisitor that it hardly mattered, the blade just flashing out again. Jeld leaned, brought his sword down, and sucked in a breath as the inquisitor's blade disappeared into his gut.

Searing pain. Shock. He'd known he couldn't beat them, but just like that? The end. And for Lira, too? No. Had to buy her time. Just another blink maybe. Something, damn it!

He grabbed the inquisitor's wrist and tugged, the blade sinking deeper, the inquisitor's throat drawing nearer. Then he swung. A good way to go, finishing the job on this scar-faced monster. But the inquisitor dodged with lightning speed, and the second inquisitor charged into him, blade a blur.

Suddenly a third blade sailed just a finger from his face, steel rang, and white robes charged past like a storm. Jeld wheeled his horse, doubled over and breathless as the sword in his gut pulled free. One inquisitor toppled from the saddle. Handsome, already still on the ground. The new arrival charged into the scarred one and their blades met.

It was Fhide, Jeld realized, the inquisitor trainee he'd befriended in Khapar. Fhide drew a line of red across the other's white chest, but it was a shallow wound and the greatsword pushed him back. Light in the scar face's hands, it came down again and again, fast as a dagger, until it slammed the sword from the Fhide's grip.

Scar face wrinkled his nose at Fhide and raised his sword again. And suddenly he spun and the blade came down. Fen caught it on his own, gritting his teeth as their swords locked. Lira stabbed at the inquisitor's chest but he threw Fen back, caught Lira's attack, then gasped as a blade protruded from his chest. Fhide twisted his blade and scar spilled limply from the saddle.

"Jeld…" Lira breathed, shaking her head, eyes fixed on his blood drenched shirt.

Jeld cried out in pain as he turned over his shoulder. More inquisitors broke through their line and charged toward them. "If Naelis gets my bag—he'll be unstoppable. Get—" Jeld gritted his teeth in pain. "Get away from me, all of you. Fhide, go with them. Go!"

Lira grabbed his reins. "Come on. Just a bit further."

"No! I'll lead them…" Jeld's head spun. He blinked his eyes back into focus. "I'll lead them away. Rally your army, Lira. Save Avandria."

"Jeld, no. I—"

"No time! I'm already dead, Lira," Jeld said. Never taking his eyes from hers, he raised her hand and kissed it.

"Go," he whispered.

Then he turned and kicked his horse into a gallop. Even with blood gushing down his legs and agony at every stride of his mount, it took everything not to look back. Not to turn around. He opened his mind and felt her there, wanted just to sooth her every worry, but he shook that away too and found the inquisitors. He showed them the bag. Showed them the forest. Showed them him.

But there was something else there. Another presence. Full of conviction, faith like the others, only warm in all ways they were cold. Benam.

"Go back!" Jeld called, breath catching as pain shot through his gut.

"Get rid of the bag!" Benam said as he sped after. "Just push it into itself!"

"I will. After the inquisitors come in to get me. We've got to stop them or they'll defeat Lira. You don't need to die today too, go back!"

Jeld could hardly breathe through the sharp pain as he turned to look over his shoulder. Six or so inquisitors not far back veered toward them. Never had he imagined he might be so glad to see such a sight, but so he was.

Jeld and Benam galloped past the medical tents, then the rear supply lines, and soon only open country. Jeld could almost be upon a wagon with Niya riding for Tovar. He could smell Cobb's sole stew, soup, whatever. Jeld smiled. Home, if ever there was one.

"Wake up!" Benam's voice came.

Jeld started awake. Benam had his reins now. Jeld managed to peer behind. The inquisitors were closing. Jeld's breaths were short and fast, vision cloudy. But he pulled his reins free and pressed into the trees.

"In there," Jeld said, veering into a thicket. "Here. Help me down. Hurry."

Benam slid from his horse and eased Jeld down. Already Jeld was pulling Kelthid's bag from his shirt. He laid it out upon the ground.

"Inside, quick. Quick."

Benam did as bid, then reached back out for Jeld. Jeld cried out through clenched teeth as Benam pulled him up into the nexus. Jeld rolled onto his back and lay panting.

"Up," Benam said, pulling him to his feet.

"There," Jeld said, averting his gaze from Reverie's door until it came into focus.

Benam looked confused, but didn't argue. His eyes widened as Jeld pulled open the door as if from nowhere. They hobbled into a grove and shut the door behind them. Benam eased Jeld to the ground beneath a tree, head upon a mossy root. Jeld started to pull his shirt up to see his wound, but Benam grabbed his hand.

"You'll rip the clot. Let me." Benam trickled some water from his canteen onto the wound and slowly started peeling it away.

"Ahg!" Jeld cried out. It felt as if a hot iron were filling his gut.

Benam sprinkled something from a vial over the wound and set to binding it, for all the good that would do. Benam's eyes fell closed and he began humming a soft song over the rustling of leaves, chirping of birds, and trickling of a stream.

Jeld stared up at the green canopy above, rocking in the wind with the blue sky beyond and sunlight streaming in through the leaves. Benam's song. Peaceful. He wished Lira was here to see it. To feel the peace. Lira...

Jeld snapped back to the present. Lira. Had to save Lira. Had to stop them. He shut his eyes, and opened his mind.

There was Benam, soothing and tranquil as a warm hearth, somehow still full of hope. Jeld smiled and pressed out further still.

"Don't close your eyes," Benam said firmly.

"I'm watching for them," Jeld whispered, eyes still closed. "I'll tell you when there's an opening, and you can get out and push the bag in."

Jeld felt Benam's skepticism flash, but the old knight said nothing.

"They're inside," Jeld said. "Four. Five of them." He dove into one of them, shuddering at the cold mind, and the inquisitor's thoughts took shape like nebulous images in his head. "There should be more."

Maybe they went to fight, Benam seemed to say in Jeld's head.

"No, something else," Jeld said, probing, listening. "They're taking the bag to Naelis."

Five inquisitors. What a ridiculous plan it had been, anyway.

"We'll figure something out," Benam said, soft like a lyric amidst his song.

Jeld's pain felt small now. Small compared to losing Lira's war. Compared to giving the kingdom to Naelis.

"I should have listened to you. I should have gotten rid of the bag."

"Never mind. All will be well, in the end."

Jeld could have screamed if he wasn't so tired. If it wouldn't have made him pass out from the pain. Even as the thought occurred to him, he felt himself sink toward sleep or something worse. He forced his eyes open.

It was a bit darker now beyond the canopy, the shadows of the trees long. His torso was wrapped, though blood was soaking through. Benam sat beside him, a hand on Jeld's chest, humming still. Jeld tried to sit up but pain shot through his abdomen. He cried out but fought his way upright then lay back against the tree panting. More blood seeped through the bandage.

"How long was I out?"

"Perhaps a bell or two. Hard to say, everything seems different here."

Something brushed Jeld's mind like a shiver crawling down the spine. He closed his eyes and, forcing himself not to slip away again, reached out.

"Naelis," Jeld breathed.

He felt another stab of guilt. Of loss. Of failure. But Benam's song pushed it away, and suddenly he knew his next ridiculous plan.

***

Naelis grunted with effort as two of his inquisitors hauled him up through the bag. He came to his feet upon a floor of pure blackness and looked about. His breath caught, eyes wide with awe and hungry with greed. A huge glowing orb floated in the middle of the room.

"By dreams..." he breathed, then looked about. Thirty odd inquisitors filled a vast cavity. The floor was not black, actually, but rather emptiness. A void, somehow bearing him. Everything was somehow completely dark despite the bright, shimmering thing and countless dimly lit hallways all around. He approached the orb of light and raised his hand until his palm hovered just above the surface.

"Circle around it," Naelis ordered, lowering his hand. "Quickly now, the suffering outside continues until our task is done."

The inquisitors did as bid, raising one hand as their master had, their other out toward Naelis. The old priest only stood silently, his white robe looking almost black against the shimmering orb, eyes growing distant. Finally he sighed.

"Forgive me. Forgive us all." Then, sharply, "Begin."

At first nothing happened. Then, tiny fibers of the shimmering light reached out and touched one of the inquisitor's hands. Then to each of them. The shimmering in the orb quickened. Swirls writhed and coiled like wounded snakes. The reaching fibers thickened until bright beams poured into the hands of the inquisitors. Their hands glowed like suns and the energy began streaming between, rolling like a wave toward Naelis.

Naelis reached out toward the flowing energy. The magic. The One. His eyes were hungry, tired, disgusted all at once. Then the light pressed into him and he cried out, back arching, teeth gritted. Not pain. Not pleasure. He felt like he didn't need air. Didn't need a body. But it was so much. So much he could just break apart, but there was so much to do still. A world to save. He had to hold. Had to hold!

The inquisitors pulled more and more, the river of energy flowing around and into Naelis. Slowly he lifted from the invisible ground, energy pouring into him. Decades of his labors came pouring back as his plans, his master's original aims, came near to fruition. Decades of sacrifice. Decades of pain. Of suffering. Of unforgivable evils. Of necessity. Finally he would have the power to save them all. Just had to hang on. Had to hold together.

Then in an instant the energy was gone and he was on his feet again somehow. The currents in the orb were almost still now, the dark chamber silence. *Close, master. We are close.*

The nearest inquisitor was splayed on the ground, bright red blood soaking his robes. The next, dead again. And the next. All of them. All the way around the glowing sphere, bloody white robes. He shuddered at the loss. A shame, but it didn't matter now. He had what he needed. He looked down at his hands, in awe that such power must reside within him now, and wondering how to tap it.

The room began to grow brighter, then. The sphere began to fade. Had he taken too much? No. No, this wasn't supposed to happen...

Walls took shape around him, like a star with five great corridors at its points. Narrow hallways lined the walls still, as they had around the room with the orb. Then a form took shape, a man, gray haired, bright blue eyes reddened and full of tears, face a blood spattered mask of anguish. Sir Benam Visleigh. His sword hung from his grip, running with blood. Behind him, the boy with the bag fell to his knees, then spilled to the floor, a tired smile at the corner of his mouth.

Naelis's eyes were wide now as he took it all in. The orb was entirely gone, as if it had never been there at all...

"What... How—" Suddenly Naelis glanced to the unmoving boy, realization spreading across his face. "No... What have you done!"

"This is the end," Benam said, and stabbed him through the chest.

High Priest Naelis sucked in a short breath. "I was—so close," he whispered, as if to the years. As if to the world. Then he turned to Jeld. "You've doomed us all."

With that, High Priest Naelis slumped to the ground. Looking on, with Lira on his mind and a smile still upon his lips, Jeld's eyes fell closed.

Benam ran to Jeld's side, sword clattering to the ground. Head shaking, he stared down helplessly, then looked over the dozens of dead inquisitors, then down at his own bloody hands. What kind of god allowed such things? He'd told Jeld it would all be okay. But why? Why have faith in a god that lets such things happen?

"Why?" Benam asked.

He spun as something caught his attention. Orbs of lights, like that of The One but small and tinged red, rose up from Naelis and the fallen inquisitors. They hovered above the bodies for a moment then one by one shot down the narrow hallways. Benam stared after them. Souls? Or had they really taken a piece of The One, despite the illusion, and now the power returned? He understood now why Jeld didn't like this place. *Hadn't* liked this place.

Suddenly, a blinding red flash filled the room. Filled everything. The ground shook. Red light pierced through the world all around, like angry fire between the boards of a smoldering cabin. Again in that moment Benam's faith shook. Everything would *not* be all right. He wondered how many people he'd let die in his faithful inaction even as the red light brightened, consumed everything.

Then a sharp crack like shattered lightning, and the light was gone, just a lingering red cast all around to convince Benam it had happened at all. Forehead wet with blood and sweat, face with tears, Benam shook his head and looked back down to Jeld. Another ball of light was rising from Jeld's chest, this one bright white and blue.

"No…" Benam said, voice cracking, but like the others, it shot away.

Then, the thing froze just before reaching one of the halls. Benam's hand was reached out toward it.

"No!" Benam boomed, not pleading, but inevitable. His skin began faintly to glow, blue like summer sky, chest rising and falling, muscles straining as if lifting a mountain.

"No," he whispered, and the ball of light began to backtrack. Slowly, ever so slowly, it came to hover atop Jeld. But no further. Benam strained his will, body trembling with effort, but it would not return. His hold wavered and the thing inched away.

"Lira needs you," Benam whispered, then pushed again with all his might.

Benam's voiceless song filled the air. His blue light wrapped around Jeld's still form, around the blue orb, and heaved them together like two halves of a great rent glacier. The ball sunk back into Jeld's chest, and he sucked in a breath.

CHAPTER THIRTY-FOUR

Dralor dodged a blade, head-butted its owner in the nose, and tugged at his sword, stuck tight in the crimson mail of a man's chest. Another blade came at him and he blocked it with the dead man's shoulder, pulled his blade free with another mighty tug, and cut the attacker down.

Spinning, he turned a spear away, then took a fist in his nose and went down. He landed on his face in the mud, conscious enough to roll over before taking a breath of muddy water. Then, blinking, conscious enough to roll again as a boot stomped down, then a spear. He came to a stop against someone's boots and a strong hand hefted him upright.

"Least you saved some for the rest of us, eh Del?" Lans said, smashing the edge of his shield into a spearman's throat.

A bowstring *thwipped* and an arrow slapped right into the eye of the last of the nearby enemies.

Lans gave something between a groan and a laugh. "Ahg, Kep! Now that's a hell of a thing to do to somebody, isn't it?"

"I—I didn't mean to," Keply stammered. The big man had lost some of his excess weight, gained even more in muscle, but grown no less squeamish. As such, he'd taken a liking to the bow, which felt a little less gruesome—usually.

Lans clapped Keply on the back then turned to corporal Davit. "What now?"

Their fit young leader looked out over the battlefield, the rest of their troop just behind. The army of inquisitors had made a mess of things, and the battle had descended into pockets of fighting strewn all about.

Just then there came a blinding red flash. Dralor flinched, then again as a deafening crack boomed over the battlefield. For a moment Dralor thought he'd been struck by lightning. Then, more likely, hit on the head. But the light faded, save just a red tinge to everything that could have merely been burned into his eyes.

"Bleedin' mother was that?" cursed Lans.

"Fire?" Keply said.

"What kind of fire you seen, big man?" scoffed the sturdy Isler, Lalow. "Odd kinda lightning, maybe. Or a mountain fire? Seen one blow with my own eyes. All red, melted rock."

"Look there," Keply said.

Dralor followed his gaze up into the sky. To the north, just beyond the reach of dawn's glow stretching up from the horizon, the star Hearth glowed an angry red. A chill went down Dralor's spine. They all fell silent, until the shouts and screams and clatter of battle rose back up all around.

"There," Davit said, pointing.

Forty or so enemies had re-formed a tight formation and were wreaking havoc on Liraelle's scattered army. Dralor spotted a grizzled sergeant at their center, barking orders and directing his men. The power of a leader. The difference between the chaos all around, and this small but mighty fighting force. More enemies were rallying near them.

"Up the side of the hill, you think?" Davit asked Dralor. "Might get the jump on them."

Dralor nodded, grabbing a shield from a fallen enemy. "Need them well engaged first or we'll just dirty their shields. Where's Captain Heath?"

"Haven't seen him for a while now."

Dralor frowned, then marched over to another gathering and grabbed the shoulder of a pale, blood-spattered corporal.

"We're taking down that bunch before they rally the whole blazing enemy!" Dralor called over the racket. "You're hitting their front. Don't get yourselves killed, just hard enough to distract them. C Troop will hit their flank. Got it?"

The corporal frowned at Dralor. For a moment it seemed he might protest.

"Now?" the corporal asked finally.

"They'll only get more organized. Go now, we'll follow your lead."

The corporal swallowed hard, then nodded. Davit already had their thirty odd men together by the time Dralor returned. Davit waved Dralor toward the front to give the orders, but Dralor shook his head and pointed back at him.

Davit took a breath. "Alright, Crauuls. We fight our way to the hillside as separate squads so we don't attract too much attention. Gather at the base of that hill and wait for my signal. Fourth squad watches rear and flanks while we assault."

Men murmured their agreement. The other troop soon was on the move. Dralor shared a nod with Davit, then the young corporal waved him back out into the carnage.

"Stay close!" Dralor shouted, his squad at his back.

Lone enemies veered from their path. Friendlies broke from scuffles and fell in with his squad. The ground was still flat and Dralor's legs burned already. Damn but he was getting too old for this.

A group of ragged northmen was getting overwhelmed not far off. A tired lot, both sides of it. Small weapons held with two hands and swung more with hips than arms. Two were locked together like this was a drawn out wrestling match and they were keen to wait it out. Another northman fell. Dralor gave one more look up the hill, then charged toward the faltering northmen.

One enemy went wide eyed and fled. Another tried the same but, held tight by a northman, got Dralor's sword through his armpit instead.

"Please, no!" a young Tovarian soldier shrieked, falling back into the mud.

Dralor pushed past a northman, stuck the fallen soldier through the heart, and twisted his blade.

"Join us," Dralor said to the cheering northmen, then called out to his men. "Up! Take the hill! Up!"

He charged, not looking back. The enemy showed no sign of noticing Dralor's charge, their exposed flanks in full view behind the shieldwall. Dralor's mouth practically watered to sink a blade into that defenseless meat before it could turn.

"Right!" a shout came.

The old sergeant, looking Dralor's way. Then an arrow hissed past Dralor and took the sergeant in the chest, dropping him from the saddle. The closest enemy glanced over at Dralor and cried out. He brought his shield around, Dralor caught it on his own, and smashed the side of his helmet in with a heavy swing of his sword.

Dralor jumped back as the next enemy swung a spear his way. The rest of Davit's troop had other ideas, smashing him forward. He flinched aside and the spear sliced down his cheek and split his ear. Suddenly he was pressed into the side of another enemy, who turned and went wide eyed. Dralor jammed his shield into the man's knees, swung his sword, and with another jostle from behind he was stabbing someone else through the gut.

The fight lost shape after that. Just places to stick his steel, bodies underfoot, blood, and faces. Backsides, before long, but those were just more places to stick steel. Not a single weapon swung his way after that spear, actually. Poor bastards never stood a chance.

Dralor stood panting at the top of the hill. The whole thing cost only two men, both in the other troop. Two troops in exchange for perhaps thirty should be a good trade in the business of redemption. Certainly was in the business of war. Why, then, did it just feel like two more wrongs to right?

Dralor turned sharply to a booming shout from behind. A big northman was riding down the battlefield, the scattered clumps of men converging around him. Ralegus, Dralor recognized at once. King now, he'd heard. He found himself smiling, wanting very much to greet his one-time friend. His brother's friend, anyway. But no, Prince Dralor was best left dead. Honestly, Del might well be dead too were he to show his face to Ralegus, and deservedly so.

And so Dralor turned away from the king of the north as the big man rode by. More and more men converged on the hill, and to either side the lines began to solidify, then advance. Funny how battles were like that, Dralor thought as he followed Davit amidst his comrades. Fickle, for better or worse. The day—and war—had seemed lost not long before when the inquisitors had struck. And maybe it would be yet when they returned from wherever they'd gone.

He cleaved a man down through the shoulder and waved his squad toward two knights. The smallest ripple could cascade to victory or destruction. One hill taken. One king with a big sword and a bigger voice.

Dralor lost himself in the rhythm of battle once again. Regrets forgotten, if only for a moment. There was just his men. Just the enemy. Just his damned blistered hands and chafing pants and a screaming cut down his arm, another through his ear. Then, sword raised in a near worthless grip, lungs aching for air, and face caked with blood, he froze.

Just ahead, a full company of enemy soldiers had thrown down their swords, hands up in the air. A commotion rose up from behind. Something being said, echoing through the ranks. *Naelis is dead.*

Dralor whispered the words himself. "Naelis is dead..."

More enemy swords were hitting the ground. More hands rising into the air. More of those words. *Naelis is dead.* Dralor shook his head as he looked out over the quieting battlefield. It should have felt better, but somehow he felt suddenly empty. Without his vengeance. None of the lives he'd taken returned. What, then?

Then Dralor's eyes fell upon a black tower in the distance. He stared at it for the longest time, then he was moving.

"Where you going?" Lans asked.

"I've got to take care of something," Dralor said, not turning.

Lans jogged up beside him. "Could be dangerous. Not everyone will have heard the fighting's done. And the rest might not be so glad about it."

"Where you all off to?" Keply said, following after.

"Wait here," Dralor said. "I—"

"Del's taking care of something," Davit said from somewhere behind, then called to the rest of the troop. "On me, Crauuls! We'll rest soon enough."

Dralor shook his head and marched on, the whole troop wrapping around him. Tovar men gave them wide berth, hands going higher, more swords going to the mud. One man wept with what looked like joy. Others stared off toward Hearth, still red in the dawn sky.

Fewer and fewer bodies littered the ground as they pressed beyond where the bulk of the fighting had taken place. They came upon a soldier laying on his back, chest rising and falling fast. He had a stab wound through the chest, and by the look of him little blood left to leak. A seasoned soldier, by the look of him. Dralor stopped over the man.

"It's done, then?" the dying soldier asked.

"Aye," Dralor said. "Naelis is dead, it seems."

"Almost made it." He gave a sad chuckle, wincing in pain. Then his distant eyes met Dralor's. "Put this old dog to bed, would you? Do me that?"

Dralor's hand closed on the hilt of his sword. He pursed his lips. Death was not the gift he wished to give Tovar today. No more of that should be dealt by his hand, even as a favor.

"Go on. Please."

Dralor stared down at the soldier. Probably spent his entire life fighting for the crown by the look of him. So many had. Even before Naelis was pulling Dralor's strings. Silly wars, for a bit more land, more power, more taxes. Taxes just to fund more war.

He drew his sword. Death might not be the favor he'd like to give Avandria, but he had a debt to pay. He had a debt to pay, and making others do the dirty work would only add to that debt. The soldier actually looked grateful as Dralor's sword came down. Somehow that only made it feel worse, though.

Dralor found his men staring at him as he turned from wiping the blood off his blade. The tears upon his cheeks he left, though. He walked on, the black prison tower looming taller with each step, and the surrounding wall with it.

The familiar, fell stench stopped him cold, gripped him, set his legs trembling. He felt like a child standing alone in the dark. But, mind on all the other souls he'd subjected to the same rending, he walked on. Each step was heavier than the last. The gate came into view, then a faint hint of the first of the miserable barracks. He signaled a halt.

"What?" Davit asked, looking up at the tower. In answer, several arrows sunk into the ground a few leaps ahead. "Ah."

"Oy, battles over!" Lans barked.

There was a pause, then a voice came back from one of the figures atop the wall. "Who won?"

"Me, shitface!"

Another pause. "You sure?"

"You think your army just let us pass? Naelis is dead. Now put your bows down and..." Lans looked over at Dralor. "And what is it you want?"

"Open the gate!" Dralor shouted.

Hushed voices, then, "You sure?"

"Goddamn open the bleedin' gate!" Lans roared.

More voices. "Fine! Hold on, we're coming to the door!"

"The gate!" Dralor said.

"But—you don't want the—"

"The gate! And the rest of you throw down your weapons and come out here!"

A moment later, swords and bows fell with a clattering. Dralor could see them moving up there on the wall above the thin gate that separated life from hell. Couldn't tell if they were following his order though, or plotting ways to kill him, but a door in the wall opened and ten guards came out, empty hands raised. Then, the gate began to open. It reached the top with a resounding crash that left everything in complete silence, or so it seemed to Dralor, who stood staring into the prison.

"Bring the guards in with us," Dralor said quietly. "Keep them under watch."

Then he started forward, slow footsteps squelching in the mud. He stopped before the gate, looking in at row after row of dilapidated barracks. He saw one of the kitchens and could taste the sour slop. Two new smithies, feeding the war effort no doubt, but everything else was the same. Smoke rose from one of the incinerators toward the red star fading now in the brightening sky. There was nobody in sight. Too late, maybe. Too late.

He pressed inward, feeling a chill as he passed beneath the gate. One of the barracks doors opened. Dralor let out a breath, but it caught at the sight of the man emerging. Legs as thin as the spokes of a wagon, face gaunt and eyes sunken. He shambled toward Dralor and they stopped not far apart, staring at one another. Somehow there was still hope in the man's eyes.

Dralor tried to speak, but nothing came out. He cleared his throat and tried again. "You're free," he managed, voice cracking. "You're free."

The man just stood there, staring. He looked about, at the gate, the rounded-up guards, Dralor's troop gathered behind, and back at Dralor. Then, ever so slowly, he hobbled closer, and fell to his knees before Dralor.

"Thank you," he rasped, and began to sob. "Thank you!"

Dralor stared down at the man. Shouldn't he feel at peace finally? Shouldn't he feel redeemed? Vindicated? But all he felt was guilt. He was an imposter. A villain in a hero's clothes. He'd put this man here!

The only more cruel deed was taking thanks for it. The man's thanks burned like a hot iron.

"No, no. Please," Dralor stammered.

He pulled the man to his feet, but the man only wrapped him in a bony embrace, laughing, sobbing. Dralor loosed a quavering breath. Exaltation. Guilt. Both. Every flicker of joy met with a searing condemnation. Tears ran down his face. He was here, wasn't he? Wasn't that something?

When he looked up, there were others. Ten. Twenty. Hundreds, and more doors opening, more filthy, gaunt wretches shuffling forward on stiff, knobby legs. The walking dead, no longer.

Dralor disentangled himself, gave the man a pat and a firm nod, and turned to his soldiers.

"Get the people whatever they need. Clothes, water, food, medicine. Benam... send for Sir Benam. And get the kitchens fired up. Man them. We're serving."

The troop was quiet, many eyes wide or wet as they watched the starved and tormented prisoners, many of whom had broken into sobs, fallen to their knees, or even lay silent in shock upon the ground. Then Davit slammed a fist to his chest and began issuing orders, and the somber men set to their tasks. Dralor was the last among them to move, then set to showing the men about.

CHAPTER THIRTY-FIVE

Jeld started awake in a sweat, some bad dream already at the edge of his memory. He smiled though. The sweet smell of Lira's hair filled the air. Her body was pressed against his, his arm wrapped beneath her. Above the heavy sheets, her shoulder caught the orange glow of the fire crackling across the room. He smiled again and drifted back to sleep.

He woke again. Craning his neck as much as his pinned arm would allow, he looked past Lira to the fire. It was reduced to simmering coals now. A hint of light peeked in around the shutters. A bell chimed, just once and done, recalling a sleepy memory of the bell that must have woken him. With a silent sigh, he began carefully working his arm free from beneath Lira. Slow and steady. Timed with each of her soft breaths. Smooth as a thief.

"In a hurry to leave?" Lira asked.

Jeld winced. "You know, just a bit simpler if I sneak out before the whole palace is awake."

Lira rolled over, sleepy eyes full of humor. "I make the rules around here, you know."

"Even so. I don't know, I just feel a bit like a chicken caught in a hen house, you know?"

"Ah," Lira said. "So you take me for a chicken."

Jeld frowned. "Well, a very royal chicken."

They shared a laugh, then she kissed him. He pulled her tight against him. Then a knock sounded at the door and Jeld jumped back.

"Lira?" came her mother's voice. "Lira, will you do breakfast with me before council?"

Jeld shot out of the bed, feeling every bit a fox, and set to collecting his clothes. It wasn't the first time Lira took breakfast with her Mother since reclaiming Tovar, but usually Jeld was out before then. Lira's relationship with her mother was better than ever, the queen a different person entirely since they'd found her locked in her apartments on retaking the city. Perhaps like many of the upper crust, she'd just needed a taste of hardship.

"Yes, Mother!" called Lira. "I will meet you there soon!"

"Very good, dear."

Lira shared a guilty grin with Jeld as they both set to dressing.

Jeld stared off for a moment. "You haven't changed your mind about having a high priest, have you?"

"Hmm? No... I haven't. People need it. Benam will do much good."

Jeld winced as he pulled his shirt on, his once-fatal wound already just a mere annoyance. Lacing the shirt up, he snuck a peek at Lira as she slid into a dress. He smiled, not as much for the glimpse of her body as for the simplicity of her dress. It was beautiful, but it was not some uncomfortable, overdone, flowery thing.

"What did you have in mind?" Lira asked. "The skies turn red and you wish to disavow the one thing people might look to for comfort?"

"It's just, every time there's religion, there's war. Or death camps. Or red priests lobbing off heads."

"It can teach good things, too."

"It doesn't matter what it teaches, it just makes people stupid. Teaches them to believe anyone with robes instead of thinking for themselves."

Lira sat before a mirror and worked at her hair. "You've seen The One. Is that not real enough for you?"

Jeld pulled on a boot. "We wouldn't need a high priest and a whole religion if it was just about telling people there's really a floaty ball of light in the Halls."

"If the Crown doesn't give religious direction they'll find it elsewhere. Red skies, Jeld. People are hysterical!"

Jeld took a breath and sat beside Lira, picking at his own hair. "And have you decided whether you'll tell Benam to keep it secret that the Idols are actually dead?"

"He can tell them what he pleases. If he does reveal it, there's still The One. And besides, being killed doesn't mean they have not ascended anyway."

Jeld shook his head. More stories. More deception. More robes. But then, maybe she was right. Maybe he was the naive one for thinking people could handle the truth. Another necessary evil.

"Perhaps you could convince Benam to give you the job," Lira said with a playful smile.

Jeld laughed. "Me? The last time I pretended to be a priest it was to kill a priest. The time before that I ended up—" He cuts off. *Ended up infiltrating the palace and setting it on fire while my colleagues killed your father?* Could he really take that secret to the grave?

He cleared his throat. "Well, I ended up killing a priest that time, too. And a damn good baker, he was."

"And as I recall, you saved a princess."

Jeld gave a little smile. "So, I think priesthood doesn't suit me." His smile faded and he paced away. "What *am* I going to do? I can't just forever be your..."

"Mistress? Paramour?"

Jeld couldn't help but grin, but it fell away quickly. "You're the queen! You can't just..."

"Actually I was rather hoping to marry you."

"Can you even imagine? A queen and—" Jeld blinked. "What?" He snorted as if it were a joke, but she only raised an eyebrow. "You're s—you're serious."

Then he laughed and his smiling cheeks pinched tears from his eyes. He walked back to where she sat facing him now on her vanity bench, slowly as if she were a bird that might fly off. He reached to her, but his heart sank and his hand fell.

"What is it?" Lira breathed as Jeld sat beside her again, eyes haunted.

"This would never work... You're a queen. I'm a..." He shook his head. "You'll need to marry for some alliance. You're supposed to be some greater power for the people. Can you imagine anything more ridiculous than a queen marrying some... street rat?"

"Ah," Lira said, nodding gravely. "I've read this story a time or ten. Usually a prince, but sometimes a princess. Protocol forbids it. Or the council forbids it. Or, elevated, our young street rat realizes that it simply won't work, then tragically or heroically rides off into the sunset."

"And you talk about giving more power to the people. They would never approve—"

"Not that power!" Lira snapped. "The people need love. I need love. And I never liked those tales. As bad as those where the hero leaves the girl for her own protection. No, I'll write my own story, thank you."

They fell silent, then Jeld blew out a breath of laughter. "Married. I never imagined we might..."

"You didn't?" Lira exclaimed in mostly feigned offense.

"I suppose it was always all I could hope for just to see you one more time. That you'd be at the temple again. That you'd somehow survived the slavers. That you'd still be there once I got out of the Halls."

Lira took his hands and kissed him. "Well, now you can hope to see me at council. I must be off. Are you sure you don't wish to join us for breakfast?"

"Mm, I've rarely been so certain of anything. Perhaps after you announce your betrothal to the beggar fox-rat he'll be proudly embraced by the mother in law."

"She already knows."

Jeld choked on nothing. "What! Don't you think it would have been appropriate to consult me first?"

"She likes you. It was her idea actually. Getting married."

Jeld's mouth opened and closed wordlessly. "Her idea, or she just brought up the topic? Probably only seeing what she was up against."

"She was one of those tragic tales, you know. Set up from birth to be married off." She patted his hands and stood. "Must be off. You're sure you won't join still?"

"Certain. I think Benam wanted to do breakfast together today anyway."

"Never thought you two would grow so fond of one another."

Jeld scratched the back of his head. "Yes, well, I suppose our differences are what makes the conversation good."

"It's cute."

They shared a final embrace and a soft kiss, then she was off, leaving Jeld staring after her with a full heart.

***

Jeld was seated in his old spot at the big, rounded council table. It was a place of lesser status, not beside the raised monarch's chair, nor directly across from it, but rather off to one side. Lira had invited him to sit beside her, but the idea of being elevated above such men as these... Well, suffice it to say he was not looking forward to whenever their supposed betrothal was announced.

Nice as it was to be back in the familiar setting, in truth he couldn't have felt more out of place. Last he was here, he'd been Arvin. Now, Jeld. Lira had fed a good enough lie about her father having inserted Jeld to watch over her, but whether anyone believed that or not they now knew Jeld for a sneak.

All that aside, there was no denying he found joy in the familiar faces. Except for Lord Governor Tydel Demerious, anyway. Sitting at Lira's side might be worth the reaction from that sod, actually. There was also Handan, Benam, Krayo. Olind was there, best Jeld could tell without building up the nerve to look him in the eye. Lira, of course. Old Tutor Reiman, Chancellor Cerus, Queen Darene. Renae as well, while Ralegus had returned to the north. It was odd not having Dralor there. Odder still how different the contentious prince in Jeld's memories was from the man he had become.

Lira's page, Wesslund, sat off to one side of the broad table, looking as ever like he'd rather be mucking stalls than taking notes. Jeld couldn't help but feel bad for the poor bastard, even knowing he was luckier than all the starving, illiterate wretches across the city.

Chancellor Cerus cleared his throat. "Let us call this council to order, if it please Your Highness?"

Lira nodded. "Please."

"I must first say again how very glad I am to have this group back together." The soft chinned, usually stern-browed fellow looked like he might actually cry. He cleared his throat again. "Now, our first order of business is the war in the east. General Handan?"

"Little new to report," Handan said, leaning forward in his chair. "Good progress cleaning the scum out of our ranks. Ours, Caldemoor's, Havaral's, Harborstone's. My guidance on Warrinton remains unchanged."

"As does mine," Tydel Demerious cut in. "You've gone to lengths to reclaim the kingdom and you don't want to risk it all reclaiming Warrinton, fine, but you risk more in not acting now. The problem will not get easier with time."

Ralegus grunted his agreement, then the room fell silent, all eyes fixed on Lira as she considered. Finally she spoke in a soft voice.

"Thank you, gentlemen. I see your point. However, you assume the east will encroach further. Also, we must remember that they have even more claim to Warrinton than we do. If we ever want peace, we must—"

Lord Tydel scoffed.

Lira continued, louder. "Must consider compromises."

"Did their people not inhabit these very shores?" Tydel said. "Will you give them all of Avandria to avoid a fight?"

Jeld glared at the lord governor. Where was his fight when he handed the kingdom to Naelis? But, he narrowly managed to silence himself.

"It's a good thought experiment, actually," Lira said. "Where to draw the line..." She trailed off and her eyes grew distant.

"Continue as planned," she said finally. "Secure the surrounding lands, make ready in case they should attack, and continue preparations for our delegation. I'm sorry, Renae. However things evolve, the lands are yours, and the people will need you greatly."

Renae's eyes fell closed a moment, then he gave a deep nod. "Your Highness is wise to be cautious."

Chancellor Cerus looked from face to face, bit tongue to bit tongue, then spoke. "Very good. Those working the matter will convene tonight once again. Next, then is..." He looked down over his papers. "The matter of our next high priest. As noted, there is growing hysteria over this matter of red skies. Some feel it validates Naelis's means. Others simply are afraid. Last noted, our Sir Benam Visleigh was considering the position."

Cerus set down his papers and looked to Benam, who in turn glanced at Lira. She bid him speak with a wave.

Benam took a breath. "I've decided to... decline the position. I will forever serve Queen Liraelle, but I have other matters to attend to. And—"

"Other matters?" Tydel pressed. "I should think this is quite an important matter."

"Research. I will not preach to the kingdom when there is so much we do not know. Perhaps I would, but there is simply not enough time for both. Besides, there is another who will be far more capable."

Lira gestured to one of the servants, who returned a moment later with a man in tattered gray robes. Lira and Jeld shared a smile as Prishner Walson took a seat not far from Lira.

"I'm beyond pleased to introduce Prishner Walson. This wonderful man has been serving our people tirelessly his entire life. The number of lives he has touched is beyond counting. Once, the Temple of One was a magnificent institution that lit the kingdom. *High Priest* Walson will be returning it to its former glory, and the temple will spread hope and decency throughout Avandria during these troubling times."

Walson beamed, tears welling in his eyes. "My queen. Great council. My heart is full. The children we can help... the spirits we can lift...

the peace we can bring—" His voice cracked. He pressed his palms together and bowed. "Such good we'll do."

Jeld looked away and wiped a tear from his cheek. A good thing happening to a great man. Power given to a great man. Rare things in this world. And as much goodness as Walson had managed with nothing but ragged robes and a hot pot of stew, the potential was beautiful, if Jeld dared to hope. More monumental still—that a solid majority in a room full of nobles might feel much the same. Could the world truly have come so far since the sweeps and slaughters and injustices that had led him here plotting vengeance?

At this Jeld wondered what the very object of his former hatred must be doing right then. Harder to believe even than decency among nobles was that Jeld could ever have grown fond of the black prince. Even Handan had embraced Dralor, in the end. But, despite Lira's efforts to convince Dralor to stay, they all knew it would never work. The people could never know, and Dralor was not one for deceptions. Nor was Dralor interested, for that matter. Other plans.

"Onto the coronation," Chancellor Cerus was saying when Jeld's mind returned to the present. "Last we—"

"Thank you, Chancellor," Lira interrupted, "but I've decided there will be no coronation. The people have sacrificed too much. To put on such a vain and frivolous show undermines all that. It's tone deaf and positions us as no better than the last bunch."

Cerus's mouth opened and closed repeatedly, jowls wobbling. "But—but, my queen, the people don't see it that way. They see the Crown as something greater than themselves. They need—"

"Maybe once, and maybe again, but not now. Now we must regain their respect. The savings from the cancelled festivities will be added to High Priest Walson's budget for use as he sees fit."

Lira looked around the room as if daring anyone to protest. Tydel Demerious looked affronted, Cerus dismayed, and Lira's mother—proud.

"One thing, though," Lira continued. "In place of the coronation, we'll welcome the citizenry outside the gates, and topple the black prison."

This time it was Handan who spoke up. "Your Highness, the strategic importance of such a lookout is significant. And we could house an entire garrison there, with proper improvement, of course."

"I know. I know. But it is a stain on our kingdom. A sculpture at the tower's base will be commissioned to ensure the mistakes of the past are not forgotten. Krayo, Sir Olind, you'll see the quarry opened for industry. The rest, all destroyed."

The room was silent for a time, then Prishner Walson spoke, voice soft and soothing as ever. "I wonder, Your Highness, if we might instead turn it into a hospital? Perhaps an orphanage? A school, too? Topple your tower if you wish, but the whole facility need not be entirely wasted."

Lira smiled. "A demolition, and a rebirth. Very well, I look forward to reviewing your plans."

"Very good," Cerus said. "Next is the matter of the ball. I assume Your Highness wishes it cancelled as well? Will you have the savings likewise allotted to the priesthood?"

"Actually, we will keep it. However, we shall once again invite the public. My father had a message for the people, and I mean to see it delivered."

"Er, Your Highness, you do realize—"

Lord Tydel cut in. "You do realize our queen knows damn well how her father died! She's right, and so was King Loris, if only we'd had the sense to see it."

Lira frowned in surprise, then gave Tydel a nod. "But do cut any of the more frivolous costs please, Chancellor."

"Very good, Your Highness," Cerus said, penning a note. "Moving right along. Rumors of our own Prince Dralor Tovados living still. Returning to Tovar, even. Does the Crown have an official response?"

Lira's eyes fell to the table and she was silent. Finally, she met Jeld's eyes as if for strength, then spoke. "Dead. He's dead."

Council dragged on to more mundane matters for nearly two bells before Cerus adjourned the session. The others filed out. Krayo approached Jeld as Lira looked over Wesslund's notes.

"I don't think I'll ever be able to look Olind in the eye again," Jeld said, shaking Krayo's outstretched hand.

Krayo smiled his slight smile. "Oh he rather likes this new reputation. An operative of King Loris, inserting you to watch over her. Pretty well saved the kingdom, but mostly he likes how tough it makes him look."

Jeld grinned. "So tough." His grin fell away. "I suppose I won't be taking on more of the business with you. Seems I'll have plenty to keep me busy here."

"This *is* my business now, Jeld, and you seem to be taking over plenty."

Krayo gave another touch of a grin and departed. Lira patted Wesslund's shoulder and gave the tired boy leave. Only Lira and Jeld remained. Lira's eyes flicked to her pile of papers.

"It's alright," Jeld said.

He sat and pulled a pile of papers from his collar. Lira smiled, brushed his cheek with the back of her hand, and set to her work. Jeld watched her for a time before turning his attention to Director Sammel's latest work. The director's own tangled edits already filled most of the margins. Jeld chuckled.

"What is it?" Lira asked, her pen still scratching.

"It's nothing," Jeld said.

He dove into the story, squeezing the occasional note of feedback into the odd space not yet filled by ink. After a while he found himself just watching Lira work. Like the weight of the kingdom was upon her shoulders. He glanced down at his own work. Just a play. He chuckled again, this time Lira not seeming to notice, and fell back into the story.

"There," Lira said after a good while. She let out a breath. "Shall we go to the library again?"

"Actually I was rather hoping you'd join me for a show tonight. I have great seats."

Lira lit up. "Seats, you say? Or tickets?"

"Four of them," Jeld said, not quite answering. I've arranged for Fen and Roba to have the night off. And dinner with the crew, after. What do you say?"

Lira was already on her feet. "I might still have some street clothes stashed somewhere."

***

Dralor hacked down a branch crossing the path and pressed his horse onward. The trail was just a line of younger overgrowth cutting through the denser woods, occasional patches of packed dirt showing through underfoot. He cut another branch aside and came to a stop at the crest of a hill.

There was a valley below. An unkept orchard looked little more than just more woods. Only traces of a split-rail fence showed through the overgrown grass of a stock field, a few goats grazing at its edge. Beyond the field was a farmhouse. It did not look its sharpest, but the blemishes were only skin deep. It stood tall and proud and sturdy, a testament to its builder.

A horse stopped beside Dralor, a little girl upon it. Claritte stared down at her old home. Too young for those haunted eyes. Dralor's horse whinnied impatiently and he patted it. Even in the afternoon sun the beast's breath smoked in the frigid air. They were lucky to have beaten the snow, but by the look of the clouds and bite of the air, their luck was nearly spent.

Finally, Claritte kicked her mount and started down into the valley without a word, Dralor following after her. She went slowly, as if at any moment she might turn away, might change her mind and ask to return to Tovar. She nearly had several times already along the way, but it never lasted. He'd offered her a fine education, or a trade. Whatever she wanted, aside from doing nothing. A far easier life than working a farm full of haunting memories. He wouldn't blame her one bit.

Claritte stopped before her old home. Another few breaths and she climbed down from her horse, suddenly just a little girl again beside the big mare. Dralor came to stand beside her, and again they stood in silence. A little hand grabbed his, and after a while longer she towed him toward the door.

The hand fell away and pressed at the door. It was stuck. Dralor stopped himself from helping her, and sure enough she managed to free it. Claritte stopped just inside, eyes flitting about.

"Da' would have a fit seeing it like this," she said softly. "Ma' too."

"We can sort it," Dralor said.

"It seems different."

"I know. I know."

She walked about, picking up this or that.

"I think the past is never the same when we return to it," Dralor said.

He'd considered staying in Tovar. Supporting Lira somehow. But that was the past. Best left alone. She didn't need him anyway.

"I think it's we who change," he added. "We see the place differently, even if it hasn't changed."

Dralor watched Claritte as she sat upon the little sofa, her distant eyes filling with tears. That was that, then. Hardly a wasted trip, though. She'd always have wondered otherwise. Probably have taken it all the long way to the grave. If they were lucky they'd make it back to the last town before the snow piled up. He had enough money to take a room, wait it out. Then... who knows.

"We should get the fireplace and firewood sorted first," Claritte said, wiping away her tears. "Round up the animals next, and see if we can dig up the last of the winter crop."

Dralor smiled and came to his feet. "Alright, my girl. Let's get to it."

CHAPTER THIRTY-SIX

J eld looked down over the radiant ballroom from a corner of the loft encircling it. People danced, laughed, and politicked below to the festive songs of harp and lute. Lira stood below with her mother, both all smiles as the wolves cycled by to court favor. Or perhaps merely to pay their respects, Jeld supposed.

"I guess you were right all along," Jeld said. "It all worked out."

At the rail beside him, Benam lowered a fancy pink drink and wiped some from his neat beard. "Perhaps for now. But there is much still to do. And, it will never truly be done in full."

Jeld bit his tongue, then spoke anyway. "All that faith and you don't think things will ever truly be good?"

He looked over at Benam. The old knight wore a green doublet, a pin of a tree on one shoulder and another of a sword on the other. One of the tall arched windows behind framed him in the black of night.

"I do think goodness will prevail," Benam said after a while. "Maybe not this time. Maybe not the next. But eventually."

Jeld's eyes followed Lira through the gathering. "Maybe after a thousand more Naelises."

"Maybe."

Jeld bit his lip again. "You have no evidence to even think so, though. All you have are wishes, and even your wishes are bleak."

"A tiny light in the darkness," Benam breathed.

Jeld's mind went to the void beneath the Halls. The fear and hopelessness that had gripped his heart. Even the faintest prick of light would have lifted his spirit then. Would have shown him the way, even.

Benam turned to Jeld. "There's something, actually. That light that rose above you. It tried to return to The One. You see? We all have the light of The One in us, Jeld. All of us. We don't need to steal it to make change, as Naelis tried. We don't need to await great acts from The One to solve our problems. The One acts already, through us. We are her hands, Jeld. All of us! We can do anything together if we bring the people together!"

Jeld felt bad to not share the old knight's enthusiasm, but in truth it seemed to change little. Maybe The One did have a hand in the battle. In him, even. But knowing where your weapon was crafted did little to decide the battle. Clearly he'd done a shit job of improving the world this far either way. He tried to feel within himself that touch of The One that Benam had supposedly glimpsed with his own eyes, but felt nothing. Probably just Benam had imagined it. Faith had that effect—*was* that effect, after all.

Still, it was a little comforting to imagine. A touch of The One in him? In everyone. An ally in this misery. A spot of light in the darkness. In his own darkness, even. Of course, there were other explanations, weren't there? If The One did act through them, surely there'd be peace if not for some limits to his power. Maybe life slipping away in the Halls just manifests as these lights for no other reason than the Halls being strange. Or what if these lights weren't—Jeld froze.

"Jeld? What is it? Jeld?

Jeld cleared his throat. "Ah, nothing. Nothing, sorry, just, well, we are contemplating the world's deepest secrets, are we not?" He forced a smile.

Benam forced his own smile. "Theories and decisions that will impact so many lives..."

Jeld shook his worries aside. "Well, if you're wrong about everything working out, we'll be dead, but if you're right, you'll look pretty smart."

Benam chuckled, shaking his head. "I'd best go speak with High Priest Walson. We have so much to prepare."

Benam patted Jeld's arm and departed toward the stairs, leaving Jeld to himself. The tune of "Fires of Khapar" rose up over the chatter and Jeld looked to the lute player. Seemed a shame to dampen such a jovial mood but you couldn't have ups without downs, Master Edlin always said. Jeld could feel the notes upon his fingers. *Idols* but he needed to get his lute out more.

Jeld's mind drifted back over Benam's words as he watched Lira. Like most of the others, she'd gone silent and watched the musicians. She turned and looked about before spotting Jeld atop the loft. Her smile filled his heart, filled his vision as if she were standing right before him. She beckoned him over. Back to her side. Back into the thick of things.

He kindly waved the invitation away with a smile. She'd been trying to get him to stop wearing masks, but he didn't much like being in the spotlight without one. She gave a shrug and turned away, not looking terribly put off, at least. He cursed to himself anyway for not going to her.

The song stole him away again before long, then his mind drifted again to Benam's words about the One's Light, then to that thought. He stood frozen for a time, eyes flitting in thought. Probably nothing. Probably nothing. He pushed it away and smiled, eyes on Lira below, but there was no escaping it. Best to squash it now. Probably nothing.

With a sigh, he donned a mask of calm and started down the spiral stairs. Pleasantries came easily as he made his way toward the corridor that led to the palace proper. Brief words. Gentlemanly nods. Smiles.

With one last, long look to Lira, Jeld swiped a handful of rolls from a table and slipped from the ballroom. He left a brief note upon Lira's pillow, then made his way down a hallway in the bowels of the keep. Passing through an unremarkable door into a room lost in time and dust, he turned the lock behind him.

Jeld laid his bag open inside an empty dresser drawer. He pulled his lute out and set it in the drawer beside the bag opening, then crawled inside, closing the drawer behind him. He emerged into darkness, picked up the bag on this side, stepped over his ring of possessions, through the expansive void with no less anxiety than ever, through a door, up a ladder, and into the nexus.

Five main halls, countless narrow ones between. Jeld made his way to one of the narrow halls. Probably they all led to the same spot, but still he made sure to select the very same one he'd once traversed. Of course, the others might not stretch for three days, but best not leave things to chance when it comes to losing oneself in infinity.

His heart began to race as he stood staring down the hall past doorway after doorway. It was not being lost that worried him this time, though. His mind was consumed by another worry. Jeld set his jaw and started onward. Sweat dripped down his forehead as his anxious heart thudded in his chest. Funny that he could sweat here but need not to drink. See? Simply a place of oddities. Probably explained the matter of Benam's ball of light. Probably he'd soon be heading back to Lira, this insane notion put to rest. Probably.

Doors. Doors. Doors. His old chalk marks from his first time through were still there. Judging from them, he'd been going for about one bell now. One bell. All that and one bell? He quickened his pace.

Slap, slap, slap, went his footsteps. *Idols* but it was quiet. He remembered his lute and pulled it from the bag. He let out a long breath as his hands touched the strings and the first notes filled the terrible silence.

He walked on. It occurred to him after nearly a full day into his journey that he needn't make it all in one go. He could crawl back out into the real world. See Lira. Make a bit of progress each night. But alas, he sighed and continued on.

What felt like days later, but was only mere bells, he sat for a break and thumbed through one of Vincet's journals.

I have written at length of the hypothesized cyclical destruction and rebirth to which the world as we know it is bound. The hungry fire, said the legend of one lost people. The red destroyer, another called it, but always it appeared in legends, by some name or another.

He stared at the words until they were a blur and his thoughts ran free. Then he was on his feet again, doors passing by. More music. More journal. More doors.

Married. He smiled. Perhaps it would never work out, but that she wanted it at all was something magical. It seemed more far-fetched than walking some dream hall toward The One, but there it was. Maybe Benam was right. Maybe everything did work out, in the end. At that, his worry swept back in.

Two days. He closed Vincet's journal and continued. He wished he could be hungry. Wished his legs would ache. Wished he could grow tired and sleep. But that wasn't the way of things here. The doors passed, one after the next. His old marks had ended. Close now. Bells away. Maybe a day, but no more.

Hungry. Red.

The red skies. The red star. The destroyer, awakened? Scholars at the great library had ancient record of a distant star seeming almost to explode, Vincet wrote. If merely that again, poor timing to say the least. Right as Naelis had died, though? Were people right to worry the end had come?

Doors, and more doors. The ever-present point where the walls of the halls pressed together in the distance was suddenly a black point. The end, at last. He stopped, wanting both to run toward it and away, then only walked on.

Eventually the black point grew to a gap. Then he could make out the end of the walls in the distance. Then, in the black void beyond, a point of light. He froze. Stared. Blinked. But it changed nothing. The light was tinged red.

Jeld crept forward, pulse beating in his ears, heart pounding. Perhaps it was something Naelis had done. Damaged it, even despite Jeld's illusion. Perhaps the destroyer was risen indeed, and gripped the very heart of The One. A horrible prospect, yet far preferable to another.

He reached the end of the hall. There was no mistaking it, lines of red light like lightning shimmered on the surface of the sphere that was The One. Jeld walked into the void toward it, feet silent against the unseen floor, like walking across a starless night sky.

Jeld came to stand just before it, eyes fixed on the red tendrils of light covering it. He'd not forgotten what he felt the last time he'd succumbed to the draw and touched its mind, but he had to be certain. So, with a heavy breath, he reached out his sense. There was its vastness. It was everywhere. Everything. Too much to comprehend. Too much to dare trying.

He felt its welcome, its embrace, and thought again of Benam's lights. The One's touch, his spark, the very soul. Life itself, returning to this great creator upon death. *Returning.* Was that not a conclusion of the faithful, though? Assuming Benam hadn't just imagined the whole thing, what were the facts? The lights had come from Jeld, Naelis, the inquisitors, yes. They'd gone toward The One, yes.

He focused on The One's touch, careful not to open himself too much to its awesomeness, just peeking at the sun through a pinhole. There was its touch. Its welcome. Its draw. More than that, though. A pull. A *hunger*.

Another red light snaked across the surface, and Jeld broke away with a shudder. His stomach dropped as it all came together with a terrible certainty. What if the light wasn't returning? What if it was Jeld's own... Not returned, but stolen. *Consumed.*

He closed his mind tight and stared into the sphere of pale red. Then, he breathed a single word.

"Destroyer."